OMEN OF ICE

OMEN OF ICE

JUS ACCARDO

Entangled Publishing, LLC
644 Shrewsbury Commons Ave., STE 181
Shrewsbury, PA 17361
rights@entangledpublishing.com

Entangled Teen is an imprint of Entangled Publishing, LLC.
Visit our website at www.entangledpublishing.com.

Edited by Liz Pelletier and Lydia Sharp
Cover design by Bree Archer
Cover art by LJ Anderson, Mayhem Cover Creations
Cover images by
FORGEM/Gettyimages, KHIUS/Shutterstock
Interior design by Toni Kerr

ISBN 978-1-64937-402-8
Ebook ISBN 978-1-64937-426-4

Manufactured in the United States of America

First Edition August 2023

10 9 8 7 6 5 4 3 2 1

an imprint of Entangled Publishing LLC

ALSO BY JUS ACCARDO

THE DENAZEN SERIES

Touch
Toxic
Tremble
Transcendent

THE INFINITY DIVISION SERIES

Infinity
Omega
Alpha

For my dad...

At Entangled, we want our readers to be well-informed. If you would like to know if this book contains any elements that might be of concern for you, please check the back of the book for details.

1

Keltania

Magic is a funny thing. It can be infinitely powerful yet, at the same time, as fragile as the most delicate bloom. All it takes to lose it is a single sacrifice.

Or a single mistake.

I breathe in deep and do my best to block the chatter from the small crowd gathered across the field. There's excitement in the air, and even the trees seem eager for the ceremony to commence. Every few moments, showers of red and gold leaves flutter down, coating the ground for several seconds before dissolving back into the earth.

"Are you ready for this?" my cousin, Alainya, whispers. She's a bundle of nerves and excitement, fidgeting nonstop, more like a toddler than an eighteen-year-old. "Because I'm not sure if I am."

"You are," I promise, then grab her hand and give it a firm squeeze—to comfort her, but also to get her to stand still. The constant movement is making me twitchy.

I understand her enthusiasm. I'm excited, too. I'm just better at containing myself.

We're barefoot, wrapped in simple white shifts made of

silk. Our limbs are adorned with flowers, and vines wind between our fingers, up and around our arms. The elders say the vines signify our connection with the land. To me, the vines represent our bond with the Winter Fae. Our histories are interwoven, our fates connected with loyalty and love. We're one. Partners, allies—friends.

We owe them everything. They ensured our survival in the days before—and during—the war. When the rest of the humans fell, the Winter Fae used their magic to make sure the druids had enough food and protection, that our shelters withstood the elemental forces from the other Fae courts.

After the war, after the Great Drain, we began repaying their kindness. Now, some of us stand at their side as guards, protecting them from harm with what little magic we retain.

Alainya turns around again. This time, there's mischief in her eyes. "What kind of gifts do you suppose they'll greet us with?"

I roll my eyes. "Shh!"

"I'm hoping for one of those rings I've heard so much about. You know, the ones that allow you to change your appearance?" She shimmies her hips. "I bet I'd look fantastic as a redhead!"

Levina, our high priestess, steps to the front of the crowd. She pins Alainya and me with a stern glare, then begins. "Thousands of years ago, Servis, the lord of the Winter Court, fell in love with our high priestess, Aphelian. When war broke out among the courts and the druids were in danger, the Winter Fae protected them. The battle raged for a decade, each court leaving behind charred forests and lands drenched in innocent blood. In the dawn of the eleventh year, the Great Drain started—the depletion of Fae magic."

"I love this story!" Alainya squeals loud enough to coax my other cousins to *shh* her as well. "It's so romantic."

"Yes," I say under my breath. "*War* is so romantic... Add it to the loss of all Fae magic, and you've got an epic fairy tale on your hands."

Levina glares at us again, but this time Alainya bows her head, cowed. "Servis's magic was, like that of all the other Fae, failing. Though the other courts were just as badly hampered, Aphelian feared total annihilation of her beloved and the Winter Fae. She appeared before the council of elders and begged them to give just a little bit more—half their magic. A normal Fae could never wield druid magic, but a Fae royal? Her beloved would be able. With the survival of the Winter Fae at stake, they agreed so long as Servis returned their power when it was over.

"Twelve days of meditation, and she channeled the land's power. She harnessed it and forced half of it into a single glass tear, which she bottled and offered to the Winter Lord to give them the edge they needed to end the war victorious. Alas, the safe return of our magic was not to be. After the final battle, as Servis made to return the tear, he and Aphelian were attacked and the tear taken. Badly injured, Servis fought with everything he had to recapture his love's magic. He sacrificed his remaining power to reclaim the tear...but it was destroyed."

Soft chatter whispers through the crowd. We all know this story. We can recite it in our sleep. Yet each and every year, on this day, everyone in the village stands riveted, like the tale is new. Eighteen times. I've heard this story on the eve of the Fall Harvest Moon each year I've been alive.

It reinforces the bond we, as descendants of Aphelian, make with the Winter Fae. A sacred partnership forged by our ancestors and carried out across generations.

One by one, the girls ahead of me, my cousins, step up. There are four of us this year. Two fewer than last. Heads held high and shoulders squared with barely contained excitement, they move with the grace of the wind. Well, all except Alainya. She's a skilled fighter and has a knack for herbal remedies, but sometimes it's hard to believe she's my age. She practically bounces forward with the enthusiasm of a small child riding a sugar-cane high.

"Are you excited?" Alainya lets out a soft giggle. "I'm so excited!"

I give up trying to quiet her and gently nudge her forward. We grew up together, and though her unbridled and irritatingly persistent optimism is annoying, I'll miss her. She always balanced me. Where I was *narrowly focused* on training—her words, not mine—she remained light and full of humor. I'm the boring one—again, her words, not mine—and she's the fun one. Night and day. She would say she's sunshine and I'm the violent storm that rolls in from the mountains, drenching our rain-starved fields. Merciless yet healing.

Alainya always had a flair for dramatics.

When it's my turn, I breathe in deep and step forward.

Alainya giggles, and Levina's gaze meets mine. She holds it several seconds longer than she did the others', and I wonder if anyone notices. We've always been close, and on more than one occasion, the other girls accused me of getting preferential treatment. An extra roll at dinner time, the better bunk in the dormitory tent. I've never seen it before, but looking at her now, seeing not only the pride in her eyes but pain as well, I know it's true.

"Aphelian's golden heart and Servis's noble sacrifice are what bring us together today. Though our magic was destroyed in the war, we honor her bond with the Winter Kingdom. The past has proven that if we stand together, we can overcome anything. I, as one of her descendants, feel great joy in sending you into the loving hands of the Fae. I pray that the Goddess shines her grace upon you."

"May the Goddess grant me her favor," we say in unison. I've waited my entire life to speak those words. The thrill is nothing short of euphoric.

"Keltania Tunne." Levina bows her head and offers me the slightest nod. "You are by far the most skilled fighter I have seen in over a decade. Your agility and cunning, as well as your superior knowledge of our most obscure inkings, are an assurance to me that you will do well in their world."

I hike up my garment and kneel before her, sinking into the soft earth. Its comforting embrace calms my fluttering nerves.

Levina rests her hand atop my head. "You are no longer Keltania Tunne. You are Aphelian, an extension of the selfless Priestess Aphelian. You are nature's fury and her sword and the embodiment of the bond. Wield them well."

Levina smiles and bends to retrieve the last burlap sack at her feet. It contains my share of our people's most prized possession. Our blood ink, the last small bits of our magic. Dipping her pointer finger into the bag, she traces a symbol onto my forehead. Our crest. A large circle with a vine of ivy wrapped around it. It's the sacred mark that will identify me as a *Fae protector*, an agent of honor and respect. The sigil of Aphelian.

The sensation is unpleasant, like a million tiny needle pricks breaking my skin at once. It steals my breath away, making me dizzy. But, as fast as it comes, it dissipates, leaving me with an all-over warm feeling as the magic absorbs into my skin.

"I will make our ancestors proud," I whisper.

We call it ink, but it's dirt. Scraped from a sacred section of earth and mixed with deep red pigment, it's blessed by the acting high priestess and imbued with a tiny kernel of the remnants of our power. Every descendant of Aphelian gets her own share, for times of crisis when we need a boost of power or strength. It allows us to channel what's left of our people's magic and temporarily reclaim a small bit of the glory we once knew by tracing sigils onto our skin with the ink.

From somewhere behind me, Alainya lets out another excited squeal. Levina's lips quirk, and my other cousins whisper for her to stay quiet.

Levina steps back and closes the pouch, careful not to spill any of the ink. "You have all been marked and have the ink of Aphelian in your veins. Make our people proud."

From this day forward, each sigil I use will mark my skin with a red tattoo. The marks are alive, churning and shimmering with power. It's unsettling to some who see them, but our sigils are worn with pride, symbols of bravery and unyielding loyalty. Like Aphelian before me, I'll use the magic to protect the Fae as they once protected us. With their own power gone, the Fae of the Winter Lands— once called Aroberg—are vulnerable. Their prosperity breeds hatred among the nomadic survivors from the other courts as well as the magic-starved creatures that border their lands.

Levina takes my face in her hands as the crowd around us cheers. "Go with the Goddess, my child. I *know* one day we will meet again."

"Thank you for all you've done for me." Because of Levina, I've trained harder than the others, studied longer, and pushed myself further. Because of Levina, I earned one of the most coveted assignments the Order has ever received. "I *will* make you proud."

"My dear…" She brushes her hand across my cheek and smiles. The pride I see in her eyes, the confidence in me, makes my chest ache. I just hope I can live up to her expectations. "I know you will."

I smile and move to turn away, but Levina holds tight. For a moment—just a moment—I swear I see a flicker of regret in her eyes.

The next morning, after changing and gathering my things—everything I own easily fits into a single pack—I'm shown to a chestnut mare with an intricately braided mane, then led down the overgrown path at the northern corner of the Order grounds. The other Aphelians left the night before, in the pre-twilight hours following the feast. I wished them well, knowing I'd likely never see them again.

My Winter Fae companions—a broad-shouldered Fae who'd introduced himself as Kopic as we began our trek, and a Fae named Wella with silvery-white hair and an expression that could easily sour milk—lead the way to my new home. We travel north on horseback for three days, stopping for very short periods of time to rest. The Fae seem eager to get home, and there's little conversation. As we travel, I run through all I've been told about my charge.

Levina didn't say much. Not his name or placement in the Winter Court, but I know he loves books and learning, has a small degree of fighting skills, and is well-liked — particularly among the females. With his love of books, the logical guess would be that he has some kind of advisory position. But given that the only other thing I know about him — he's just a year older than my eighteen — that seems unlikely. Then again, the Fae do things differently than we do.

Eventually, I give up speculating. Whatever he does, whoever he is, we'll make an amazing team. The details don't matter.

I've never been outside Lunal. The terrain is both beautiful and terrifying. Our lands aren't exactly lush, but the decay I see here is brutal. Shriveled and calcified tree trunks and eternally rotting foliage dot the landscape. But, as disconcerting as it is, there's something strong about it. Something unwilling to yield. The magic drained from the land, yet the forest has refused to fall.

The farther we travel, the narrower the path becomes. When I start to think passage will become impossible, we emerge from the mist-laden brush, the temperature shockingly colder.

Even though I've spent hours reading about the Winter Lands and know to expect the abrupt temperature change, I still can't fight off the involuntary chattering of my teeth.

Ten steps out of the woods, the shriveled brush and rotten foliage are gone, replaced by a thick blanket of glinting snow. It's more beautiful than I could have ever imagined, and the paintings I saw in our books haven't done it justice.

"Wow…"

"Impressive, isn't it?" Kopic laughs. It's a warm sound that eases my nerves just a bit. It's the most he's said to me since we started out. "I was born here, and it never fails to steal my breath away."

His companion isn't nearly as friendly. She snorts and rolls her eyes. Where the other Fae's disposition now seems sunny and warm, hers matches the cold landscape as she adds, "Yes. Stunning. Maybe we can gawk at it after we're settled back at the estate?"

In the distance, there's a sprawling manor at the end of a long, snow-covered path lined with miraculously blooming fruit trees. Apples, pears, and… I pull up hard on my reins and lean closer to the tall, white-barked tree closest to me.

"No… It can't be!"

I rub a silky leaf between my fingers, half expecting it to be fake. It isn't. Despite the falling snow and freezing air, the leaf is warm and undamaged. Thriving, even. I inhale. A long-forgotten scent fills my nose and brings a rush of childhood memories flooding to the surface. "Is this a *hilpberry* tree?"

Kopic nods, smiling.

"When fungus came in my tenth year, we tried to save them, but in the end, the decision was made to let them perish. A painful choice, but our dwindling resources were better spent elsewhere." Channeling what was left of our magic to save a single species of plant, possibly risking the extinction of many others, hadn't been worth the risk.

"Understandable," he says.

I shift in the saddle and nod to the rest of the trees, all just as vibrant and alive as the hilpberry. "How is this possible?" A gust of wind blows, and I shiver. The trees should all be dormant in this kind of weather. "It's almost like you still have —"

"Magic?" Wella supplies. She doesn't smile as much as bare her teeth. "We do."

I nearly fall off my horse. "What?"

"That's not totally accurate." Kopic glares at her. "There are trace amounts of druid power still left in the land. From the war, and…" He points beyond the gate, to a statue of a Fae man and a human woman, both kneeling in front of each other. "There. That's where your priestess presented Lord Servis with the magic to win the war. It was on that same spot, nearly twelve years later, he tried to return it. When they were attacked and the vessel shattered, it bled the power into the grounds, imbuing the land."

"Come," Wella says with the smallest hint of irritation. I get the feeling she doesn't like me for some reason. It's fine. She doesn't have to. "The Winter Lord is waiting."

She nudges her steed, and away they go, bounding down the lane toward the estate and leaving me to gawk at her words. "The *Winter Lord*? My charge is the Winter Lord?"

Kopic cocks his head to the side and studies me for a moment. "Not the Winter Lord, exactly, but a member of the royal family. Did you not know?"

"I was only given a few details about my new partner and told he was a member of the court. Have you been acting as his guard?"

"No. I've been the emissary for the Lady Liani for the last twenty years." He offers a slight bow from the back of his horse, then gestures toward the estate.

"Twenty years?" Even though I try not to gawk, I know I'm staring. He doesn't look a day over that. Glittering eyes, snow-white hair—he's beautiful. Just like every other Fae.

"I'm much older than I look." He smiles. "Excuse Wella's disposition. She's…an acquired taste. You'll be taking her place as Valen's guard."

"Valen." The name rolls comfortably off my tongue. "He's my new charge?"

"Yes. He's Lord Orbik's only nephew. The Winter Lord has no heir, so I suppose Valen is technically next in line—not that Orbik has any plans of abdicating."

"I look forward to meeting him. He must be very special."

"Not really." He looks back and forth, then leans in a bit closer. "He's actually kind of a pain in the ass." Kopic points to the hilpberry tree. "You're welcome to sample it if you'd like. They're one of my personal favorites."

Memories of the sweet fruit tempt me. Popping berries by the handful as a child, sucking on them until they exploded in my mouth. Unparalleled sweetness followed by a small burst of bitterness. I remember the tartness of the seed splitting against my tongue like it was just yesterday.

When a Fae offers you something, it's considered deeply disrespectful to decline. I'm not hungry, but the last thing I want to do is insult anyone so early into my assignment. "I appreciate it. Thank you." I pluck several berries from the tree and pop them into my mouth.

Kopic does the same. His eyes roll back into his head, and he lets out a moan. "Delicious, aren't they?"

"My memory doesn't do them justice." I straighten and gather my reins, unable to wait any longer. The berries are a nice surprise, but I'm dying to meet Valen. Plus, I'm freezing. Frostbite isn't exactly how I want to start my time in the Winter Court. "Shall we continue?"

With a nod, Kopic spurs his horse forward, and we canter down the path. When we reach the grand gateway, there are two hulking guards stationed on either end. Their armor is sleeveless, offering no protection from the harsh wind and cold. I'm jealous. I've heard the cold doesn't bother Winter Fae. Me? I stopped feeling my fingers and toes a day ago.

We ride through the gate and around the back of the estate, to a massive brick-faced stable. Like the pathway leading to the house, it's surrounded by flowering plants despite the harsh winter conditions. Large blooms in varying shades of blue and purple hang from vines that grow up the side of the building. The roof, covered in slightly frosted moss, comes to a high point, then drops low to overhang a small receiving area, where two stable maids, both in riding leathers, wait.

"This...this is all residual magic from the tear?"

Kopic smiles. "I've heard druid magic was truly a wonderous thing. It rivaled our own in fortitude. Some Fae were envious of it. Even with the destruction of the tear, it remained in the land, unlike our own power, which ebbed from all things."

It seems like such a far distance from the destruction site for residual magic to still be affecting the land. But maybe there's still a bit of Fae power left. Maybe, like the Aphelians', it partners with the druid power to create this small miracle.

"Did you journey well?" the shorter of the two stable maids asks as Kopic pulls his horse to a stop and dismounts. She brushes a stray cerulean lock from her face and smiles as she positions herself close, eyes greedily soaking up every inch of his impressive form.

"I did," is Kopic's response. He seems oblivious to her attention as he extends a hand to help me from my horse. "Is Valen on the grounds?"

The other maid shakes her head. She's taller than the first, with well-toned arms and deep red hair gathered in a severe ponytail. "He's with Buri. Lord Orbik intends to present the Aphelian to him this evening, at the festivities."

Kopic groans. "They still haven't told him?"

Both stable maids shake their heads.

"Wait..." I hold up my hand, sure I'm misunderstanding. "Are you saying Valen doesn't know he's been assigned an Aphelian guard?" Getting assigned an Aphelian isn't something generally kept a secret. It's an honor worth bragging about because there aren't many of us anymore. Why haven't they told him?

He's kind of a pain in the ass...

An ember of concern works its way into my chest. Is Valen going to be a handful? Not that it matters. I'm adaptable.

Still... It would be nice to know what I'm walking into.

Kopic sighs and gestures for me to follow him. We walk away from the stable, onto a path lined with red and pink roses. The fragrant scent reminds me of summers in the field behind the training arena in Lunal.

"Valen is under the assumption that he needs no protection," Kopic says. "Unfortunately, that's not the case."

I pull my attention from the blooms and force my mind

to focus. Okay. So maybe he's just proud. Determined to maintain independence. I can see how having a partner, a protector, forced on you might be unpleasant. "I'll need a list of his enemies. His daily schedule and—"

"Everything you need has been gathered and is waiting." Kopic points toward the estate. "For now, we must get you ready. You can't go before the royal family of the Winter Lands looking like *that*."

2

Valen

My uncle's party is going strong, and as I reach the edge of the courtyard and slip into the main hall of the estate, I pause. The sound of chortling and music drifts out from the ballroom on the other side of the hallway. Another extravagant ball thrown to celebrate some pathetic event he's declared a victory. At one time, we celebrated real triumph. Far back before I was born, but I've heard the stories. Now, we reward the smallest mediocrities, because they're all we have left.

Kopic rounds the corner at the opposite end of the hall, and I spin, hoping to duck into the alcove before he sees me.

"Valen! Wait."

"Damn it," I mutter. My aunt Liani's head guard, the ever-present thorn in my ass, starts toward me. Ladies to be charmed, drinks to be consumed—sleep to be had—and Kopic's favorite pastime is to get in my way. He's not a bad guy…he's just missing a personality. And a sense of humor. Possibly even a libido. I've never seen a Fae so oblivious to the adoration of those around him.

He crosses to me in three large strides. I'm not offended by the perpetual grimace on his face. It's a greeting reserved solely for me. But I suppose I've more than earned it — a fact I take great amounts of pride in.

"I've been looking for you."

"I'm sure you have." I turn and start walking back to the east wing. There's a flask in my pocket and at least one more bottle of wine left in my room. I just have to remember where I hid it… "I'll save you the trouble. I was not the one who raided the wine cellar last night."

Not a lie. Technically, I sent someone else to do it for me.

"Lady Liani wants to speak to you." He sprints past and positions himself in front of me, arms folded and lips set in a grim line.

I stop short, study him, and sigh. "You look like you're in pain, Kopic. Constipated, perhaps?" I jab a finger at him. "You should eat more fiber."

He ignores my sarcasm — like usual — and maintains his stony expression. "Liani wants to confirm you'll be in attendance tonight. She and Orbik need to speak with you."

"Have you ever known me to miss a party?" The same group of Fae drinking, eating, and cavorting until they can no longer stand on their own provides an endless source of amusement. Plus, I'm never at a loss for company. My uniquely colored violet eyes have garnered many admirers over the years. The royal blood in my veins probably doesn't hurt, either.

"Lord Orbik and Lady Liani would like you to join them promptly."

I flash him my most practiced grin. "Kopic, I believe

my aunt wants me there, but my uncle? I think we both know better." Unlike my peers in the court, the Winter Lord finds my presence disturbing. I once overheard him tell Kopic that he wanted me tossed into the woods as an infant. A feast for the wolves that lurk outside our gates.

Kopic's expression softens. "You look so much like his beloved sister. I'm sure—"

"Not to worry, old-timer. I'm not about to cry over it." I wink. "Look at it this way. His treatment of me is the perfect excuse to drink!"

The grimace returns to his face as he nods at the door. "I assume you can find your way inside?"

I wave toward the ballroom with a flourish. Escaping him at this point is out of the question, so I might as well go with it. Kopic puts up with my antics, but he'll drag me into the party kicking and screaming if need be. That would end badly for both of us. "I don't think it'll be a problem."

"Just to be sure, I'll wait here. You know—in case you get lost along the way."

I bow. "Your *kindness* knows no limits. I owe you a gift. Perhaps something to unclench your ass?"

He grumbles and points to the door. I whirl and start walking, shuffling my feet to the beat of the music coming from the ballroom.

I feel his gaze on me as I make my way toward the party and slip inside through the southern entrance. The hall outside the ballroom teems with party guests. They offer enthusiastic greetings as I pass, dressed in their finery, the most lavish silks and jewels the kingdom has to offer, all in the Winter Lord's bland signature colors—silver and ice-blue. I once suggested changing them to orange and green. No one was amused.

Music drifts from the cavernous room, a spirited melody that has a generous portion of the guests dancing with a frenzy. Cheers and laughter ring out. They mingle with the sound of clinking glasses and clanging cutlery. It's a familiar—and somewhat predictable—scene of revelry that my uncle has become known for.

Orbik sits at the front of the hall, seated with my aunt behind the main table. He's talking to Fedica, one of the winter nymphs who oversees Havierst, the small forest that borders the Winter Lands in the south. His crown glints, the ice-diamonds making Fedica wince each time he tilts his head and they catch the light. There are rumors that he wears the damned thing to bed, and it wouldn't surprise me in the slightest. In fact, I wouldn't be surprised if it has become fused to his huge head.

Several wood nymphs join the conversation, and they look less than thrilled. Relationships with the nymphs have become tense in recent months. Stragglers from the remains of the other courts are becoming more brazen, their desperation pushing them across our borders. They steal and ransack the villages in search of supplies. There was a time my uncle would have moved mountains to stop them. I'm told he would rally his guard and lead them himself until the last of the scavengers were driven from the land. Now, he rarely leaves the estate. Probably a good thing. Going into battle with that ridiculous crown on his head would cause balance problems.

"Valen! Over here. We have Geela wine!" a male voice calls from the crowd, while a small group of Fae along the far wall bat their eyes and pose provocatively to catch my attention.

"Val!" another shouts from a cluster of men by the bar. Several in the group lift their glasses and cheer before tipping their heads back to drain their drinks.

I move farther into the room, colliding with a small but surprisingly solid obstacle.

"Have you forgotten me so soon?" The estate chef's daughter, Kitara, wraps a soft hand around my arm. "I called on you this morning. Are you avoiding me?"

She's pretty. Stunning, really, with chestnut hair that just barely brushes the bottoms of her ears. Her gauzy white dress leaves little to the imagination, adorned with crystals of ice-blue and silver. I should be struck by the sight of her. Breath stolen and heart pounding at the sound of her delicate voice. Kitara is strength and beauty — everything someone like me should want.

Should but don't.

"The only one I have the energy to try avoiding in this place is Kopic." I extract myself from her grip. "Did we have something to discuss? Because I thought we were just having fun."

Her lips press thin, and the lines of her jaw twitch as she fights a grin. "Are you implying you don't believe us to be destined for a claim?"

"Save it for fables and wistful romantics." I laugh. We enjoy each other's company occasionally, but a *forever bond* isn't in our future, and she knows it. "You're more sensible than that."

"You have a point." She pouts, then gestures toward the door with a wicked grin. "Should we find someplace quieter to *enjoy each other*? I might even be willing to share you this evening."

"As tempting as that is, I'm afraid I'm going to pass."

I turn to my uncle. He's still talking with Fedica, but it seems the conversation is winding down. "There are court matters to discuss with my uncle."

"*Court matters?*" Kitara lets out an undignified snort. "Is there a party to plan? A drinking contest to participate in?" She leans close, her breath smelling of Geela wine and sweet fruit. "What could the Winter Lord possibly need of you?"

Her words aren't meant to offend me, but they do. A pampered royal with too much free time and no filter— that's my reputation around the estate. It's fair. I've more than earned it. When my nose isn't buried in books, my lips are poised at the mouth of a bottle. If I'm not out working off nervous energy with a run, I'm sweating it out in bed with anyone willing. I might be a royal, but I don't have the heaps of responsibilities the others do.

I have *one*.

It's that solitary responsibility, that singular job I'm so uniquely able to do, that has me seeking out unique—and, at times, destructive—ways to deal with my existence.

When Orbik *requests* an audience during a party, it's never about revelry. He needs something from me.

A *donation* I have no desire to give.

3

Keltania

"This gown is beautiful but...impractical. How in the Goddess's name am I supposed to fight wearing"—I grasp the front of the long green dress and tug it away from my body, the fabric whispering as it moves—"this?"

Roriel, the dark-green-haired Fae tasked with getting me ready, rolls her eyes.

They scrubbed me, spritzed me, twisted and curled my hair to the point of tears, then stuffed me into a flowing dress. Absurdity aside, it's the most stunning thing I've ever seen. Floor-length and the color of fresh pines, it swishes and flows as though made of air. The color is amazing and makes my bright red hair and hazel eyes stand out.

The straps are thin, the right one covered in flowers and ivy leaves that spill down across the center of my chest and wrap once around my waist before cascading down the left front side of the skirt. The dress is backless, adorned with matching floral and ivy strands, three of them strung horizontally across my back—the first going from shoulder to shoulder, the second mid-back, and the third just above my waist.

I feel naked. Though not transparent, the material affords no protection if something noteworthy should arise.

Or the wind should blow too strongly in the wrong direction.

"Where am I supposed to keep my weapon?"

Roriel's delicate laughter sounds like wind chimes, but there's a cutting undertone to it. "Silly Aphelian. You've no need of a weapon in the Winter Lord's estate! Valen is beloved. No one would dare harm a hair on his handsome head."

I hold my tongue. If that were true, I wouldn't be here.

A knock sounds at the door. A moment later, Kopic pokes his head into the room. "Is she ready yet? They're waiting for her."

Roriel sighs. She fiddles with the tiny white flowers she's woven into my long hair, then steps aside. "Take her. There's not much else I can do with"—she makes a sweeping gesture in my direction and scrunches up her nose—"this."

An acidic retort lingers on my tongue, but I bite down hard to keep it from spilling out. Give me five minutes alone with her, and I'll show her what she could do with *this*. Or more accurately, what *this* could do with *her*.

No. Breathe. I'm here for Valen. This particular Fae's snobbish opinions don't matter.

Kopic leads me into the hall and steers me toward a winding glass staircase while sneaking sidelong glances every few moments. "You look…interesting. You present better than expected."

"What were you expecting, exactly?" I haven't met many Winter Fae yet, but so far, Kopic has been the friendliest.

No one has been outwardly rude, but I expected more fanfare. Growing up, I heard tales of Aphelians arriving to long paths of rose petals, feasts lasting for several days—even a parade. All I can think is, *Alainya would be so disappointed if she were standing here in my place.* I hope her new assignment is all she dreamed it would be. Gifts and parties and perfection.

To me, things aren't relevant. In fact, I'm actually relieved there's no huge fuss. I've never been one for attention. It used to make me uncomfortable when Levina insisted I take the center ring and demonstrate maneuvers for my cousins. Their eyes, their expectations… There were only four of us, but that was three too many. It will be nice knowing that my only responsibility is to Valen going forward.

"You're new, I take it?" Kopic slows his pace but doesn't stop. "I only see your induction sigil."

"I was anointed just before we left Lunal." The sigil on my forehead itches, almost as if responding to his question. "I look forward to adding more."

"I've always wondered how the druids felt about them." Kopic chuckles. "We Fae are, dare I say, quite shallow when it comes to our beauty. Intentionally marking our bodies? Most would sooner die."

"The sigils are badges of honor," I tell him. "Visible proof that we carry forth the bond between Servis and Aphelian."

Kopic frowns. For a moment, it seems like he might say more, but instead, he focuses on the hallway ahead of us and quickens his pace. "You can relax, you know. You don't need to be so…official."

"I'm sorry?"

"Well, the whole bond thing. Honor, duty, and so on." He stops walking and turns to me. "A little advice, if I may?"

"Of course."

"I've met several Aphelians in my time. I know how you're trained, how strict your teachings are. How regimented…" He shakes his head. "Valen won't respond to those things."

"You're saying he's not the formal type?"

Kopic laughs. "No. He's most definitely not the *formal* type. Valen is… Well, he just isn't interested in the, um, courtly side of things."

"So, he's more relaxed?" That's good. I've studied Fae tradition and rules, behaviors and appropriate conversations, but keeping them all straight in my head terrifies me. Nobles are different. There's a bit of wiggle room. But members of the royal court? That can get tricky.

"Relaxed is…one way to put it."

"I understand. Thank you, Kopic. I appreciate the heads-up."

"You're going to need it."

"What?"

"Nothing. Nothing… Are you ready?"

"Might I ask what's expected of me this evening?" I haven't been allowed my weapons, and they've wrapped me up like a gift to present to Valen. Am I supposed to smile? Bat my eyes and offer an array of ego-boosting compliments? Perhaps I'm expected to simply stand there and look pretty. Deceptively demure and hiding my deadly skills until there's need of them. A party isn't an ideal situation for Valen and me to get to know each other.

Kopic pushes through a set of double doors framed in

silver and gestures to a room across the way. "Have you never been to a party?"

"We don't have parties in the Order." Brutal training, constant bruises, rationed food, and bare bedding—but parties? The closest I ever got to a party was the farewell feast the night before I came here, and I skipped it.

"Well, then… Prepare for the time of your life." He pushes open the doors so I can peer inside, and everything spins a bit. My stomach pitches, and I swallow the sudden lump forming in my throat.

The expansive room is full of Fae. The revelers are dressed in flowing gowns and sharp tunics. Heads of intricately curled and knotted coifs bounce about as they move.

"Amazing, isn't it?"

I've never seen anything like it. The laughing party guests, the upbeat music—the tables and tables of food! "It's…unbelievable."

Everyone dances and drinks and laughs as a lively tune drifts from a trio of musicians in the corner. They are triplets, all dressed alike, their hair twisted into matching knots atop their heads.

I follow Kopic as the crowd parts to allow us passage to the dais at the front of the room. "Lord Orbik, Lady Liani," he says, bowing low. "I've brought you the Aphelian."

Orbik stands and steps around the table. He's tall with broad shoulders and a lean frame draped in a satiny blue tunic. Fae age differently than humans, so it's impossible to guess his age—as proven with Kopic—but I know he's been ruling the Winter Lands for at least four hundred years.

Really, he doesn't look a day over two hundred.

"Your name?" His deep voice booms, and when our eyes meet, it takes all my strength not to turn away. I don't intimidate easily, but Orbik is a force of nature. The air around him is chilled, and there's a storm brewing behind his eyes.

"Aphelian." Short. Simple. I hadn't expected to get so nervous in the presence of the Winter Lord. He's imposing, yes, and has a commanding air of leadership and strength, but I've heard how kind he is. How thoughtful and welcoming he's been to the Aphelians who ended up in his court in the past.

Lady Liani laughs. Like Roriel, it sounds like music. But there's also the smallest hint of menace. Sitting before me, on an ornate chair lined with silver, is an ethereal creature. Delicate and blindingly beautiful, with long raven hair and eyes that match the clearest blue skies. But underneath all that beauty is a viper looking for an excuse to strike. The truth of it flickers in her eyes as they rake across me, assessing. Warning. Protective, I realize. I'm here to guard Valen. If I mess up—if I allow him to be harmed—she'll come for me.

I like her.

"You must have been given a name at birth?" she asks.

"My name is Aphelian," I repeat as evenly as I can.

"I suppose it is. Her *gracious* blood runs through your veins, after all." She laughs and bends to look me in the eye. "I hope your loyalty is as unflinching as hers was."

"I promise you, my loyalty to Valen is my highest priority." I stand a little straighter. "We will be—"

"You summoned me, Uncle?" a profoundly resonant voice asks from behind me. I turn to find a tall Fae with night-dark hair gathered into a low ponytail. He adjusts his silver tunic and squares his shoulders, giving me a dismissive once-over from the corner of his eye.

Orbik points a meaty finger in my direction. "Valen, this is—"

Valen holds up his hand and barely glances at me. He sighs. "A human. Yes, I can see that."

Lady Liani frowns. "Dear one, this *human* is an—"

He turns to fully face me, and I gasp. He has high cheekbones, generous lips, and a chin that comes to an understated point. But his eyes—they're what draw my attention. In my years at the Order, I've seen many Fae come and go. Hundreds of them, eye colors ranging from every shade of blue, gray, and gold—but never violet.

His gaze immediately goes to the mark on my forehead. "...Aphelian." He offers a bow. Something akin to sadness flashes across his features, but it's gone so fast that I'm not even sure I saw it in the first place. "I apologize. I wasn't aware—"

"Enough," Orbik snaps. Color flames in his cheeks as he glares at Valen. "This Aphelian is here to act as your guard. She is here to serve!"

Oddly, it's more his tone than the actual words that has me cringing. It's true—we come to the Fae to protect, to use what little magic we've retained to ensure their survival. In some way, I suppose that could be viewed as serving. But to hear it said like that, with anger instead of adoration, is jarring. "I—"

"You will address her with respect." Valen's deep voice spits the words out low and cool. "Aphelians are no more servants than you or I."

His aunt rises and nods. "Excuse your uncle. It's been a long day, and he's tired." To me, she says, "Please excuse the Winter Lord. He means no disrespect. Of course, you are welcome here as a part of the Winter Court."

I nod, not trusting myself to speak.

Valen's lips part, and he seems to hold his breath for a moment. "Regardless, we've talked about this, Uncle, and you know my feelings." He turns and bows. "With respect, I don't need—or want—a new guard. Mika—"

Orbik steps back around the table and settles into the chair beside his mate, then snaps his fingers high in the air. Seconds later, a petite Fae with deep-purple hair hurries over with a goblet of pink liquid. "This is not open for discussion, Valen. The sight of you may sicken me, but your life is far too important to risk. The Aphelian goes where you go. That is the end of it. Are we clear?"

The sight of Valen sickens the Winter Lord? What is that supposed to mean? What kind of a mess has Levina dropped me into?

Valen grits his teeth, a muscle twitching in his jaw. His fists clench tight, and it almost looks like he'll make a scene. From the not-so-subtle hints Kopic dropped, it wouldn't surprise me. Fury churns in his eyes, and every muscle tenses.

I have no idea what to expect, so I ready myself for anything. Winter Lord or not, Valen is the one I'm here for. He's who I will die to protect. After a moment, though, he turns on his heel and strides into the crowd, leaving me no choice but to hike up my ridiculous dress and follow.

"I'd like for us to go somewhere and talk, if that's okay?" I ask as I race to catch up. I'm not even sure he can hear me over the loud music, but his pace increases.

"There's nothing to talk about," he calls over his shoulder as we pass a blue-haired Fae carrying a tray of drinks. Valen snatches two as he passes. I expect him to hand one to me, but instead, he downs the first in a single gulp, then chases it with the second, depositing both glasses on the next server's tray without looking back or slowing down. He reaches the large double doors and kicks at them in a single, brutal assault. They fling outward and clatter against the wall. "I respectfully ask that you go back to where you came from."

"I — Go back to where I came from? Do you understand why I'm here? Are you confused?" I bite out each word.

He keeps walking but finally slows just a bit. "It's possible. You'd be surprised at the number of times I've been asked that."

"Wait." I race ahead and jump in front of him, effectively bringing him to a stop. He sighs and slumps against the wall next to a darkened alcove. One eyebrow raised, I press on. "Look, you're obviously unhappy to see me. Could you at least tell me why? Most Fae would be thrilled to have an Aphelian guard. Yet you…"

The muscle in his jaw flexes again. Once. Twice. Three times… He pushes himself off the wall and gestures to the hall. "I officially release you of your duties here. You are free to go wherever you want."

I put my hands on my hips. "I *want* to be here."

"You don't know anything about *here*. *Here* is highly overrated," he mutters as he fishes into his pocket and pulls out a handful of coins. "How about I pay you?"

I stare at the coins in his hand, blinking several times to make sure I'm not hallucinating. "Pay me to what?"

"To leave. Buy a boat. Sail around the world." He grabs my hand and dumps several coins into my palm. "Purchase your weight in cheese or ferrets. I don't care what you do, as long as you don't do it here."

"You want to pay me —"

"Yes."

"To leave?"

He quirks a brow and winks. "You pick things up quickly. Are all Aphelians as smart as you?"

"Wow." This isn't happening. Maybe it's a joke? Some weird hazing ritual everyone forgot to tell me about? Whatever it is, I'm done.

"Impressed by my negotiating skills?" He laughs. "You're not the first."

"You got me. I'm impressed. But it's not your negotiating skill that has me stunned."

He pulls out a flask and raises it to his lips, but I grab it and throw it over my shoulder before he can take a sip. It bounces off the wall and clatters to the floor, spilling bright red liquid onto the marble.

He stares after it, mouth hanging open. "You — did you really just — I can't believe you wasted perfectly good wine!"

"What's stunning about you is the level of immaturity and lack of appreciation. Aphelians are hard to come by! Your uncle obviously cares a great deal —"

"My uncle is trying to protect a resource and nothing more."

There's anger in his tone, but also pain. Whatever the situation here, it isn't a simple one.

"Valen, I —"

There's movement in the corner. Then, a rush of footsteps. From the shadows, a tall form cloaked in black lunges for us. Silver glints against the dark, and I knock Valen aside and spin, reaching for the weapon's hilt as it rockets toward us. I miss—*shit!*—and wrap my fingers around the blade instead.

The skin of my palm splits open, and I cringe against the sharp sting. A string of curses spills from my lips as I pivot, bringing my elbow up hard. It lands against the assailant's jaw with a satisfying *thwack*, and he stumbles back, quickly righting himself for another round.

"Get back," I growl at Valen. He ignores me, standing by my side as the enemy roars with fury and charges.

"I gladly sacrifice myself, and my house, if it means saving our people from the Omen!" The attacker draws back to throw another knife at Valen.

I twist and kick out, sweeping my leg into the back of Valen's knees. The action sends him down, cursing as he lands safely outside the path of the blade. As the robed figure lumbers closer, I grab his forearm and twist, changing his trajectory. He crashes into the adjacent wall, and the motion displaces his hood to reveal an older Fae with thinning silver hair and golden eyes.

Valen makes a choking sound, and when I glance down to check on him, he's pale and staring at our attacker. "Keeper Fleeting?"

"You two have met?" I toe off my ridiculous shoes.

"He was my childhood tutor…" Valen's eyes are wide, but there's no hurt there. I see only anger.

"Seems like you made quite an impression," I tell him as I circle the assailant. "Misbehave during lessons?"

Fleeting mumbles something and prepares for another attack. As he lunges, I twist and grab his shoulders, bringing my head forward. The resounding *crack* as our skulls collide sends a wave of vertigo through me and topples him off-balance. He stumbles back, grabbing the wall so he doesn't crumple to the ground.

Valen smirks. "Maybe he heard about the things I did with his daughter—"

With a roar, the elder Fae launches himself at Valen. It's a foolish move; if he'd had any sense, he would have aimed for me. Given the angle he charges in at, I simply have to pivot and kick. The blow nails its mark. He flies backward, then drops like a sack of grain.

"Are there other *tutors* I should know about?"

"Everyone here loves me," Valen says, narrowing his eyes. He's leaning back on his elbows, casual as can be, like he hasn't a care in the world.

"Apparently not." I bend down and extend my hand to help him up.

He grumbles something, then reaches for it, stopping just shy of touching me. His expression morphs from annoyed to horrified, and he throws both hands out to stop me from coming closer. "No!"

I resist the urge to flip my pinkie at him, an insult among polite Fae society and something I never would have entertained doing until tonight. Kopic is right. He *is* a pain in the ass.

But I realize it isn't me he's shouting at. His eyes are focused on something over my shoulder.

Fleeting. *Goddess.*

Turning my back on the enemy, even when victory appears inevitable, is a rookie move. I've been in the same scenario during training a hundred times back home. My first time out in the world, and I blow it?

The hairs on my arms and neck jump to attention, and a curse lodges in my throat as I whirl to find the blade hurtling straight toward my head.

No, not toward my head. *At* my head. Directly in front of my left eye. But it isn't moving. It's frozen—in every sense of the word. The blade is encased in ice and suspended a mere inch from impaling me. It hovers there for a moment before falling to the floor and shattering into a thousand small pieces, and behind me, Valen lets out a wheezing breath.

He didn't just—

Instinct kicks in, and I lunge for Fleeting. He's produced another weapon, this one a smaller blade with the subtlest gleam of green. Poison. I catch his hand as he pounces, pivoting and twisting the knife inward. It pierces his shoulder, and he screams and hits the ground. It only takes seconds for the poison to kick in, and he begins to convulse.

I sink to the floor in front of Valen, knowing what I've seen, knowing it's impossible. This kind of magic doesn't exist in the world anymore. Druid power is rooted in life, in nature, and because of that, it couldn't be drained completely. But Fae enchantment over the elements? That's been gone for millennia, drained during the war. Yet...

"You have magic," I whisper. *Goddess.* A Fae exists with magic.

He glances around the courtyard and, satisfied no one has seen him, nods. He watches me for a moment, then sighs and says, "Aye, I have magic."

4

Valen

After the Aphelian alerts the Winter Guard and they promptly take the dying Fleeting away, I try to give her the slip, to gain some kind of distance. I fail.

I'm almost back to my bedroom, and she's right on my heels. *Slap, slap, slap.* Her footsteps have now replaced Kopic's irritated *cluck* as my least favorite sound.

"Who else knows about the magic?" she asks.

She's the strangest human I've ever met. They come from Lunal to barter occasionally. Trade their wares for threads and pelts of native wildlife. They're always treated with kindness, offered fair deals, and given gifts of friendship. In return, they share their stories and their passion for life. The rumor is that's what made Servis fall so deeply in love with Aphelian in the first place. Humans are short-lived. When you survive as long as we do, you tend to forget how to *live.* Through their eyes, we're able to see beauty in the world long after our own senses have dulled to it.

I don't answer her until we've reached my door. "My aunt and uncle know, of course, as well as a few members of the staff. Kopic and Buri know, too."

I push through the door to my bedroom, then settle on the edge of the bed as she leans against the wall to watch me. Something tells me that no amount of bribery, no measure of pleading, will get her to leave.

The last thing my miserable existence needs is someone trying to push themselves into my life. It's already complicated and messy—not to mention dangerous—and I don't have room to share it. Not anymore.

On the other hand, a small voice in the back of my mind says that maybe she'll be good for me.

Maybe it's her dark eyes and red hair I find engaging. She has curves and a definition to her frame that sets her apart from the others at court. A strength and hardness that make me curious what her life was like before coming here.

"Who is Buri?" She turns and closes the door, giving me an unobstructed view of her backside. When she turns around, she catches me staring. "Were you just—are you staring at my—"

"What? It's a very nice…form."

"I—you—" Her cheeks flush, and I like the color. It brings out her eyes.

"Oh, relax. Think of it as a compliment. I mean, it's not like I'm the only one who saw it. The fabric back there is nearly see-through."

If possible, the red in her cheeks gets brighter, and her mouth hangs open. She drops her hands to cover her rear and backs up against the wall. "You were saying? About Buri?"

"She's been helping me focus my magic." If I can learn to control it, then maybe I won't have to donate the magic

Orbik uses to keep us safe.

"What makes her qualified?" Her lips quirk, both thin brows lifting in question. "No one's had magic in thousands of years, right?"

"She was born before the Great Drain and used to teach magic to the younger generations in town. My uncle sent her to me."

The druid rolls her eyes. Brownish green with tiny flecks of gold, they remind me of the jasper vines that grow in the field behind the estate. Creeping things that twist around whatever they touch, luring you in with their beauty…then choking the life from you. So far, the comparison seems dead-on. "Is that wise?"

I stare. "Is *what* wise?"

"Trusting someone so implicitly." She pushes off the wall, forgetting about the dress, and steps farther into the room. "Considering a beloved teacher, someone you knew from childhood, just tried to gut you not an hour ago…"

"I never said he was *beloved*." I point to the empty decanter on the table next to my bed. "This conversation might go better if we both have a drink. I have a bottle of wine around here someplace…"

"So, he *didn't* like you?" She clasps her hands behind her back and tilts her head. Several strands of hair fall across her face, but she ignores them. Why the hell do I feel the urge to brush them aside? It's the color. That must be it. I've never seen hair the shade of wildfire.

"Like I said, maybe he heard about his daughter and me." There's far more to it than that, but I have no reason to tell my new *friend*. If I have my way, she won't be sticking around. "I suppose he might have been annoyed."

"*Everyone here loves me. That's what you said less than*

an hour ago, isn't it? Seems you were wrong." She leans against the wall a few feet from the bed. Her dress is torn in several places. The vines in the back hang, swaying loose over her bare skin, but that, too, escapes her notice. "Who else might *like* you the way he did? Maybe this Buri is harboring deep-seated feelings of hatred?"

"Buri harbors deep-seated feelings, but they aren't hatred." She would be easier to deal with if they were. "And I doubt my uncle would have me trained by someone he hadn't properly vetted." I touch a finger to the bedspread. A small section of it ices over, the frost glinting against the soft light coming in from the moon. Tonight's been stressful. Sometimes it helps to release the magic a little at a time to keep it from building. "I'm the only known living Fae with magic. I'm too important for Orbik to risk."

"I bet it's a lot of pressure, huh?" She sits on the other end of the bed. The mattress barely dips beneath her small frame. Cunning and agile... My mind wanders to her fight with Fleeting, to the way she moved.

Definitely agile.

"Ahh. Now I get it." She's just trying to be nice, to form the bond that's supposed to take root between us. Problem is, I don't want it. Bonds like that only cause more problems in the long run.

"Get what?" she asks.

"Why the druids picked you to come to the Winter Lands. They found you completely annoying."

"Yep. That's it." She rolls her eyes. "You've uncovered their secret. They wanted to get rid of me."

I brush the frost off the bedspread. "Makes sense. You just got here, and I find you irritating."

"I guess you're going to have to learn to live with the

irritation, then, Valen. I'm not leaving."

"There has to be someplace else you'd rather be." I jab my finger toward the large map tacked to my wall. "Anywhere in Derriga! Say the word, and I'll send you."

"I'm right where the Goddess wants me to be." The corner of her lips twitch, and a pang of regret washes through me at the hint of sadness in her eyes. "The relationship between a Fae and an Aphelian is special. It's a bond unlike anything else. It should come easily, but if you insist on fighting it, then I can't stop you. But that doesn't change things. My job is to ensure you continue sucking up oxygen."

"And wine. Don't forget the wine."

She sighs and gets to her feet, shaking off defeat and smiling. "It's getting late. Where am I supposed to sleep?"

I glance at my bed. "Plenty of room in here."

She stares at me.

Fantastic. She's got as much of a sense of humor as Kopic.

"Pick any one of the rooms down the hall." I stand and cross to the door, pulling it open. "They're all empty."

Her brows lift as she pokes her head around the corner and looks down the right side of the hall, then the left. "How many people live in this wing?"

"One. If you aren't leaving, then two. The entire east wing of the estate belongs to me."

Instead of going to one of the rooms, she points to the door across the hall, directly in line with mine. "What about this one?"

I look from her to the door. "That's a…closet."

She pushes past me and pulls open the door. It's full of clothes and boxes and layers of dust. It's used to store the excess things my aunt keeps sending along. Useless trinkets taking up room that could otherwise be used for books. "It'll work."

"*It'll work?* The other rooms—"

She stares at the small space across the hall. "If it's my choice, then I choose this space."

I don't argue with her. For all I know, she slept in a closet where she came from. "Whatever." With a bow, I say, "If you need anything, don't hesitate to call someone else."

"I want to ward all the ways in and out of this wing before I turn in. Is it possible to get someone else to clear away the empty boxes?"

I shrug. "I'll make sure it's taken care of."

"Thank you." She turns and hesitates. "And Valen?"

Gods. "What?"

"I know you don't want me here, but I'm going to grow on you. Just wait."

I close the door and groan, then head back to my bed and flop down like a dead weight. "Yeah. Like fungus, maybe."

Footsteps echo, and a moment later, her face hovers above mine. "You know, there are actually quite a few beneficial fungi out there." She's grinning, and it's impossible not to notice the way the right-hand corner of her lips tilts at an odd angle. It gives her face character. Makes it interesting...

I hate myself for noticing.

"Good night, Valen."

"Good night, Fungus."

As the bedroom door closes, the relief I feel at her absence quickly turns to worry. I fear someone else— someone like Fleeting—will make the Aphelian's stay here unnaturally short. After all, it's happened before...

5

Keltania

Using my finger, I trace the druid sigil for alarm—a circle with two long curved lines through the upper right-hand corner—onto the underside of my left forearm. The needling sensation has me biting down hard to keep from crying out. The pain will get worse with each sigil I use, and as it absorbs into my skin, I hold my breath and wait for it to pass. When it does, I'm left with a deep-red design. It shimmers and churns, rippling with the magic. The more "alive" one of our sigils is, the more power imbued in it.

I move to all the possible entry points in Valen's wing of the estate and trace the same symbol with my finger without using the ink. The power is inside me, now residing within my left arm. It won't last forever. Eventually—probably within a month—the energy from the symbol will fade. The connection between me and the things I've warded will dissipate, and I'll have to retrace the design with more ink or the wards will be useless.

It's not foolproof by any means, but it's more than Valen had yesterday.

Doors, windows, hallways—it takes me three hours to secure everything. I'll be alerted if anyone tries to enter, which is good news, as I'm exhausted by the time I make it back to the closet. It's been a long day with a lot of change.

In less than a week, I've been anointed and moved from Lunal to the Winter Lands, had my mettle tested in true battle for the first time, and found out my Fae partner wants nothing to do with me.

Valen's door is closed, and the hall beyond our rooms is dark and quiet. I push open the door to my new room, half expecting the space to remain untouched, but to my surprise, the clothing and boxes are gone. More than that, there's a cot wedged in the corner with a pile of expensive-looking linens and sleep clothes upon it, and a small silver tray atop a newly added dresser, with an assortment of cheeses and some sausage.

The new furnishings, save for the cot, look ridiculous crammed into the small space. Like someone is trying to pretty up a hovel. I could move into one of the rooms, but they're too far down the hall for my comfort. If someone managed to slip past my wards in the middle of the night, there's too great a possibility the sounds of struggle could go unheard. I won't risk anything happening to Valen. We owe the Fae. If not for them, the druids would have perished with the rest of humanity during the War.

I pop a piece of cheese into my mouth and sink onto the cot to remove my shoes, then remember I kicked them aside in the fight—no wonder my feet are sore. In the chaos, I forgot to go back for them.

The cheese is sweet with a slightly nutty flavor. Much better than what we had back home. I sample a small piece of the sausage—also delicious—and look down at myself.

I'll have to find clothing tomorrow. Something that will allow me to blend in better—despite the rounded tops of my ears. No doubt there's an entire wardrobe of the finest silk and leather waiting for me. I just hope I can find something practical. Fae fashion is better known for its aesthetics than its functionality.

The morning after the ceremony, I changed into my training gear and left the Order with nothing more than my ink, my blade, and the clothes on my back. The simple green leathers I arrived here in were the standard garb for Aphelians. They were left behind when I changed for the party, and I hope they haven't been discarded. They aren't in the best shape, worn through to the stag-hair lining in some places, but they're familiar, and I need that.

Not even a full day here, and nothing is as I expected it to be.

I shed the dress and slip on some thin linen pants and a halter—which, like most Fae fashion, leaves little to the imagination—then lay back. It's quieter here than I'm used to. The trainees' quarters in Lunal are nothing more than a canopy of vines hanging over a collection of hammocks in the middle of the forest. All my life, I've fallen asleep to the sounds of nocturnal animals going about their evening routines. Now the absence of those sounds is a vacuum, and I miss it more than I imagined possible. Though only our priestess, Levina, can connect to nature in the same way our ancestors did because of a special sigil, the rest of us druids still crave the outdoors. The small, closed-off space of my new living quarters is near suffocating, but I'll adjust. It's what we do.

Getting Valen to accept me? That might be another problem entirely.

This assignment is special because Valen is a member of the royal family. Levina put her trust—and so much extra time—into training me. I have no intention of letting her down.

"Do you know what this sigil represents?" Levina slapped the drawing down on the table. Sweeping lines and complicated swirls formed what looked like a bird on fire. I'd seen it in the old books, the ones containing the sigils we dared not use anymore.

"Rebirth."

She nodded. "Study it. Memorize it. Draw the sigil over both your hearts. If anything should happen to stop your Fae's heart, this will restart it again. It will give you one second chance. Just once."

I traced the outline with my finger. "Aren't we forbidden from using these?"

"We are, so tell no one I've given this to you. When you've memorized it, burn the parchment."

"But why? If this isn't allowed, why show it to me? Why let me use it?"

Levina's notoriously stony expression softened for a moment. She brushed my cheek with the back of her hand. "Child, you are special to me. I simply want to do everything in my power to help you succeed."

But she didn't know Valen would want nothing to do with me. How am I going to get his permission to ink the sigil that might save his life? It certainly complicates things, but I'll just have to do everything in my power to change his mind. If I can't…well, then Valen is in for a world of misery.

• • •

I wake up the next morning with a stiff neck and a kink in my back. Having no real ventilation, the air in the closet is musty and too warm, and I'm happy to get out.

Across the hall, Valen's door remains closed. I lean closer and listen, and when I hear nothing, I knock twice.

"The door is open," he calls from the other side.

Of course it is.

I steel myself against what I assume will be the start of a long day and push inside. Valen is on the edge of the bed, lacing up his boots, shirtless. He doesn't look up as I enter, and I'm grateful because I know that I'm staring.

I heard rumors of Aphelians and their Fae becoming intimate — mostly from Alainya, whose mind was never far from the bedroom — but I swore it would be impossible for me. I could never see my charge that way. A distraction like that could endanger them as well as myself. But standing here, I can't dismiss the perfection of the boy sitting across the room. Exquisitely sculpted muscles span a broad chest under deep-blue-ink-covered skin. Most of the tattoos are symbols I don't recognize, but there's one across his heart that's eerily familiar. One that chills me to the bone.

Valen clears his throat, and I realize he's caught me watching him.

"See something you like?" The right corner of his lips lift with a grin. "I can stand if that would make it easier to appreciate my God-like physique."

"That's a druid symbol." A series of lines vaguely resembling a broken lover's knot inked over his heart. But…it can't be!

His grin slips into a frown. "You know it?"

"It's called the Heartbreaker." Every Aphelian candidate is inked with the Heartbreaker sigil the day we turn fifteen. "It blocks the heart, closing it off to any kind of romantic love." We're allowed to enjoy physical relationships—there's no rule dictating a celibate life—but the Order decided more than that would be a liability.

The look on his face tells me he already knows this.

"What could possibly possess you to let someone put such a mark on your skin?" I didn't have a choice. It's simply the natural progression of being who I am. But to think someone would willingly do that to themselves…

"I'm the first Fae born with magic since the Great Drain. One day, the truth *will* get out. I'll become an even bigger target than I am now. It won't be just those who wish to stop my heart, but also those who wish to win it. I could be manipulated."

"If someone were to turn you into a lovesick fool, you mean?"

"When a Fae falls in love, it's forever." He shrugs. "It wasn't my idea."

Someone made him do it. Forced it on him? Anger burns in the pit of my stomach at the thought. "I've never seen a druid sigil inked directly on someone who isn't a druid. I didn't think it was allowed." We could ward someone else. Ink ourselves and use the magic to trace an invisible ward. But using the *ink* on someone? Unheard of.

"Must be. A druid did it. She used some of your magic dirt mixed with Fae ink. Hurt like hell." He laughs, but there's no humor in it. I can't help watching the lines of his sigil churn. It's not nearly as chaotic as mine, and I wonder if it's because they mixed it with Fae ink.

"Now…" He grabs a shirt from his bed, stretching out and flexing his muscles. With his free hand, he makes a sweeping gesture in the air, from his head to his toes. "If you've had your fill?"

"Sadly, you're going to have to stomach me a bit longer." I move to the large mirror across the room and pull the pouch of ink from my belt. "But I promise I won't enjoy it."

I tug down the collar of my halter.

"Not that I'm complaining, but if you intend to undress…"

I turn over my arm to reveal the sigil I inked to ward his rooms. "Don't you know how this works? To use what little magic we have left, we need to bind the power onto our skin. I use the ink to trace it, then, when it absorbs into me, I can ward other things. Like you."

He pales, and his expression turns stony for a moment before seamlessly melting back into the same indifference that seems to be permanently plastered to his lips. "I knew. I just haven't seen it done in a long time."

Of course he does. Someone inked the Heartbreaker…

He shrugs. "Please try not to spill your dirt on the carpet."

"Feel free to look away." I wait for a moment, and when he doesn't turn, I sigh. I picture the rebirth sigil Levina showed me the night before the ceremony. I spent the entire night studying it. Committing every line, every curve, to memory. Unlike most of the charms we use today, our ancient symbols were complex. Exact lines and dimensions need to be obeyed for the power to take. If even the slightest miscalculation is made, the consequences will be unpredictable and dire.

They also require much more ink. Much more power.

I reposition my finger and start the sigil. The sting of it makes my eyes water, but I tamp it down, stashing it deep. The stronger the sigil, the more it hurts. Add that to

the cumulative cost of the sigils, and the pain is horrible. I
tense and hold my breath as I begin to trace the sweeping
lines and intricate details.

"You look like you're in pain…" The concern in his
voice almost causes me to stop.

"It's…a bit uncomfortable." I grit my teeth and
continue.

"It wasn't always this way," he says, voice a bit softer.
"The way your magic worked?"

"Our marks were beautiful. Glowing golden lines that
glittered in the sunlight." I wasn't alive to see them in
person, but the paintings on the wall in the Order Hall are
breathtaking. I used to spend hours just staring at them,
dreaming about what mine might have looked like. "But
when the tear was lost, our magic only barely accessible,
the beauty faded, replaced by dull red ink."

Ink runs down the front of my sleep clothes and onto
Valen's carpet, despite his plea to keep things clean. He
cringes at the mess and offers me a cloth. "Thank you." I
blot the front of my shirt, then dip my finger into the ink
bag to get more.

"Looks like it's a bit more than uncomfortable." He
shifts closer to get a better look.

"It's not that bad." I bite back a hiss as I come to one
of the farthest edges, just below my collar bone. The area
is sensitive, and there's a good chance I use more ink than
needed. "Kind of tickles," I lie.

"There are much better ways to indulge a tickling fetish.
Ask me to demonstrate for you sometime."

"You have a better chance of being shit on by a dragon,
Valen." I bite the inside of my cheek as I hit another
sensitive spot.

"Hey now. You shouldn't joke about that. I knew a blacksmith that happened to. Poor guy was crushed. Do you have any idea how big dragon shit is?"

I straighten and wipe the ink from my hands. "Is this normal for you? The annoying, weird, borderline gross chatter? I mean, it's fine if it is. I just want to know what to expect. Unless, of course, this is just residual awkwardness from last night."

"Awkwardness?" His eyes widen. "I've never been awkward a day in my life."

"Well, you did seem to like my dress. Maybe you're trying to find a way to impress me."

"Impress you," he says flatly. He blinks, and I get the feeling I've caught him off guard. Good. "With my knowledge of dragon shit?"

I shrug. "How should I know what Fae girls like?"

He paces back and forth. On the third pass, he stops with a smirk and points at me. "You're *unconventional* for an Aphelian. Let me guess. You spoke to Kopic, right?"

"He *did* have some words of wisdom for me before the party. Implied that you were a bit hard to handle."

"Did he?" Valen leans in closer. "Did he tell you I drink too much? That I'll brash anything that walks?" He winks and brings his lips to my ear. His breath is like fire, and it takes all my focus not to shudder. "Did he say I'd try to bed you?"

Despite my determination not to let him affect me, my heart hammers. I keep my cool, though, and gently push him away. I need to finish what I've started.

Once I trace the mark onto Valen, if his heart stops beating, the magic will restart it. It will save his life. I hope to never be in a position where it's needed, but considering his distaste for me, it's an extra measure of protection, and I'm grateful.

He sighs and nods to the ink pouch. "If you plan on doing that to me, I'm going to stop you right there…"

"Don't trust me?" I twist so we're face-to-face.

"If it makes you feel better, I don't really trust anyone." His lips curl into a truly devastating grin. He inches even closer, invading my personal space, and squints for a better look. "What does it do?"

"Once I'm finished tracing the pattern onto your skin, it will alert me if you're in danger." Levina swore me to secrecy. Granted, the Fae probably don't know which sigils are forbidden and which aren't, but why take a chance? "I still can't get over the fact that you have an actual sigil…"

"Like I said, it's a mix of your mud and Fae ink."

I watch as his sigil twitches, barely moving, almost as if it's struggling to survive. I've never seen anything like it.

He sobers, his entire body relaxing for a brief moment. "I know what it means. I understand the weight it carries—and I respect it. It reminds me to keep myself…separate."

He's been hurt. Whatever it was—*whoever* it was—goes beyond the conflict with his uncle. I'm dying to ask questions, but if I push him, chances are good that he'll shut down. I gesture to his chest. "May I? It will be invisible, so it won't look weird over the one you have."

"This isn't necessary…" He regards me skeptically for a moment before nodding once. "But if it will move things along, fine. Just hurry. I have to meet Buri on the hill."

Nudging him back, I push him into the chair a few feet away. "Try not to move. This has to be exact."

He raises a brow and settles in. "You know, there are some Fae that find pushy humans extremely appealing. I could introduce you."

"And there are some humans that find obnoxiously flirtatious Fae filthy." I press my pointer finger to his chest, just above his heart. Like the touch of his hand, the skin is abnormally cool, but not in an unpleasant way. I find it...comforting.

"Make no mistake, Aphelian. I'm filthy. But the kind of dirty I am doesn't rinse off."

As my finger begins to move, the steady rhythm of his heart picks up, and with each line I make, the motion of his breath becomes more apparent. He closes his eyes, and I tilt my finger, skimming his skin with the tip of my short nail. I have more control over the lines this way and can work with more precision.

"That feels..." His muscles shudder beneath my touch. "Amazing."

I've never transferred a sigil from myself to another person, but I've heard the effects can sometimes be euphoric. As the magic seeps from the druid's fingers into the sigil wearer's skin, it mimics the buzz one might get after overindulging in drink or substance.

Valen's head tips back even farther, and he groans. The sound causes the tiny hairs on my arms and at the base of my neck to jump to attention.

"It's not supposed to feel good," I lie. I can't help the small thrill that races through me at the thought of making him squirm.

"Well..." He moans again, this time shifting in the seat, almost as though he's trying to move closer to my touch. "It does. Feel free to do this all day."

I flick his ear, and his eyes pop open. "Ow!"

I finish tracing the sigil and step back. For a moment,

I see the outline of it over the Heartbreaker. It pulses several times, then fades from sight. "There. Done."

He stands, watching me with an odd expression before pulling his shirt on and pointing to the door. "Are you planning to change first?"

Heat flushes my cheeks. I've forgotten all about being in my sleep clothes. "Oh. Yeah. I should do that, huh?"

"There are brand new articles for you in the *room* down the hall. You'll also find a place to wash." When I say nothing, he points toward the door again. "The sooner you go, the sooner we can leave—unless you'd like assistance?"

I glare at him.

"Also, Fae bathing facilities can be tricky. I'll gladly offer my assistance, if you'd like."

I look from him to the door. "You'll wait for me to come back?"

"I promise." He taps his chest above his heart. "In the meantime, if anyone sneaks in to assassinate me, I'm sure you'll know somehow."

"I won't be long."

I close the door and step out into the hall. Despite his improved mood, I don't trust him. A part of me wonders if he'll still be here when I return…

If he's not, I'm going to kill him myself.

6

Valen

I don't break my promise. I told the Aphelian that I'd wait, and I do. I wait until she disappears into the other room—then wait another few moments before leaving to find Buri.

Aphelians are a dedicated and determined bunch. No amount of asking, no measure of sniping, is going to get her to leave. I can see that now, so I need to change tactics. Catch her off guard and wear her down. If I make her job impossible, surely she'll give up and leave.

Because I need her to give up.

I head out to find my tutor on the hill behind the estate, her long silver hair twisting in the wind. "Valen," she says, her voice light. "You're fifteen minutes late. I was worried."

The daughter of the most renowned dressmaker in the Winter Lands, Buri grew up surrounded by luxury. Pampered, adored, and never refused, she was born several decades before the Great Drain. She'd been a prodigy when it came to controlling her magic—a particularly brutal tier of the element of water. When my uncle enlisted her to help hone my skills, she jumped at the chance to gain favor with the Winter Lord.

"Sorry." I bow. Even if I'd shown up three hours late, Buri would still be here waiting for me. "What's on the agenda for today?"

"Our last lesson focused on manipulating ice to create objects. Perhaps we could take it a step further. I was thinking—"

"Valen!" The Aphelian stomps toward us. Despite being five foot nothing, with her red hair blowing wildly in the wind, she looks like a creature out for blood. "Are you trying to get yourself killed?"

"If I said yes, would you leave?"

"You— I—" She stops in the snow a few feet in front of me and throws both hands in the air.

Buri glares at the interruption. "Was there something you needed to take care of before we begin, Valen?"

"Buri, it is my utmost displeasure to introduce you to my Aphelian." I wave offhandedly at the druid. "Just think of her as fungus. Annoying but mostly harmless. Supposedly, she'll grow on you."

"Your uncle got *another* one for you? She looks far punier than Mika."

I glare at her. Mika is a subject that's off-limits. Everyone knows that.

Buri clears her throat and surveys my new companion, then pulls her lips back into a sneer. The action distorts her delicate features. "How...nice."

Humans are a source of contention among a small group of Fae. Some believe them to be untrustworthy and vile. Stories of the fabled land of Vey Brill, where humans are said to whisk away the brightest of us—no one knows why—are peppered throughout our history. But it's nothing but myth. A tale told to make Fae children behave.

Buri cocks her head to the side and stares. If the scrutiny bothers the Aphelian, it doesn't show. She meets her gaze head-on, expression stony. Buri continues, "I never saw the last one up close." She steps forward, and for a moment, I think she'll be brazen enough to poke my new guard. I can't imagine that going over well, and a part of me is curious to see what would happen. "Send her away so we can begin."

"She's amazingly persistent. Where I go, she follows, apparently."

Buri blinks. Her gaze lingers on our unwanted guest before meeting mine again. "She can't stay here. This"— she gestures to me with a grimace—"I won't have an audience while we work."

The Aphelian takes a single step forward and draws her sword. It's an extraordinary blade. But as impressive as the weapon is, the girl herself overshadows it. Fierce, with a wild look in her eyes, she's shorter than Buri but still somehow manages to make the other Fae look small. "Refer to me as though I'm not here one more time, and I will bury my blade so far down your throat that you'll be crapping steel."

Buri's mouth hangs open. "I know the rules, druid. You cannot lay a finger on me unless I am a threat to Valen's life." She narrows her eyes. "Valen is far too precious to me. I would sooner die than see him harmed."

Her words would be comforting if I didn't know the truth behind them. It's not me that's precious to her—it's the power. It makes her seem oddly obsessive at times.

The Aphelian grabs the front of my tunic, then seizes Buri's arm before she can react and uses it to slap me across the face. Hard. "There," she says. "Now you've hit him, and I've perceived you as a threat. Irritate me again, and we'll revisit the argument." She steps away and gestures to the clearing with a devilish grin. "Carry on."

I bite down on my tongue to keep from laughing. This is a side of her I didn't see yesterday. Less formality and more attitude. I don't want to like it, but the truth is, I do.

And it just reinforces that I have to get rid of her, the sooner the better.

An hour and a lot of ice later, Buri sighs. She's barely taken her eyes off the Aphelian the entire time. "That's enough for today. Same time and place tomorrow."

"Actually, no." The Aphelian stands and brushes the snow from her clothes. She shivered through most of the lesson, but I choose to ignore her discomfort. It would call attention to her humanity, her *weakness*, as Buri would undoubtedly label it. I don't want her here, but I have no desire to embarrass her.

The Aphelian declares, "Tomorrow's lesson will take place somewhere else, and at a different time. Someone will contact you in the morning with the details."

"How dare—"

The Aphelian moves her cloak and rests a hand against the hilt of her sword. Buri seethes but doesn't say another word.

We leave her stewing on the hill and head into the woods. The Aphelian keeps my pace and says nothing as we move, though she constantly scans the area. Looking for threats? Taking note of all the small details? Maybe she's simply looking for a place to shit.

I insisted there was no need for protection, but the truth is, my enemies have become increasingly brazen with each passing day. It's only a matter of time before someone catches me unaware. I'm moderately skilled in hand-to-hand combat, but living each day without letting my guard down has become exhausting. It's resulted in one too many close calls, and sooner or later, someone is going to get the better of me. I'll need her to watch my back, at least until I can figure out a way to get rid of her.

And, in order for her to do that, she needs to know a bit about me.

"Keeper Fleeting's attack had nothing to do with his daughter." The words come easier than I expect. The truth is, I barely know his daughter. She tried to seduce me once, and I politely refused. Angry, she started the rumor to save face, and I never corrected it. She has no idea that she did me a favor. Fueling my already lecherous reputation only helps keep focus off my lesser-known traits.

The Aphelian shrugs but doesn't look at me. "I never believed it did."

"Obviously, she found me irresistibly attractive, but nothing happened between us—which I'm sure her father knew."

"Mmmhmm." She keeps walking.

"Fleeting is one in a small but determined group of Fae who will never tolerate a bastard on the throne. Since Orbik has no heir…" I let go of a pained chuckle. "It also doesn't help that several years ago, I did something.

Accidentally used my magic in front of someone. My aunt did her best to cover it up, but, as I'm sure you know, rumors spread. Because of that, some believe I'll be their end."

"The Omen…" She stops walking and turns, and I almost suggest heading back to the estate. She's trembling from the cold, and her lips have an almost blueish tint.

"Heard that, did you?"

"I'm fairly observant, Valen."

"Yes, the *Omen of Ice*. There's an ancient scroll that foretells the destruction of the Winter Court. A child born of two factions will have the power to freeze the world and bring an end to our way of life." It's largely regarded as the stories of Vey Brill—a cautionary tale. But some believe. Some, like Fleeting, believe so fully that they're willing to die for it.

She snorts and rubs her hands together. "That's ridiculous."

"I agree, but added to other things like my eyes…"

"What's wrong with your eyes?"

"Have you ever seen a Winter Fae with violet eyes? It feeds the whole two-factions bit—even though, as far as I know, none of the other courts have hereditary violet eyes."

"That's the problem with prophecies. People read into them as is convenient." She starts walking again. "So, your eyes are different? They're unique. Personally, I think they're beautiful."

"Beautiful, eh?" I jump in front of her, grinning. "I'll allow you to gaze longingly into them if you'd like."

She rolls her eyes, shoves me aside, and keeps walking. Every once in a while, when she thinks I'm not watching, she shivers. There's no point in suggesting we head back, though. Less than twenty-four hours, and I already can tell she's stubborn.

She slows as we come to the next ridge and holds her hand out to catch several flakes of falling snow. Bringing her palm up, she inspects them with the smallest hint of a smile tugging at the corners of her lips as the snow melts away. "Where are we?"

"We're approaching Hiffen, the home of the Grove Wardens," I answer as we continue to cross through the brush and over the frozen stream that marks the border.

"Grove Wardens?" she asks.

"Creatures said to have inhabited Derriga even before the Fae. When the Great Drain came and the other courts crumbled in the war, they migrated here. They're a sentient race deeply attuned to the land. I'm surprised the druids don't know of them."

She shrugs. "Some might."

"This is my favorite part of the Winter Lands." This part of our territory holds an odd kind of peace, and most days I need that. A voice in my head says this is a mistake. That sharing even the smallest bit of myself with her will draw her in, not push her away. But the words come anyway. "Sometimes, as a child, I'd come here and stand in the snow, watching the flakes fall and listening to the total absence of sound for hours."

With her head tilted toward the snow-capped trees, the Aphelian sighs. "There was a place like that for me, in Lunal. Not that it snowed, but the quiet, the peace. I get it." When our gazes meet again, she's smiling.

It's infectious, and I can't keep myself from smiling back. Maybe it's something about Aphelians in general.

Maybe they have a way of drawing you in, making you want to be near them. I was a small child when I met Mika, but I remember instantly wanting to be near her, craving her attention...

"What do you normally do after training with Buri? I assume it's more than stomp around in the snow all day?"

It's the sound of her laugh that snaps me back to reality. The pleasant timbre threatens to warm my frozen heart—and that can't happen.

"Usually, I go for a run."

I'm edgy when I'm cooped up too long. Everyone at the estate knows this. They write it off as me being spoiled, always wanting my own way, but the truth is so much more than that. I have another secret. One I've managed to keep hidden from all of them, my aunt and uncle included. If the Aphelian is going to be here—even if it's just for a short time—then she has to know this truth.

For both our sakes.

Her brows lift. "You run in the snow?"

What I'm about to do is risky, and it will undoubtedly piss her off. "As my Aphelian, your loyalty is to me, correct?"

"Haven't we covered this already?" She frowns and leans forward. "You're stuck with me, Valen."

"There's a stream a quarter mile east. Follow it, and it will take you back to the estate. It's not far."

Her eyes widen. "Take me back to the— And where the hell will you be?"

"You need to truly understand what I am." With a bow, I say, "Tell no one about this, druid. I do not command but request your silence." I bring both arms up. A second later, I use my power to make the snow swirl until we can no longer see each other. I drop to my knees and draw in the cold, welcome it until it fills me. My back arches, and my bones snap, changing, rearranging. My vision enhances, sharpening, as the sounds of the forest, ones muted to even Fae ears, come alive to animal ones.

My mother, Orbik's sister, was stolen away. To this day, we know nothing of her kidnappers, of who my father is. She was found stumbling in the woods nearly two years later, half dead, with me cradled in her arms. She didn't survive the night.

Highborn Fae don't have animal forms. There's no way my father is royalty.

When the snow clears, the Aphelian stands in the center of a small indentation left by the vortex, staring at what I would guess is the largest wolf she's ever seen. Not with fear or even awe, but utter surprise. "Valen?"

My reply is a roar that sends her stumbling back several feet.

I lower my nose to the snow, huff out once, twice, and then turn and lope into the woods without looking back. Maybe seeing my wolf will send her running.

It's midday by the time I return to the estate. Under normal circumstances, I would stay out until dusk, prowling through the forest, stretching my legs. But Gods help me, the guilt for leaving the Aphelian behind gnaws at my conscience the entire time I'm away. She's probably worried sick—unless she finally gave up and left. Curiosity has me picking up my pace.

My wing of the estate is dark and silent, and when I slip into my room, I'm a little surprised to find it empty. The human is dauntless. I was sure she'd be waiting here when I returned. The fact that she isn't fans those embers of guilt. Maybe she really did leave. Or what if she never made it back from the woods? She could still be out there, stumbling around in the snow looking for me. *Damnit.* Now I have to go find her.

I whirl back to the door and yank on the knob.

Nothing happens.

I try again, with the same result.

"Something wrong?" a familiar voice calls from the hallway. The sound of it both relieves me and irritates me. She isn't dead or lost; she's still here.

"The door is stuck," I say.

The Aphelian laughs. "Is it? Huh. That's inconvenient."

Clarity strikes, and the air in the room cools. *Trapped.* I'm trapped. "What did you do?"

Something brushes against the other side of the door. "Me? Why do you think I did anything?"

"Because my damned door was fine before you arrived." I kick at the heavy wooden barrier in a barrage of merciless assaults that should have the thing in splinters strewn around the room ten times over.

If she'd chosen to retaliate any other way, I wouldn't care. I know I earned her anger by leaving her behind when all she wants is to keep me safe. But this? This is a mistake.

My mind reels, recalling in dizzying detail the childhood days of being locked in the tunnels below the estate each time my aunt went away. The damp, dark passages still haunt my dreams, and sometimes, when

I wake in the middle of the night, I can still smell the rot and mold. That was before I found the lower level of the tunnels. Before the estate itself seemed to take pity on me... Orbik always let me out hours before my aunt returned. I never told Liani, because it would have broken her heart.

For my own good, my uncle always said. I knew better then.

I know better now.

The Aphelian taps twice on the door. "Promise never to do that again?"

"I will say this just once. Let. Me. Out." The glass decanter on the table next to the door begins to fog. The softest sound of cracking fills the room as the decanter chills, then freezes solid.

"As soon as you promise not to ditch me again." She sighs, and something thumps against the door. "This is serious, Valen. If what you say is true and this group of Fae is out to get you, I can't have you running off."

"You have no idea what you're doing. Open. The. Damned. Door. *Now*." The decanter shatters, and frozen bits of glass scatter across the floor. The room begins to tilt and spin. I brace myself against the small table. Each breath sends a razor-sharp jab of pain through my chest. The wood beneath my grip ices over. The corners of the large mirror on the wall fill with thin veins of frost, cracking the glass midway up.

"Valen? Did something break? Are you okay?"

Fog rises around the edges of the room, the warmth in the air rebelling against the dropping temperature.

I roar and slam my fists into the wood.

My breathing grows ragged, and the ice in my body, in

my heart, *in my blood*, takes over. Clinking and crackling, the wood before me lightens until it's nearly transparent. The door is gone, now nothing more than a thick layer of ice. Involuntary flashbacks quicken my pulse and tighten my fists. Confinement. Darkness. Loneliness.

One strike. That's all it takes to smash through the barrier.

Chunks of ice explode outward and rain into the hall as the Aphelian stumbles away, her mouth agape.

"If you ever do something like that again—"

For a moment—a single split second—there's fear in her eyes. A disturbingly welcome reaction that both sickens and excites me. Perhaps a callback to the feral blood that secretly poisons my veins. Some Fae outside the estate walls are said to harbor volatile tempers and have little self-control. Depleted, we call them. Fae driven to different levels of unrest due to their magic-starved lives.

Her fear is short-lived, though, and when it dims, instead of the anger I expect, I see concern. Compassion. "I—I'm sorry. I had no idea you were afraid—"

"I'm *not* afraid," I snap, forcing myself to take a deep breath. *In. Out. In. Out.* This. This is what happens when I lose control. It's bad but could have been so much worse. I could have killed her...

No, she needs to go. I don't need more blood on my hands.

"Buri mentioned you had another Aphelian. Mika? Valen, tell me what happened to her."

"She died early last year." Damn Buri. Aphelians are so few in numbers, if a court Fae requests one, they're limited to one a lifetime. Orbik never bothered with one of his own. He had the entire Winter Guard at his back. Liani had Kopic and his small group. But me? I was different.

I needed something more.

"How—" Her voice catches, and she swallows. "How did she die?"

I move a step closer. A spike of adrenaline courses through me, equal parts anger and guilt. "Her heart stopped beating."

Because of me.

7

Keltania

Valen refuses to give an explanation about his first guard, and after his explosion, I don't want to push. Not that it matters. She's gone, and I'm here. He's my responsibility now, and what I did obviously affected him. The guilt gnaws at me.

I shadow him for the rest of the day, waiting for another outburst. He behaves, though, eventually requesting that I accompany him back to the eastern section of the estate. There's no hint of the wolf I came face-to-face with in the woods. It's misplaced, but my disappointment is undeniable.

The creature, much like Valen himself, was stunning. The feral spark in the beast's eyes, one that is uniquely his, makes me long to connect with nature the way my ancestors did. The idea of running my fingers through his snowy white fur, of understanding him in a way some humans never could, is as thrilling as it is impossible.

We wander the halls of the eastern wing, going from room to room. Valen peers inside each one, then moves on a moment later. Everything is immaculate and unlived-in.

The only area that shows signs of wear is the large library at the south end of the wing, the depreciation obvious in the books on the shelves. Most of the spines are cracked and worn, the bindings rubbed smooth and the letters faded.

I follow behind him, keeping a bit more distance between us than I had earlier. "What is it you're looking for?"

He's calmer now. Reasonable. For a moment in the hall, I worried he'd kill me. The frenzy in his eyes had been untethered, but he pulled himself back. Exercised restraint—which isn't something that comes naturally to Fae. We've been taught they're driven by magnified emotions. Everything is amplified. A simple argument can easily turn to war, just as an act of jealousy can effortlessly slip into a crime of passion. Ultimately, their heightened emotions ended up being their downfall.

Valen pokes his head into a medium-sized dining area. A long marble table sits in the center, set with elegant placings and silver goblets. "Sometimes when I have— when I get angry—there are unwanted side effects in the surrounding radius." He nods to something on the other side of the room. "There. Such as that."

I follow his gaze. The second chair on the far side of the table is white.

No. Not white. Frozen.

The closer I look, the clearer the steam is as its chill meets the warm air. "So, you didn't do that on purpose?"

"No." He glares at me. "That chair did nothing to me. The same cannot be said about others in this wing."

Ouch...

He cranes his neck to see into the corner of the room,

then spins in a slow circle.

"Is there something else you're looking for?" Surely the amount of scrutiny he's giving things has to be about more than frozen furniture.

"One of the cooks has a dog, Mouse. The timid thing has recently decided she likes this wing of the estate. Probably because it's quiet."

"You think you froze a dog?" There's a good chance I'm going to be sick.

"Let's hope not."

The guilt wells up again, and I frown. What kind of an Aphelian am I? Not one deserving of Levina's trust, that's for sure. Torturing my Fae—possibly causing harm to a dog? "I'm sorry about that. If I'd known you'd get so upset—"

"I didn't *get upset.*" He squares his shoulders and starts back down the hall. "I don't like being confined."

I stare at the chair for a moment before following him down the hall. "Is that why Orbik keeps you in a different part of the estate? In case you lose control?" Fewer people coming and going means fewer potential complications to worry about. It makes sense. Though I can't imagine how lonely it must feel for Valen.

"That's one of the reasons, yes." Valen stops walking and turns. His lips twist, face contorting into a sour expression. The contrast to his usual grin makes him look like an entirely different Fae. "You don't find me... unsettling?"

Valen is beautiful—strange eyes and all. If he weren't mine to protect, things might be different between us. I'm not dead, after all. I can appreciate a stunning male. Though strictly forbidden because of Servis and

Aphelian and the events that led up to the Great Drain, relationships between Fae and their Aphelians still take place in the shadows. How can they not? We live with them, eat with them, share our lives... The Heartbreaker may quell deeper emotional attachments, but physical needs still remain. Everyone knows it happens, but no one brings it to light. It's a dirty secret, a sinful pleasure. With the Heartbreaker, there's no danger of a mutual claiming.

In my case, Valen and I are both inked. Double protection. If I were the kind of druid who allowed herself to blur lines... I shake my head and push the thought out. "If you're fishing for what you believe to be another compliment, you can forget it."

His lips twitch. There and gone in a half beat of my still-pounding heart. "And what you saw in the woods? Does that disgust you?"

"I'm a druid, Valen. That wolf is the one part of you that actually excites me."

He steps close, locking his gaze on mine. "Really? That's the part of me that excites you?" Lifting his arm, he flexes and grins. He puffs out his chest and, squaring his shoulders, pouts out his lips. "My rippled muscles and swoony swagger don't do it for you? How about my delectably kissable lips?"

He's trying to get a reaction, and the truth is, it's hard not to give it to him. His lips *are* kissable, his muscles ripped. But beneath his teasing, I can see something more. Something deeper that I force myself to focus on. There's a vulnerability in the way he watches me, a rawness in his voice. It's almost as if he's afraid I'll reject him because of the wolf—even though he swears he doesn't want me here. It's the first crack I've seen in his armor, and I'm desperate to open it up.

"Your uncle knows about the magic but doesn't know about the wolf?"

"He doesn't," he confirms, and I'm not at all surprised. He drops his arm, shoving his hands into the pockets of his leathers. "The magic was impossible to hide. It manifested before I could speak. The wolf came later, a sign of my mysterious father's bloodline. Highborn don't have an animal side. There is no one living—aside from you, now—who knows."

I press two fingers against his chest, over his heart. "I will tell no one what I saw. You have my word."

Beneath my fingers, his heartbeat explodes. Eyes wide, he lifts his hand to mine yet stops just shy of touching me. "What are you—"

"I didn't mean to—" I blink and yank my hand away. "An oath. When a druid swears something over the heart, it's binding."

His eyes are still on my hand as he takes a step back. Nodding once, he says, "Thank you. If Orbik knew about my wolf, he'd have me gutted and hung on display in the center of the estate, magic be damned."

"That's barbaric!" My gut twists. The Winter Lord seems the opposite of everything we've been told he was. How could we have gotten it so wrong?

He shrugs as if he hasn't just informed me his own uncle might one day flay him like cattle. "It would be an excuse to be rid of me. He might want the magic in my blood, but he fears it just as much." Valen turns and walks toward an open doorway, sticking his head into another room. A quick scan, and he moves on again.

"Right. The omen thing. Like I said before, prophecies

are tricky things. Easily warped to suit an individual's needs."

"It's not just that. I'm technically next in line to the throne—not that I want anything to do with it. I imagine Orbik is unhappy about that because I'm a bastard with no clue what my bloodline is. I don't know my father."

"You don't know who your father is?" I can sympathize. Valen and I, it seems, have much in common.

"My mother was abducted. There are theories, but we never discovered who was to blame. She found her way back home years later with a baby in her arms. She died shortly after. Where she was, what was done to her... It remains a mystery."

We come to another room. He peers inside, and when nothing seems amiss, we continue on.

"I didn't know my parents." The confession tumbles out with more emotion than I mean to give. Most Aphelians don't spare this fact a second thought, but for me, it's always been a sore spot. "My father was an unnamed volunteer from the only remaining druid village, and my mother, an Aphelian, was assigned to a Fae shortly after I was born."

He nods and says, "I'd like to ask you a question."

"Okay...?" The serious tone of his voice makes me nervous.

"I would like to know your name."

"Aphelian," I answer immediately. It should make me happy that he's trying to establish more of a connection, but this is something I'm not willing to offer.

"I would like to know your *real* name."

"Aphelian," I repeat, this time stiffly. My birth name was given to me by my mother, the one and only thing I ever received from her. I'm an anomaly among my kind in that respect. Normally, we're simply handed over to the Order moments after birth—no name, no connection. A blank slate to train and hone as they see fit. But, for some reason, my mother was different. She gave me a name, and though I'm not supposed to use it anymore, I keep it close.

His brows lift. "That can't be the name the Order gave you at birth."

His request shouldn't surprise me. His last Aphelian apparently shared her name with him. He must have worn her down, somehow—but I'm not her. "Why does it matter?"

"Because we're going to be spending a great deal of time together."

"So, does this mean you've accepted that I'm here to stay?" Hope blooms in my chest.

He makes a show of taking a deep breath, and when he blows it out, the air turns frosty. "What is your name?"

I square my shoulders and meet his steely gaze. One word. That's all I need to give him. But I can't push it past my lips. It's something that's mine, the only thing I truly own. I want my relationship with Valen to grow, and maybe I *will* tell him. Eventually. But not now. Not yet. He hasn't earned it. "Aphelian."

"Fine, then." His posture stiffens, the tightly corded muscles of his arms taut. "I'm retiring to my quarters for the evening."

I watch him go, waiting until he turns the corner to start moving. A few moments later, his door—obviously replaced by estate staff after we left to search the rooms— slams hard enough to rattle the pictures on the walls in the hall.

A moment later, his room is quiet and there's no light bleeding from beneath the door. I'm tempted to knock and apologize, but I'm tired. My first full day might not have been as bad as the day before, but it still hadn't gone the way I hoped.

Tomorrow is another day.

I shiver as I grip the doorknob to my room. It's colder than it should be, and when I pull open the door, more than a foot of snow spills from the small space. It comes to just below the mat of the cot and covers my old boots.

He's still trying to get a reaction. Probably wants me pounding on his door and screaming bloody murder as *he* had. Maybe he wants to watch as I struggle to somehow dig the space out, but I refuse to give him the satisfaction. I'm better than that. More disciplined. I sink onto the dry cot and pull my tunic tighter. I don't know if this is retaliation for me locking him in his room or for the fact that I refuse to give him my name. For all I know, this is another attempt to convince me to leave. Either way, I get the feeling Valen isn't used to hearing the word "no."

I'm here to protect him, and nothing can change that. But Valen needs to learn a lesson. You can't bully an Aphelian into getting what you want.

8

Valen

hear the Aphelian in the hall and pull open my door. I can see a puddle seeping out from her room. "Have a good sleep?"

She steps past me, into the room. "Of course. You?"

"Like a dry, toasty log."

"Good. I'm glad." She smiles, giving no indication that she's angry about the stunt I pulled.

Part of me is disappointed when the Aphelian doesn't offer even the smallest hint of a reaction. What I did was childish, but the trick worked with many caretakers when I was young. Liani doted on me night and day, when possible, but she had duties to tend to—many that took her away from the estate. I don't know what they were. I never asked. But before Mika showed up, my aunt enlisted the services of many nannies. I got rid of each and every one.

I was furious after we parted last night, and anger clouded my judgment. Guilt seeped in not long after, but the damage was already done. I lit a blazing fire in the room next to hers so that the heat would help melt the snow. I might not want her here, but there's no true venom on my part. She's an Aphelian, after all. She deserves my respect and reverence. Unfortunately, it's too easy to forget who—what—she is. I've never met someone who held such mystery in their eyes, such fire in their demeanor. No one has haunted both my dreams and waking moments. This human—this woman—is supposed to be the safest soul for me to be around. If only the reverse could be said.

She shifts from foot to foot and clears her throat. "What's on the agenda for today?"

"I'm taking a ride out to the market on the edge of the Winter Lands. Have you been?" I stretch and flex, yawning loudly. Ideally, I'd go alone, but, like a fungus, she's unyielding and invasive.

"Have I been to the market?" She blinks several times. "Of course not."

"You're in for a treat." I hesitate. "Or maybe not. You don't believe in having fun, do you?"

She grabs the cloak hanging on the back of my chair and throws it at me. "Is there a reason you need to go to the market?"

"Do I need a reason?"

"Isn't there something you should be doing at the estate?"

"You haven't been here long, so I'll let you in on a little secret. I don't *do* anything around here. I drink, I brash, sometimes I drink *while* brashing…" I roll my eyes. "It gets a bit tedious."

She studies me for a moment, and even though I was trying to catch her attention, now that I have it, I find the scrutiny unwelcome. There's no judgment in her eyes, but there is…something. I can't put a name to it. All I know is that it does odd things to my chest, and I don't like it.

...

Mika and I used to come to the market once a week when I was a child. My first Aphelian was stern, but I figured out pretty quickly how to win her over. Orbik had forbidden the trips, but Mika managed to sneak me out. I found out later that was only because of Liani's help—which didn't surprise me.

I haven't come here in several months, but the place doesn't seem to have changed.

"This is how you want to spend the day?" The Aphelian looks around, cringing. Behind us, a Fae stumbles from the tavern, drunk, and proceeds to double over and vomit in the street. "Because I thought even you had some small semblance of standards…"

"Are you always this much of—"

"Valen?" a musical voice calls from the edge of the crowd. "Valen, is that you?" Kitara waves and approaches with an enthusiastic bounce.

"No wonder your uncle has safety concerns." The Aphelian stiffens. "More fans?"

"As a matter of fact…"

Kitara reaches us and throws her arms around me, and I return the embrace. Briefly. "Kit, this is my Aphelian… Aphelian. Aphelian, this is Kitara, the daughter of the estate chef."

She turns to my guard and bows. "It's nice to see that they're taking Valen's safety seriously after everything that's happened."

"Why? What's happened?" my guard asks.

Kitara looks from the Aphelian to me, then back again.

"Doesn't she know what's been going on?"

"She's been informed."

"Oh, good." Kitara sighs. "We wouldn't want another episode like the one we had last month."

"Last month?" The Aphelian's brow lifts.

"Nothing," I assure her. "It was nothing."

"It was absolutely not *nothing*!" Kitara folds her arms. "Valen and I were in the gardens last month, *occupied* with—"

The Aphelian rolls her eyes. "Skip ahead, please."

"Well, we were come upon by three Fae who tried to kill Valen." Kitara frowns. "Some Fae think that because Valen is a bastard, he'll make a horrible monarch one day, but I—"

"I would sooner cut off my own hands than become the monarch of the Winter Lands. You know that."

Kitara smiles. "*Anyway*, they tried to kill him, and—"

"Obviously, they didn't succeed."

Kitara shakes her head, smiling, her gaze going from the Aphelian to me. "Valen managed to scare them off."

I remember being furious that day. Partially because of the interruption and partially because I'd been in a foul mood to start. When Kitara found me, I wasn't interested in her as much as I was interested in the distraction. Any distraction. My magic, so intertwined with my emotions, had been erratic. She'd given me something else to focus on for a time. When the three intruders came...

"It was my impressive physique, no doubt."

The Aphelian snorts. "More like your *winning personality* sent them away screaming."

Kitara chuckles. "I like her. She has a sense of humor."

"Not really," I say.

"Valen faced them, and they must have seen that he wasn't to be trifled with."

"They ran away?" the Aphelian says, and it's impossible to miss the note of suspicion in her voice.

They did run away, but I suspect it was more because my control slipped. While there weren't any obvious signs of my magic, the air grew noticeably colder, and I'm sure they saw something in my eyes... There's no doubt in my mind that was the incident that spurned Orbik to seek out another Aphelian. The attacks have increased since that day. We chalk it up to the whole bastard thing, but I have my suspicions that it's something more.

I spread my arms. "What are you doing here, anyway, Kitara?" We need a change in subject. I haven't known the Aphelian long, but I can tell she's already gearing up to launch a barrage of questions—ones I'm not in the mood to answer.

"Oh, you know..." Kitara winks and swishes her hips. The material of her skirt sways in the breeze. "Father sent me to fetch some special ingredients for tonight's supper."

The Aphelian stiffens just a bit. She narrows her eyes at Kitara. "Doesn't the estate have someone who does that for him?"

"Oh, well, normally, yes." Kitara beams at me. "But some ingredients Father deems too delicate to allow the kitchen staff to handle."

"Such as?"

Kitara's smile fades. She looks from me to the Aphelian and frowns. "Hammond root is extremely delicate. It bruises far too easily."

The Aphelian cocks her head to the side. "What's he making?"

"There's no need to be suspicious of Kit." I laugh. "We've known each other forever."

"Yes." Kitara nods. "But I can understand the caution. He's making ansted pie—Lord Orbik's favorite."

I grin. "Now that we've cleared that up…"

Kitara leans close and, as the Aphelian looks away for a moment, whispers, "Let's ditch your babysitter and have some real fun."

It's not why I came to the market, but it would undoubtedly irritate the Aphelian. And that's what I vowed to do, wasn't it? Make her see that there was no way this would work? Send her running for the hills?

I nod to Kitara and sigh. "Aphelian, I wonder if you might fetch the hammond root while I stay here with Kitara."

"Why would I do that?"

"Because I'd like to spend some time with Kit." I shrug. "I mean, I could just go with her to get it, but the dealer is notoriously edgy. He only allows two at a time in his shop, so you'd have to wait outside anyway…"

"You'll stay right here?"

"Naturally."

She rolls her eyes and takes the pouch of gold Kitara holds out, then stomps off toward the food section of the market.

"Huh." I crane my neck to make sure she's actually gone. "That was far easier than I expected it to be."

Too easy.

Before I can give that another thought, Kitara grabs my hand and tugs me around the small building and to the edge of the woods. Pushing me back against a large tree, she smiles. "Much better."

"And what wicked intentions do you have today?"

She drops her hands to the waist of my pants and grins. "Only the wickedest."

"As enticing as that sounds…" I grab her hands and cup them between mine. "I'm going to have to pass."

"Pass?" Her expression sours. She pulls her hands from mine and wraps them around my neck, tugging me down just a bit. Leaning in, she brushes the tip of my ear with her lips. "That's the second time you've turned me down. Why send the Aphelian away if not to be with me? You're going to give me a complex."

She trails a line of kisses along my neck, and I can't deny it feels sensational, and I've never been shy about public displays—if for no other reason than to anger my uncle—but something has me pushing her away. "Please don't view it as a slight. You…" I gesture to her, from head to toe. "Are exquisite."

"But?"

"But my mind is elsewhere today."

Her eyes narrow. She looks toward the market, then back to me. "Elsewhere? Or…*someone* else?"

It takes a moment for me to understand what she's implying. "Don't be ridiculous. That human is infuriating and has all the fun-loving tendencies of fungus—her words, not mine." But even as the protest spills past my lips, I find myself thinking about wild red hair and eyes that blaze with determination.

Would kissing the Aphelian interest me? Of course it would. She's stunning and moves in a way that makes my mind wander to dirty, forbidden places…but I would never—

Kitara snaps her fingers in front of my face. "Valen?

You were saying?"

"I'm just not in the mood right now."

She snorts, and her face contorts with anger. "You? Not in the mood? That's rich."

"Kit—"

"Spare me," she says, her tone changing to something far less heated. "I suppose you've done me a favor, really. It makes this all so much easier."

"Makes what easier?"

"This." A hulking shadow emerges from the trees, and something flies at me from the right. There's a *thwack* and a small kernel of pain, and then...nothing.

My head is pounding, and there's a knot forming in my lower back. I force my eyes open and am greeted by nothing but darkness. "Kit, if this is your idea of fun, I have to tell you, I could have done without the whack on the head..."

"Oh, Valen..." Her voice drifts from somewhere to my right, very close. "This isn't how I wanted it to go." Light floods my vision as the cloth covering my eyes is removed.

"That makes two of us." I shift in my seat, realizing my hands and feet are tied tight and there's a rope around my neck. I'm not sure of its purpose until I try to move and it pulls taut, threatening to squeeze off my air.

"Please don't do that," she says. "I'm not looking to kill you."

"That's a relief." I sit as still as possible and plaster on my most charming smile. "What, if you don't mind me asking, are you looking to do, exactly?"

She's sitting on a chair beside me. As she stands, her head tilts just a bit to the right. It's a move I've seen countless times, yet now it seems troubling. "We need your cooperation."

Who is we?

I yawn, giving her my most practiced bored shrug. Whatever is going on, I need to stay calm. "You know me. I'm always willing to lend a helping hand."

"The people need to know that the Omen is on their side, not the side of the court." She comes to stand in front of me. "They need to know that you'll do what you can to topple the current rule."

"First of all, since when do you believe in such dragonshit? The Omen? Me?" I try my hardest to keep the anger from my voice, but it's impossible. "And second, do you have any idea what you're saying? The consequences that come with threatening the Winter Lord's rule?"

"We're well aware," a deep voice says from the shadows. A moment later, a tall Fae with black hair and hazel eyes to match Kitara's steps from the darkness. "As I'm sure you are of your uncle's inadequacies on the throne."

"My brother is right," Kitara says. "I know you've seen the fault in Orbik's rule."

"Brother? I didn't know you had a brother." I flash him a toothy grin. "Nice to meet you. I'm the Fae who's been brashing—"

Her brother snarls and punches me in the face. The blow knocks me sideways, and the chair wobbles, stopping just before toppling to the ground.

"*Roan.* That won't get us anywhere. Stop it."

"This oversize child isn't going to help us, Kit. If we kill him here and now, it will ensure he doesn't fight on the wrong side of the people."

She sighs. "I was really hoping—"

"Um, excuse me. But as Kit can attest, I don't fight at all. Too much effort, and it cuts into my drinking time."

"Will you help us or not?" Kitara pushes Roan away and kneels in front of me.

"I am not the Omen," I say through gritted teeth. There's mutual respect between Kitara and me. A friendship based on years of antics and a multitude of capers that usually ended in equally satisfying encounters that left us both breathless. But this? This is betrayal. It's betrayal, and it stings like nothing has in a long, long time.

"Valen, we've all heard the rumors. You can't deny them!"

"Rumors? Really?" I snort. Kitara is the last person I would have expected to behave this way. "Even if I was," I say, "I wouldn't help you."

Her eyes go wide, and she jumps to her feet, shocked. Why? It's like she doesn't know me at all. She glances at her brother, then back to me, before taking a step away and brushing her hands down the front of her skirts.

"Fine. Then Roan gets his wish." She starts toward the door but pauses in the doorway without turning back around. "At least promise me you'll make it quick, painless. If nothing else, he was…amusing."

She disappears, leaving me with her brother. His expression is stony as he pulls out a wicked-looking knife. "I told her that the Omen was too dangerous to play games with. My sister never listens."

He lifts the knife and brings it to my throat. I hold my breath, focusing on the power thrumming through my blood. If I release it, his fate is sealed. He can't see my magic and survive. But I don't want it to come to that unless I'm left with no other choice.

The blade presses into my skin. Something warm rolls down my neck—blood—and Roan chuckles. "Huh. Maybe you're not the Omen. Either way, I'm more than happy to be rid of you."

The blade twitches, and I ready myself to release a fatal blast of ice, but Kitara suddenly stumbles back into the room.

No. Not stumbles. She's been thrown.

"If you do it, I will gut your sister and make you watch as she bleeds out in front of you." The Aphelian grabs Kitara by the hair and hauls her to her feet.

"Roan!" Kitara struggles, but it's pointless. The Aphelian's grip is like iron.

A moment later, there's a commotion outside, and several Winter Guards storm into the room. They take Roan and Kitara away without a word, and the Aphelian comes to stand in front of me. Just stands there.

"Well?" I say.

"Well, what?"

"Are you planning to untie me? Or..." I grin. "You could leave me tied up and we could play a game."

She studies me for a moment before lifting her foot and bringing it up to rest on the back of my chair. "A game, huh?"

I swallow as she leans close, the inside of her knee brushing my shoulder. My mind spins, a whirlwind of scenarios and wild images that have no place banging around inside my head. "I promise I'm very good at it."

"I'm sure you are." She pushes my chair over. It topples backward with enough force to shatter the wood and rattle my head around until my vision blurs. "But my game is so much more fun."

I cringe and dislodge myself from the bindings, then climb to my feet. "That wasn't very nice, you know. I just went through something traumatic."

"I'm sure you were terrified." Gesturing to my neck, she rolls her eyes. "That cut looks bad. Should I summon a healer? Call the guards back to carry you out? Maybe I should get you a bandage and a candy?"

"A *wine-flavored* candy would be nice."

"Come on." She rolls her eyes and hitches a thumb over her shoulder. "We should head back to the estate."

I nod and follow her, trying not to think of what might have happened if she hadn't shown up when she did.

If Kitara can betray me, then anyone—anywhere—is a potential threat.

We get our horses and ride for several miles in complete silence—which is good. By the time we make it outside the market borders, I don't trust myself to speak.

Kitara and I were nothing more than amusement for each other. But there'd been a certain level of trust and friendship. Of respect.

Or so I thought.

"You're unusually quiet. That worries me." The Aphelian urges her horse forward to keep pace with mine.

I keep my eyes on the trail, focusing on my breathing. I feel anger bubbling inside, and with it, my magic. Each step away from the market, closer to the estate, feeds the flame burning in my gut. "Missing my lyrical voice, Aphelian?"

"More like wondering what you're plotting inside that devious brain of yours."

I don't reply, and she sighs.

"You know, there's no hammond root in ansted pie."

"Huh?"

"The ingredient Kitara sent me to get, the one she said she was there for—it doesn't go in the pie."

I pull up on the reins and bring my horse to a stop. "How do you know that?"

"I used to help with the cooking in Lunal. Twice a month, the Order makes a feast for the village. We don't attend, of course."

"What are you saying?" The anger in my gut churns, turning darker, more volatile. "That you knew she was lying?"

"I did."

"And you let me go off with her?" I twist in my saddle as she pulls her horse to a stop beside me.

"Would you have listened to me if I'd told you the truth?"

I want to insist that I would have, but we both know I wouldn't. It just makes the whole thing worse, and I know what's coming. I feel it building, and there isn't much time. "I need a moment. Wait here."

I swing my leg over and jump from my horse, walking fast off the trail and into the woods.

"Valen—what are you—"

There's a soft *thud* behind me as the Aphelian dismounts, but I don't turn around and I don't slow down. I should demand that she stay back, but the anger is choking me now, forcing the magic in my blood to boil and churn.

I stop in the middle of the clearing and fall to my

knees in the snow. A howl escapes my lips, otherworldly, and shakes the powder from the trees. Birds scatter, rocks tumble—the very ground quakes—and snow begins to swirl around me.

"Valen!" From the corner of my eye, I see her fighting her way forward, through the violent squall. "Valen, you need to calm down!"

She's right, of course. Always around, always the voice of logic...always not far from my mind. And though I know this, it's impossible to tamp down the building pressure.

She manages to get to me, dropping to her knees in the snow, her body shuddering from the cold. She's so slight, the wind and snow knock her from side to side, yet she keeps her balance and stands her ground. "Valen!" she screams.

That's when I hear the cracking ice.

9

Keltania

The storm is localized, and though it's chaotic and violent and threatens to tear me apart, there's an odd beauty to it. It's Valen's doing. Triggered by his emotions, no doubt. How he hasn't done any real damage to himself—or worse, someone else—yet is beyond me.

The squall is so bad now I can hardly see his face through it. I feel him, though. I thrust out both my hands, clasping onto his shoulder with an iron grip, and refuse to let go. Even though my fingers are numb. Even though every limb of my body feels ready to snap and fall off.

"Valen, listen to the sound of my voice. I'm here. You need to calm down."

"—need to go." A shudder rolls through him, and he gasps. "Get—away."

"We'll go together or not at all." I'm terrified, sure. This kind of magic hasn't existed in thousands of years. No one knows the extent of it. And Valen… I have a feeling I've only seen a whisper of what he's capable of. He's right. I *should* be putting distance between us.

I just can't do it. I can't abandon him.

He screams, and something icy latches onto my forearm. There's a sound like cracking glass, and what little light manages to penetrate the violent storm disappears. Something forms above my head, solid and cold. The sound of the storm doesn't fade completely, but it's drowned out by something—a barrier made of thick ice.

There's an explosion—I can't tell exactly where it comes from—and the ground beneath us shakes and trembles. The icy enclosure shudders for a moment, then shatters into a thousand tiny pieces. They rocket out in all directions. I gasp as they skim my skin—Valen's, too—but luckily, we're both still whole.

"What the hell was that?" I stumble to my feet and glance around the clearing. As the swirling snow clears, I see nothing but devastation. The outlying trees are down, knocked over and shaken bare of snow and ice. The snow on the ground is displaced, some spots down to the bare earth.

"That…" Valen stumbles to his feet. He sways, and I rush forward to steady him. To my surprise, he lets me, leaning on my frame for a moment before shrugging me off. "That was me losing control. Again."

"You're upset about Kitara." It bothers him far more than he's admitted. I knew it the moment I entered that building. She wasn't overly special to him, but they'd had a kind of bond. One he'd trusted. One she'd destroyed.

He spins in a slow circle, exhaling sharply before shaking his head and slumping down to his knees. "I'm upset because…I need you."

He…what? "I don't understand."

"No. You wouldn't, would you?"

"I see you're feeling better." I kick a patch of snow

at him. The powder swirls and settles around him, never quite meeting its intended target—his head. "Back to your arrogant, cryptic self."

"No. That's not how I mean it. I simply mean…" He sighs and lets his head fall back. "I don't need a guard, Aphelian. I am more than capable of protecting myself and then some."

After what I saw back in the market, I don't agree. "Okay…"

"I could have overpowered Kitara and her brother, stopped Fleeting without blinking an eye…"

"But you didn't. Why?"

"Because, while I don't agree with many of my uncle's policies and tactics, I do agree that my magic must be kept a secret. For now, at least."

"And if you used it to stop them, the secret would be out."

"The secret cannot get *out*. I would have had to *kill* them."

The emotion in his voice cuts like a blade to my gut. There is so much more to Valen than he lets the world see. He is by far the most powerful being in the Winter Lands—possibly all of Derriga—and he has to keep his power hidden. I understand now that his confines are far worse than simply not being able to shift into his wolf form. He's essentially a prisoner in his own body.

"And you didn't want that," I say.

He lifts his head and meets my gaze. "No. I didn't want that." A laugh escapes him. Brutal and sharp, it bounces off the trees and echoes through the woods. "I don't want you. I don't want the royal blood in my veins or the magic in my blood. Yet here we are, stuck with these things. Stuck with each other."

"There are worse things you could be stuck with." I picture Alainya and how she'd relentlessly pursue Valen if she were here instead of me. "Be happy they assigned me here instead of my cousin."

"Is she more annoying than you?"

"Some might call it that, yes."

He sighs and climbs to his feet, dusting the snow from his leathers. "You have working legs. They allow you to move from place to place, to have freedom."

"Don't be so dramatic." I snort. "Your legs work just fine."

"Yes, but consider how you would feel if you were told you couldn't use those legs the way nature intended. That you could walk but never run. You could bend but never fully stretch. You would exist—you would breathe and eat and sleep—but you would not use the things nature had gifted you. You would feel a constant itch, unable to scratch it."

"I won't lie, Valen. I can't imagine how complicated things must be for you. And Orbik—"

"Orbik's *protection* suffocates me." The venom in his tone takes me by surprise. "I've been forbidden to use magic outside of my time with Buri, forbidden to leave the grounds unescorted. Every move I make is watched and measured by the calculated risk of losing their precious resource."

That isn't the first time he's referred to himself as a resource. Knowing what I know about his uncle, I can only imagine, but this isn't the time to ask. He's already been pushed too far today.

I position myself directly in front of him. He's not

looking at me, focused on something over my shoulder, so I grab his face and force his gaze to mine. "You are not alone anymore, Valen."

"I know," he says, his expression pained. "That's the problem."

Life at the estate isn't what I imagined it would be. The next several weeks pass in a haze. I watch the strained relationship between Valen and his uncle bounce from rocky to indifferent and everything in between, and with each passing day, I'm more and more convinced that the monarch of the Winter Lands is a monster. He's lazy and uncaring. He's always snapping at his wife. And the way he treats his people… Just the other day, I watched as one of his guards asked for time away because his wife was dying. Orbik suggested he kill her himself to *speed things along.*

How have the druids gotten it so wrong? I'd heard countless stories about the benevolence of the Winter Court, yet walking among them makes it clear those tales were fabricated—or at the very least greatly embellished.

Earlier this evening, Valen was summoned for dinner with Lord Orbik and Lady Liani, and, by extension, I was summoned along with him. I was made to stand in the corner while they ate, their discussion hushed and too low for human ears. By the time he rose from his seat, Valen's face was flushed and his expression stony. He stormed from the room, and I followed.

"I don't suppose you want to tell me what has you in such a mood?" I settle on the edge of his bed as he stalks from one end of the room to the other.

"My uncle asked me to check in with one of our villages to the north tomorrow. They've been having issues with a small band of rebels stealing supplies."

"And that's bad?"

He stops pacing but doesn't turn to face me. Instead, he pulls open his door and steps aside. "We should get some sleep. It's a long ride to the village."

I stand and make my way to the door but pause halfway across the room. Something glints, catching my attention. I look up and over. There's a weird collection of ice on the ceiling I hadn't noticed before. "What is that?"

He follows my gaze to the far corner of the room, to a section of the ceiling covered in what looks to be icy vines. "Oh. Yeah. That happens sometimes."

"It's so strange…" I walk back and rise onto my toes, running a finger along the bottom edge of the ice that has spread halfway down the wall. "I haven't seen anything like this anywhere else on the estate. Does it just happen in here?"

"Seems to. I think it has to do with me. Fae magic interacting with the latent druid magic in the ground."

"And you don't find that odd?" The sprouting plants and flowering fruit trees are strange enough, but vines made of ice? That can't be a result of latent magic, can it?

"There are a lot of things you'll find odd if you're here long enough, Aphelian." His demeanor is different tonight. The overconfidence and swagger that normally precede him are darker. The mood is heavier, and I feel it leeching in to affect my own state of mind. A sense of foreboding washes over me, along with the distinct twinge of anger—which I don't quite understand.

"Now, go get some sleep." He ushers me toward the door.

"Do you anticipate problems tomorrow?"

He snorts and snaps his fingers. An icy bubble forms in the palm of his hand. It's stunning, a crystalized ball that glints in the light. His thumb twitches, and his fingers curl inward, crushing the delicate ball and sending tiny pieces of ice bouncing across the floor at our feet. "There are always problems."

10

Valen

We reach the edge of the village by late afternoon. Unlike the trees on the estate, which are vibrant and thriving because of the residual druid magic that remains in the ground, everything in the wild is dead and encased in ice. Spindly branches reach for us as we walk, glistening like glass. I catch the Aphelian staring all around her, open-mouthed, eyes full of wonder. She touches the tip of her finger to the snow-covered leaves, then smiles as the superfine flakes scatter in the wind.

As we cross into the village, several Fae stop to watch us. They smile and wave and offer gifts as we pass. Homespun threads and pottery fresh from the kiln. And wine. Several bottles lay tucked away, stashed in saddlebags for the ride home. I've made many routine trips here as an emissary of the Winter Lord over the years. As a child, I was greeted with dismissal and caution, but as I grew older and made the trek myself, the reception warmed.

Mostly.

Wanlo, the village's overseer, stomps toward us through the snow. He's tall, with dark hair and eyes, and walks with a limp. The injury, he claims, was obtained while defending the village from an attack several years ago. But whispers claim the injury was caused by the owner of the tavern when Wanlo refused to pay his tab.

"Valen," he says. "I wasn't expecting to see you again so soon."

"Lord Orbik told me of your recent troubles. I came to see if I could offer my assistance."

"We greatly *appreciate* it." His words drip with thinly veiled sarcasm. Wanlo, unlike most of the village, never liked me. He gives my companion an assessing once-over, ultimately deeming her not worth his time. When he turns his attention back to me, he's sneering. "I see you've taken precautions after your last trip."

"What happened last time?" The Aphelian looks from him to me, eyes narrowing just a bit. She's so out of place here. Her vibrant, red-hued hair is a discordant splotch of color in an otherwise crystalline setting. She chose a set of black leathers with ice-blue accents today but still wears her own boots. The worn green leather is an odd combination that sticks out, but it's also uniquely her.

When we started out this morning, last night's foul mood still haunted me. But half a day on horseback with the Aphelian at my side, and my mood has lightened considerably.

"Several of the villagers attacked me last month," I tell her.

It can't be proven, but I strongly suspect Wanlo knew about the attack prior to it happening. He'd been edgy that day. More nervous than usual. I managed to fend the assailants off without using magic, but they got away, their identities kept hidden. I wave a hand between us, grinning.

It pisses him off that I'm so casual about it all.

"Jealous of my good looks and charming disposition, no doubt."

The Aphelian's lips twist. She leans in close but makes little effort to keep her voice low. "And you didn't think I might need to know that before coming here?"

"You've spent enough time with me. You already know I'm charming." I swing my leg around and dismount. The Aphelian dismounts as well.

I flash Wanlo a smile. "You were about to tell me more about your troubles?"

Wanlo clears his throat and turns to gesture toward the large building behind him. Their storage house. "The rebels were here again last week. They've almost cleaned us out. When is the Winter Lord going to do something about this?"

The storage space in this village is smaller than others'. They've been raided four times this season. If the assaults continue, they'll run out of resources, and getting my uncle to help them is impossible. As it is, my presence here is merely for show. Wanlo and I both know Orbik has no intention of helping these Fae. The Winter Lord won't waste estate resources to investigate, and he certainly won't send supplies.

"How many are there?" I ask.

"No way to know for sure. They come at night. Attempts to guard the supplies have failed."

"They're killing your guards?" The Aphelian narrows her eyes, and I don't miss the suspicion in her tone.

Wanlo frowns. "No way to know that, either."

The Aphelian and I exchange a glance, and he sees it. His lips twist downward, and he shakes his head.

"There are never any bodies. They're just…gone."

"That sounds like the rebels." It's what they do. Steal Fae away—like my mother—and sell them as slaves. Trolls, ogres—even other Fae—pay top coin for a chance to enslave a citizen of the court that prevailed in the war. The Winter Court has many enemies. The only reason the rest of Derriga hasn't come for us is the magic soaking our lands. Thanks to the druids' aid and sacrifice, as well as the magic I donate for Orbik to use, we're protected.

"Of course it's the rebels." Wanlo's face reddens. "Didn't you hear what I said?"

"With respect," I say, "it could be anyone. Piskies are known to pillage food supplies this time of year. Harpies, too. But since you've found no bodies, no indication of violence… Is it possible they defected and took supplies with them?"

Wanlo's brows disappear beneath his shaggy hair as he blanches. He clenches his fists. "How dare you—"

"I'll report my findings to my uncle."

"Lord Orbik is well aware," Wanlo growls. He straightens and puffs out his chest, not unlike the way he did when I was a child. A tactic meant to intimidate. Fae like Wanlo have nothing else to work with. "You're not going to *do* anything?"

I spin in a slow circle and spread my arms. "What am I to do? Are they here? Do you know where they are? Should I send out a messenger bird and invite them for a chat?"

He glowers, then takes a step back and offers a stiff bow. "*Thank you* for your time." The words are terse and forced—it probably kills him to speak them.

Still, I understand his anger. He's an ass, but I know he

cares about the town. These are his people, and he's only trying to keep them safe. Like my uncle should be.

We watch as his retreating form is swallowed by squalls of snow. The wind kicks up, and the Aphelian shivers. She tries so hard to hide it, but it's like a blow to the gut. We must be spending too much time together, because I can almost *feel* the cold seeping into her limbs.

"That was fun." The Aphelian pulls her cloak tighter. "And he seemed like such a fan. You win over everyone you meet, don't you?"

"My charm knows no bounds." I pass the horses and start walking toward the woods.

She fumbles through the deep snow after me. "Where are we going now?"

"I just want to have a look around the edge of the village."

"You think you might find something?" She catches up to me, instantly alert, scanning the horizon for possible dangers. I'll never admit it, especially to her, but the Aphelian's presence gives me the opportunity to relax more than I have in a long time. Plus, she's grown on me, just as she said she would. Like fungus.

Very attractive, deceptively innocent-looking fungus.

"Whoever raided the village is long gone, and if it was the rebels, they know how to cover their tracks." I sigh. "Still, it feels like we should at least check the area out."

We make a wide sweep on foot, carefully scanning the woods that surround the village. There's nothing amiss. No suspicious tracks in the snow, no signs of blood or struggle. If Wanlo's guards were killed, they were taken elsewhere first. The only thing that interrupts the stillness of the forest is an occasional gust of wind and the intermittent cry of a snow crow.

The Aphelian's gaze is a weight on my shoulders, both comforting and irritating. How can something be both wanted and unwanted at the same time? I know I should embrace her presence. Not because my uncle went out of his way to bring her to me, but because her position is one of sacrifice and honor. The idea of giving her an inch scares me, though. I've accepted that her presence here is necessary for the time being, but there are still aspects of it that make me uncomfortable.

My relationship with Mika was starkly different. I was so young, I viewed her as a protector, a mother figure. This Aphelian is unlike her in every way, and we're nearly the same age. I see something familiar in her eyes. Something I could connect with deeply.

"I've always been isolated." The silence is heavy, and even though I know it's crossing a line, I say, "Self-imposed to a degree because of what I am, and by my uncle's hand because of what I can do."

Several moments tick by, and when I'm sure she won't respond, she finally says, "You don't need to be isolated anymore, you know. We're supposed to be a team. We can be friends, Valen."

"We really can't."

"Why not?"

"Because I don't want to be your friend. I don't want to be anyone's friend." I've lost too much already, and I refuse to give someone else the power to take from me— by accident or of their own volition.

She doesn't answer, and we continue to trek through the snow. About a mile in, I can't stand the silence anymore.

Or maybe I've become so lonely that I'm desperate

for conversation. "You never regret this? Your lot in life?"

"Lot in life?" She laughs. The sound sends goose bumps across my skin and makes my heart thump ten times faster than normal. She's been lucky so far. No one has tried to harm her; no one has threatened her. Aside from protecting me, she's unscathed. But, from past experiences, it's only a matter of time. "What I'm doing here, with you, is an honor."

"And you never wonder if there's something else out there for you? Another path?"

She groans. "I thought we were past this? I'm not leaving—"

"No. I don't mean it like that. I'm simply wondering if you ever wanted…more?"

"This is all that I've ever wanted." Her answer is instant and spoken without hesitation. Unquestioning faith. That's what it is. How can she not see how wrong that is?

"Because it's all that you've ever known." I stop walking and spread my arms wide. "Have you ever considered the possibility that you've been brainwashed?"

She sighs and shakes her head. "Are you really that desperate to be rid of me?"

The hurt in her eyes, in her tone, is like a sucker punch to my gut.

"You're a human. Not to be blunt, but you're far frailer than I am."

"So?" Her lips curl into a snarl, and she narrows her eyes. I've obviously offended her, and for once, that's not my intention.

She shakes her head again, some of the anger fading. "I don't see us as unequal, Valen."

If that were true, then she wouldn't be here as my

guard. But I can see getting her to understand is pointless. At least right now. "I'm not trying to hurt you. It's just... No one can *see* me. I'm not interested in forming any kind of bond."

"Buri sees you."

I sigh. "Buri doesn't see me. It's not like I can reveal myself. I must always wear a mask, hide the truth."

"You don't need to hide the truth from me."

"No. I don't. And in an attempt at transparency, I hate it."

"Wow." She lets out a whistle that echoes through the trees. "No wonder you're so popular with the ladies."

"I'm simply saying I don't want to blur things between us. Do you understand?"

She laughs. "Trust me, Valen. Things between us won't be blurring any time soon."

"Well, that's a relief." Or at least it should be.

"So why not leave?" She tugs on a low-hanging branch as we start to walk again. The snow on the leaves scatters, drifting slowly to the ground in a fluffy white puff. "You're obviously not happy at the estate. Orbik can't technically stop you from going, can he?"

"I suppose he couldn't." I try to picture walking right out the front gate, and I snicker. It would never happen. But I *could* sneak away, if that's what I wanted. "I stay for the same reason you remain by my side despite my best attempts to get you to leave. *Duty.* Responsibility to my people."

"You mean because of the magic?"

"The power in my blood will save my people one day."

She stops walking. "Is that a goal? A hopeful thought? Are you basing it on anything particular—or do you just have a savior complex?"

Her tone is combative, but I breathe in and keep my voice even. This was the information she wanted. "Mika told me."

She hesitates, and I know she wants to ask more pressing questions. She takes a breath, closes her eyes for a moment, and sighs, then opens her eyes again. "How could she have possibly known something like that?"

"She did what you did with your tracking sigil. She traced a symbol onto her arm and used her ink. She saw that one day I'll be able to bring back Fae magic."

Her brows furrow. "Is she the druid who inked the Heartbreaker?"

I nod and rest my hand over my heart. I was twelve when she placed the sigil onto my chest, too young to understand the long-term ramifications of what had been done.

The Aphelian's expression softens. "How did she die?"

"I told you. Her heart stopped—"

"Everyone's heart stops when they die," she says gently. "What caused it, though?"

I should have known better than to think she would let this go. And, really, can I blame her? This is information she should have, considering the same thing could happen to her...

"Valen...you can talk to me."

"She was killed." My fists clench tight, the smallest traces of frost creeping across my knuckles.

Her lips part, eyes darting to my hands. She tries to hide it, but the sadness in her eyes is impossible to miss.

"I found her on the floor in my room. They'd slit her throat." The frost moving across my knuckles thickens and continues to spread over the back of my hand and toward my wrist. "Aside from Liani, Mika was my— They took her away. With her out of the picture, it would be easier for the fanatics to get to me."

"That's it, isn't it?" Her voice is so soft, so tentative. It's like she's afraid I'll run if she speaks too loudly. And maybe I will. This was just the thing I wanted to avoid. Opening up, connecting in a way that would bond us.

"In your place, I would have slaughtered them all." Her tone calls to something deep inside my chest. It's icy and razor-sharp, each word more dangerous than the last. With her gaze still on my hands, she takes a step back. "I can see that you cared a great deal for her."

"I did." The admission burns my throat, but I can't keep it in.

"If I had someone, a…a person who cared for me as much as I imagine Mika cared for you, I would rip the world apart if they were taken from me."

I roll my eyes. "You? You don't seem like the type."

She smiles. It's a sad grin that doesn't quite reach her eyes. There's something severe in her expression. An emotion far stronger than any I've ever felt. I'm jealous of its intensity. "I understand now, I think. Why you seem so resistant to me."

She's right…yet she's also wrong.

I flex my hands. The thin coating of ice covering them cracks and scatters in every direction. I stare at the small pieces that fall into the snow. It's dark, now, and the moon makes a rare appearance through the clouds. It shines on the glassy fragments of ice, causing them to twinkle like stars fallen from the sky. "The ones who took Mika's life were repaid in kind. Liani found them. She gave them to me."

"And you killed them. For her..." It's not a question, and she doesn't seem upset. She inhales and blows out slowly. For a long moment, she stares at me. "Keltania," she says finally.

"What?"

Her shoulders sag a little, and she draws her cloak tighter, shifting from foot to foot. "You asked for my name. That's what it was."

"Keltania," I repeat with a laugh. "Did you know that Tania, in the old language, means stubborn?"

"Stubborn is just another word for determined." She smiles. "Which is exactly what I am, Valen. I know me being here isn't what you want. And now, I have a better understanding of why that is. But I'm not Mika. I'm sure she was an amazing Aphelian, but no one is taking me out."

"I suppose we'll see."

No, she's not Mika, who was like the mother I never had. Like Liani.

Keltania is something new entirely. I don't understand it, and though I don't want it, I see now that it's something I'll have to deal with.

And part of me—a very senseless, misguided part of me—is happy about that. My reasons to be rid of her have become so much more complicated than they were when she first arrived.

11

Keltania

Valen cared a great deal for Mika. The anguish in his eyes might have dissipated, but I feel it in my chest. An inexplicable ache that gnaws at my subconscious.

We start walking again—thank the Goddess. My new clothing is warm and does more to protect me from the elements than my old leathers, but I refuse to give up my boots. Unfortunately, the snow is seeping through holes in the heel.

"What will your uncle do for the village?" I ask him.

"Probably nothing."

"Why did he send you, then?" Somehow, I'm not surprised. Everything I've seen of Orbik is a glaring contradiction. I doubt he'd spill his drink if someone were set ablaze in front of him.

"It was probably more for my benefit than theirs. To get me off the estate. To give me purpose, to keep me from causing trouble for him."

"Their food will run out." I stop walking again. With the magic gone, most forest creatures have moved on or died out. Even the animals that didn't need to survive on enchantment left. It's said that the woods themselves, angry at the Fae over the war, chased the life from the trees. "They'll *starve*."

"Many villages have starved." He shrugs casually. Like hundreds of lives are nothing.

"But they don't have to."

"You're the expert, then? On Fae? On the affairs of our court?" His eyes darken. "So, tell me, Aphelian, what *should* I do?"

"If your uncle won't help them, then you should. All your power and wealth must be good for something."

"I have no power and wealth." He breathes in slowly, then out. In, out. In, out. Like he's trying to keep the ice at bay. Thankfully, we aren't close to the village, but if he loses control, I'll be squarely in the blast zone. I got lucky that day after the market. I'm not eager to tempt fate.

"I'm essentially a prisoner," he says once he's calm.

If Valen looks the other way as Orbik allows his people to starve, doesn't that make him just as guilty? If he's that complacent about something so dire, what else is he willing to ignore?

"Then fight your way out of captivity," I say.

"You make it sound so easy. I have responsibilities. Things that I must—"

A high-pitched whizzing sound, followed by a blurry projectile, flies past my head. An instant later, another. The second is accompanied by a sharp pain across my shoulder. "What the—"

Another object zooms by, this one impaling the thick trunk of an oak to our left.

An arrow.

I grab the back of Valen's tunic and hurl him sideways

just in time to escape the next arrow. From the brush on the other side of the clearing, several figures emerge.

Four large Fae, all armed, cross to the center of the clearing. "Do I have your attention now?" the one in front calls. He holds up his bow and bares his teeth.

"Wanlo said you've refused to help us," the one beside him yells. He's the shortest of the four, with onyx hair and a rusty broadsword.

"That's not true." Valen tenses but plasters on a smile. He spreads his arms for a moment in a placating gesture, then tugs at the edge of his collar. "I offered the lot of you lessons to attract the fairer sex, but he turned me down."

The shortest swings his sword, twirling it in an impressive display.

Show-off...but impressive.

I curse. Our argument is going to have to wait, because there's a good chance Valen's mouth is going to get us in trouble. "Could you be serious for a single instant?"

Valen snorts. "Have you ever considered you're more than serious enough for both of us? Besides, tell me I'm wrong. I mean...look at them. They need all the help they can get."

He turns to the group of Fae and opens his mouth again, but I jump in front of him. "Wanlo is a damned liar," I shout at them. "I was there. Valen told him we would inform Orbik when we returned to the estate."

They laugh for a moment before the leader quiets them with a wave of his hand. "So, as I said, you refuse to help us."

"We've got a resolution. One where everyone wins," another of them shouts. He's wearing a wolfskin cloak and stands several heads taller than the others. The side of his face is pocked and rough, like he's been badly burned in the past.

"What is your idea?" Valen steps around me. "I'll be sure the Winter Lord hears it."

The one in front lifts the crossbow. "It's not a what. It's a who. *You*."

"The way we see it, the only way to get Orbik to pay attention is to do something drastic." The tallest grins. "Maybe if we send you back to him one piece at a time, he'll finally help our village."

"Is that any way to treat someone who's trying to assist you in finding love? Or, at the very least, a good time." Valen delivers the words with his trademark jest, but the tone lacks amusement. Beneath each syllable is a razor ready to slice. His body tenses, shoulders rigid and arms taut.

The air around me grows frigid. One look at Valen, and I know what he's thinking. I lean just a bit closer, keeping my voice low and my eyes on the enemy. "If you do it, they'll know about the magic. You'll have to kill them all. If that's something you can live with, then proceed. If not, take a deep breath, calm yourself, and stand down."

He hesitates for a moment before his fingers go slack. He isn't a cold-blooded killer.

But I can be—if I need to.

"Turn around and go back to the village," I say to the group of them. "I don't want to hurt you, but if you force my hand, I *will* cut you down."

There's no verbal response, but the spark of fury in their eyes says it all.

I tug at the strap securing my cloak, and it falls to the snow.

The leader of the group lets out a roar and sprints toward us.

"Fool," I mutter and charge forward, unfastening the blade on my belt, then throwing it. It slices through the air, but in the dark, I miss the mark by inches, the knife claiming only a wisp of his sleeve before embedding itself in the tree a few feet behind him.

He retaliates, dropping his bow and producing a small dagger of his own. When he lunges toward me, I'm ready. Left and right, up and down. His attacks are graceful, and I appreciate the skill it takes to move like that. He slashes; I shift. I swing; he ducks. We're well matched, but he's repetitive. His style is flawless but lacks imagination. There's no improvisation. One more cycle and I can—

"Aphelian, look out!"

I bring my blade up to protect my face as I whirl toward the sound of Valen's voice, effectively blocking what would have surely been a mortal blow. Always meet a new direction with your guard up. Always be ready to swing. I bend and pivot as the second attacker strikes again, twisting my body just beyond his range.

"It's a pitiful human, Royza. Kill it already," the leader says with a growl.

Royza, the one who came up behind me, swings. I duck the blow and dip my fingers into the edge of my boot. As he rounds once again, I bring my hand up hard and bury another tiny blade in the soft flesh beneath his chin.

For a moment, everyone freezes. Royza's eyes are wide as I watch the life drain from them, and then he drops, falling face-first into the snow. Bright red leeches out, soaking the white drift.

I turn my attention to the leader, who stares not at

me but at his friend's lifeless corpse. "He was my brother."

"I warned you. I'll give you one last chance to go back to the village—"

He roars in fury and throws himself forward. The two remaining Fae do the same.

Valen runs toward us, eyes glowing bright violet and a snarl on his lips. A spear of ice flies past me. Large, solid—and cold—it slices the air with enough force to tug a chunk of my hair free of the band holding it in place. The projectile strikes the leader as he dives for me. He goes down, dark red staining the snow surrounding him, his face frozen in surprise.

I face the next assailant—he's the tallest of the group—as the last one circles Valen. He's the fastest of them, clumsily dodging the sharp, icy projectiles. He's unnerved by Valen's magic, his eyes frantic, and it makes him sloppy.

"It appears that there's more to the Winter Lord's nephew than we knew." My assailant's lips rise into a wicked grin as we circle each other, both waiting for the other to make the first move. "Step aside and let us take him," he offers. "We'll let you live."

I incline my head toward his fallen comrades without taking my eyes from his. "I'm not leaving until you join them."

He shrugs and lifts his sword. "I was hoping you'd say that, human."

We meet in the middle, blade to blade. He's bigger than me, stronger, but I'm faster. More agile. I give in to the pressure of his weapon, letting mine fall back, then duck. His strike sails harmlessly above my head. When he rounds again, I drop my blade and tuck my fingers. As he brings his weapon down for the killing blow, so sure of himself with the loss of mine, I jam my hand forward, into his throat.

He clutches his neck and stumbles, sputtering flecks of blood as he falls backward into the snow.

His friend's curse and the sound of Valen's ice hitting the rocks and trees roar behind me. I turn, ready to leap forward, but as I start to move, Valen takes his opponent to the ground with an icy club.

I stop halfway to him and brace my hands against my knees to catch my breath. The remnants of adrenaline course through my system, and my head is still buzzing from the fight. "Are you all right?"

There's no response, but the sound of Valen's feet stomping through the snow has me tensing up.

"What—"

Valen crashes into me, twisting us so that our positions are reversed. The opponent I thought I'd taken down charges toward me with his blade up. He collides with us seconds before we all hit the ground.

The assailant's skin pales, then turns translucent, finally crystalizing into solid, glass-like ice.

"You…"

Valen saved me.

Again.

"Tania—" Valen stares at me for a moment, then grunts and rolls onto his back. He's breathing heavier than he should be, even after such an intense fight, and a wave of icy fear nearly steals the air from my lungs.

I push myself onto my elbows, and my body numbs. The villager's blade is buried in Valen's side, and there's a growing pool of blood soaking into the snow beneath him.

"No!" The word tears from my throat like a million

shards of jagged glass.

I tear at his tunic. The sound of ripping material echoes off the trees, as does the sound of my breath, coming in quick, uneven rasps.

"Brace yourself," I say, gripping the handle.

One.

Two.

Three.

I pull the blade from his side. He grunts and grits his teeth. The injury between his ribs and hip bone is bad but not life-threatening. At least not for a Fae. Several inches higher, though…

"Thank the Goddess." I exhale and press one palm against the wound while I yank at the sleeve of his tunic with the other. Balling it up, I press it tight to staunch the blood flow, which is already beginning to slow.

"If you're done groping me, I'd like to get up now." He cracks his left eye open and pushes my hand away, replacing it with his own.

I roll my eyes and shiver against a rush of sudden cold. Lunal wasn't perfect, and life there wasn't easy, but Goddess how I miss the sunshine and warmth. I stand to retrieve my cloak from where I'd dropped it, but when I go to step away, everything spins wildly out of focus. Pain sears my side. Scorching hot, it steals the air from my lungs.

My legs give out, and I collapse. "What—" I wrap my arms around my middle and look down. Blood. There's so much blood.

Valen is beside me in an instant. "Tania?" His voice is tight with concern. "What happened? Let me see!"

I try to focus on the surrounding area, on his voice, but everything swims in and out. Have more Fae appeared?

Have I been pierced by another arrow? Nicked in the fight without knowing it? Maybe the adrenaline kept me from feeling the wound?

No. I was fine. Untouched save for a few cuts and bruises and that very first graze. "Nothing to warrant this much—" I gasp. "Blood. Where's it coming—"

Valen mimics what I did to him. His search reveals an identical wound to his, one that wasn't there moments ago.

One that for a human *is* life-threatening.

Supporting my head, he tilts me down. There's a wild look in his eyes, and his breathing is rapid and uneven. Panicked. He's *panicked.* "Lie as still as you— I need to stop the bleeding!" His hand presses against my side, to the left of the wound, and my body numbs. "The cold will help constrict the blood vessels. Slow the bleeding."

"Or freeze me solid." My teeth chatter as he presses something into the wound. Despite the numbness, I still feel the sting of it. "Do you know what you're doing?"

"Human anatomy is similar to Fae. I won't freeze anything internal you might need." The pressure increases. "Now be quiet or I'll freeze your lips shut."

I bite back an acidic retort and let him work, relaxing a little when some of the pain ebbs.

A few moments later, he rocks back on his heels, calmer. "I think I got the wound to stop bleeding. We'll have to have someone in the village look at it before making the journey back to the estate, just in case."

"Someone in the— Absolutely not." I bite back a scream as I push myself into a sitting position. If I don't get off the ground soon, my ass is going to be a permanent block of ice. "People from the village just tried to *kill* us. We, in turn, *killed them.* You want to go to one of them for medical attention?"

He folds his arms, completely unbothered by the missing sleeve. "To be fair, they were nothing more than thugs. Maybe no one in the village will care?"

I shake my head and brush some snow from my leathers. "We'll just take the ride a bit slower and be careful. I'll use a medical sigil, then deal with it when we get back to the estate."

"If you don't bleed out by then."

"Don't be dramatic. You stopped the bleeding." I'm trying to stay as calm as I can, but inside, I'm screaming. The pain from the wound is nothing compared to the bigger picture.

Valen was the one stabbed—and I suffered the wound right along with him.

A mistake... I made a mistake while inking the rebirth sigil. That's the only explanation.

I need to get back to the estate and figure out how to fix this.

"This is a bad idea," he prods.

"We'll both survive the ride." I point toward the outskirts of the village, where we left the horses. "We can make it back to the estate before morning if we leave now and ride hard."

"Ride hard?" he says with a snort. "You just said we should take it easy! You don't look like you can get into the saddle, much less *ride hard*."

"I'm an Aphelian, Valen. I'm used to doing unpleasant things. I'll be fine." *I hope.*

I start moving forward, and when he doesn't follow, I stalk back to where he stands, a few feet from our frozen Fae attacker. He's probably dead, but just to make sure...

Drawing my sword, I swing. A single, brutal blow that shatters the ice and sends bits and pieces of frozen Fae scattering about. It costs me, and I know I don't hide the cringe as well as I want to, but I don't care.

"There. *Much better.*"

Now we just need to get back to the estate without anyone else trying to kill us.

12

Valen

We're just over three hours into the trip home and still haven't spoken about the attack in the woods. I wrapped my own wound after tending to hers, then waited for her to explain. So far, she's said nothing. Guess I'll start. "Obviously, we have some things to talk about…"

She sighs but stays silent.

"Look, we're going to need to be on the same page when we arrive home. About the attack…and what happened after it."

"I don't *understand* what happened."

"Neither do I." I glance down. A slight throb in my gut needles me. It's enough to make me squirm, which means she must be in excruciating pain. "The sword that pierced me didn't make contact with you. How is it possible that you were injured?"

Her gaze remains focused on the path ahead. She's stiff in the saddle, and every so often she closes her eyes and inhales deeply while pressing her lips tight. "As I said, I'm not sure."

"Is it possible we —"

Her skin is pale, but her breathing seems more even than when we started out. "Do you love the sound of your own voice so much that you can't go five minutes without hearing it?"

"You should hear my singing voice."

She growls and nudges her horse into a faster walk.

"Tania—" I catch up to her.

"Keltania," she says, exasperated. "But you should be calling me Aphelian."

"If it truly bothers you, I will call you—"

"It's fine." She sighs. "There's nothing conventional about this assignment, so why not."

"Good. Because Tania suits you better." A nudge of my heel, and my horse speeds up a bit, pulling away from hers. Once I'm a few feet ahead, I slow and step into her path. "You need to tell me what happened back there. You might not know *exactly*, but I get the impression you have a theory."

She sighs, and some of the tension in her shoulders eases. The stiff set of her jaw slackens, and her head tips back. "The only explanation is that I made a...*mistake*... when inking you."

The disgust in her voice makes me cringe. The self-loathing I hear is a blow to my chest. She's been trained for a single purpose from the time she could walk, and clearly the thought that she isn't up to the task terrifies her.

I know—because I feel the same thing. My magic could save the Winter Fae, yet what if I'm not strong enough? What if I'm discovered and manipulated somehow? After what happened with Kitara, it's all I can think about. How many would have suffered because I trusted the wrong person?

"Seemed like a pretty complicated mark." The need to make her feel better is like a fog creeping in. Heavy, thick, and impossible to ignore. "Besides, you did have a colossal distraction that morning."

"Huh?"

I gesture to myself. "I was shirtless. Obviously, the sight of me caused your thought process to lapse."

"I— You— You're impossible."

"Thank you. That's quite a compliment."

She grumbles something, and I know that my attempts to distract her haven't done any good.

"Like I said, it looked complicated. I bet plenty of druids have messed it up."

She lets out a laugh that borders on frantic, then melts into a fit of hysterical giggles. I have no idea what I've said that's this funny, but at least she's laughing. "I'm the first druid to use that sigil in a very long time," she finally explains.

"Oh. Well, I…um…" Now I have no idea what to say.

"Even the smallest miscalculation in the lines can have vastly different results with a sigil like that."

Gods. "What kind of results?"

She rests a hand against her side. When she realizes what she's done, she stiffens and sits up taller in the saddle. Gods forbid she look vulnerable. "We seem to be linked. The injury you received manifested in me."

That could be potentially disastrous—for both of us. "Do you suppose it works both ways?"

Her scowl fades, giving way to a truly wicked smile. "Let's find out." She pinches her thigh—hard.

I swallow the urge to yelp. "Good news—I felt it. We've now proven that it works both ways."

"How," she says, brows disappearing beneath her hair, "is that *good* news?"

"It's possible that *good* is a slightly exaggerated term for the situation." I grin. "Unless you take into consideration the recreational possibilities. I wonder…" I run my finger across my bottom lip with a featherlight touch.

She gasps and slaps a hand over her mouth. "Stop that!"

"Apologies. I'm just trying to lighten your mood." I wasn't sure she'd feel it. Whatever happened to link us came on suddenly. Because of the injury?

"That's not a possibility, since now I have to go back to the Winter Court and tell Orbik that—"

I hold up my hand. "There's no need to tell my uncle what happened today. In fact, it'd be far wiser if we kept this between us, at least for now."

She stares, open-mouthed. "I don't know how to fix this!"

"We'll figure it out."

She rests her left hand against the wound again, fingers curling into the dressing. The pressure of it is a ghost at my side. "And I don't know if it will get worse."

In that moment, there's something strangely vulnerable about her. She's deadly, but she's also just as insecure beneath her mask as I am. She tries so hard to hide it, and maybe it's because of this thing that's happened between us, but I can see it just as clearly as I can my own hand. I see her differently. Not as a guard or even as a woman, but as someone I want to protect with unfamiliar ferocity. It's strange and unwelcome, but I can't stop the soothing platitudes. "We'll take it one day at a time. We'll figure this out together."

"Oh. So now it's *we* and not *me*?" She snorts. "That changed quickly."

"I told you. I've made peace with your presence, Fungus. We're stuck with each other."

She seems like she wants to argue, but she says nothing, instead threading her hand through her hair before straightening in her saddle.

I gather my reins, trying to shake away the ghostly feeling of her fingers running over my scalp.

D espite my protests, we travel through the night, making it back to the estate by late morning. I informed Orbik what we'd discovered at the village—leaving out, of course, the scuffle that ended in both of us getting a nice new hole in the gut. As predicted, the Winter Lord decided not to act. Tania fumed silently beside me, and I excused myself, telling her that I was retiring for the rest of the day. I gently suggested she do the same.

I try and try, but sleep doesn't come. Normally in cases like this, I'd simply wander down to the courtyard, possibly the ballroom, and find myself a companion. There's always activity at the estate, at all hours of the day and night. But after Kitara…

Draining the last of the wine I have and knowing I'm in for a long night, I set out in search of more. Past the gates of the east wing and into the kitchen, I find the cabinet has been emptied and a note left from Kopic stating the Winter Lord wishes to keep the rest of his wine hidden. The bastard even has the nerve to *apologize*.

"Asshole," I mumble as several of the kitchen staff whisper from the other end of the room. I salute them and leave, heading for the lower levels of the building.

The tunnels below the estate used to terrify me. They're endless and confusing and extend far past the main house and its exterior buildings. But beneath the main layer is a hidden, deeper layer. Tunnels within tunnels. Rumor is that Servis had the deepest level dug and bespelled during the war as an emergency escape for the royal family if the need arose. The walls and rooms change, along with the pathways, never in the same place twice.

Since the days of the war, the tunnels and their various rooms and nooks have been ignored. No one alive now knows the origin of the spell used to enchant the tunnels, and no one understands how it works. In my lifetime, at least nine staff members had come down here and were never seen again.

In recent years, I started coming down and exploring. Part of me secretly hoped the tunnels would swallow me whole. If the hallways changed, if I couldn't find my way back, then my disappearance couldn't be blamed on me. It never happened, though. It's almost like the walls have come to know me, allowing me to pass through unhindered, as if in apology for the terror Orbik heaped on me as a child.

I take one of the torches that burn on either side of the landing and start down the hall. It seems narrower than the last time I was here, but I don't give it much thought. There's always something new to see.

One of the last times I ventured down here, several months before Tania showed up, I stumbled upon a room I'd first thought to be a torture chamber. Restraints and cruel-looking instruments lined a small, padded room. After a bit more inspection, I remembered the rumors that my grandfather, Lord Envrill, had engaged in various forms of bondage for fun.

Dragging my hand along the wall as I go, I breathe in deep. An odd smell wafts through my nose. "Something down here stinks, old friend."

A breeze rushes through the hallway, like someone, somewhere, opened a window or a door.

I laugh. "Thanks."

Something creaks, like the sound of a door cracking open, and the walls begin to shift again. The hall in front of me constricts and changes, forming a sharp right corner.

"Huh. I take it you'd like me to go this way, eh?" I shrug. "Sure. Why not."

I make the right and stride to the end of the hall, then set the torch in a holder beside an oversize metal door. That's when I feel it.

Power.

The air is thick with it, almost cloying. It's wrong in a way I can't explain. I feel it in every limb and with each breath I take. Resting my hand against the door, I do my best not to vomit. In all the times I've been down here, I've never felt anything like it. "Why are you showing me this now?"

As if in answer, the walls shake, small bits of debris coming loose from the stone.

Acid bubbles in my gut, my gorge rising. I swallow it back and try the handle. It doesn't turn. "Well, that's no fun. Why show me the door if you won't let me inside the room?"

Again, the walls shake, this time a bit more violently.

"Sure wish you could, you know, actually talk." I bend down to inspect the door. The lock is ancient and more than likely easily broken, but when I try to freeze it, nothing happens. "Performance issues. That's a first."

Picking it is impossible. I haven't brought anything with me to try. But maybe I can *unlock* it.

I press my palm against the lock and close my eyes. Letting the cold settle over me, I push out as lightly as I can. Ice forms around my cuticles, frost creeping across the back of my hand. When I move slowly away from the lock, a thin rod of ice follows. If I've done it correctly, the ice will have seeped into the crevasse of the lock, forming a makeshift key.

I twist the ice. It snaps instantly.

"Damnit." I glance up at the ceiling and frown. "A little help?"

I cover the lock and try again. This time, I make the key too thick. The ice fills the entire lock and then some, making it impossible to turn at all.

Thirty-seven attempts later, still no luck. "Okay. Now it's just pissing me off. The harder you try to keep someone out of a room, the more they're going to want in. Could you please just open the damned door?"

There's a loud metal *clank*, and the handle of the door twitches—then turns.

"Are you kidding me?"

With one last glance behind me, I retrieve the torch and push inside.

I was born with magic. I've seen a number of amazing, virtually unexplainable things happen because of it. However, nothing in my life has prepared me for what I see now.

The space is empty save for a single slab of black granite in the center. There are two small items on the slab, but I can't bring myself to move closer for inspection. No, my feet remain rooted, my attention captured by the room itself.

Four walls, all covered in jagged peaks of ice. In some places, the outcroppings reach several feet; one in particular juts almost to the center of the room. The ceiling is the same. The sight is strange and wondrous and hardly the oddest thing I've seen. But what makes the room a sight to behold, the thing that causes my heart to slam unevenly against my ribs, is the thick, thorny foliage that appears to be growing from random patches on the ice. Much larger versions of the strange vines that sometimes grow from ice on my own walls.

There's a phantom breeze, and something inside my head whispers… "*Druid magic.*"

I force my gaze away from the walls and look to the slab in the center. On it is a pearlescent flask—the one Liani uses to store the magic I donate. The glimmering liquid churns, the glass nearly empty despite the fact that I made a donation not long ago. It seems odd to me that there's so little left.

Beside my flask is something considerably smaller. An oddly shaped vial no larger than a grape. It's nearly translucent with the smallest tint of blue. I bend closer to get a better look and realize that it's shaped like a teardrop…

"No…"

I reach for it, pausing when my hand gets close. The liquid inside swirls, glowing for a second before going dormant again. Stepping back, I take in a deep breath.

Determined, I reach out again, this time picking it up and slowly, carefully, pulling out the cork. Tipping it just a hair, I spill some of the liquid onto my index finger. It pools for a moment before dissolving into my skin. A moment later, a jolt of energy courses through my body, and I know...

I know exactly what this is. Replacing the cork, I set the tear-shaped vial down and stumble away, as though at any moment, the thing might lash out and punish me for touching it. In doing so, I accidentally knock the other vial—the one containing my magic—off the slab. The glass doesn't break, but the contents spill out onto the floor. "This cannot be," I whisper to myself.

"Valen?"

I whirl.

Liani comes inside and closes the door behind her. "How—" She looks at the door, then peers down the hall. "How did you get in here?"

"I..." What am I supposed to say? That the tunnels led me here? That the estate itself showed me the way? Liani is the one person in this world who loves me. But, despite that, I've never told her about my strange relationship with this place. "I'm not sure."

She looks skeptical but nods. Pointing to the slab, she says, "I am so sorry that you had to see this."

"Tell me that I'm wrong." My fists tighten, and I stalk to where she stands. I point a finger violently toward the slab. "Insist that isn't what it looks like."

"My dear child, I will never, ever lie to you..." A single tear slips down her cheek. "I cannot."

The air rushes from my lungs, fast and brutal, as though she's landed a mortal blow. We would never hurt the druids this way, but the evidence is right in front of me.

"We stole the druids' magic," I say. "The tear was never destroyed. We betrayed them."

"Servis betrayed them." She shakes her head. "*We* had nothing to do with it."

"How is it still full?" I lean closer to the strange tear. The power emanating from it makes me dizzy. "After all these centuries, how has it not dissipated, like mine does?"

"Druid magic is different than Fae. Ours can be spent; it can be diminished. The Great Drain sapped our power, but there was never any doubt it would one day return. It was just a matter of time. Druid power can't be depleted. It's part of them, tethered to their souls. It's why we honor them. The gift Aphelian and the druids gave us was boundless."

"And we betrayed them. How loyal of us." I feel sick. "Why haven't we given it back?"

She pulls me close and wraps her arms tight around me. "Without it, you would die. The frequency of your Fae magic donations needed to sustain us would increase, and I don't believe you would survive."

"But—"

"I will not risk losing you over some foolish moral dilemma. I regret that it has to be this way, but you are far more important to me than any human."

Her embrace, normally a comfort, feels lifeless and cold. She knew. All this time, she knew the tear was down here and she never said a word.

"How did it even get here? My flask is here, as well, which means you've been here before. How did you find this room?"

She pulls away and cups the sides of my face. "The magic that spells these walls took pity on me long ago. It considers me...an old friend. If it allowed you to find this room, then I imagine it sees you in a similar manner." She brushes a stray lock of hair from my face.

"I can't keep this from the Aphelian."

Her expression darkens. "What do you think she'll say if you tell her? Do you think she'll be happy you've been hoarding her people's magic all this time?"

"*I* haven't been hoarding anything."

Liani's expression softens. "I'm sorry. You're right. You're not to blame for this mess. If anyone is, it's me."

"Servis betrayed the druids, not you."

"But I knew about it. I did nothing..."

Liani's desire to protect me often gets in the way of logical thinking. It has been that way since I was a child. Is it so hard to believe that this was just another murky decision made for what she viewed as my well-being? No...

Especially since she knew what a toll the donations take on me.

"I know you didn't want the human here and that you were angry we brought her, but you've grown fond of her, yes?"

"She's...not completely horrible."

"She's your age and pretty... I'm sure you've been *enjoying* your time with her. She's definitely safer than the chef's daughter you were messing around with."

It takes a moment to realize what she's insinuating. "She's an *Aphelian*. I would never disrespect her like that." I joke with Tania, but I would never— Not to mention that she wouldn't overstep that line between us. She's had plenty of opportunities.

Liani waves offhandedly. "Well, whatever it is you do with her, if you want that to continue, then don't say a word about this. You might not be to blame, but she'll blame you nonetheless."

It's been a little over a month now, and while I don't know the Aphelian as well as I could, I do know that if I told Tania the truth, I would lose her.

I can't lose her. Especially now that we have this strange connection.

I sigh, feeling defeated. "You're probably right."

"And if you did tell her—if she didn't turn on you—that would put me in a precarious position..."

"What do you mean?"

Liani frowns. There's a glimmer to her eyes, and a single tear rolls down her cheek. "I will not sacrifice you for her magic. If it came down to her or you, I would have her *removed*. Permanently."

I stare at her.

"I... I understand." I don't believe for a moment she'd hurt Tania. But I never thought Liani would have the druid tear stashed in our basement, either, so I suppose anything is possible.

"Now, please, go back to your room," she says. "I'll send something up to relax you. Try to forget this awful secret and know that it's for the good of all those involved."

She leads me to the door, down the hall, and up the narrow set of stairs. With each step, my mood darkens. I don't want to lose Tania, but is lying to her even an option? Will this damned link give me away?

We have no idea how deep this connection between us goes...

13

Keltania

Valen did a decent job of staunching the blood flow of my wound, but I retraced the medical sigil to ensure the skin has knitted together. Satisfied the wound is closed, I venture down to the outer courtyard to work off some steam after trying—and failing—to sleep. It's foolish, given the injury, but I need a clear head to think. Things have changed, and I have no idea where to go from here.

I've created a mess by linking us together. I have no idea what I did wrong. I stared at the picture Levina gave me for hours—I had been so sure of myself.

The moon is nearly full, its light throwing oddly shaped shadows across the courtyard. If I can close out the rest of my surroundings and ignore the not-so-subtle throb of my injuries, I can almost pretend I'm back in Lunal. The feel of the brisk night air caressing my skin as I practice, the sound of nocturnal animals filling the silence. I inhale, fighting to remember the scent of our fields—lilacs and fresh grass accompanied by the faintest smell of whatever concoction the kitchen had planned for the following day.

Stance steady, I lift my blade and begin the calming

motions of Kravik, the druid form of combat. I spent so many sleepless nights practicing in the clearing behind the barracks. The fluid movements and razor-sharp discipline did more to ease my mind than anything else. When practiced outside the battlefield, the motions are serene, beautiful to watch and calming to complete. When used against the enemy, it's deadly.

Aphelians are never coddled, never held or sung to sleep as the childhood monsters creep out from under our beds. Food is rationed. What little magic we have comes from the land; we live connected to it. When Aphelian gave half the power away, we were weakened. We could no longer manipulate the lands, so our harvests were meager. The Order is afforded a small portion of the crops in Lunal, with the majority going to the villagers.

Training was harsh and often cruel, and I know I'll never shake the nightmares of it as long as I walk this plane. But the Order did its job. I'm stronger, faster, less likely to let this life break me. Things like hardship and pain aren't hurdles but motivations that force me to do better.

And that's what this is. Another hurdle. This is the Goddess testing me to see if I can overcome.

I can.

I breathe in slowly and adjust the grip on my blade. In, out. The air moves through my body as though the sword and I are one, filling me, fueling me. Up, down. Eyes closed, I move to the sounds of nature, an echo of my long-forgotten heritage. Old tales of peace and greatness intertwine with rich magic that once connected us to nature in a way I can never fully comprehend. We were far more docile then. Existing to better our surroundings, taking pride and reverence in all living things.

Now... Now, we're darker. The shadow of Aphelian's act of kindness hangs over us. We have edges where soft corners once were, and vicious bites.

My breath quickens. I pivot and swing violently. The sound the blade makes as it slices through the wintry night air is sharp yet comforting in a way I should find disturbing. My wound throbs despite the sigil, but it's good. A reminder of the path I walk.

Sword pointed down, I brace the tip against the soft earth and use it to propel myself up and sideways. A powerful move, yet graceful enough as to not send the blade plunging into the earth. When I land, I tighten my hold and bring the weapon up. An intricate circular motion above my head, ending with a vicious swipe. I picture Orbik's face cleaved in half. Next, the Fae from the village, Wanlo, hewn from nose to navel.

"Good evening, Aphelian." Kopic approaches from the far end of the courtyard. He's dressed as he was the first time we met, in a mix of leather and Fae mesh atop a tunic of silver and blue. "I trust you're having a good evening?"

I holster my sword and adjust my jacket, which is not nearly warm enough for the chill in the air but is thin enough that I can move mostly unhindered. It's Fae leather—thinned wolf hide pressed in a way humans don't have the machinery for. Like the rest of the clothing left for me, it's of the finest quality, buttery smooth and supple. "As well as can be expected, I suppose."

"Where is Valen tonight?"

"He's gone to bed early. Long day." Of almost getting killed, of having our life forces fused together. Just the usual activities.

"If you've nothing left to tend to for him, then Lady Liani requests your presence in the main hall."

I nod and follow Kopic down the now silent corridors of the estate. When I came through the first time, it'd been bustling with sounds of the party. There was no real opportunity to take in my surroundings. Then, as time passed, I was always rushing here or there. Now, at a slower pace, I'm able to get a good look around.

The wide hallways are lined with flowering bushes. Blue and white roses and ivy with scattered wisps of white and pink baby's breath. The foliage isn't anchored in dirt but seems to spring from the marble floor. Thriving despite being deprived of its nutrients and the life-giving power of sunlight. Above us, the ceiling also teems with life. Thick bushels of white and silver wisteria hang, some so low they brush the top of Kopic's head.

He notices me looking at the flowers and says, "Amazing what the latent power in the ground can do, isn't it?"

"This is all from residual magic?" I still can't wrap my head around it.

"The tear was powerful. It helped us win the war, after all. I don't think Aphelian knew just how much of an advantage it would give us."

We turn the last corner, and I see her—the lady of the house. She sits alone at the front of the large room and flashes a feline grin I suspect hides a vicious bite. "Aphelian." She stands and steps down from the dais. Her brows furrow. "I trust that your wound is nothing serious?"

For a moment, my heart stutters. Did Valen tell her we were attacked?

When I don't answer, she nods to my tunic. The blood

from my wound is seeping through. I should know better. There's no way to tell how my body will react to the sigils now that it's tied to a Fae. The sigil sufficiently numbed it, but the skin is still thin and easily torn.

"Oh." I breathe out, relieved. "This is nothing. A scratch. Several of the villagers were unhappy about their situation."

About the fact that your court refuses to help them.

She offers a knowing tilt of her delicate head. "Our encounter was so brief the night of the party, and things have been hectic the last few weeks. I simply wanted to see how you were doing. Inquire if there was anything you might need."

"The hospitality has been adequate."

"Is that so?" She laughs so hard it borders on unladylike. "You are truly bold for a human. Fair warning that Orbik won't find you quite as amusing as I do."

The room grows abruptly warmer. The clothing that only moments ago fit as if made specifically for my body now smothers me as sweat begins to bead. I tug at my sleeves and roll them up, allowing my skin to breathe. "If I've disrespected you in some way, then you have my apologies."

"Not at all." She settles back in her chair and folds her long, slender fingers in her lap. "I find you to be a breath of fresh air in this court, Aphelian. One that's long overdue."

I slip a finger beneath my tunic collar and tug it away from my skin. The reprieve is brief but magnificent, and I have to bite down on my tongue to keep from giggling. "That's kind of you to say, Lady."

She leans back and watches me for a moment. "Yes... I think you'll be good for my Valen. If nothing else, having a pretty thing like you around all the time will keep him on his toes. Maybe we can avoid another incident like Kitara…"

Pretty thing? I grind my teeth to keep from saying something I'll regret later, and I smile. "I'm sure the relationship will benefit us both, Lady."

"I'd like to discuss my nephew's security situation. Obviously, my biggest concern is keeping him safe from any who would do him harm. After what happened at the market…"

"Of course." I shift from foot to foot, trying to tug at my leathers without making a fuss. With each moment that passes, the material becomes heavier and heavier. Suffocating. An odd taste fills my mouth. Bordering on sickeningly sweet, it's cool and has the slightest hint of berry. I swallow, feeling the phantom liquid slide down my throat. A second later, an insane giggle slips past my lips.

"Aphelian?"

My fingers curl into fists, nails gouging my palms. Goddess. Valen must be drinking. If I'm feeling it, this is so much worse than I feared. "So sorry, Lady. I, um, had a tickle in my throat."

She nods and toys with the ring on her pointer finger. A large blue stone glints in the light. "My husband can be a bit…cold, if you'll pardon my wording. But Valen is very dear to me, and though his interactions with most here are positive, there are those who would see him harmed. You must vet his company more carefully."

Every scrap of material touching my body itches, sensation heavy and unwanted. I shift again, and with each move, the need to shed the weight becomes more urgent. "I understand. It's my job to keep him safe. No harm will come to him."

She leans closer. "Yet you allowed him to be alone with Kitara at the market."

"With all due respect, Lady, Kitara was the daughter of your own chef, was she not?"

"Yes." Her tone is terse, and she narrows her eyes.

"She lived on estate grounds, correct?"

"All staff and their families live at the estate."

"Then, and I say this with the utmost respect, shouldn't someone have caught on to her intentions much sooner?" My head is fuzzy, and I bite down on my tongue to keep from laughing out loud.

"Well said… I'll see that it's investigated. Thank you." Liani folds her hands in her lap. "This must be hard for you, being so far away from home."

An explosion of warmth hits me again, but this time it's pleasant. Relaxing. In an instant, my muscles, my bones— my entire body—feel like they could melt happily into the floor. "Lunal was always a placeholder until I could find a place beside a Fae partner."

Liani quirks a brow. "Are you unwell? Your cheeks are flushed."

I swallow hard. "No, just a little warm."

She relaxes and leans back. "I want to know that you'll come to me with any concerns or issues. We want you to feel at home here, comfortable and safe."

"I appreciate the hospitality." I clench my teeth to hold back another laugh.

"I am unable to have children. I love Valen like he is my own flesh. You understand, right?"

I open my mouth to agree with her, but instead of words, a relaxed sigh slips out.

"Aphelian?"

"I, uh." Goddess. How much can one individual consume? "It's just very warm in here."

"So you said." She clucks her tongue. "I always forget that you humans are so temperature intolerant."

I clear my throat and tug lightly at the hem of my tunic. "You were saying? About Valen's security?"

"He can sometimes be—"

She keeps talking, but her voice fades as an invisible force thumps my head. The room spins a bit, and I swallow back a phantom mouthful of something sickeningly sweet. "Wow. That's...disgusting."

This time, Lady Liani stands. "Aphelian?"

White-hot embarrassment barrels through me, completely warring with the euphoric sensations my body is still reeling from.

"I am sorry, Lady. I am, in fact, ill and need to take my eeeave." I bite back another gasp. "My *leave*."

I don't wait for her to excuse me, turning on my heel and inelegantly sprinting from the room. Down the halls I walked with Kopic, I turn the sharp corner and nearly topple as I stumble across the courtyard toward the eastern wing of the estate. I'm almost to Valen's door when my knees buckle. A wave of dizziness washes over me, making it hard to keep my balance.

I'm going to kill him myself!

It takes a moment for my vision to even, but when it does, I'm able to stand and stumble the rest of the way to his door.

I lift my boot and kick hard. The wood groans and gives way, falling into the room with a thunderous clatter. Valen is sitting on the bed, two nearly empty bottles of wine in front of him.

He glances at me over his shoulder, the same obnoxious grin he always wears glaring back. "There was no need to kick the door down. It wasn't even locked."

A problem to deal with another time.

"You." I jab my finger at him, trying hard to focus despite the not-so-subtle tilt of the room. "What in the Goddess are you doing?"

"What does it look like?" He rolls his eyes and picks up the fuller of the two bottles, then waves it at me. "Seems like you might need this a bit more than I do."

"If I count to ten and you're still holding that bottle, I'm going to start swinging my sword." I clumsily draw my weapon and aim the point in his direction. The fact that I don't drop it is a miracle.

"Violence? Really, Tania—"

"Aphelian," I grind out, desperately trying to keep from swinging my sword in his direction. Several locks of hair, an ear, possibly an entire limb… There's plenty I can do without actually *killing* him. My pain threshold is high. I can take it. "You are to call me Aphelian."

"But that's not your name. Your name is Keltania." He swings his legs over the edge of the bed and stands. "You told me so, remember? And I told you that Tania—"

"What were you thinking?" I demand.

He grins and takes a long pull from the bottle.

"Stop doing that!" I lunge forward and smack the bottle from his hands. It shatters against the edge of the table, bits and pieces plinking to the ground. "I'm about to fall over!"

He stares, his now empty hand hanging mid-air. "Fall over? Are you saying you're—"

"I'm drunk!" I grip the edge of the bedpost to keep from falling down. "I was with your aunt! I stood in front of the Lady of the Winter Court while you guzzled Goddess knows how much wine and stumbled around like a fool."

For the briefest moment, he's stunned. Eyes wide and face—somewhat—apologetic. Then he smiles, beaming like the sun as it chases away the moon. Smug, satisfied, and utterly guilt-free. "Then you're welcome, of course. It's quite pleasant. Wouldn't you agree?"

"It's not just your life you're gambling with anymore. It's mine now. If you do something foolish and get yourself killed, then I'm dead, too. I can't protect you if I can't see straight! No more wine."

He has the nerve to shrug. "You're overreacting. Liani sent this to me." He hesitates for a moment, lips tugging downward. "To take my mind off troubling matters."

"Such as random villagers trying to kill you?" I supply. "How about friends?" It's a low blow. I know he's still raw from what happened with Kitara, but I can't think of any other way to snap him out of it.

He leans against the wall. "You seem to be worrying enough for both of us. Honestly, it frees up a lot of my time."

"You're an ass."

"You're going to need to work on your flattery, Fungus. Here, try this: Thank you, Valen. That was amazing. It was nice to relax for the first time in my sad, boring life."

I want to scream but bite down hard on the inside of my cheek. "Get someone here to fix that door and *keep it locked.*"

14

Valen

I sleep fitfully, nightmares that I imagine stem from guilt waking me every hour. It's an impossible situation.

Telling her about the tear would be a betrayal of my own people. Plus, if Liani's theory is right, it would put my own life in jeopardy—which would, in turn, put Tania's life in danger. But deep down, I know that's not the real reason I'm keeping it from her. Losing her just isn't an option—and I hate myself for feeling that way.

After what happened to Mika, I swore never to let anyone get that close. Aside from Liani, who is…essential. She loves me despite my flaws and inadequacies. Tania doesn't love me—our relationship is nothing like Mika's and mine—but doing something that would likely cut her from my life feels like planning to lop off a limb. It's an odd feeling, but it's inescapable.

The problem is, I'm not sure this link between us won't give me away…

Buri meets us in the dining room of the east wing. The long table and all its chairs are pushed to one side, allowing us space to work. She's unhappy, preferring to do our lessons outside where she doesn't feel so closed in. But Tania insisted. We're better protected here, less vulnerable.

And it's far warmer for her.

"No." Buri tries to be supportive, but the deepening furrow of her brow and increasing twitch in her right eye are telltale signs that she's coming to the end of her patience. "You've got to dig deeper." Her goal today is to get me to create specific weapons using my ice. Swords, clubs, shields… It's not going the way either of us hoped.

I slump back against the wall and flick several chunks of ice from my knuckles. A frosty projectile with a pointy tip? No problem. An intricately designed frozen sword with a curved handle? "It doesn't work that way. Maybe if I had some wine…"

"No," Buri and Tania snap at the same time.

"Is it because the human is here?" Buri narrows her eyes at Tania, who is perched atop the table in the far corner of the room. Every once in a while, she swings her feet and grins like she's in on some big secret. No doubt she knows what her presence here does to Buri—and enjoys every last moment of it.

The Fae keeps stealing glances over her shoulder, glaring at the druid with enough menace to send even the most stalwart winter guard scrambling for cover. I understand her unease. It rankles to fail in front of Tania. She's not here to judge, and I shouldn't care what she thinks, but being unable to do as instructed makes me feel small. She's already witnessed two meltdowns due to my weakness. I could have easily killed her that day on the way home from the market—or the day she locked me in my room. This is just adding insult to injury.

"We could make her wait outside," Buri suggests.

"Maybe it's hard to perform under such scrutiny." Tania hops off the table and crosses the room. "Perhaps if you didn't drool over his magic every time you looked at him, he'd find it easier to do as you asked."

"You dare blame me?" Buri moves from my side. "If I had my magic—"

"But you don't—and that's the problem, isn't it?" Tania flicks a finger in my direction. "He has the one thing you desperately covet."

Buri's cheeks pink. "I don't—"

Tania holds up her hands. "You've been in the service of the Winter Lord for a long time. It's kind of weird that you watched Valen grow up, maybe changed his diaper a few times, and now you're obsessing over him, over his power. It's disgusting."

I've never voiced my discomfort over Buri's attention, but here Tania is, putting it *eloquently* into words as though she's known me my entire life.

Buri's mouth falls open. She makes a stuttering sound, gaze flickering to me for an instant before narrowing on the Aphelian. "Your kind used to be scattered across these lands like vermin."

"Buri," I warn. Anger bubbles in my gut like acid. I taste it, the foul tang coating the inside of my mouth. A part of me doesn't understand, while another part—the one feeding off the fury—wants to gut Buri like a fish...

"Some used to view you as equals, but others—we saw you for what you were. Amusing." She ignores me, advancing a single step. "You used to beg us to take you in. To *use* you."

Tania blinks. Momentary surprise at Buri's boldness quickly melts into red-hot fury that blazes in her eyes. Her hand goes to the hilt of her sword, and as my own haze clears, I shoot forward and wedge myself between them before the situation can escalate further.

"I think we're finished for today," I say. Blood pounds in my veins, and my heart hammers. It's a struggle to get the words out in an even tone.

Buri snorts. "I'm sorry, Valen. I'll be informing your uncle that I'm unable to continue these lessons until you properly restrain your new pet."

She turns to Tania, mouth open, but the Aphelian holds up her hand and shakes her head slowly. Just once. "Think very carefully about the words you want to speak. You've burned through my patience allotment for the day. Say the wrong thing, and no one will find your corpse."

Buri, smart enough to know better, spins and stalks from the room. Her footsteps echo down the hall, followed by the slam of the door.

I pull a chair out from the table and sink into it. "I didn't know you had such a keen understanding of Buri's motivations."

"I don't."

"Is it at all possible that you've taken a fancy to me? Your impassioned defense was…sweet." I grin despite the glare she's aimed my way. "You couldn't be blamed, of course." I stand and turn in a slow circle, giving my hips a wiggle for good measure.

She scrunches up her nose and frowns. "I honestly don't know why I said all that. How I knew…"

"I might know where it came from." I pick up one of the intricately folded napkins and pull it apart. I'm not sure if it's supposed to be a bird or a frog. Liani makes the servants come in twice a week to change the design even though I've never used the room for a meal. "Our problem is more serious than we thought."

"*You?*" Her skin pales. "That came from you?"

"It makes sense, doesn't it? You felt the wine I drank... And I think I felt your anger over the whole thing, too. You've got quite a temper..." I nod. "We need to get a handle on this, or we're both going to land in a lot of hot water."

She levels a gaze at me. "We're going to have to find a way to fix it."

"And if there is no way?"

"There's always a way."

She sounds sure. Her shoulders, her stance—it all screams of confidence.

But I don't miss the glimmer of worry that flickers through our new link.

Kopic arrives the next morning to bring Tania before my uncle. I don't know what the meeting is for, but my best guess is that it's a discussion of security measures, since she ran out on Liani the day before. While she's gone, my plan is to sneak out for a quick run, but someone knocks on my door before I can slip away.

"Valen." My aunt breezes in from the hallway, looking out of place against the bright tile. She reminds me of darkness. Not necessarily the bad kind, but cool nights and starless skies. Peace and tranquility. "I hoped we could talk."

"Is everything all right?" I step aside and wave her to

the chair. "Sit, please."

The grateful smile she flashes lights her entire face. "Yes, yes. Everything is fine." Liani is the daughter of the court's healer, Zomade. With her elegance and beauty— not to mention intelligence and quick wit—no one was surprised when she caught the eye of Orbik, the son of the previous monarch, Envrill.

Her smile falters as she crosses the room and perches on the edge of my bed. "I'm afraid the conversation isn't a lighthearted one."

"Orbik sent you to fetch another donation." My tone comes across flat, but inside…inside, I rage. This isn't her fault. Orbik is just as careless as our ancestors when it comes to squandering magic. Liani always tries to stop him, but he does as he pleases, stating the Winter Lord answers to no one.

I knew it was coming. After being down in the tunnels and finding that room, after knocking over the flask… It was only a matter of time.

I take her hand and squeeze. "Please don't be upset. I'm not angry with you." Sighing, I add, "I'm never angry with you…"

"You are the purest soul I've ever known, dear child." She cups my face and smiles. There's so much sadness in it, and I hate that my uncle makes her do this. I've suggested many times that she ask Kopic to come for the donation, but she always refuses. If it has to be done, she sees to it herself to ensure my safety.

"The party drained most of it. Then, when you were down in the cellar…"

While Fae lost their magic in the Great Drain, certain powerful individuals, such as someone in a royal bloodline, can still manipulate it. My uncle can't manifest his own power, but he can use mine.

"I spilled the rest of it." I sigh. "I wonder if you might convince him to wait a day or so. I haven't been feeling well lately. The last donation he took sapped me for a week."

"You're still upset about what you uncovered in the tunnels, aren't you?"

That isn't the reason I'm asking her to wait, but since she brought it up... "It doesn't bother you?"

"The druids sacrificed a great deal for us. I *am* deeply bothered by what transpired. But I will *not* put my feelings ahead of your safety." Tears gather in the corners of her eyes. "Orbik is...careless. If the burden of keeping our magic stores full fell solely on you..." She ducks her head for a moment. "Besides, we did keep them safe during the war. And Servis did use the remainder of his magic trying to get the tear back..."

"That was lifetimes ago!"

"For them, maybe. But not for us."

I want to keep arguing with her, to make her change her mind, but the last thing I want is to upset her further. "I suppose you're right."

"It's why we honor the bond to this day," she says. "Not for Servis's sake—for Aphelian. Her descendants are brought here to live in comfort, never having to worry about filling their bellies or seeking shelter."

"If it's about honoring them, why do they come to us as guards? We're physically stronger, live longer, and can withstand more damage. Why do we not act as *their* protectors?"

Her eyes widen, and if I hadn't been staring at her,

I would have missed it. "I suppose because it's the role Aphelian herself played. She was a very powerful druid and, while accompanying Servis's caravan on a mission to the Autumn Lands, saved his life. They were unlikely friends before that, but it was on that trip they fell in love. It's also when she met Avastad, the Autumn Lord who wanted her for himself."

"Which is rumored to have started the war," I say. I know my history, but recent developments have me questioning everything I thought I knew. "So, could we wait another day or so for the donation?"

The process is painful for me, but how would Tania feel? If it's even a whisper of what I endure, the thought of it makes me sick.

She lowers her gaze and presses her lips tight. It's a look I've seen a thousand times. Absolute and utter shame. Regret and apology mingled with more guilt than someone as pure as Liani should ever have to endure.

"Oh, Valen." She stands, hands shaking slightly. "I wish it could. Obviously, your uncle can manipulate the magic in the druid tear, but it's much harder than using yours. Lately, even yours has begun to take a toll on him. It seems the stronger you get, the quicker it fades from the flask."

If that's true, they're going to bleed me dry if they aren't careful. How much can they take without killing me?

This is my responsibility, though. The one thing my presence within these walls is good for. The process is agonizing—both physically and mentally. In the days before the Great Drain, the procedure, called panashere, was used as a form of corporal punishment. Criminals would be strapped down, a needle inserted into their chest, just below the heart. Our magic is in the blood, extractable only using a needle made of iron. Criminals would have their magic bled slowly over the course of several days. The pain was excruciating, and most didn't survive.

I was very young the first few times it was done, and it almost killed me, but I adapted. Found a way to fight through and ease my own discomfort. As I got older, it was easier to endure. Liani never takes that much.

But Tania is human, and I'm tied to her.

Despite my concern, refusing isn't an option. Orbik has a temper, and if Liani goes to him on my behalf, there's no telling how he'll react. I won't take that chance.

A single tear slips down her cheek. "I am truly sorry, Valen."

"It's okay. I understand." I stand. "But before we start, I need to—"

Liani grabs my arm and gently guides me back to the bed. "I'm afraid Orbik is waiting in the hall for this as we speak."

If I don't warn Tania… "But—"

"I won't take much. It will be quick. I promise."

I nod and settle beside her on the edge of the bed, steeling myself against what's to come. "If this is what it takes to ensure our survival, I will do my part."

She brushes a hand against my cheek as her breath trembles. "These Fae do not deserve you, Valen. *Orbik* does not deserve you."

I remove my shirt and lay back. She's gentle as always, yet I still know the moment the needle pierces my skin. It starts with an uncomfortable rise in temperature. Sweat beads against my brow. I swallow as I inhale deeply in an attempt to fill the void Liani creates. *Hollow*. That's how it always feels at first. It's like the needle draws out my soul, sucking away the thing that makes me who and what I am. Then, the ache starts. First dull and faint, progressing slowly toward a pressure that threatens to crush my chest.

"Almost done," Liani soothes.

Around us, ice begins to encase the room. I feel each item as it freezes. The chair in the corner, the table and decanter by the door…the wine inside.

I close my eyes and chase the pain. Anything is better than the vacuity left behind in the wake of withdrawal. The encompassing numbness has grounded me in the past. During the early years, for days after, I could do nothing more than lay in bed and stare at the ceiling. Food, frivolity, and even simple bodily functions were too great an effort.

Until I learned to embrace the pain.

"Shh." Liani's fingers trace a light circle against my forearm. I barely feel her touch. "Just a bit more."

A spike of anxiety breaks my reverie. The magic surges inside me, exploding outward in a crash of ice and hail. An assortment of pops and clinking fill the room as it pours out, blanketing every last surface.

Liani gasps. Her hand, resting against my chest, shudders from the cold. "Valen, please. Try to stay calm."

It takes all my effort, but I force my eyes open and make a halfhearted swipe at the syringe. "Enough…"

My aunt continues to pull up on the plunger.

The panic surges, blooming into stone-cold terror. *Tania*. She feels what I do. She doesn't understand what's happening. I should have tried harder to warn her!

I swat at the needle again, this time a little harder. Liani doesn't seem to understand. "I know. I know," she croons. "I'm almost finished."

"STOP!" I violently grab for the needle, and this time she pulls it out. It clouds, then freezes solid, the magic inside crystallizing.

Liani looks from the needle to me, her face ashen. "What— What's wrong?"

An acidic retort bubbles up, but I swallow it back, reminding myself that none of this is her fault. My reaction is rash and uncharacteristic, but it's not really mine, is it?

I force a steadying breath into my lungs, hold it for a moment, then blow out slowly. "Like I said, I haven't been feeling well. It was a little rougher than most donations."

"Valen—"

I hold up a hand to stop her. "It's all right. I just... I'd like to rest a bit."

"Of course." She cradles the frozen syringe and hurries from the room, and I slump back against the pillows.

I almost have my breathing evened out when the door bursts open and Tania stumbles in. Her eyes are bloodshot, her breathing ragged. She surveys the ice-encased room. Her skin is so pale... "What—"

She sways on her feet, eyes rolling back. I launch myself from the bed. The room spins, but I manage to catch her just as she passes out and drops to the icy floor.

I follow her down, the room growing dark around the edges for a moment before I chase her into oblivion.

15

Keltania

My entire body is numb.

I force my eyes open and fight back a shiver as I try—and fail—to move any of my appendages. There's something heavy on top of me. Not quite as cold as the surface I'm lying on, but not at all warm, either.

A familiar sigh fills the silence.

I open my eyes.

I'm on Valen's floor, just inside the door. *Drip. Drip. Drip.* The entire room is encased in ice, slowly melting into large puddles all around us. Valen lies on my left side, one arm beneath my head while the other is across my midsection.

"What are you— Get off me!" I bat his arm away and scoot back. I make a move to stand, but the room dips and sways so violently that there's a good chance I'll lose the contents of my stomach. "What happened?"

He stirs and groans, slowly lifting his head from the wet floor. "I would have warned you if I could. I tried… I wasn't set to donate for another few weeks."

"Donate what?"

"My magic." With wobbly effort, he stands and practically has to drag himself to the edge of the bed. His shoulders are taut, his fists clenched so tight that his knuckles have gone pale. "It's called panashere. Technically, the practice was outlawed centuries ago, but there's no other way to extract the magic. They take a small portion of my power from time to time to keep the wolves at bay, so to speak. Orbik uses it to enforce protection over the Winter Lands."

I press the heel of my hand into my temple, breathing in and out slowly. The spinning slows just a little—thank the Goddess. I can't remember ever being so nauseous. "*Donate* and *take* are two very different words…"

"I do it willingly. To help my people." He's shaking just a bit, trying to hide it, and he squares his shoulders. Sitting up a bit straighter, he says, "Unfortunately, it…takes a toll."

"I felt as though the air was being sucked from my lungs. It was like my internal organs were all collapsing." I brace my hands against the small table beside the door and shudder at the memory, sure I've gotten a taste of what it will feel like to die. "I still can't see straight."

"We're going to need to fix this…whatever it is, before they have to do it again."

"Agreed." I'm not going through that again. Valen shouldn't have to, either. I don't care if I have to kill us both to prevent it.

"Ideas?"

I've gone over everything a thousand times, and I can't understand what I did wrong. At this point, there's only one place I can turn to fix my mistake. "The only thing I can think of is to send a message to my high priestess."

I hate the idea of admitting I've screwed up so badly,

but my life — Valen's life — hangs in the balance. While we're connected, there are too many variables. Too many possibilities that something could go wrong. I'm human, after all. What would happen if I was mortally injured protecting him? If I was killed? What would that mean for him?

"If there's a way to fix this," I say, "Levina will know."

She has to. If not, there's a good chance Valen's life will kill me.

It takes just over two weeks for Valen's messenger hawk to return with word from Levina. It's hard to judge her tone from the sprawling cursive and druidic seal, but I get the impression she's disappointed in me.

Or maybe that's my own shame eating me up slowly.

I wait in Valen's room with Levina's message clenched between my fingers. He went out with Kopic early this morning. A Fae solstice hunting tradition, they said.

Valen is moody and obnoxious with an overly inflated sense of self-worth, but he's also thoughtful. He treats me with respect and as an equal, seeming to genuinely enjoy my company now even though we bicker constantly. Some days it's a toss-up during any given hour as to whether I want to laugh with him or kill him. He has no regard for his own safety and doesn't take anything seriously, but it's hard to imagine my life without him now. This isn't what I expected our bond to be, but it's something I'm not sure I could live without.

He's the closest thing I've ever had to a friend, and

sometimes, when I catch him watching me, I feel like there's something more brewing between us.

Even though that's not possible.

The door handle jiggles, and a moment later, Valen appears in the doorway. Kopic is right behind. "Tania!" He blushes when he realizes his mistake, and he corrects himself. "Aphelian…"

When we're alone, he uses my name. When we're not alone, though, he uses my title. He insists it's a sign of respect, but the way he says my name when it's just the two of us—like he's whispering a prayer to the Goddess—makes me wonder if he doesn't understand me more than I give him credit for.

He holds up a small rabbit. "It took six years, but I finally did it."

I cross to where they stand, bending down to inspect the pitiful creature hanging limp in his grip. It's a little breed of rabbit I've never seen before. Long black ears and pinkish fur. Several sets of wicked-looking red fangs peek from behind tiny white lips. "Took that down all by yourself, did you?" I clap slowly. "Good thing you still have all your limbs."

He rolls his eyes and laughs. "It's a Verreza. They only come out of hibernation on the eve of the solstice, for nine or ten hours."

"Catching and eating a Verreza is said to bring good fortune and health to the individual," Kopic says with pride. "They're extremely rare. In my six hundred years, I've only caught two."

"They're rare, and your answer is to slaughter one?" I frown.

We've surmised the link is strongest between us during

amplified emotional situations. I can't feel him constantly, but during times of heightened emotional responses—like when he was drinking—I felt it all. Now, Valen's excitement over the small rabbit allows me to feel the cool fur in his hands, the dry, crusting blood on his fingers. I can almost taste his elation over the kill, but I also feel my own regret. Senseless slaughter of a creature—especially one so rare—seems stupid. "Have you asked yourself why they're so rare?"

Valen sets the creature down on the table by the door, and I can tell he feels what I do. My intention isn't to dampen his excitement, but I can't help the way I feel.

He looks to the paper in my hand, then turns back to Kopic. "I need to talk to the Aphelian for a minute."

"I'll have this prepared." Kopic takes the animal carcass. "If I leave you two alone, there won't be any bloodshed, right?"

The last time Valen said we needed to talk, I threw a half-full decanter of wine at his head. It was justified. He'd suggested I start wearing a new uniform. Something more *Fae*.

"There's nothing sharp in the room." He grins. "We're good."

Kopic nods, then offers me a slight bow before disappearing through the doorway with the dead rabbit.

"The answer is yes. It's exactly what you think it is." I stand and wave the paper back and forth.

The small, fanged rabbit is forgotten, and a new emotion—hope—floods between us. "Well? What did she say?"

"She thinks she can fix it." Reading Levina's words lifted a massive weight from my shoulders. When I sent the message, I wasn't sure there'd be a fix. Or, if there was, the specifics could be lost to time. It's been centuries since we used a sigil like this. No one even remembers them. Thankfully, Levina pored over our oldest books when she was young. She soaked in as much of the lost knowledge as possible, saying once that paper was fragile but human memory passed from one to another was endless.

His head tilts back, and relief floods through me—both his and mine. "Thank the Gods."

"But we have to meet her in Ventin Peaks."

His eyes narrow. "Ventin? Isn't that an old, untethered town in the south?" He snatches the parchment from me and skims the message, his brow furrowing. "She estimates the journey to take *two weeks*?"

"Give or take." I'm not thrilled about that part, either, but if it solves our problem, then it's worth it. Plus, Valen needs some time away from the estate. He never says anything, but I know he fears his aunt coming to him for another donation. I understand because I fear it, too. With each passing day, he's gotten edgier and edgier. It's starting to affect us both—which triggers the link more often. He tries to hide it, but I know he feels guilty about it. Every now and then a wave of it hits me, so strong that I need to focus or I'll topple over.

"You think she's right?" He stares at the paper as though he's trying to see some kind of hidden message in the text.

I snatch it back from him. "I think if anyone can do it, it will be Levina. She's truly magnificent. The most revered priestess we've had in decades." Still, a part of me *does* worry. What if she's wrong? What if something she does makes this worse? "The question is, are you going to be able to leave?"

He keeps his expression neutral, but I can tell—by both body language *and* the link—that he's concerned. "You're worried Orbik won't allow me to take the journey."

"You said it yourself—he keeps you where he can see you. Fear for your life and all." The words drip with sarcasm, and I know Valen hears it, too.

I don't trust the Winter Lord one bit. There's no way he'll let Valen—or, more to the point, Valen's *magic*— scamper off without a fight. The question is, will it be a fight we can win? My loyalty is to Valen, but waging war on the entirety of the Winter Court won't go over well with anyone. Things have been quiet recently, but I feel like I'm always on guard—if not watching for attackers, then protecting him from his own family.

Valen says he trusts his uncle's motives, but I'm not sure that's the whole truth. There are little things. Small, almost unnoticeable tells. The way Valen stiffens whenever Orbik enters a room, or the cold, unimaginable terror I feel from him in the dead of night as he sleeps. I can't see his nightmares, but some nights, the chill of them—the utter desolation—steals the air from my lungs and has me waking covered in sweat.

My palms tingle, and when I look up, Valen's fists are clenched, digging his fingernails into his own palms. He catches me watching, then glances down. Regret fills the space between us. "Oh. Sorry. I didn't mean—"

I ignore the sting in my own palm and snap my fingers in front of his face. "Focus. What should we do?"

"My first instinct is to sneak away." He shakes his head. "But that won't work. We wouldn't get to the gates before being spotted. I think we only have one choice…" There's a flicker of hesitation through the link, as if he's bracing himself for my reaction. "We need to tell my uncle the truth."

"Let me be sure that I have this clear." Orbik sits on his throne while Liani hovers like a shadow behind him. It's impossible to miss the look of accusation, of hatred, each time her gaze lands on me. "You were attacked at the village and told no one?"

"I thought it prudent to minimize the spread. Each time Valen is attacked, it seems to entice his enemies to act. Makes him appear more...vulnerable."

Orbik considers this for a moment before nodding sharply. His gaze goes to his nephew. "The attacker was thwarted, and you're safe. The Aphelian has honored her ancestor. What is the complication?"

"The complication," I say as calmly as I can manage, "is that you nearly killed me when you siphoned more of Valen's magic a few weeks ago."

The Winter Lord and his lady exchange glances. Something unspoken passes between them, and his right hand twitches. They're surprised I know. Do they really think Valen would keep such a secret from me? Don't they know how this works? No, we don't have a conventional Fae/Aphelian bond, but really?

"Whatever magic the druid ink holds seems to have linked us together," Valen rushes to interject. "It creates a...liability."

Liani clutches her husband's hand. "How so?"

"The wound I received wouldn't have been fatal for me, but it could have killed the Aphelian." Valen catches my gaze for a moment before quickly looking away. "When I'm injured, she will be injured. When she is injured, I'll be harmed as well."

"You believe this link works both ways?" The panic in Liani's voice is impossible to ignore. She slips into her seat beside Orbik and grips the arm of his chair hard enough to turn her knuckles snow-white.

Valen nods. "We've tested the theory. It's all true."

Orbik shrugs. "We are far hardier than humans. She would have to be beheaded for you to—"

"Is it a risk you're willing to take?" Valen makes a slicing motion across his throat.

Liani glares at Orbik, then at me. Her lips twist in a way that I can only describe as poisonous. She's a snake, coiled and ready, and I'm the mouse. "*You* must fix this at once."

"That's easier said than done," I reply coolly. They simply make a demand and wait for it to be carried out. Don't they understand that just wanting something doesn't mean you can have it?

"You've obviously made a mistake. Your part of the partnership is to protect him, and that cannot be done while he shares your human frailties. Was this not the result of one of your silly little druid markings? Simply erase it and start over."

"Erase it?" I hold out my forearm, the one I traced the alarm sigil into, as an example. The deep red symbol glares back at me. "The magic has seeped into my skin. I've used it to ward Valen's rooms. Does that seem like is can simply be *erased*?"

With a sigh, Orbik says, "I will allow you to contact the druid priestess in charge of the Order. She may know a way to fix this."

"We've already taken the liberty, Uncle." Valen stands a little straighter. "I—"

Orbik stands. "Good. Then we'll wait for her reply. Until then, the Aphelian will be confined to the east wing for your safety and, of course, for her own. I will issue you an additional guard in the meantime." He gestures to the guards standing by the door. They cross the room and settle, one on either side of me, while Kopic takes the lead. "Please see our esteemed friend back to her quarters. Be sure to get her anything she desires. Valen, if you'll remain for a moment, I'd like a word…"

Valen starts to speak, but the guard on my right gently nudges me forward and out of the throne room before either of us can protest. We navigate the halls in silence, swiftly moving through the courtyard that connects the rest of the house with the eastern section.

When we get to my door, Kopic bows. "I wish you a speedy resolution to the matter, Aphelian."

I try to thank him but don't trust myself to speak. Whatever Orbik is saying to Valen has him worried, and the sudden flood of it makes me dizzy.

Closing the door, I sink onto my cot. This is bad. I don't want anyone else to look after Valen. Plus, would distance make the link better—or worse?

I lay back and fold my arms across my chest. Weeks have passed, and the creation of the link still bothers me. I know I memorized the sigil perfectly. Made sure to duplicate every curve, each twisting line, from a meticulously studied picture. How could I have gotten it so wrong?

Sigils that give strength—both physical and mental—are shaped vaguely like trees, their edges resembling branches reaching toward the sky and roots running deep. There are marks for altered senses—a collection of inkings that appear as an eye, more or less. The rebirth sigil, used to restart a stopped heart. It has to be placed over the heart. Then there's the Heartbreaker, also drawn over the heart...

A chill creeps across my skin, and I bolt upright and jump from the cot. The sinking sensation in my belly almost brings me to my knees.

The Heartbreaker.

The rebirth sigil.

I drew one over the other.

"How could I be so stupid!" I pace like a caged animal.

There's no rule about overlapping sigils when it comes to everyday use. We do it all the time, many of the marks having to be traced on the outsides of our wrists, bases of our spines, or in the hollows of our throats. Power calls to power, and there's nothing stronger than life force. But the ancient sigils, the ones nearly forgotten—those are different. They hold more magic.

They need their own space.

What I did must have altered the sigil. Changed it to grant us this unforeseen—and unwanted—outcome. Levina told me to trace it over Valen's heart—but she had no way of knowing someone already inked the Heartbreaker there. This is on me. I should have known better.

I stop pacing and kick the cot. It rattles against the wall, the pillow tumbling over the side. I take aim again, intending to kick harder, and an urgent knock sounds at the door. I reach for the handle, but it bursts open before I can touch it.

Valen stands in the hallway, and the set of his shoulders and the fierce gleam in his eyes make my stomach roil. His unease rolls over me like a tidal wave, as warm and real as the breath in my own lungs. Something is horribly wrong.

"Gather supplies." His words are frantic. "We need to leave. *Now*."

16

Valen

I turn and stalk across the hall to my door, shouldering it open with more force than necessary. Tania is right behind me. "And where, if you don't mind me asking, are we going?"

I pull a pack from beneath the bed, then proceed to fill it. Warm cloaks, blankets, spare clothing… "We need to get to your priestess so she can fix whatever it is you did to us."

"I thought we covered that." She glares at me but there's a hint of confusion in her tone.

Concern floods the link between us, and guilt bubbles to the surface, so thick that I almost choke on it. Between what I've learned about Servis and the tear, and what my uncle just said, I don't know how she hasn't seen through me yet.

"We made a mistake." The confession kills me. We said too much, put too much faith in my uncle. Pointing toward her wound, I add, "Telling them about that, about the link." The moment Kopic led her away, my uncle questioned me further about what happened outside the village. He came up with a simple solution to remedy the link between us.

One that doesn't require me leaving the safety of the estate.

"I'm still not following," Tania says.

"The wound I received wouldn't have killed me."

She nods. "Right…"

"But chances are it would have been fatal for you had I not intervened, correct?"

Understanding creeps into her features. Understanding tainted by the hint of cloying panic that coats the inside of my mouth and nearly makes me gag.

"We gave them all they needed to fix this problem themselves." I stuff a pair of gloves into the bag. I won't need them, but Tania might. She's so damned determined to shrug off any hint of discomfort, but I have a new awareness of her now. One that makes it impossible to ignore. "I told them that when they took my donation, it almost killed you. They believe that if they do it again, if they take just a little more, it will do the trick."

"*Do the trick?*" Her mouth falls open. The horror, the disbelief, that rolls off her nearly brings me to my knees. If she only knew the whole truth… "They want me *dead*? They're willing to *torture* you for it?"

There's a small bit of skepticism in her tone and in her emotion, but more than that, there's a profound sense of astonishment—and I can't blame her. What I'm implying is unthinkable to her. Until recently, it would have been unthinkable to me, too. Aphelians are honored. Revered. They hold the highest standing and are given the deepest of respect. To harm one is unthinkable.

But knowing what I know now, finding out the truth about Servis and Aphelian, Orbik's reaction makes so much more sense. These druids, these descendants of Aphelian, are nothing more than tools. How many before me knew the truth? How many carried on without batting an eye? How many druids were used and discarded?

Like Mika.

By not telling her, I'm just as bad as the rest. But I'm also protecting her. If she found out, it would only cause problems for her. For her people. It would cause problems for *us*. "Apparently, some don't find your position as revered as others. Having your life tied to mine puts the magic in jeopardy. That's not something they can allow."

She glances over her shoulder, at the large window behind us, then at the door. Her entire body tenses.

"You would never get to the gates," I say softly. Fight or flight. My own legs itch to run in answer to her fear. Every thunderous beat of her heart pounds inside my own chest, each breath coming slightly quickened. "The guards would cut you down."

"From what you've just told me, I don't have anything to lose." Her lips split with a wicked grin, and I have to remind myself that our situation is dire. It's impossible to tear my eyes from the flame that flares to life behind her eyes, or the way her entire body tenses, straining her leathers in all the right—or wrong, depending on how you look at it—places. While she might be fearful of the situation, she's still Tania. Brave and dangerous and unwilling to go down without a fight. "You Fae might be physically more resilient than me, but slicing open an artery would still probably kill you. Do you think they'll take that chance?"

She wants me to believe she's considering it, but I know better—and it has nothing to do with our *situation*. "I'm proposing a way for us to both make it out of this alive. If you'll hear me out—"

There's a rustle at the door, and a moment later, Liani slips inside. Her eyes are swollen and red, and she has several brown bags in her arms. The scent wafting from them tells me she's just come from the kitchen. "You must hurry." She thrusts the bags at Tania. "Orbik's men will be here shortly."

Tania sets the bags on the bed and glares at her. "Then I will meet them with my sword in hand."

Liani laughs at the Aphelian before dismissing her completely and turning her attention on me. "You must find a way to break this link. Orbik won't risk your life, but he's not above hurting you to be rid of an insignificant human. I cannot allow that!"

Insignificant human… No doubt a slip, but it tells me more than enough about the court's true feelings. About my *aunt's* feelings.

Liani closes her eyes for a moment, and when she opens them, tears gather in the corners. My aunt has worried about me my entire life, but the spark of fear I see now is brighter than ever. "I won't see you harmed, Valen. Not because of her or anyone else. I would kill her myself if I didn't think it would hurt you so."

I refuse to acknowledge what she's just said. I know it comes from a place of love, but my bond with Tania makes the words sting. "We received word from Lunal. The druid priestess can help us. We just have to get to Ventin."

My admission seems to lift a ten-ton weight from her shoulders. "Then that's where you must go." She grabs another pack from the floor and shoves it at Tania. "In ten minutes, be at the east gate, and one of my guards will let you out. Follow the road south. I will make sure Orbik's men believe you've gone north."

She throws her arms around me, and I return the embrace. "Thank you."

"Be safe. Not because the Winter Lands need your magic or because your uncle has convinced you it can save us, but for me. Be safe so that we may be together soon."

The woman who's been like a mother to me turns toward the door and slips through, and I wonder if I'll ever see her again.

We made it to the gate in time for none other than Kopic to usher us through. He offered a simple *journey well* before stealing into the shadows like he'd never been there at all.

Daylight fades fast, and by the time the moon breaks through the small cracks in the cloud cover, we've almost made it to the edge of Winter territory.

"I still don't understand why we couldn't take horses." Tania has the lighter of the two packs slung over her shoulder, secured with her right hand, while the left rests on the hilt of her sword. Her eyes dart every which way, body tense and ready for an ambush. "This is going to take forever on foot."

"I told you—the northern terrain would be impossible for a horse to navigate. If we'd taken them from the stables, my uncle would suspect Liani's information was false." Gods only knew what he'd do if he found out my aunt helped us escape.

Tania grumbles something under her breath, then sighs. "If we're going to travel this way, we need to be smart. Camp at night and make as much progress as we can during the daylight."

"Agreed."

She stops walking and glances back at the trail behind us. It's dark, the scant light from the stars barely reaching us through the tree cover. "Do you *really* think they'll believe her? That we went north?"

"For a while, yes. I don't think it will last forever, though. Eventually, he's going to send scouts out in all directions, but we have a fair head start as long as we remain cautious." I've been covering our tracks in the snow using magic, but my uncle would anticipate that. If they come this way, his men will push on despite the lack of evidence.

"I'm betting these woods aren't friendly after dark. I don't love the idea of going much farther before morning."

"These woods are unfriendly any time of day." Even forgetting about the rebel bands of Fae scattered throughout Derriga, this part of the forest houses lethal occupants. "Aside from an assortment of venomous snakes and vermin, these woods are known for having venom stalkers."

"What are venom stalkers?"

"They look like cats but much larger and with the mandibles of a spider."

She scrunches up her nose. "That's…disturbing."

"Their venom kills you slowly over the course of a week, giving the stalker time to drag you back to its nest to feed its young." I shiver. "Trust me when I tell you, it's not a creature you want to encounter."

Tania is somber, her gaze trained intently on something over my shoulder. "I could have lived happily without the experience."

The tightness in her voice wraps around me like a vise, and a chill that has nothing to do with my power creeps across my skin, penetrating deep into my bones. "Would I be wrong to assume your experience was *very* recent?"

She sighs. Her fingers twitch against the hilt of her sword. "You wouldn't be wrong."

I move as she draws her weapon, and by the time I turn, the venom stalker is already leaping. I lift my hands, and the air around me chills. My fingers numb as ice cascades from the tips, encasing the stalker. It's mid-leap, so the momentum is still there, but Tania is ready. She swings her sword, just once, and the creature shatters into a million tiny chunks of ice scattered across the forest floor.

She looks down at her hands, wiggling the fingers of her free one. "That was…odd."

"What do you mean?"

"I felt it. As you froze the stalker, I think I *felt* it." She shivers and sheaths her weapon. "It was…"

I know exactly how she feels. "When I froze larger things as a child, my entire body went numb for three days." Liani had wrapped me in layers of blankets, then set me up in front of a roaring fire. She never left my side. I don't think I would have survived the early days of my magic without her.

Tania gives her fingers one more twitch before making a tight fist. "My hands are cold but not numb. Not really."

She spins in a slow circle, eyes scanning the area. This part of the forest is thick with henwood trees. Defined by unusually gnarled trunks, their wide branches are densely covered in silky blue leaves tipped with white. Just before the leaves fall, the edges turn from white to black—one of the only remaining signals to mark the subtle season change in this area of Derriga.

"How are you at climbing?" she asks.

"You mean to hide us in the trees?" Stalkers are solitary, so the chance of there being another in the immediate area is slim. Still, it's not a bad idea. There are other things, more dangerous things, that prowl these woods after dark.

"It's really too late to continue on for the night. Safer to batten down." She swings her pack across her shoulder, looping the handle over her head. "If we get high enough, the leaves will easily cover us should someone—or something—happen by."

She's right. We'll need to sleep so we can cover more distance tomorrow, and doing it above ground will be safest. I'm confident we'll go undetected. Unfortunately, there are other issues to factor in besides wildlife and my uncle's guards.

"You've never spent a night in these lands unsheltered." The temperature is already dropping. It makes no difference to me. While I'm not immune to the cold, my tolerance for it is much higher than hers. Even though we're close to the border, the wind chill is brutal and will only continue to dip as night falls. With her sensitivity to it, we might both freeze. "We won't have the ability to light a fire up there."

She shrugs. "It wouldn't be a clever idea to light one on the ground, either. The smoke or the light could attract your uncle's men—or something worse." Her gaze falls to the frozen pieces of the stalker, and she shudders. Bracing her foot atop the lowest outcropping of the tree, Tania begins to climb. "I know this must be a foreign concept for you—Fae privilege and all—but sometimes you just have to knuckle down and push through."

I wait until she's several feet ahead before starting up behind her. "While having you freeze to death would remove your constant nagging presence in my life, I've no idea what it would do to me."

"A little cold won't kill me." The annoyance in her tone screams of overconfidence. Whether she wants it to be true or not, the facts are the facts. She's already shivering.

"I suppose we'll see." My only hope is that my tolerance to the cold will transfer onto her, at least in part, instead of the other way around. "I could offer my services as a body warmer."

"How generous of you." She missteps and slides a few inches, and a spike of panic floods the link.

"It's the least I can do. You would have to promise to keep your hands to yourself, though." I pause to give her a chance to get a bit higher. "This is a life-and-death situation, and there's no time for you to indulge yourself in the near-perfect planes of my—"

"I think I'll manage without your *perfect* planes."

We climb the rest of the way in silence, easily traversing the tree's massive limbs, and when we're high enough, we settle on the thickest branch we can find. Tania fastens a rope around her waist, wraps it several times around the smaller, surrounding branches to secure herself, then tosses the end to me—presumably to do the same. Without a word, she leans back and closes her eyes. It doesn't take long for her breathing to even out.

There's more than enough room on the branch. Henwood trees are known to have limbs large enough to dance on. I know—I've done it a time or two. We're in very little danger of falling. Still, I watch her for a while just to be sure, cringing each time a gust of icy wind breaks through the leaves and she shivers. Something growls from the ground below, and above us, somewhere in the trees, a crow caws. It's like the forest is saying, *I see you. I know you're here...*

When I'm sure she's asleep, I release my wolf and curl around her, my thick fur acting as a barrier against the brutal elements. I tell myself that it's self-preservation. If she freezes, I will undoubtedly suffer *some* kind of blowback. If she falls, I will endure the injury.

Yes. Self-preservation...that's all this is.

17

Keltania

Something tickles the tip of my nose. No. Not just my nose. My cheek, as well. Every few seconds, it brushes against my skin, skimming an oddly warm softness that beckons me to move closer. I lift my hand, but nothing happens. Panic wells in my chest, and when I force my eyes open, all I see is white.

"What—" I thrust my hands out, momentarily forgetting that I'm precariously balanced atop a tree limb thirty feet from the ground. Despite the rope I've tied to secure myself, I tip to the left. If not for the keen reflexes of a massive white wolf poised beside me, I would have gone over the edge.

One thick paw rests lazily across my lap, its nails secured to the trunk of the tree, while the other front paw wraps around the far side. "I swear to the Goddess, if you've given me fleas…"

I free my hand and mean only to rest it atop the wolf's hindquarters, but the moment my fingers touch his soft fur, they seem to take on a life of their own. I run my hand across the unparalleled softness and can't help the tiny sigh that escapes my lips as it chases away some of the cold. It's intimate in a way I've never experienced, in a way I've never imagined possible. There's a connection there, and a part of me wants to chase it with all that I've got, while another part wants to run as far and as fast as my feet will carry me.

The wolf's form blurs and changes, melding seamlessly back into Valen. In an instant, my hand is resting not on the hindquarters of a wolf but on Valen's thigh, dangerously close to—

I jump and yank my hand away, sending the snow on the leaves scattering in all directions.

"Sudden movement isn't advisable this high off the ground. You could fall and break *my* neck. As for fleas..." He stretches and yawns. "Don't insult me."

I try not to shiver at the loss of warmth. At least, that's what I tell myself. If I was honest, the shiver was more from the way Valen's eyes catch mine, the momentary flash of heat I see there... I wait for him to make a joke, to break the tension I know we both feel, but he doesn't look away. For the first time, it's me who breaks eye contact.

Small slivers of the early-morning sun shine through the cracks in the leaves. A rare thing in this part of Derriga, from what I've been told. We're at the very edge of the Winter Lands, and most days are bleak and sunless. Occasionally, though, the clouds break, and the sun makes an appearance. I want to take this as a good sign. That our plan will work. That we'll get to Ventin Peaks in one piece.

I untie the rope from my waist and swing my legs around to dangle over the edge of the massive branch. "We should start moving. We need to make as much progress during the light hours as possible."

• • •

The sunshine turns out to be an overwhelming disappointment. Unlike the fields in Lunal, where the warmth from the light soaks everything, the sun here makes no impact on the brutal cold, and each step is a challenge.

"We're almost to the edge of the Winter Lands," Valen says. He has on a light cloak over his leathers and hasn't so much as quivered once from the chill. "It will warm up considerably soon."

"I'm fine." It annoys me to see the ease with which he moves. How he swaggers gracefully while I stumble along like a newborn foal in the nearly knee-deep snow.

"My previous suggestion still stands…"

He offered to shift and carry me until we were clear of the snow. I declined. There are rumors of a time when druids were able to connect so wholly to animals that we could *become* them. Travel with catlike grace and speed or soar high into the sky. But those days, if they ever really existed, are long gone. Riding on the back of a massive wolf—one that's also the Fae I'm supposed to protect— would be a bad move. It feels like an oddly intimate action. Then again, running my fingers through Valen's fur this morning felt like a line that shouldn't have been crossed. I know he felt it, too, but we've both chosen to ignore it, and that's more than fine with me.

"Like I said, I'm fine."

He shrugs and pushes forward, leaning into the wind. I keep my head down to block some of the force from a newly formed squall, following the movement of Valen's feet. I don't realize he's stopped until I slam into him. "Why the hell—"

"The good news is that we've reached the end of the Winter Lands…" He points to the snow-barren land a few yards in front of us. "That's Autumn territory."

Like the border between the Winter Lands and Lunal, the change here is extreme. An invisible line in the earth. On our side, wildly swirling snow and brutal wind assault the terrain. Everything is encased in ice, and not a trace of life is visible. On the other side, a dense forest awaits, the scant leaves on the trees swaying slightly as if caressed by a soft breeze. The forest ahead isn't the frozen wasteland we're standing on, but neither is it a thriving ecosystem. Even from this side of the invisible line, I can smell the decay of the woods. An unnatural state brought about when the Fae magic leeched from the lands. Still, there must be *something* left for the terrains to differ so significantly.

Desperate to rid myself of the chill, I step forward, but Valen grabs my arm. "What do you know about the Great Drain?"

I stare at him. "I'm about to turn into a block of ice, and you're asking me questions about history? When ten steps ahead I can defrost my toes?"

"I thought you were *fine*?" He drops his hand from my arm.

I tamp down the urge to slug him. "Is there a point to your question?"

"There is."

"The stories tell us that the Fae from every court burned out their magic. The war was brutal, and it required every last ounce of power they had." I move my fingers—more to keep them from freezing solid than for effect. "It all drained away."

"It's a bit more complicated than that," he grumbles. "Did your Order tell you how the lack of magic destroyed the other courts?"

I knot my fingers into the thick material of my scarf and try not to let my teeth chatter. He'd better be going somewhere with this. "Fighting, stealing, general debauchery—more than usual, I mean. As the power faded, everything turned to chaos. Your people didn't *know how* to live without magic. It drove them to chaos."

"We didn't. And the world around us? It didn't know how to live without our magic, either. Druid power is rooted in nature, in life. Fae power? That's nature, too. The elements. It all stems from the same place. Once it faded, the land, the animals…things changed. Some said the very soul of the ground outside the Winter Lands shriveled and twisted."

"Your point?"

"The *point* is that we're protected, on some level, on this side of that invisible line. The lingering druid magic in the ground, the presence of my magic, calms the land. Orbik uses the magic I donate to build an invisible wall. I need you to understand that once we cross the border, we forgo that protection. Anything can happen."

"Oh, please. Surely you're overreacting." I push him aside and cross the line in the snow. "See—" I step across and breathe a sigh of relief when the bitter cold abates almost instantly. Hefting the pack over my head, I let it fall to the ground. Like the warmth, the lightened weight is a welcome reprieve. "Nothing disastrous has happened."

"Tania." He stares at me. "It's been ten seconds."

I fold my arms and snicker. "And here I thought you were the overly optimistic one."

He grins, then offers me a mock pout. "Normally I am. I don't like it when you make me play the realist. It's no fun."

"Aww. You poor, poor thing. Should I get you a warm blanket? Maybe some milk and cookies?"

"Wine would be nice." His lips slip into the kind of grin I've come to recognize as dangerous, and despite my best attempt to steel myself against it, my heart thunders. "I wouldn't say no to a nice big hug from you, either. The less clothing the better."

"In your dreams, Valen." In mine, as well. I hate myself for where my mind has wandered recently, but there's something magnetic about him. His wit and charm and overconfident humor…

He leans closer and pins me with his gaze. "Every damned night, Tania. Every damned night."

Even though there's no danger of complicated emotions entering the equation, I know the physical is a bad idea. Still… "Hmm. Maybe we should do something about that sometime."

I'm just kidding.

Mostly.

"You—I—we—" he sputters.

I can't contain my laughter. Valen gets flustered so rarely that I've decided it's my new favorite thing. "Take a breath, Valen. I'm just messing with you."

"You, Fungus, are purely evil."

I punch him playfully. "You know you love it."

"I—" He freezes and tilts his head to the sky for a moment.

"What is it?" I look around and scan the horizon, but there's nothing that alarms me.

"Damnit!" He lunges forward, and it isn't until the reverberating roar of a beast pierces the silence that I understand the mistake I made in crossing the line.

I turn, but I'm too slow. The creature is already on top of me by the time I draw my sword. Its massive claws puncture my shoulder, and it hefts me high into the air.

Valen stands very still. "Try not to move," he calls as he slowly flexes his shoulder. A small amount of blood seeps from the same place the claws are piercing me. His eyes dart from the creature to the line of snow behind him and back again.

The animal's talons twitch, and I grit my teeth against the pain. Long, black nails tip a four-finger-like grip. The beast is covered in what looks like dragon scale—but I've never heard of one this color or without wings. Bright orange with patches of black that almost resemble stripes. It's beautiful. Or it would be, if not dangling me four feet in the air. "What is this thing?" I whisper, afraid to anger it.

"A tragon. We drove them from the Winter Lands decades ago. I tried to warn you." He flexes the fingers of his left arm, rotating his shoulder again with a cringe.

"Blame later. Now, tell me how to get this thing to drop me."

He takes a small, careful step to the right, toward my discarded sword. The tragon, as if sensing his intentions, rears onto its hind legs and roars. The sound reverberates in my chest and echoes in my head.

"Let's not enrage the dragon while it's flinging me around like a sack of flour!"

"Tragon," he corrects calmly. "It's a cross between a

dragon and—"

"Valen," I snap. "Focus! Freeze it or something before it eats me."

"They don't eat humans. Or Fae, for that matter. It will rip you to shreds for the simple sport of it."

I stare at him. "Is that supposed to make me feel better?"

"That depends." He keeps his eyes on the beast, but his shit-eating grin is all for me. "Did it?"

"Valen," I warn again. The pain in my shoulder brings an involuntary sting to my eyes as I struggle to keep my voice even.

"All right, all right." He takes an even smaller step toward the sword. This time, the tragon watches him, silent. Encouraged, he takes another, slightly bigger, step.

That's all the beast seems willing to stand for. It thrashes again, shaking and twisting my body, sinking its talons deeper into my shoulder. I try—and fail—to stifle the scream that builds.

Valen curses.

The tragon roars, then breaks into a sprint, moving unbelievably fast on three legs while keeping me secure with the fourth. Valen's panic surges through our link first, followed by a spike of anger. Something tickles my skin. Like a feathery touch skimming the surface, everywhere all at once. There and gone.

A vicious snarl splits the silence behind us.

Valen.

He's shifted.

I fumble with my belt, searching for the hidden compartment where I keep a small retractable iron blade. My fingers probe the opening, and I pull out the knife, almost dropping it as we bound along the uneven ground. With a silent prayer to the Goddess, I bury the blade just above the talon piercing my shoulder. The beast howls and thrashes. When I drag the blade through the tender flesh and straight through the middle tendon, the pressure in my shoulder releases. I slip from the beast's grasp and crash to the ground, tumbling at breakneck speed over jagged rock and dirt.

The tragon stops short and spins with a snarl.

A massive white blur shoots past me. Valen's wolf lands gracefully between the tragon and me, hackles up and fangs bared. The beast rises onto its back legs and snaps its teeth. The sound echoes through the clearing and sends chills down my back.

The tragon swipes at the space in front of Valen. A warning. *Back off.*

Valen, in turn, snaps his jaw and growls. It's ferocious and protective and sends a ripple of gratitude through me. Gratitude, then guilt. Our positions should be reversed. I'm supposed to be protecting him. Not the other way around.

His form blurs, then melts back into Fae.

The tips of his fingers begin to ice, and as he lifts both hands and holds them out toward the tragon, he says, "Tania, back up." But his voice is wrong. Deeper than normal with an eerie warble. I realize I don't feel the adrenaline surge through the link that I should. I feel... chaos.

"Valen—"

"Get back." There's no room for argument in his tone, so I do as he says and creep around to stand behind him, then watch in awe as the tragon wails, each of its feet quickly becoming fused to the ground, encased in ice.

It's subdued. Now is our chance! "Come on. It's stuck. We need to move."

The beast lets out a wail, and Valen smiles. The slightest twitch of his lip and rise of his brow. In another situation, I might think I was looking at a mischievous child. One covered in mud and smirking as he stood in the center of a once pristine white hall. But I know better. The jolt of power that fills the air caresses my skin, and the hairs on my arms and at the back of my neck jump to attention. Confidence flares in his eyes a second before he closes them. For a moment, I don't understand.

Then my entire body goes numb.

The tragon screams, this time full of fury. The creature thrashes, and the ice cracks. "Valen," I say. "You've immobilized it. We need to go before it gets loose."

There's no indication that he hears me. He doesn't blink, doesn't speak. It's like he's in thrall to the magic, as if he's allowed it to take control.

His heart stutters, the erratic thump stealing the air from my lungs and making me dizzy. Anger unlike anything I've ever known pours over me.

The tragon flails as the ice continues to splinter. Tiny bits break away and fall to the ground, bounce several inches, then dissolve into liquid.

I gasp, trying to clear away the toxic emotions permeating the air. "Valen, snap out of it!"

No response. If this keeps up, the tragon will be free and gnawing on our bones in moments.

"You're going to get us both killed!" I grab his arm and curse. Stinging cold bites at my skin, ripping away the top layer on two of my fingers.

The ice keeping the tragon rooted shatters, and the beast stills. Valen blinks once. Twice. Three times... Awareness filters back, and his mouth falls open.

"Tania, I..."

The tragon lets out a bellowing roar and charges straight for us.

18

Valen

The haze clears as the tragon frees itself from the ice, and my brain snaps into place, telling my feet to move. I rush back to where Tania's discarded sword lies.

Tania grunts and throws herself sideways as the animal charges, tucking and rolling safely out of reach. "Don't just stand there," she yells. "Use the damned sword!"

"I'm no good with blades!"

She picks herself up off the ground and bares her teeth. "*But I am.*"

In that moment, the druid's sword is lighter in my hand, and my fingers wrap comfortably around the hilt. The blade and I are one. I lift the weapon and pivot as the tragon lunges, swinging up and stepping several inches to the left. The move is just enough to avoid the animal's blow, whispers of its scales skimming across my face as I turn away. The blade hits meat. The distinct resistance, then smooth, eerily familiar slice as it tears through my prey is like euphoria.

The tragon bellows. It skids to a stop a few yards away, the large gash in its belly oozing deep green fluid. A bad wound but not fatal. It crouches and readies itself for another round.

My pulse thunders in my ears. The blood rushes to my head, focus narrowing on my prey with razor precision.

"Be ready," Tania shouts. She drops to one knee and slams her hand against the ground. Her eyes glaze over, from the deepest hazel to a crystalline blue. I feel warmer, like the cool of my magic is being leeched from my veins. The dirt between her and the tragon shimmers and lightens, turning slick—just as the beast starts to run.

With the ice beneath its feet, the animal can't control its trajectory. I'm able to lift the sword and cleanly plunge the blade into its heart as it passes.

The tragon convulses several times before falling still. Watching the light leave the animal's eyes both turns my stomach and feeds a boiling rage I hadn't been aware of until that moment.

No. Not my rage.

"You're angry," I say, understanding. These aren't my feelings—they're Tania's.

"I'm not," she returns, brows furrowed. She retrieves the sword and holsters it, then drops her gaze to her hands. They're tinted blue, slowly returning to their normal coloring.

"About the tragon." My tone is softer. Careful. Being linked to a druid, someone whose people were once able to speak to animals, puts things into a sharper, *harsher* perspective. Guilt, even though I had no choice, washes through me. "You didn't want to kill it."

She leans against the nearest tree and huffs out a breath. "Please, don't. The guilt… It's suffocating. I thought once we left the estate, it would get better—"

"What do you mean?"

Her expression softens, and she tilts her head back. "I know you felt bad about the donation. The guilt was eating us both alive."

She's right. The guilt *was* eating us both alive—but it wasn't the donation that was doing it. It was the tear. "I'm sorry. About that…and the tragon."

Her gaze shifts to the beast. Reaching forward, she runs a single finger along the length of its massive claw. When she draws back and turns, there's a spark of concern in her eyes. She holds up her hands. "True or not, don't you think there's something more pressing to concern ourselves with?"

I nod to her sword, remembering the feel of it in my hands, the exhilaration. "It was your skill with the blade that guided my hand."

"And your magic that flowed through mine," she says, frowning. "This could be a problem."

"We already knew the link intensified during emotional situations." Until now, it's just been a heightened awareness. What does this change mean? "How did you know we could do that?"

"I didn't. It was just something I felt. In my gut. And we survived…*this time*." She paces from one end of the dead tragon to the other. "We have no idea how to control this, and it seems to be getting stronger."

"Maybe it was a one-time thing. A spike in the connection brought on by our situation." I grab her arm as she passes. "Try to do it again. Freeze something."

Her frown deepens. "It only happens when one of us is worked up."

I wink. "Well, if you come a little closer…"

She glares at me, but I don't sense any anger. If anything, I feel an ember of amusement...and something else.

I throw my hands up. "Okay, okay. But, really, try to do it again."

Her brows form a deep *V*, but she nods and steps back. Holding out her hands, she closes her eyes and sighs. "Anything?"

At first, there's nothing to see. There are no traces of frost on her fingers, no change in her overall coloration. Then I catch sight of the grass a few feet from where the tragon lies. It isn't much, but a small area, several inches at most, has frosted over. It isn't my doing.

"Nothing," I lie. Telling her the truth right now would only cause her more distress—which would cause *me* more distress. That's the last thing we need... I need to keep my emotions in check or I'm going to make this worse—for both of us.

We walk in silence for half the day. Tania keeps her hand on the hilt of her sword, constantly scanning the terrain. The quiet isn't uncomfortable, but it isn't easy, either. When the tragon grabbed her, a stone settled in my gut. I told myself it was fear. For myself, for the magic—but there was more to it. More than the Fae/Aphelian bond. The idea that something might happen to her, might take her from me, is suffocating, and I can't seem to shake it.

"Does that happen often?" Tania asks. The sun is setting, and our pace has slowed considerably. We'll have to stop soon to rest. "You losing yourself so completely?"

"That's not what happened." The words flow effortlessly, but inside, I snap them. It's a sore spot. A constant reminder that Orbik is right to segregate me. She quirks a brow, and I wonder if she feels my anger, as I had hers earlier.

"Fine," she responds, equally cold as the voice inside my head. "Whatever you need to call it. How often does it happen?"

"Like you saw back at the estate, little slips happen all the time. Sometimes, like after the market, it's a bit more... complicated. When it comes to the magic taking control and leaving me in a haze? That's only the second time it's ever happened."

She peers at me, and I don't need to see the look in her eyes to know she doesn't believe it—and can I really blame her?

"I was aware the entire time. The magic had me locked away inside myself. When the power took over, I was nothing more than a bystander."

"Like you were trapped," she says, almost to herself. "What caused it the first time?"

"It was right after I found Mika." The memory of finding her on the floor is razor-sharp, like the blood on my hands is still there, slick and warm. I didn't remember half of what happened by the end of that day—only that those involved paid dearly.

She nods but says nothing. I appreciate the moment of silence.

I maneuver around a large boulder in our path. "Buri can teach me control, but magic like mine hasn't existed in thousands of years. No one really knows how to deal with it anymore. She even theorized that it came back different—stronger and less controllable as a way of protecting itself from us."

"And is it just anger that brings it on? Or can fear cause it?" Tania slows for a moment, leaning against the large rock to readjust her pack. She's tired. I feel it. And even though I want to stop to let her rest, I know it's not safe. Not yet. We need to go just a bit farther.

"Fear? Why would you say that?"

"If I'd been eaten, you'd probably be dead. No one, human or Fae, wishes to greet death. Not like that."

"Maybe I do." My life is less than ideal. The one true joy I have, aside from wine, of course—releasing my wolf and running free—is controlled by my uncle's suffocating security measures.

She turns back to the path and sighs. "I was seven when I was placed in training. I'm not sure how much you know about the Order, but training is *hard*. It's brutal and unforgiving, and some don't make it past the first year."

"Why have children, then?" I step over a large, fallen tree, then reach out to help Tania over. To my surprise, she lets me. "Surely your mother knew what was to become of her offspring."

"It's an honor to bear an Aphelian. A joyous thing." A sad laugh slips past her lips. "To know your child will one day live among the Fae. Lavishly clothed, exquisitely fed, and offered every comfort beyond human reach."

What I know about our ancestors burns the inside of my mouth and begs me to release it. I know what it's like to have my beliefs destroyed. Do I really want to do that to her? For Tania, the truth would be so much more devastating.

She turns back to me, smiling sadly. "Don't feel bad for me, Valen. I have no regrets."

I bite down on the inside of my cheek to try and get my emotions in check. Surely there won't be a way to explain the guilt every time it needles me?

"I have three brothers, all older," she says. "Since Aphelians are female, my mother kept going until she had me."

"And what do they think of all this? Your brothers…"

"I doubt they know I exist." Another laugh, this one weaker than the last. "They don't even know my mother exists. She was forced to surrender them the day they were born, just as she was me. The fact that I know they're out there somewhere is a small gift. We're not usually told anything about our families. But Levina always favored me."

"You've never met them?" I feel for her.

"And I never will. The Order doesn't keep records, and even if they did, I'm sure they wouldn't disclose the information."

"Why not?"

"For the same reason they ink us with the Heartbreaker, I suppose. They fear the emotional connection might get in the way one day." She laughs once more, but this one is forced. An almost choked sound that implies she's trying to cover up bitterness. "The only reason I know of them, know their names, is because Levina told me."

"You know their names?"

"Only their first names. Duren, Wellan, and Larkin."

"The whole thing seems cruel." To have living family out there and be kept from them must be torture.

"I used to dream about meeting them one day. But, as I got older, I understood the reason behind keeping us apart." She stops walking and spins in a slow circle. An odd emotion pulses through our link—a spike of sadness and a pang of regret. It only lasts a moment before hardened determination takes its place. "Do you think this is far enough to camp for the night?"

The frozen trees at the border of the Winter Lands have long been replaced with thick, reddish trunks and branches scattered with dull gold leaves. The moss has a sickly yellow tint and grows scattered reddish-brown flowers, their small petals ragged and torn, like something has shredded them. It's warmer here, too. Not uncomfortably so. At least not yet. I've never ventured this far from the estate.

I've spent innumerable hours reading. Page after page about the other courts and their lands. About their bounties and people...about their downfall. Before my time, this part of the forest was the site of the Stedfel bloodbath. What little remained of Autumn and Summer had waged war here just after the Great Drain, when a rumor spread that Autumn had taken in a mysterious druid who'd somehow retained full power. It'd been nothing more than chatter; otherwise, they would have survived. But countless Fae lost their lives in these woods, chasing that hope. Enough blood soaked the ground to drown this entire continent.

"We should hike to the edge of this forest before settling down for the night." We're both tired, but there's a wrongness to this place that sets me on edge. I know Tania feels it, too. The air is heavy, and the absence of all sound makes it feel as though Death itself is creeping toward us. I don't care to linger. "This land is drenched in blood, and I doubt the spirits lurking here would welcome either of us tonight."

...

We agree a fire still isn't wise. There's still too great a chance that someone would see—or smell—the smoke. If my uncle's men are tracking us, they'll have to give up eventually. Given that I've covered our tracks and they have no knowledge of where we're headed, it'll be challenging to follow for long. There are too many ways we could have gone by this point. Still…they might get lucky this close to the Winter border. By now they'll have realized we hadn't gone north as Liani said.

I pray she's all right.

Sleep comes fitfully, and when I open my eyes the next morning, I know right away that I'm alone. Whatever this thing linking us together is, it's growing. Tania's presence is like a familiar itch I can't quite scratch. It grows worse the farther away she is.

Scanning the area, I climb to my feet. "Tania?"

"Worried I left you out here to fend for yourself?" Her voice drifts from the trees. She appears a moment later, tunic untucked and pulled up with the ends gathered in her hands. In the well of the material is a small pile of slightly shriveled apples and peaches. "I thought we could conserve the dried food we brought. There's only so much to scavenge from the land these days."

Without the Fae magic, the lands are sick and nearly fruitless. Liani said druid magic was harder for Orbik to manipulate than Fae. The rumors are that he's stronger than even Servis himself. So why had my great-grandfather taken the magic if he couldn't use it? Was it spite? Had something gone wrong between him and Aphelian that history has forgotten?

"What happened to Aphelian?" I pick up a small apple and clean it against my tunic. It's bruised and soft—completely unappetizing—but I'm starving. I take a bite. It's bitter, so I pull out the flask of wine I brought and take a long pull. "Our history tells us that she died protecting Servis, but the details are fuzzy."

I'm no better than the rest of them. I've had multiple opportunities to tell her the truth, yet I keep the secret hidden out of fear of losing her. Do I really want to be responsible for upending the balance between Fae and the last of the humans?

What I need to do is find a way to return what Servis stole so long ago without destroying all that we both know. Fae magic has started to return. I'm the first, but Orbik is sure more will come. It might take decades—centuries, even—but our birthright will return. We simply have to wait. Knowing that, possessing the power I do, should be enough. I'm already giving the court infusions. What if I just give a little more… I might be able to return the druid power without damning my own people.

Tania dumps the fruit onto the blanket between us, then kneels and begins separating the pieces. "Death to protect the one you love. It's the oldest fairy tale around." Her lips twist into a sad smile. She takes a bite of one of the peaches, grimaces, then tosses it into the woods. "We tell our people the same tale, but the truth is—from what we can tell—Aphelian took her own life."

"Really?" The guilt threatens to swallow me whole, but I tamp it down. "Why would she do that? Did something happen between her and Servis?"

Servis died almost three hundred years after stealing

Aphelian's power. Murdered by a jealous courtesan. Envrill, his son, had taken over for him. When he died—also a victim of foul play—his own son, Orbik, took the throne. Servis, Envrill, Orbik... It didn't matter. Aphelian's death, the druids' squalor and suffering... My entire bloodline is responsible for so many reprehensible actions. Any one of them could have done the right thing.

She shrugs and tries an apple. "No one really knows. Like I said, the Order doesn't like to keep written records. All we have are our stories passed down from person to person. As I'm sure you know, things like that can warp with time." She deems the apple distasteful and sends it into the woods to join the peach. "For all we know, she died of old age, tucked away in one of Servis's many estates."

The apple in my hands frosts over, and I let it fall to the ground. I can't do it anymore. Maybe it would be easier if we weren't linked, or maybe I've just grown too fond of her to lie. Whatever the reason, the idea of standing in front of her spitting these lies for another instant makes me sick. Not telling her out of fear of losing her is selfish. Normally, something like that wouldn't bother me, but with Tania... "I have something to confess to you."

"Valen, if you're going to attempt flattering me into kissing you, I'll stop you right there." She grabs another apple and waves it at me. "Goddess knows you must be starving for attention out here in the woods with no one to fawn all over you."

For the briefest moment, an image of kissing her is all I can see. Threading my hands through her wild hair, pressing her close and pushing her back against one of the trees... I shake it off and force my breathing to even out. "It's not that."

"Whatever it is, don't hurt yourself. I'm not a fan of unnecessary pain." She tosses the apple, plucks another peach from the pile, and stands. "Do you think—"

"Your people are wrong." The link between us flares, warm and electric. She stops, brow quirked as the second peach hovers in front of her lips.

"Wrong about what?"

"About Servis. He wasn't who you think he was."

She's absolutely still, watching me with confusion but also something darker. Deep inside her, there's a black thing brewing. It should scare me, but for some reason, I find it comforting. It's everything and nothing all churning at breakneck speed.

"He was…" I take a single step toward her. She remains where she is, but the way she watches me makes my breath catch. My head clouds, the words on the tip of my tongue slipping away.

"He was what?" Her gaze meets mine, and she's quiet. So deathly quiet. If a feather were to fall, the entire forest would hear it in this moment.

"Beautiful."

"Servis was beautiful?"

"You." I swallow back a lump that's formed in my throat. My heart is pounding, and I can hear it beating, *thumpthumpthumpthump*… "You're beautiful."

"Will you stop playing games?" She rolls her eyes and turns to walk away, but I touch her arm.

I can't do it. Looking in her eyes, seeing the trust she has for me, the loyalty, I can't destroy that. I can't lose it. No one has ever looked at me with such adoration, such favor. It's not physical, and it's not greed. It's…pure. I'm far too weak to let go of it. In the short time she's been here, I've come to rely on her. If I tell her the truth, what's to stop her from leaving? Certainly not me.

I blink and shake away the haze. "I just mean, I value you. For all that you are and all that you have to offer."

"All that I have to offer?" She gives up on the fruit entirely and tosses the last of it into the woods. "Can you really not go a day without—"

"No!"

She folds her arms and stares.

"I mean, yes. I can. But no, that's not what I'm getting at. I certainly don't want to—no, actually, I do." I grin. "You're stunning, and I would jump at the chance, but at the moment, I'm referring to your other qualities."

"My other *qualities*?" She laughs. "I hoped you were almost out of wine."

"Huh?"

"You're drunk. Obviously." She sighs and starts gathering the supplies. In the distance, a crow cries. The sound of it echoes through the woods, bouncing off the trees in an eerie wobble. "That explains why I feel such... chaos coming from you. You know, we really don't have time for this."

"You're right. Sorry." I grab the heaviest pack and sling it over my shoulder, hating myself just a little bit more. This link between us is growing by the hour. I'm not so delusional to think that she won't see through me eventually. But right now?

Right now, there are other things to worry about. What happened in the past is ancient history. We need to focus on the *now* if there's any hope of seeing the future...

19

Keltania

Kadakard is the small expanse of neutral forest between what used to be the Autumn Lands and the Summer Lands. I imagine it once held flourishing plant life, singing birds, and crystal-clear streams beneath a flawless blue sky. The Derriga of old. A place where the Fae and humans—not just druids, but all branches of our family tree—once lived in harmony.

A place, if it was ever real, that is long gone.

Though not as badly as the area just beyond the Winter Lands border, the woods here are decayed. It's a different kind of rot, though. Oddly beautiful. Through the trees, the crumbling remains of ancient housing stands like ghosts, covered in moss and vines. Inside, they're no doubt rotting and foul, but on the outside, the structures are just as stunning as the forest. Like nature knew the previous inhabitants had been betrayed, and, out of pity, had taken them in, made them its own.

The path is overgrown but not unused. An assortment of tracks smatter the dirt, the edges of some of the leaves gnawed by passing wildlife. We see several mice, a rabbit, and an abnormally large crow, which seems to make a game of following us for a time, but nothing more.

"Do you know anything about these lands?"

Valen snorts. "Other than the fact that we shouldn't be here?"

There's something he's not telling me. Every once in a while, I feel it filter through the link. It's guarded and filmy but unmistakable. A foul, metallic tang on my tongue that reminds me of blood. Part of me knows he'll tell me if he has to, but another part is so curious that I want to demand a confession. Knowing Valen, though, it's likely something scandalous or paltry—maybe something he's embarrassed I'll find out. He should know by now that none of his antics surprise me. Still, there's a whisper about it that scares me and makes me worry that it's something far worse.

I slow as we approach a rabbit standing in the center of the path, and I wait, expecting it to scamper into the brush, but it sits motionless. Watching us.

"*Tro.*"

"What?"

Valen cocks his head and stops beside me. "What do you mean, what?"

"You just said *tro.*"

"I did?" One brow lifts as the corner of his mouth quirks.

"Yes. You did." After everything that's happened in the last forty-eight hours, my patience is wearing thin. "My question is, why? Did you see something? Hear something?"

"I'm seeing what you are," he says. "And one of us is hearing things, but I assure you it isn't me." He reaches

around and plunges his hand into his sack. When he pulls
out his flask, he gives it a shake. "You haven't been stealing
my wine, have you?"

"*Bidge.*"

My fists curl. "Don't tell me you didn't just say —"

His eyes go wide. "I didn't—but I heard it."

Our gazes drop to the rabbit still in the center of the
path. The small creature is the only other living thing here.
It hops once. Then twice.

"*Tro bidge.*"

Valen shifts from foot to foot. He spins in a slow circle,
scanning the area, and when he sees what I have—that we
are alone—he turns back to the bunny. "Did that rabbit
just..."

"*Tro bidge.*"

"That rabbit just... Fuck." He shakes the flask, then
takes a long swig. "Fuck..."

I sink to the ground, balanced on the balls of my feet,
and stare at the white-and-brown ball of fluff. Slowly, I
reach forward, a single finger extended to stroke it between
the ears. The rabbit doesn't recoil or run away. Instead, it
leans into my touch, lightly thumping its back leg.

"*Tro bidge.*"

Before the Great Drain, before the loss of our power
pushed us into the dark, we lived side by side with nature.
All manner of plants, every living creature, all harmonized
by the bond of druid magic. When Aphelian gave Servis
the tear, it was said that the forest animals all over Derriga,
no longer able to communicate with the druids, sank into
a kind of depression, forever changed.

"How is this possible?"

Valen kneels beside me, his eyes wide. The astonishment

on his face is trumped by the wonder filtering through the link. Wonder and that same metallic tang. Whatever it is he's hiding, this rabbit is making him feel guilty about it.

The rabbit regards him warily, scooting closer to me. "I...I have no idea." He tries to pet the creature, but it hisses and leaps into my arms. "How are we able to hear it?"

"Fae bad. Fae bad. Fae bad. Fae bad."

I laugh and snuggle the rabbit close, stroking its soft fur. "This one is just slightly less vile than the rest." I glance at Valen. "You sure this has nothing to do with your magic?"

He shrugs. "I mean, it could? Remember, we don't know much about my magic. Fae power didn't use to work like that, but now? Who knows?" It's a lie, and it takes all my effort not to call him on it.

"Since you were born with magic in your blood, it doesn't seem unthinkable that you're more attuned to power. Maybe living at the estate, with the latent magic in the ground..."

"That has to be it." He cringes a little, and I know damn well he doesn't believe it.

"And since we're linked..."

"You have much stronger access to druid magic," he finishes for me. There's a tentative smile on his face. "And I'm hearing it talk because you're hearing it. I mean, I assume..."

Even though his explanation is pure fiction, the idea sends a thrill through me while being just a little terrifying. If it was even remotely true, then I'd be the first druid— other than our priestess—to speak with an animal in centuries. I gesture toward the rabbit. "Do you have any idea what a *tro bidge* is?"

The rabbit squirms from my arms and begins hopping frantically from one end of the path to the other. *"Trobidge Trobidge Trobidge Trobidge."*

"No. Unless it means…" Valen groans and stands, dusting the dirt from his leathers. "Troll bridge." He narrows his eyes and glances down the path. "Maybe it's telling us there's a troll bridge ahead—which would be extremely inconvenient."

I get to my feet and stare at the rabbit. It's still hopping back and forth, now whispering *tro bidge* under its breath, over and over. "We didn't have trolls in Lunal."

"We won't be able to pass unless we offer them something."

"Like what, exactly?" We have no money and can't spare what little food we have left.

He shrugs. "Depends. I suppose the best way to find out is to head to the bridge."

"Thank you, little one," I say to the rabbit. I give it one last scratch, then nod down the path. "Shall we?"

Valen falls in step beside me. I keep my gaze on the trail ahead of us, cautious of anything that might cause us harm, but his scrutiny is like a weight pressing down on my shoulders. The silence that comes with it is suffocating. Whatever he's hiding is going to make me scream. I don't want to push him to tell me, but I might not have a choice.

"If you don't spit it out, I'm going to turn you upside down and shake it out of you."

He sighs, and both our breaths shudder. Warmth engulfs me, an invisible, featherlight touch skimming the surface of my skin—inside and out. "I suppose I'm just wondering how it felt. Being able to understand the rabbit. That's what your ancestors could do, right?"

"We were able to communicate with animals. The strongest of us could even become them."

"Was it everything you imagined it would be?"

"I never gave it much thought, honestly." I hesitate, not sure I want to open myself up to his mocking. "I still don't understand how it happened."

"Regardless of how, I bet it was amazing." A spike of something floods the link—there and gone far too fast for me to get a lock on it.

Even if I wanted to lie to him, I couldn't. The link saw to that. A hesitant grin spreads across my lips. "It was… different."

His lips twitch. "How? Good different? Bad?"

"*Very* good," I say. The smile that follows is completely involuntary. I'm the first druid in centuries to access our magic without a priestess sigil—if that's what happened. There isn't anything I can think of to compare it to. "Better than a good brashing."

"Is that right?" His eyes widen a little, but the surprise only lasts a moment. "I, uh, joke about it, but I didn't know Aphelians were allowed to—"

My cheeks heat. "Why wouldn't we?"

"Well, to be honest…" He clears his throat. "You humans have, uh, fickle hearts."

"Fickle hearts? What is that supposed to mean?"

He waves his hand. "One proper brash, and you think you're in love. Humans in love do foolish things. They hurt themselves and others and turn their back on their responsibilities."

"So, you assume Aphelians are prohibited from having a physical relationship with another because we will—and let me be sure I have this correctly—fall in love, hurt people, then run away?"

"Well, when you put it like that…" At least he has enough sense to look apologetic.

"How does that make us fickle?"

He sighs. A surge of regret—probably for bringing it up in the first place—filters through the link, followed by a blast of confidence. "Your human nature makes you fickle. There is nothing constant about you when it comes to relationships. Nothing sure." There's no accusation in his tone, no teasing. Only what he considers fact. "You brash and kill each other at random or for insignificant reasons. You are always in love and then out of it, or angry or sad over the smallest consequences."

"So, the fact that we *feel* makes us fickle? Aphelian damned her people because she loved Servis and the Fae. What about that is *fickle*? And let's not forget about the war. It wiped most of you out!"

"Technically, the Great Drain is what took out the courts," he says. "And Aphelian was the exception, not the rule. It's the fact that humans, in general, feel so little." He thrusts both hands into his pockets and shrugs. "It's probably generalizing to say *humans*. Aphelians are… different. But for the most part, humans are like stars in the sky. Like the sun. They change position constantly. Their loyalties, affections—their promises—all as solid as a rotting carcass. Most human attentions shift as quickly as the wind."

I put my hands on my hips. "And you can say this because you know so much about humans?"

"I've seen them come and go for years. Liani told me stories about them from before I was born. The Winter Court actually employed humans at one time. Obviously, this was a long, long time ago, but my point is, they had to stop. It caused too much trouble."

"What kind of trouble?"

"Exactly the trouble I stated. They fell in and out of love with every new Fae they met. It caused quite a bit of chaos, from what I'm told."

I wonder how many of the stories he's been told have been relayed truthfully.

You used to beg us to take you in. To use *you.*

Buri has been around a long time, too. I wonder if what she said held more fact than I wanted to think about. "And I suppose the Fae are superior?"

"You sometimes see us as cold, but when we love, it is with only one other for the entirety of our existence. When we pledge our loyalty, it's eternal. We don't offer ourselves easily. The word of a Fae is more than a promise. It's our lifeblood. If you manage to win the trust of a Fae, you have an unwavering, ceaseless support system. There is nothing we won't do for those in our circle. That doesn't change. It doesn't fade. Petty squabbles don't interfere." He puffs out his shoulders and grins. "So, yes. In many ways, we are superior."

"Interesting." My tone is casual, but on the inside, I want to throttle him. "That doesn't sound superior to me."

His jaw clenches, the muscles in his neck twitching. "Oh no? Enlighten me, then. What does it sound like to you?"

"Have you ever considered that what you view as superiority is really more like a flaw? Take yourself, for example. You've pledged your loyalty to Orbik. You allow him to take your magic—to, as you put it, treat you like little more than a prisoner—so that you might one day help your people. All this, while you stand idly by as he does nothing to save those within his power."

His shoulders stiffen, and I feel the argument rising inside him, but I keep going.

"Yes, human loyalty can shift. But sometimes that shift is necessary. Not even the Fae can predict someone's path. What starts out as a noble service might one day turn bitter and cruel. And love? Don't get me started on that bit of crap."

"You seem to have the lives of the Fae so perfectly figured out." There's no malice in his words, just an abundance of sarcasm. "Please, continue."

"You fall in love once during your lifetime. Is that right?"

"If it ever happens, yes. It is with just one individual."

"And if tragedy strikes, you're alone. You're never able to find someone new? How is that better?"

"It's not like we live celibate lives."

"So I've heard," I retort. "But sex isn't love."

"We can still enjoy the company of another; we don't lose the ability to feel. It will just never be the same."

"Still sounds like a flaw to me." I shrug. "Besides, I think you're oversimplifying things."

"How so?"

"You're spinning it like the Fae are so much more controlled than humans—"

"We are."

"Yet you're far more prone to heightened responses than we are. A bit of a contradiction, don't you think?"

The bridge is a few yards away. I don't see anyone near it, but an uneasy feeling stirs in my gut. With each step, it gets worse.

"Have you ever loved?" His brow quirks, and a strong pulse of curiosity blasts through the link. There's something just beneath it—an emotion he's trying hard to hide.

I think back to the warm nights, the stolen moments with a dark-haired boy in the shadows of the forest that bordered the Order. "There was someone I was particularly fond of. His name was Arjen. He was the son of the Order's blacksmith."

"Do you miss him?"

"I think of him sometimes, but I suppose not. It's not like I could have loved him."

"Because of your position?"

I hold a hand over my heart. "I wear a Heartbreaker, remember?"

"That's right!" He throws back his head and lets out an exaggerated sigh. "That's actually a relief."

"It is?" I ask. We approach the edge of the chasm, just shy of the bridge. Still, there's no one around. Maybe the rabbit was wrong. Confused or disoriented. Or maybe the trolls have moved on in search of greener pastures. It would be a small break of luck.

He stops and takes my hand with a dramatic bow. "I won't have to worry about you falling in love with me."

I choke back a laugh, but I can't help smiling. Valen brings me from anger to hysteria in a few short words, and a part of me enjoys it. "You're not my type."

"Well, then spill, please. What is the mighty druid *Keltania's* type?"

He's still holding my hands, and a whisper in my head says to pull away, yet something just a bit stronger tells me not to. "Someone humble, for starters."

"Bah. Humble is boring."

"Also, my ideal match would have to be selfless."

He drops my hand and lifts a low-hanging branch as I pass under it. "Hero complex. Gotcha. Overrated, if you ask me."

"And definitely someone who understands the value of common sense."

He snorts. "How is *that* a desirable trait?"

I shrug and pull my hand from his and step onto the bridge. "It's desirable because it would mean less time spent having to save his sorry ass from his own bad decisions."

"Sounds to me like you have your priorities mixed up."

"It doesn't surprise me that *you'd* think that."

"You're, well, I hate to say it, but a bit…bland. You need someone exciting and energetic to balance that out. Someone who's not afraid to throw caution to the wind. Someone with a sense of humor." He winks. "It might rub off on you, and let's face it. That could only be considered a win."

"Oh, and let me guess—this someone would be a lot like you, right?"

"Well, I *am* all of those things. And then some. But, no. Not me. You'd never be able to handle *me*."

I laugh. "That's the truth. Trust me, Valen— Heartbreaker or not, I would never fall in love with you."

Valen opens his mouth—no doubt to inform me just how wrong I am—but a loud rumble and the thunderous sound of breaking rock fill the air.

A deep, booming voice says, "I could love you, little Fae…"

20

Valen

Two paces ahead of me, Tania freezes mid-step as two hulking forms swing out from beneath the bridge. She drops her hand to her belt, where it inconspicuously lingers by the hilt of her sword as two massive trolls climb onto the edge of the cliff and move to block the path across the bridge.

"It has been years since we've seen the likes of you, little Fae," the first troll says, eyeing me. An expanse of well-muscled moss-green skin ripples as the creature stretches. The smell permeating the air is foul and reminds me of the swamp on the outer edges of the estate property.

The second troll lets out a mighty roar. It's slightly taller than the first—both of them are much taller than me—though leaner, and its features are not quite as sharp. A female. "If you wish to cross our bridge, you must give us our due."

Tania steps back and settles beside me. She studies the chasm that the bridge spans, thirty feet wide and extending as far as the eye can see in both directions. There's no other way across. If we're going to get to Ventin for her priestess to fix this thing between us, we need to get across this bridge. Preferably without a fight.

I pinch my nose and choke back a gag. Beady eyes hooded by puffy lids follow my every move. "Might I suggest several bricks of soap?"

The male leans forward. It sniffs me once, then turns to Tania and inhales deeply. "A human? With a Fae?" The creature lets out a horrible guffaw. The edges of the ancient bridge quake, several smaller pieces chipping off and falling soundlessly into the depths below.

"Longer has it been since a human stood at our bridge," the female says. She closes her eyes and brings a meaty hand to her lips, slowly licking each finger with a loud slurp. "That shall be our price. Give us the human, and you may pass freely."

"I'm afraid you'll have to name another price." Rage boils in my gut, and I'm not sure if it's Tania's or mine. "The human is not mine to give."

More chortling. "Not yours to give? It is your slave, is it not? What other use could it possibly have?"

"Go ahead, Valen. *The human*," Tania says, words sharply clipped, "will separate their heads from their shoulders and meet you farther down the path." She takes a step forward and draws her sword. "It'll just be a moment."

I catch her wrist and meet her gaze with a subtle, silent plea. *Don't*. Tania is a skilled fighter, but if she attacks, they'll overpower her before she has a chance to swing twice. Trolls are smarter than most give them credit for, and the sheer strength they possess makes them more than formidable. As a rule, they guard their bridges in pairs, but it's not unheard of for more to be lurking nearby.

This situation could get away from us quickly if we don't proceed carefully.

She backs down, sheathing her sword.

"There must be something else we can offer you," I say calmly. Trolls are bound to the bridge they keep, unable to wander more than a few miles. "Some trinket you are unable to procure yourselves, perhaps?"

"Maybe we'll just go around." Tania nods to the east. "There must be another way across."

The trolls laugh. It's a harsh sound that lifts the hairs on my arms and the back of my neck to attention. "There's no way around, foolish human," the female says. "This is the Lavadak Chasm. It extends into the unpassable mountain range of Feldar in both directions."

"We are willing to pay a reasonable price," I say. "Name another toll."

The pair glances at each other for a moment before the male says, "Daroose stole something from us. A small golden chest. Return it, and we will allow you to pass."

"What is a Daroose?" Tania glances at me, brows raised. Her hand still rests against the hilt of her sword, but her posture has relaxed a bit.

The male troll snaps his considerable jaw. "Sonnet Lake lies several miles east of here, just before the chasm. The kelpie lives there."

"A *kelpie*?" I take a step back. If there's a kelpie involved, then we've just gone from bad to worse. "No. Ask something else. Anything else."

"How bad could it be?" Tania asks.

"That is our final offer," the male troll says with a sneer. His mate grunts in agreement.

"Kelpies are wild, violent creatures. Shapeshifters." I

turn back to the trolls. "How do you expect us to retrieve this item from a kelpie? It will devour us before the first word."

"If you want to cross the bridge, those are your choices. Leave the human or retrieve our treasure chest from Daroose."

"Or do not cross at all." The female lets out a horrible gagging sound I imagine is laughter. She doubles over, her enormous shoulders shaking with mirth. More rubble dislodges from the bridge and falls into the chasm below, and I wonder how sturdy the thing is. Even if we manage to strike a deal with them, will we make it across in one piece?

"Go back the way you came," the troll says.

"No, we'll retrieve your golden chest." Tania squares her shoulders. I start to object, but she grabs me by the wrist and drags me back along the path.

In addition to trolls, they obviously don't have kelpies in Lunal. If she thinks this will be as simple as storming the lake and demanding the chest, she's in for a rude surprise. "We're not going to be able to get that chest from the kelpie."

"To get to Ventin, we have to get past the trolls. You said that bridge is the only passable way. I don't see another choice."

"And how, since you're obviously an expert on *all subjects*, are we going to do that?"

She shrugs and keeps her pace. "You have magic."

"Oh. Magic. Is that your plan?"

"You have Fae magic. So, technically, *I* have Fae magic, too. Yes. That's my plan."

I stare at her. "Perhaps we'll stroll up, ask it nicely to

hand over the treasure, and if it doesn't, simply freeze the water?"

"Please." She rolls her eyes. "That would never work. The chest would be buried beneath solid ice. We'd never get it back."

"Of course. Why hadn't I thought of that? How silly of me."

With a confident nod, as if she just won an argument that *wasn't* total nonsense, she starts off in the direction of the lake, and I follow her, shaking my head.

This girl is either going to be my sweet salvation or my bitter end.

The sun is about to set as we approach Sonnet Lake. I might prefer a snowier backdrop, with ice-tipped branches and crystalized leaves, but even I can admit this is beautiful. A rare section of thriving earth. Tall reeds tower over thick patches of wildflowers that sway gently in the subtle breeze. The blooms are every color imaginable, from bright red to the darkest black. Dense tree cover shades a good portion of the lake, allowing the sun to beat down almost directly in the center as if shining a spotlight.

We stop at the water's edge, and Tania spins in a slow circle. "How do we find the kelpie?"

I stoop down, balancing on the balls of my feet, and dip a single finger into the cool water.

The surface instantly ripples, and a gentle wave pulses outward from the center, directly beneath the small patch of light from the sun. When it reaches the edge, it dissolves into nothingness, only to be followed by a second, stronger one.

A head of golden hair rises slowly from the heart of the wave, followed by the body of a man. Once fully emerged, the figure stands atop the water just as solidly as we stand on the bank.

The kelpie. Its human form is slightly shorter than me, though bulkier. It has hair that holds an unnatural glisten against the light, and its blue eyes are just a shade too bright to be mortal. Its clothing—simple dark cotton pants and a matching tunic—appear bone-dry and brand new.

It quirks a brow. "It's an unwise being that disturbs my lake without invitation."

"And what would one have to do?" Tania asks. She steps closer to the water's edge, and I resist the urge to reach out and drag her backward. "To win an invitation?"

The kelpie laughs. "Wicked things," he responds with a disturbingly human wink. "Very wicked things, indeed."

"I thought kelpies preferred to appear in true form?" The creature is a shapeshifter. The most devious and vile kind. Unforgiving in nature, a kelpie is said to use its razor teeth and vicious hooves to tear apart travelers who happen upon their homes by accident. What the beast does to those it purposefully lures there is far worse. The fact that it came to us wearing a human grin puts me on edge.

"As magnificent as my true form is to behold, how would I be able to converse with you if not like this?" The creature leans forward and inhales deeply. As if savoring the breath, the kelpie closes its eyes for a moment. When it exhales, its eyes snap open. Gaze locked on Tania, it says, "Perhaps I would have been able to speak with *you*. Are you truly a druid?"

Tania bows. "I am. I am an Aphelian."

The kelpie cocks its head and studies her. "I don't know that tribe." It leans forward and squints. "The markings on your forehead are...strange. Unlike any of the druids I know." It tilts its head and snickers. "Well, I suppose *knew* would be more accurate. You humans are so short-lived."

Tania touches her fingers to the sigil on her forehead, shifting from foot to foot. "Tribe?"

"Do you not call yourselves that anymore?" It sighs. "I've been in this lake, unable to leave, for a very long time. Since long before the songs of man faded from this part of the forest."

"The songs of man have all but faded from the entirety of Derriga," I say with a sideways glance at Tania. "The druids are the only humans that remain."

"That *is* a pity. They were all so wicked." The kelpie licks its fingers. "So very tasty, too." The creature's gaze settles on me, and it's impossible to miss the spark of hunger in its eyes. "Almost as tasty as the Fae. Tell me, young one with the strange eyes. Who are your people?"

"My people?"

The kelpie cocks its head to the other side. A lock of golden hair slides forward, and it absently brushes the strand away. "Your kin? You must have someone. What court were your ancestors affiliated with?"

"I'm simply a wanderer," I lie. The truth is far too dangerous. These days, knowledge is power. My true identity could be a valuable bargaining tool to a savvy individual. "I've never known my kin."

Tania elbows me out of the way. "You're Daroose, correct?"

The kelpie nods. "I've not heard that name for a very long time, but yes. Yes I am."

"We came here for something." Her gaze flickers to the lake. "A golden chest stolen from the trolls at the bridge not far from here."

The kelpie's expression is impassive and its stance utterly indifferent. "And you would like me to give it to you? Is that it?"

"We don't ask for free," I insert. It's dangerous to ask a kelpie's favor without offering something in return. Their temperaments are like the elements—calm one moment and a raging storm the next. You never know what might set one off. Daroose can't leave the lake, but it could lure us under the water's surface as simply as it stands before us now. A kelpie's call is impossible to resist. They thrive on evil and wickedness and kill for sport when the whim takes them. "Would you be willing to offer a trade?"

Daroose approaches the edge of the lake. "Interesting. And what, might I inquire, do you have to offer?"

"What would you ask?"

"I'm a bit peckish. A tasty sinner would be at the top of my list." Daroose grins. It licks its lips and waggles its brows. "I don't suppose you might bring me one of those?"

Tania tries—and fails—to hide a soft snicker. "Try again."

"Am I to correctly assume you wish to cross the bridge? That the return of the golden chest would be your payment to the trolls?"

"Yes," I say carefully. I don't like the way it's staring at me.

Daroose considers my response for a moment before nodding once. "My price is decided. I will give you the chest freely if you agree to open it and give me what's inside. You must also agree to take me with you as you cross the bridge."

Tania grins. The wicked twist of her lip and the gleam of mischief in her eyes do odd things to my pulse. "The trolls only asked for the chest—they never said anything about what was inside. Clever." She points at the kelpie. "I think I like you."

Daroose beams.

"Don't tell it you like it! Gods know what it'll do."

The kelpie gasps and clutches its chest, mock horror on its face. "I beg your pardon! If the lovely druid wishes to compliment me, she has every right to do so." It grins at Tania. "In return, might I just say, you are spectacular for a human."

"Um, thank you?"

"Your skin is nearly flawless, and your eyes sparkle with life!" The kelpie licks its lips.

I snap my fingers between them and glare at the beast. "Careful. That's its way of saying you'd make a tasty dinner."

"That's absolutely false," Daroose says. "She's far too small for dinner. Dessert, maybe. But not even close to an entrée."

Tania stares at it.

Daroose throws up its hands. "Of course, I would never…"

"Of course…" She looks away, trying—and failing—to hide a smile.

This feels wrong. The kelpie is far too chatty, and the effort it puts into presenting itself as a friend worries me. "Didn't you say you were unable to leave the lake?"

The kelpie scowls. "The chest itself may belong to those vile trolls, but the item inside belongs to me. If I reacquire it, I will be able to leave the lake."

"Why would you want to cross the bridge with us? Couldn't you simply cross on your own?"

The kelpie shrugs. "Would you believe I'm simply trying to get out of paying a toll?"

"No," Tania and I say at the same time.

"If you must know, the trolls and I have a long-standing grudge."

"Is that why you stole their chest?" Tania tenses. She doesn't trust the creature, but the unmistakable tint of compassion thrums through our link.

Daroose bristles, losing the facade of patience. "Do we have an accord or not?"

Tania frowns. "If what's inside belongs to you, why not just take it?"

"He can't." It isn't the look of fury on the kelpie's human face that gives it away but the fact that something important is missing. "Every kelpie has a necklace, inherited from their mother. So long as the kelpie wears it, they are free to do as they please. But if someone were to take it…"

"I have been bound to this lake for a very long time," it says between clenched teeth. "Six hundred years ago, I bargained with a particularly nasty Fae. His life in exchange for stealing my necklace back from those filthy trolls. Unfortunately, the Fae double-crossed me. He returned the necklace within the box. Since the box belonged to the trolls…"

"You can't open it," Tania says. "That's horrible." There's still skepticism in her voice, but there's empathy as well. Clearly, she *doesn't* know anything about kelpies.

"Don't pity the creature." I lean against the tree growing closest to the shore. The lake is serene. The perfect mask to hide the horror that lives beneath the water. "In its long life, the kelpie has surely devoured unfathomable numbers of both human and Fae."

"That's true." There's no shame in its voice. With bared teeth just a touch too pointy to be human, it says, "But as I'm sure you know, little Fae, kelpies only devour the wicked. If someone was lured to my lake, they deserved every chomp they received."

"We have a deal," Tania says before I can respond. I glare at her, but she ignores me.

The kelpie smiles and walks to the edge of the water, extending its hand to her. "I believe this is the start of a beautiful friendship."

She shakes on it. The deal is done. There's no turning back from this shit show now.

21

Keltania

Daroose disappears beneath the water and returns surprisingly fast, a small golden chest in his hand. I expected a fight, but I open the box easily, allowing him to retrieve a silver necklace bejeweled with gems of black and green. He wastes no time fastening it around his neck and ushering us into motion.

On the way back to the bridge, Valen takes the lead, all the while sneaking glances back at Daroose and me. Maybe he thinks the kelpie will betray us somehow. Anything is possible—which is why I make sure to bring up the rear, effectively keeping an eye on both of them.

Above us, a large crow circles, letting out a shrill cry. I reach out to it, hoping that, like the bunny, I might be able to talk to it. I still haven't been able to shake the feeling of euphoria that came from touching something my ancestors did. Unfortunately, I get nothing but silence, and the bird eventually flies away.

"How many of you are left?" I've been filling in some of the time Daroose lost in the lake. The destruction of Fae magic, the loss of druid power, and the dissolution of the courts. He's full of questions, and it fills the uncomfortable silence. Valen doesn't trust our new companion, but I intend to reserve judgment.

"As far as I know, there's only one druid village left, as well as my Order. Fedavar still stands on the edge of Lunal, just south of the Order."

"And you're slaves? To the Fae?"

Ahead of us, Valen's shoulders stiffen, but he doesn't turn around.

"No." What Valen said earlier about the inequality between us bounces around inside my head. I've never looked at it that way. I still don't. But I can see how it might look to someone on the outside. And, if I'm honest with myself, I love that Valen sees it the way he does. It just proves to me that there's more to him than he shows the world. It makes me proud to stand by his side. "We're allies."

"So, this Fae with the strange violet eyes, he is your ally?"

"I'm her friend," Valen says.

Daroose snickers. He leans in close to Valen and breathes in deep. "You smell clean. That's…unusual for a Fae. Has that much truly changed?"

Now it's my turn to snicker. "Did Fae in the old days stink?"

"Most Fae I've encountered have been touched by the stench of death." He shrugs. "An unavoidable pitfall." Daroose pokes at Valen's shoulder, then scrunches up his nose and frowns. "This one has not been touched by violence, but…" Another deep breath. "I *do* scent magic. Didn't you say—"

Valen stops short and whirls around, but I'm one step

ahead of him. "As a member of the royal Winter Court, he's lived his life in a place where latent magic lives in the ground. I imagine that's what you smell."

A furious gleam sparks in Valen's eyes, and my fists tingle in response to his anger. The barest hint of cold lingers at my fingertips.

"I thought we were keeping things like that to ourselves, Tania," he says.

"That is interesting," the kelpie muses. "Interesting indeed. Little Fae is a descendant of Servis?"

Letting Daroose know we have access to Fae magic is a card we don't need to show, but there's no way to hide the power completely. If Daroose smells something, then we have to come clean—at least a little. "I'm sure you can understand why we wish to keep his true heritage a secret. Valen doesn't share his family's...views."

Daroose grins. "Oh, I wouldn't be too sure about that. The bloodline of a Fae is *very* telling."

I want to ask what he means, but Valen stops walking. "There." He points to the chasm in the distance, toward the rickety bridge that spans it. Though the two trolls aren't visible, they're no doubt lurking close by. "Remember to stay silent, kelpie."

Daroose holds both hands up and nods ahead.

Like earlier, the moment I set foot on the bridge, the trolls swing out from beneath it. "Did you bring us our..." The female's gaze lands on Daroose. More specifically, the necklace draped around his throat. She rips the chest from my hands and yanks it open. "How dare you!"

"We've brought you the price you requested." I square my shoulders and stand tall. A fight won't be ideal, but if that's what it comes to, so be it. Valen and I are crossing this bridge one way or another.

"You've done no such thing." The male roars. He hurls the golden chest at my feet. The small thing shatters, bits and pieces bouncing in every direction. The one closest, a chunk of the cover, glints in the fading sunlight before springing over the edge of the bridge, into the seemingly bottomless abyss below.

"We have," Valen corrects. "You asked that we bring you the golden chest that Daroose stole. That is exactly what we've done. You said nothing about the contents inside. You're required per our agreement—and troll honor—to let us pass."

My fingers itch, hands ready to draw my blade and cut our way across if needed.

The male troll advances. His colossal figure casts an expansive shadow over us, and in that moment, I'm convinced he'll strike, but his mate intervenes. "The Fae is right. We said nothing about the contents of the chest. They broke no agreement." As she steps aside, her meaty hand gestures across the divide. "You may pass."

Valen relaxes and starts forward. I move aside to let Daroose follow, but the troll holds out her hand to block his path. "The toll was for the human and the Fae. The kelpie has paid no price."

Daroose growls, the fingers of his human form twitching.

"What will you ask to let him pass?" Our deal included taking him with us across the bridge. I have no idea what will happen if we break our promise.

"The necklace." The male troll makes a meaty fist and sneers, baring a mouthful of jagged, rotting teeth. "I will allow him to cross, but not with the necklace."

Daroose freezes, eyes going wide. His hand goes to his throat, covering the necklace as he staggers back. "You've held me captive long enough, troll."

"Perhaps," the troll says. His blue lips curve up at the corners. "But if we allowed you to go free, you would surely return to exact revenge for our trespass." Thick fingers shake greedily. "Remove the necklace, and you may go."

Fury sparks behind his eyes, but Daroose reaches back to unhook the necklace. A satisfied rumble growls through the troll as he lumbers closer. Daroose moves like he's going to drop the chain into the troll's hand, but instead he seizes my arm. Before I realize what's happening, Valen roars and Daroose drops the necklace into my upturned palm.

"What have you done?" Valen stares down at my hand.

Daroose only shrugs. He catches my eye for a moment, and I swear I see the smallest hint of fear. It's fast and passes quickly, and when he turns back to the troll, he's grinning. "I am no longer in possession of my necklace—as requested. May I pass?"

The female is furious, but the male throws back his head and howls with laughter. "I pity you, Daroose. You have been away from the world for a long, long time. Giving your necklace to a human will prove far worse than giving it to me."

Worse?

The troll steps aside and gestures across the bridge.

"I suppose time will tell." Daroose saunters past the trolls and starts across the bridge. Valen follows, very pale, but says nothing.

When I move forward, the male troll grabs my arm. "If

you allow the kelpie to return here, know that I will make it my mission to kill every remaining human in Derriga."

I jerk from his grasp and snort. As if I have any damned control over what the kelpie does. I have my own problems to worry about. And, really, how much damage could one kelpie do?

22

Valen

We cross the bridge without incident, and the moment our feet hit solid ground, I grab the kelpie by the throat and pin it against the nearest tree. "What game are you playing?"

Daroose doesn't respond, but the sly smile on its face says it all. Tania shoulders me aside, grabs Daroose's hand, and deposits the necklace there. "I'm not sure what you're up to, but we're done. We filled our part of the deal. You go your way. We'll go ours."

"I'm afraid it doesn't work like that, druid." It's still smiling, but there's sadness in the kelpie's eyes. "You took the necklace. There's no getting rid of it now. At least not for another twelve moons."

She points to the bejeweled silver thing in its hand. "I just did. And I didn't take it—you gave it to me." She turns away from the kelpie. "Let's go, Valen. The sun is setting. We need to find a place to camp for the night."

Tania starts walking, but neither Daroose nor I move. Whirling, she says, "Well?"

I tap my neck twice, right below the hollow of my

throat. The druid may know a hundred ways to slaughter an enemy, but she doesn't seem to know the first thing about life outside the Order. She tenses and lifts her hand to her own neck. I feel the cool silver and smooth gemstone as her fingers graze the necklace, now draped around her neck.

She rips the thing from her neck and hurls it through the thick tree line. "What in the Goddess's name is going on?"

"Burn it, throw it into the ocean, gamble it away a thousand times over," I say, approaching slowly. Daroose is a few steps behind. "Once that metal touched your skin, you became its master for the next year."

"Master?" She glares at Daroose. More and more, Tania reminds me of a tornado. Swirling, chaotic fury rages on the outside, hiding a perfectly calm but vulnerable center. There's anger in her eyes, but beneath that, subtly pulsing through the link, is fear. "What did you do?"

"What I had to in order to survive." The kelpie stops in front of her and bows. "Might I have your name, druid?"

"Aphelian."

"Oh, for the love of—" I bite back a curse. "Her name is Keltania."

Tania glares at me for a moment before turning on Daroose. He bows lower and says, "Think of a kelpie's necklace as their leash—their bridle, essentially." He cringes a little. "Whoever holds it commands us. The instant it touched your skin, it bonded with you. From now until the twelfth moon yields to the sun, I am yours to command."

"Fine." Tania scowls and folds her arms. "Then I *command* you to go. Be free. Run wild, eat things—I don't care, as long as you do it far from me."

"I'm afraid that won't work. You're stuck with me for a while."

"We don't have time for this." She looks from me to Daroose and growls.

"On the contrary, you do." Daroose puffs out its chest and squares broad shoulders. "Whatever little"—he gestures between us—"quest you have going, a kelpie would be a useful addition."

"Oh?" I've never encountered a kelpie in person before now, but I know enough about them from reading. Foul tempers, wicked intentions, and an unquenchable appetite for flesh. None of that sounds helpful.

Daroose steps back and closes its eyes. As we watch, its features shift, arms and legs elongating seamlessly into powerful equine limbs. Its body darkens and thickens as tufts of inky black hair sprout all over. When Daroose steps away, it throws back its head and lets out an echoing whinny.

"Would you not prefer an alternate method of travel? My druid—not you, Fae."

A mighty stallion stands in front of us, but it's the voice of the man who'd been there moments ago echoing in my head. I can tell by the look on Tania's face that she hears it, too.

"Wait. I thought you said you couldn't talk to us in your true form..." I say.

The kelpie laughs. It's an echoing sound that grates against my spine and has me cringing. *"I can't. This isn't my true form. You wouldn't be able to handle my glorious true form!"*

"Anyway..." Tania rolls her eyes and sighs. "I really

can't just release you of your obligation?"

Daroose shakes its head and snorts. *"As I said, you are stuck with me, and I with you."*

We set up camp for the night. The moon is high in the clear night sky, dotted with bright stars shining down through small gaps in the tree cover. After an hour of Daroose crowing about a kelpie's usefulness, Tania sends it into the woods to find food. Unfortunately, it returns with little more than several piles of berries—most of which are poisonous. We're forced to use the last of our dried food from the estate. The forest has been dying for centuries, and this part is seemingly a bit further along than what we've seen before. Most of the animals have fled for more fertile grounds.

Three hours later, the fire has nearly burned out and Daroose, having returned to human form, is snoring against a thick fallen percher tree, with Tania sitting beside it.

"How far do you suppose we've gotten?" She moves closer to the dying embers. It isn't freezing like it was in the Winter Lands, but the night air holds a definite chill. I'm more aware of it now than I've been, probably because of the link.

I offer her one of the cloaks from my bag, but she ignores me and leans back against the fallen tree. "As soon as day breaks, we might be able to climb high enough to get a better lay of the land. If I had to guess, I'd say we haven't made as much time as we should have."

"Damned trolls." She closes her eyes.

The bark of the log digs painfully into her head. She shifts, eyes still closed, trying to find a better position. The move only makes it worse. "You can come over here," I say, trying not to sound too enthusiastic. The truth is, I've been wanting her to move closer all evening. For warmth. For...other reasons. "I promise, I won't bite unless you ask nicely."

She adjusts herself several more times before giving up with a grunt and stomping to where I am, on the other side of the fire.

"Isn't that better?"

She stares at me. "The view is worse over here."

"I didn't know Aphelians were so funny." I wad up my cloak and shove it into her arms before she can protest, then sling my arm around her shoulder. She freezes—both physically and emotionally. The link doesn't necessarily go dead, but there's an odd kind of static to it. Like she's holding her breath in every sense of the word.

"I like this," I say before I can stop myself. Her eyes widen, and I decide to just open the floodgates. I've been tiptoeing around my thoughts when it comes to Tania the last few weeks, but she's the one person I should never do that with. "Having you this close is—"

"Dangerous?"

She licks her lips, and I feel the link between us shudder as her heart beats faster. Or maybe it's mine. It's impossible to tell. All I know is that she's watching me with a mix of hunger and hesitation, and my fingers itch to explore the curves of her body. "Would it really be?"

"Be specific, Valen." Her breathing quickens just a bit. "Would *what* really be...?"

"You. And me. Would it be so bad if we were to—"

"Yes." Her gaze flickers to Daroose sleeping on the other side of the campsite.

"We could go someplace private."

"No. That's not— Well, it is. A little. But that's not it."

"Then what is?" I take her hand and trace circles across the back of her wrist. I don't know if I'm feeling the sensations from my perspective or hers, but it's electric.

"It would complicate things," she says.

"I like things complicated. Besides, it's not going to complicate anything too much. There won't be any feelings involved."

"Won't there?"

"I thought—"

"Valen, just because we can't fall in love with each other doesn't mean there are no feelings. I care about you."

"You trust me, right?"

"I do."

"Then how about a compromise?"

"What are you talking about?"

"We're obviously attracted to each other." I stand and dust myself off, then pull Tania to her feet and gesture to myself. "I mean, how could you not want all this? I'm magnificent."

She rolls her eyes. "Anyway…"

"Anyway, kiss me. See how *complicated* it feels."

She glances back at Daroose, who snores softly. "You're ridiculous!"

"What's so ridiculous about it?" I whisper. "One kiss should tell you everything you need to know."

"Are you so desperate that you'll try tricking me into kissing you?"

"How am I tricking you?" I grin. "You forget that we're

linked. I can feel your desire just as plainly as I do my own. So, don't play—"

"Oh, Goddess. Would you shut up already!" Tania growls and grabs two handfuls of the front of my shirt. She pulls me in and crushes her lips to mine.

I *do* feel her desire as I do my own, but to be fair, the move is all mine. I can't say I don't like it, though. Her coming for me first, along with the blazing warmth of her lips, fans my flames higher, hotter, than they've ever been.

The kiss is demanding, insistent, and when I wrap my arms around her waist and drag her close to chase away what little space separates us, I find myself craving so much more. I slide my hands up her back and tangle them in her hair, beneath her long braid. Without hesitating, I tug the string free and run my fingers through her flame-red locks.

In turn, Tania clutches the back of my head and backs me up against a large percher tree. The impact as she crushes her body to mine sends leaves fluttering to the ground around us.

I'm not sure who breaks first, but one minute we're lost in each other, the sensation nearly too much to take, and the next we're both stumbling in opposite directions, breathing heavy and batting lust-fogged eyes.

I can't make out what I'm feeling through the link. It's chaotic and muddled, and it takes me a moment to catch my breath. "See? That wasn't complicated at all," I lie.

As the forest stops spinning, I find myself more confused than I've ever been. Sure, Tania and I have a relationship that differs from any I've had before, but for some reason, the kiss feels odd. Strange in a way I've never felt. I hate to admit she's right, but anything more than this might complicate things between us.

It's the damned link. It has to be. It has us so tied up together that our emotions are a tangled mess. Without it, a simple brash would be just that.

Tania is still breathing heavily. She leans against the tree and watches me like she's trying to see straight through.

"I'll take the first watch," I manage to whisper, still not taking my eyes from her.

She swallows, and I'm sure she'll back down, but she doesn't. "That's all right. I'll take the first watch."

"Then I guess we'll both take it." I slide to the ground where I am, not daring to move closer to her.

A few moments pass, and Tania does the same, settling across from me. Her gaze skims the tree line, bouncing between the noises of the forest.

There's no way to know for sure what inhabits these woods now. Books say that centuries ago, the woods here were thick with harpies and tree nymphs, but they seem to have moved on. The only real signs of life are several large bird nests scattered about, nestled into the thick branches of the surrounding trees.

Tania is amped. The kiss should have been a tension breaker, but instead, it's made us both uneasy. It thrums along my skin, reverberating beneath my ribs. Like her presence in my head, it's an itch I can't quite scratch. "Tell me about the Order," I say.

"Why?"

"Because I'm curious. And since you've made it clear that you've no interest in passing the time in more *interesting* ways…it will keep us awake." Gods know where my mind will wander if I dare go to sleep. "Do you miss it?"

"Yes," she says. Then, after a moment, softer: "No."

"The estate was friendly to me, but I was never truly happy there. I never belonged. Not really. It was familiar, and there was a certain level of security that came from that despite the less-than-ideal conditions."

"I get that." She picks up a small rock and rolls it between her fingers several times before throwing it into the brush. "We're trained to be fearless. Taught to willingly court death with a song in our hearts if the need arises."

This is it. Another opportunity for me to tell her the truth. All I have to do is open my mouth and spit it out. "Tania…"

She lifts her gaze to mine. "You have nothing to feel guilty about."

I nearly choke on my own tongue. "I don't—"

"I feel it. Your guilt." She leans forward, narrowing her eyes just a bit. "Unless…there's something else?"

In an instant, the inside of my mouth dries out. My throat is thick, clogged by words that I desperately want to push out—but can't. "It won't ever come to that. The death part."

She studies me for a moment, then shakes her head, just once. "That isn't what you want to say, Valen."

"No. It's not." There's no point in lying to her. We're past that now. I won't add insult to injury by trying.

"What aren't you telling me?" There's no malicious suspicion in her voice, and that makes this all ten times worse. If she was angry, if she demanded me to confess, I would do it. I don't think there's any way I could refuse her. She has more power over me than anyone else ever has. I don't intend to tell her this, but if she looked—*really looked*—she'd see it for herself.

"Will you trust that I'll tell you when I can?"

"I suppose I have no choice, do I?"

The pain that flows through the link settles like a stone in my chest. "I'm sorry." And I am. I, the Fae who's never sorry about anything—who makes no excuses or apologies for who I am, what I say or do, or where I come from—am sorry. But telling her now, with the weight of the bond bringing her down, would only make things worse. "I just— I need to figure something out." After the link is broken. I can tell her then.

"That's vague."

"It is."

She laughs. Not a harsh cackle or an irritated snort, but an actual laugh. The sound of it makes the hairs on the back of my neck jump to attention. It's soft yet hearty. Genuine amusement trickles down the link and lingers for a moment before fading. "Just give me a heads-up if it puts our lives in danger, would you? I don't like surprises."

"So…" I clear my throat and try to focus on something other than the way her lips move as she smiles. "You were saying…about Lunal?"

"I was so eager to leave Lunal and find my place in the world of the Fae. I used to lay awake at night, imagining all the things we'd accomplish, how we'd make enormous strides in bringing both our people back from the brink." She lets out a pained laugh. "Then I had to go and screw it up."

The small glimpse of vulnerability is so unlike her, and I find myself wanting to chase it. To see more of the person she keeps so guarded. "What happened was a simple mistake." I'm not aware that I've inched closer to her until our knees are nearly touching. I swallow, my throat suddenly dry. Gods, she's something to see. Fierce and brilliant and deadly, all wrapped in a brazen, beautiful package. "We'll figure it out. Together."

It's hard to look at her and remember a time—not that long ago—that I wanted nothing more than to be rid of her. How has she burrowed so deeply under my skin? I was guarded, too. I was careful. Nothing was taken too seriously, and no one was allowed too close. Yet here she is, this breakable human girl with the loyalty of a Fae, the stubbornness of an ogre, and the compassion of a sprite.

What the fuck is happening to me?

"Together…" She takes a deep breath, her heartbeat thundering through the link, and shakes her head. Her brows knit, and her lips press into a firm, thin line. "I think we need to redefine *together*."

"Oh? Well, if you insist on it, we should take our clothing off and start redefining things immediately." I grab the hem of my tunic and grin.

She doesn't smile back. "I'm serious, Valen. What happened? We can't do that again."

"You mean the kiss?"

"It was a bad idea. You see that, right?"

That same, seductive hum pulses through the link, and I can't help myself. "I'm not convinced. Maybe you should kiss me again to prove your point."

She rolls her eyes and slumps back against the tree, then nods to Daroose, who's snoring several feet across from us. "What do you think?"

I know kelpies are despicable creatures that deserve the pointed end of her sword, but given Tania's love of all living things, I decide to keep my thoughts to a minimum on that matter. "Not sure. Don't trust him, though."

"Yeah. Me neither."

I gasp and offer her an expression of mock surprise. "Surely you lie! The great druid Keltania of the Order of Aphelian trusts all living creatures."

She half-heartedly kicks at me, trying—and failing—to hide her grin.

I dramatically waggle my brows, and she laughs, the rest of the tension draining from the link. "Oh. I do like it rough," I say. "A bit harder and much lower, if you don't mind."

"Careful, Fae. If you anger me, I'll command him to eat you."

"Counterproductive, since you'd essentially be eaten, too."

"If I really have to listen to your scratchy voice for the next week, it might be worth it."

She doesn't mean it. In fact, she likes the sound of my voice.

I like the sound of her voice, too.

As the night wears on, we settle into a comfortable silence. It isn't long before Tania drifts off to sleep, while I continue keeping watch. Every so often, my gaze flickers to the kelpie. I don't know what I'm expecting it to do, but I know what it's capable of. We still have a long way to go, and I don't trust it not to get in the way—or worse.

23

Keltania

Despite my mistrust of Daroose, sleep claims me. It's fitful and full of memories masquerading as nightmares, and when I wake, I get the feeling that they aren't all mine.

The link between us is evolving. It grows stronger with each passing day. I'm more aware of Valen than I've ever been. His moods, his feelings, the sensations of his body.

The dynamic between us has shifted, and I'm both oddly comforted and unnerved by it. I can't put my finger on it, but something has changed.

From somewhere close, a hawk shrieks and a crow cries out, followed by the howl of what sounds like a wolf. Definitely not Valen's. His voice is deeper, more resonant.

I roll over and force my eyes open, noting that I'm far more comfortable than I was when I laid down in the early morning hours. Instead of jagged little rocks and bits of stick pinching through my clothing, it's as though I'd nodded off in a lush field. Even the smell is different. From rotting forest floor to fragrant blossoms.

When my eyes adjust, I see that directly in front of me

sits a large crow. It stares, tilting its head to the left, then
the right. The bird hops forward, lets out a shrill scream,
then pecks my nose once and flies off.

"Bastard…" I put my hand down and start to push
myself up—and freeze. The surface my fingers brush really
isn't dirt or jagged rock.

I yelp and scramble to my feet. Valen, face down with
his arm wedged beneath one shoulder, jolts awake. "What?
Where is it?"

I don't answer him. I can't. What was decaying leaves
and an assortment of pebbles and debris when I fell asleep
is now a seven-or-so-foot section of healthy green grass
thick with wildflowers.

More than that—we aren't alone.

Valen shakes off the remnants of sleep and scrambles
upward. He backs slowly to where I stand. An assortment
of animals forms a circle around the newly green camp.
From several wivryn, their wings stretched above them, to
a group of mice huddled under a large blueish doe. That
damned crow is there, too. "Did you— What are they
doing?"

An emaciated black wolf on the edge of the crowd
lifts its head and howls. The two wivryn follow suit, tilting
their massive snouts to the sky and releasing mighty roars.
Every animal surrounding us bellows a call to the wild.
Then, as if they're one, they all lower their heads to the
ground.

Valen holds very still. "Are they—"

"Bowing," I say, breathless. "They're *bowing*."

"I don't understand." The reverence in his voice makes
my chest ache.

I scan the growing group of forest denizens, my gaze

finally coming back to the small patch of grass I woke on. The ground is no longer lifeless and decaying. It's alive— thriving, even. It doesn't make sense. "I don't understand what's going on. Fae magic can't—it can't do this."

Valen comes to stand beside me. "This isn't Fae magic." Something thrums through the link. It's dark and broken, but it's there and gone so fast that I can't quite catch it. He kneels in the grass and runs his fingertips over the soft blades. The feel of them tickles his fingers—which tickles mine.

"It's not possible," I say. It's the most beautiful thing I've ever seen.

"Neither was the rabbit." Valen stands. He glances down at his hands, splaying his fingers. "I—I can feel it."

"Feel what?" But even as the words leave my mouth, I know what he means. The land. The forest, the animals— it's one big heartbeat thundering through my entire body, a second pulse beating with renewed vigor. I close my eyes and focus on it, chasing the sensation. It's euphoric. "Oh, wow…"

"Amazing." He turns in a slow circle. The animals are all still bent, chittering softly, their eyes following our every move. "I've never felt anything like it." He meets my gaze and grins. "And that's saying something."

A small fawn, similar in color to the doe, wobbles forward, softly nudging Valen's hand with her nose. She's too thin, the bones of her ribs protruding prominently, and walks with a subtle limp. My chest aches with his sorrow, tinted by the desire to help her in some way. He stretches out his hand, and the small deer nuzzles it twice before hobbling back to her mother.

I pluck a small pink flower from the ground. Instantly,

another springs to replace it. In that moment I feel lighter—freer—than I ever have. "I want to try something. To test a…theory."

"You're smiling." He lifts a brow and flashes me a lopsided grin. "I feel like you're about to suggest something ridiculous."

"Do as I do." I drop to the ground and pull him down with me. With one hand twined in his and the other pressed flat against the earth, I close my eyes. "Think about the forest as it should be. Lush grass, blossoming trees, fresh air…"

Valen's hand tightens around mine, and a jolt races up my arm. It travels through my torso, then spreads to my other arm and down to the tips of each finger. Something raw tugs at my chest, and deeper. My soul. Completeness like I've never known washes over me. I exhale, and it's like time stills. The second pulse beating inside my chest explodes outward, seeping into the land.

"Tania," Valen whispers. His grip on my hand loosens but doesn't disappear.

I open my eyes, and my heart thunders. The entire clearing, previously brown and decaying, now hums with life. The trees bear brightly colored leaves, their bark turned from dull gray to healthy brown. Birds swoop down from the sky, some settling on the newly invigorated branches, while others land on the ground, pecking for fresh food.

My hand still in his, Valen says, "We did this, Tania. *We* did this."

The excitement in his voice, vibrating throughout his entire body and flooding our link, is infectious. "A Fae and a druid. This is what it was meant to be."

"But *how*?" I'm elated, and it feels like every part of me is more alive than I've ever been, but what's just happened isn't possible. "I'm not an expert on druid magic. No one is, anymore. But living atop latent magic in the ground? It can't do this."

Can it? What other explanation could there possibly be?

He hesitates, and I feel it again. That odd emotion in the link. Does he feel guilty about having access to my people's power? It's not his fault...

"One of the very first things Buri drilled into my head was that power calls to power. As I grew older, stronger, the druid magic in the grounds at the estate must have somehow merged with mine."

If that's true, then Valen is even more important than Orbik thinks he is. He's the future of the Fae *and* the druids.

Daroose sits up and stretches, and I start. I'd completely forgotten about him. "If you two kiss again, fair warning, I'll vomit. All that blather last night was more than I could stand. Trust me. You don't want to see a kelpie vomit. Our bodies aren't the only thing that can shapeshift."

I yank my hand from Valen's and stumble away. "Don't be disgusting."

Daroose rubs his eyes and climbs to his feet as he takes in the newly rejuvenated section of forest. "Didn't you tell me that druid magic was lost to the Winter Lands?" His nose scrunches up, and his lips tilt down. He spreads his arms wide. "This looks pretty *magical* to me."

"It was—in a manner of speaking." I drop my gaze back to the grass. The breeze kicks up, making it dance softly. "But Valen seems to have access to it."

Daroose narrows his eyes at Valen, and the anger there

surprises me.

Valen sees it, too. He throws up his hands as a rush of guilt washes through the link. "Don't look at me like that. I have no control over this!"

Daroose's brow furrows. "I heard you say *we* did this. You *and* Keltania."

I open my mouth but close it, completely at a loss. Thankfully, Valen is slyer than me. "We don't understand it, either. The truth is, we're heading to Ventin. There's an elder there who might be able to help us."

Daroose sniffs the air. "You're tied together somehow, aren't you?"

"Something like that," Valen says. He holds his ground, gaze never wavering. "We're trying to fix it."

Daroose sniffs again, then frowns. "I can scent no wrongdoing or violence on you. But the moment you slip…" The Kelpie smiles, then licks his lips slowly.

"And now it's time for some ground rules." I step between them. Valen might be mellow for a Fae, but I'm sure even he has his limits. Daroose is still a wild card. If I really am stuck with him for the next year, we need boundaries. "Even if Valen does something truly evil, you are forbidden from eating him."

The angry twist of Daroose's lips morphs into a childlike pout. "Well, that's no fun at all."

Valen grins and sticks his tongue out at Daroose.

"And you…" I glare at him. "Stop taunting him. It's annoying." Turning back to Daroose, I say, "In fact, eating people in general—no matter how wicked you deem them to be—is off-limits."

The kelpie's mouth falls open, and he stomps his foot. "How am I supposed to eat?"

"Spare us," Valen says with a roll of his eyes. "Everyone knows kelpies are scavengers. You can eat animals just as well as you can feed on…other beings."

Daroose pouts. "But the Fae taste so much better. Less fattening, too." He turns to me. "Of course, I would refrain from indulging in human sinners out of respect for my druid friend."

"Animals only." I hope the command is enough. The last thing we need with all our other problems is a bloodthirsty kelpie leaving a trail of corpses scattered across Derriga.

"How about a finger? He has ten of them, after all. Or a toe! If he steps out of line, a single digit — "

I hold his gaze.

"Fine." Daroose folds his arms and glares at me, not unlike a spoiled child. "I won't eat him. But that doesn't mean I can't hurt him if he steps out of line." He narrows his eyes at Valen, the hint of a smile playing at the corners of his lips. Holding his pointer finger and thumb a hair away from each other, he adds, "Just a little."

I drop my gaze back to the ground, to the newly grassy area. I'm the first druid in centuries to access our magic without the aid of ink — and it was amazing. A high unlike anything I've ever imagined. Now, though, I feel heavy. Like something is stirring inside me — something that doesn't quite fit. I should be dancing over what we've done.

Instead, I feel a little bit sick.

We hike south for the better part of the day. Daroose and Valen take turns sniping at each other, and I keep an eye out for palewort, an herb used for alleviating headaches.

I'm going to need it before nightfall.

"I met Servis once—he'd be your *great-grandfather*, right?" Daroose is ahead of me, walking behind Valen. "Was quite self-absorbed, even for a Fae. Servis always bragged about how superior the Winter Fae were and how they'd be the only ones left standing."

"I suppose he was right, in the end." Valen's pace remains steady, but his posture slumps a little. A small spike of shame hits me as his guilt flares again. "After the war, refugees from the other courts came to him for help. He refused them all."

"And they tore themselves apart." The whole thing makes me ill. Our history shows that humans did a fair amount of damage to themselves. There was no shortage of violence and war, but our motives were never that cutthroat. There were disagreements over beliefs and territory, but we'd never set out to wipe each other from the face of Derriga. We never stood by as branches of our race withered and died. If someone, even our enemies, was truly in need, we opened our doors. We tried to help the non-druid villages—we just didn't have enough resources to spare to make a difference.

"Aye." Valen sighs. "He said there weren't enough resources to go around. The Winter Lands were fairly desolate after the war. Then Envrill took over. He promised to take in migrants from the broken courts."

"But he never did." The story the druids were told was that there still weren't enough resources to care for the Winter Lands' own citizens. To take on more would be to doom their own people. But after meeting Orbik, I doubt that his father was much different from him.

"And the current ruler?" Daroose snorts. "What of him?"

"My uncle, Orbik." Valen cringes a little. "By the time he claimed the throne, it was apparently too late. The chaos had taken over, and the rebel bands had formed. There were far too many centuries of bad blood between the Winter Lands and everyone else."

He adjusts his pack, swinging it to the opposite shoulder. The weight of it presses down on me. The link seems to open in times of heightened emotion, but over the last forty-eight hours, it seems to also be affecting us at random. A touch here, a scratch there...

"He's got no intention of sharing our prosperity," Valen says.

Daroose grabs a handful of leaves from a nearby tree as we pass. He sifts through them, picks out the largest, then rolls it up and takes a bite. He makes sure to grimace and glare at Valen as he chews.

Valen still doesn't slow his pace. "I don't agree with what Orbik is doing. I don't agree with what any of them have done. They—"

I gasp. Pressure in my chest and leaden weight in my limbs. The ground dips and sways, and a wave of vertigo throws me off-balance. I thrust my arm out to keep from toppling, but all I get is air. Icy air. The temperature around me plummets.

Someone catches me before I hit the ground. "Keltania?" There's concern in Daroose's voice, but the panic I feel from Valen is enough to steal my breath away.

"Don't worry," I say to him as Daroose helps me right myself. The sensation is gone almost as quickly as it came. My vision snaps back into focus, and the eerie chill abates. "I'm not dying, so you're probably safe."

He frowns. "What happened?"

"I just need to eat something." I bend to retrieve my pack, which has fallen on the ground. Unfortunately, after rummaging through it, I come up empty-handed. We've exhausted our food reserves.

Valen checks his with the same results. He spins in a slow circle, scanning the area. "There should be beetberries in this part of the forest. I read that the Autumn Court used them in all kinds of desserts."

"I'm not convinced this is a nutrition issue," Daroose says. He leans closer, coming nose-to-nose. He pokes my cheek several times before straightening. "Your pupils are dilated, and you smell funny."

I swat him away. "Rude."

He ignores me and turns to Valen. "We're going to need help. I think I know someone—if he's still around."

As we make our way, my feet become heavier. My body begins to ache, and I feel like I haven't slept in days. Daroose leads us west for nearly an hour before stopping and announcing *we've arrived*. He starts a fire, tosses in some pontiweed—which turns the smoke bright green— then settles against a large tree.

Valen has been staring at him for the last twenty minutes. His irritation at the kelpie's silence is mounting. "What, exactly, are we doing?"

Daroose examines his nails, fanning his fingers and giving his hand a quick shake. "Waiting."

"For what?"

"I told you—I have a friend who I hope still lives in the area. He might be able to help."

"Help with *what*? You still haven't told us why we're here."

The tips of my fingers turn cold as the cuticles of Valen's left hand begin to frost. I hold up my hand and wiggle my fingers as the numbness settles in. "Valen, hand me my pack. It's getting *cold* out here."

His eyes go wide, and he clenches his fist, taking a visibly deep breath when he realizes the magic is affecting me. I still don't know what to make of Daroose. I already feel like we've told him too much.

Once I'm sure Valen has his magic under control, I turn back to Daroose. "What do we need help with, exactly?"

"If you told me the truth about what you two were doing stomping through the woods, then maybe I'd be able to tell you, but since I doubt you're going to give me more information than absolutely necessary, you'll have to simply settle for a promise that I'm trying to help. Both of you."

Something snaps, and leaves crackle. Valen tenses, but Daroose seems at ease. He stands and straightens his tunic, then gestures for me to stand.

"Announce yourselves," a deep voice calls from the darkness.

"I have a human in need of aid," Daroose says.

Three figures step into the green-hued light from the fire. The flame casts eerie shadows across their faces, oddly accentuating the sharp points of their ears.

"Fae?" My hand lingers at my sword. From first glance, it's not clear what their affiliation is. Then again, other than the Winter Court, there really isn't anything except nomads these days. All that's clear is that they're clean, well-fed, and don't seem at all like they're suffering. "What are Fae doing in this part of the forest?"

The one in front, tall with what looks like purple hair, takes a step forward. "My name is Benj." He squints, studying me, his eyes focused on my forehead, no doubt on my initiation sigil. "The human is an Aphelian druid?"

Valen steps up and wedges himself between us. "Before you act, know that she's under my protection. If you harm her, I'll kill you with my bare hands."

I roll my eyes and move to shove him aside but notice something odd. The three newcomers are now staring at Valen. In a panic, I skim his clothing. There's nothing overtly indicating him as a royal member of the Winter Court. I don't see any frost or ice forming. He's dirty and disheveled from traveling, and there's nothing that gives him away as anything other than a simple nomad.

"Who are you?" Benj demands. He holds a torch dangerously close to Valen's face.

"Someone you don't want to irritate." Valen's voice is deadly and cool. He doesn't shrink away from the flame. In fact, he leans in, baring his teeth. "Whatever it is you have to offer, we don't need it." He tries to step around them, but they move to block his path.

"You summoned us, and we are here. You can't leave until Delkin allows it." He turns, and the other two position themselves behind us. We're gently herded forward. "Please, for now, consider yourselves *guests* of Vey Brill."

The name is familiar, but not from histories—from legend. I frown and say, "I didn't think it was real."

"It isn't. Vey Brill is nothing but a children's bedtime story," Valen says with a laugh.

Benj stops in front of a massive tree trunk. It's dark, so

I can't see exactly what he does, but a moment later, light floods the small clearing. He steps aside to reveal a narrow staircase, lit by torches, inside of the tree.

Valen's breath hitches, and his surprise overwhelms me.

Vey Brill is real.

24

Valen

We climb a winding staircase through the center of
the largest tree I've ever seen.

"What court are you from?" I ask. It isn't easy to tell
anymore. Since the other courts fell, most rebels have given
up their colors. They cut their hair and abandoned their
traditions, some even covering court-specific markings out
of shame for the way their leaders behaved.

"We have no court," Benj says. Once we reach the top
of the staircase, he pushes on a large panel, and another
door opens.

"No, not anymore. But what court were you part of
before the Great Drain?"

"I'll let Delkin answer that."

"Who is Delkin?" I ask.

"Let's just say he runs things around here." Benj steps
aside and gestures for us to pass through.

The sight renders me speechless.

A sprawling village nestled in the hulking branches
of ancient trees. Not just any trees—giant hilpberry trees.
The canopy is so high that you can't tell from the ground

what they are.

Tania enters behind me, and I turn. Her mouth hangs open as she climbs onto the landing and spins in a slow circle. "This— I— Wow." She takes several steps and leans over the railing. It takes a few tries, but she manages to grab a low-hanging berry. Larger than an apple, it dwarfs her small hands. "How is this possible?"

Daroose lets out a shrill whistle. "Place has come a long way since I saw it last." The kelpie snatches the berry from Tania and takes a bite, purple juices dripping down its chin, before handing it back to her. "Can't say I'm surprised. Delkin has always been a bit flashy if you ask me."

Tania cringes and drops the berry over the side, then watches as it disappears.

Benj murmurs something to his companions, and the two Fae move to either side of Tania and Daroose. Then, to me, he says, "If you'll follow me, I'll take you to Delkin."

"The druid comes with me." There's no way I'm leaving without her. Daroose might vouch for them, but I don't trust it. Tania and I are stronger together.

Benj shakes his head. Just once. It's unyielding and leaves no room for argument. "You have my word that she will be unharmed."

Daroose snorts. It slings an arm around Tania's shoulder and waves me off. "Run along. *You* have more important things to deal with right now."

Tania rolls her eyes. "It's fine, Valen." She folds her arms and regards Benj carefully. "I'll be okay. Anyone lays a finger on me and I'll simply rip it off."

My lip twitches with a grin. "I would expect nothing less. Be sure it's a useful one, though. We Fae find the thumb particularly pleasing." I turn to follow Benj but pause, glaring at the kelpie. "Oh, and see if you can find me some wine. Mine has *mysteriously* disappeared."

Daroose gasps. "I'm certain I have no clue what you're babbling about."

The corner of Tania's mouth hitches, and amusement flickers through the link.

She'll be fine. If she isn't, there'll be no containing her.

I let Benj lead me up several small steps, to the highest platform. There, in the leaves, is a hollow carved from the trunk. No. Not a hollow, but…a room.

"Del?" Benj hesitates.

"What the hell was Marvis chattering on about?" A tall, white-haired Fae appears in the doorway. "He said you found a Fae that has violet—"

Benj says nothing and inclines his head toward me. Delkin growls, then turns. When his gaze lands on me, his mouth falls open. "What is this?" The anger in his voice is gone, replaced with something I can't quite place. Sorrow? Regret?

"The kelpie summoned us to the ground." Benj's voice is softer now. "He was with a druid."

It's then that I notice his eyes. Violet. Exact duplicates of mine. "You—"

"Your name—what is it?" He's utterly still. Not a flinch of muscle or even the rise and fall of his chest as he breathes.

"I'm Valen, nephew of Lord Orbik, monarch of the Winter Lands."

Delkin exhales, then breathes in deep. "Nineteen. You are nineteen now, yes? Nineteen and two hundred and six days."

I don't answer him—I can't—because my brain starts buzzing. His reaction, his eyes, the knowledge of my age…

Delkin takes a step back. It's him and me, alone now. Benj must have slipped out at some point. He closes his eyes and inhales. One moment, there's a Fae with eyes like mine; the next, a wolf with white fur like newly fallen snow.

My body reacts without thought. I melt into my own shift and crouch in front of him.

This Fae is my father. There's no doubt in my mind. The truth of it is a weight, primal and unrelenting, pushing against my subconscious. He's my father—and he stole my mother from her home. Stole her, then inflicted the injuries that ultimately killed her.

A feral roar tears from my throat, and I lunge at him.

We crash against the wall. Delkin lets go of his wolf but doesn't raise a hand to defend himself. "Whatever it is"—I snap at the air beside his face, and he swiftly jerks away, cringing—"you think you know"—another snap, this time resulting in a chunk of skin and material from his sleeve—"is wrong!"

I release my wolf and shift back to Fae form. Too easy. Ripping him to shreds with razor-sharp teeth is cheating. I want to feel it. To relish in his blood as it flows over my hands and slips between my fingers. "Fight, damnit!" Grabbing him by the front of the shirt, I slam him hard against the wall.

His lip is bloodied, and there are scrapes on his face. Blood oozes from the bite on his upper arm. Still, there's no retaliation. A glint of annoyance, maybe, but no anger. "I can allow you to pummel me until your anger is sated, or I can answer whatever questions you might have. But first, I beg you one of my own."

I don't owe this bastard anything, but there are things I want to know. Need to know. If I answer his question, maybe this will go easier. I can kill him when I'm done. "Ask it."

"Where is she? My Mori… Is she well? Is she—"

"My mother is dead!" I shake him hard. "*You* killed her."

I catch the tiniest spark of rage before I career into the adjacent wall. The air rushes from my lungs, and when my vision clears, Delkin's face is inches from mine, that tiny spark of annoyance now a raging inferno.

His unwillingness to fight me moments ago was a mercy. Had he wanted, he clearly could have taken me apart with little more than a flick of his fingers. "If you remember nothing else in this world, let this small bit of information stick in that thick skull of yours, boy. Amoriel Icekeeper was—and will be until my last moment in this place—*mine* as much as I was *hers*."

Fae can't claim a partner as *theirs* unless it's mutual. A claim is forever, and theirs was real—and judging by the ferocity of Delkin's reaction, it's something I'm glad to be spared, thanks to the Heartbreaker.

I let go of him and step away. "You're my father."

He straightens his shirt. "I'm many things, but yes. That's one of them."

"And you didn't keep her here against her will?"

Delkin laughs. "There isn't a creature in this world that could make Mori do something against her will."

He hasn't met Tania yet.

"So, you didn't kidnap her?"

Something akin to regret flickers in his eyes. "Not personally, no. But a few of my Fae did."

"I don't understand." It's impossible to wrap my head around it all. I'm standing here with my *father*. The Fae I've hated since I learned what hate was. Now I find that hate was misplaced? That he *loved* my mother? Everything I've grown up believing has been a lie. My entire world turned on its ass in a single moment.

I suppose I shouldn't be surprised. Everything I knew about Servis and Aphelian was false. Why not this, too?

"Why would your Fae steal her?"

"You have many questions. I understand. I have them, too. But your druid friend—"

"If they've hurt her..." No. She has to be all right. If she wasn't, I would know. Then again, when she faltered earlier in the woods, I felt nothing. What if—

I inhale and focus on her. The link between us surges to life. Her pulse is calm, and she's uninjured. A bit concerned—understandable, considering my outburst moments ago, which I'm sure she felt—but otherwise fine.

Delkin shakes his head. "I guarantee she's perfectly all right."

"Daroose thinks there's something wrong with her. He said you could help." But his Fae kidnapped my mother, right? Now I'm supposed to trust them?

I'm not sure I'm comfortable with that.

"Where is she?" I ask. I'll feel better when Tania is back at my side. Being separated from her makes me twitchy.

"I'm sure she's being looked after." He smiles. "Benj probably took her to meet the others."

"What others?" Just how many Fae does Delkin have in his treetop village?

"The other humans, of course."

25

Keltania

A wave of rage hits me through the link, followed by sadness—then more anger. Where have they taken Valen? Or Daroose? Why split us? I keep myself braced for any indication that Valen has been hurt, but despite his shifting emotions, he seems fine. After a few minutes, he seems to settle. A good sign, but the separation makes me uneasy. I have no control this way. No way to protect him.

Granted, he isn't helpless, but we don't want to expose his magic. If it comes down to life or death, however, he'll have no choice.

"Hello." A figure pokes his head into the room. "Might I come in?"

"You're asking the prisoner for permission?" I snort and shake off a chill. Valen's mood has calmed, but I'm still cold. The chill that normally comes when he's on the verge of losing his temper seems to be lasting longer and longer. "That's a new take on captivity."

"You're no prisoner." He steps into the room and smiles. He's short for a Fae. Probably just a hair or so taller than I am, with sand-colored hair and mud-brown eyes. His ears... His ears!

I jump from my seat in the corner of the room, and it takes every ounce of willpower not to lurch forward and pinch him to be sure he's real. "You're human!"

He laughs and offers a small wave. "Ander," he says, then bows. "And you are a druid. It is truly an honor to meet you."

"Trust me," I say, unable to keep the bitterness from my tone. "It's not as much of an honor as you think it is."

He laughs again. A head-tossing, full-belly laugh that has me fighting a smile. Goddess. I haven't heard anyone laugh that way, that *true*, my entire life.

"Would you like me to introduce you to the others?"

"Other...humans?"

He nods. "I believe at last count, there were twenty humans in the camp." He smacks the side of his head. "Oops. Twenty-one. Farrah and Wendel had a little one last month."

Surely I heard him wrong. How is this possible? "Twenty-one," I repeat, stunned. "Are you all..." How do I put it without sounding rude?

"Regular humans?" His smile widens. "Yes. Not a druid among us. Except, now, for you."

"How?"

Centuries. That's how long it's been since humans other than druids have walked in Derriga. Or, so we'd thought. After we gave the Winter Fae our magic to win the war, what remained of the other courts hunted the settlements down and snuffed them out. They sought out the villages not under druid or Fae protection and burned them all to the ground. The few they couldn't access dwindled when the Fae in their regions cut off their supply routes.

"You all died off," I say. "Victims of starvation and war with the Fae."

"Delkin and his family have been here, hidden away, for a very long time. The humans here are descendants of the ones who came with him, thousands of years ago, to escape the turbulent, changing landscape of Derriga."

We learned Fae had extremely long lifespans, but no one in the Order really knew the true extent of it.

He gestures over his shoulder. "How about a tour before meeting some of the others?"

Ander is human, but he's been living with the Fae. Just because this place is amazing and he's something of a rarity himself doesn't mean I instantly trust him. Still, I'm curious. What other secrets are they hiding?

Ander leads me from the small room and out into the predawn light. Benj wasn't rough with me on the way in, but he didn't give me time to really take in my surroundings. Now, with the ability to take a good, long look, I'm in awe.

The village is nestled into the unnaturally huge branches of hilpberry trees, hidden within the fat leaves and strangely large hanging berries. It's all connected by wooden platforms that span what feels like miles, six, maybe seven trees down.

"Delkin found this place long ago, by accident, when he was driven from his home. He and some of the other Fae climbed up and began building as the rest of us stayed hidden. Generation after generation, we've lived here in peace and tranquility. A community unhindered by the outside world."

We pass a small row of living quarters, some decorated with flowers and long sections of vine. Farther down, there are large portions of fenced-in area. Inside, several cattle, a few goats, and multiple pigs graze contentedly on a mossy carpet that's growing from the planks. He points to a small section to our right. "Over there, we have a place to grow vegetables. Other than an occasional hunt, we're mostly self-sufficient. We survive almost wholly on what we create here."

"What do you do for water?"

Ander points in the other direction, to one of the connecting trees. There's a large basin with several pipes and a huge spout. "We collect the rainwater, and that handy contraption purifies it. Invented by a member of our community no longer with us."

"It's all so… I can't believe it." A shiver races down my spine, branching out to the tips of my fingers. I ball my fists and shudder.

Ander cocks his head to the side. "Are you all right?"

"I—" I force a smile. "Fine. Just a little cold."

"Let's go see the others." Ander grins. "They've been buzzing about you since they heard."

He takes me around the pen, to the back of the massive tree. There, we climb a narrow set of steps that lead to an upper-level plateau. The large hilpberry leaves create a tunnel, encasing the stairs like a living hallway. This place is nothing short of fantastic.

We end up at the very top of one of the peaks, the tallest of the village. Low-hanging clouds kiss the edges of the tree, and an assortment of birds—ones I've never seen before—perch atop the railing.

We emerge from the stairs, and the instant my feet touch the platform, all eyes are on me. Ander gives me a small nudge forward. "Friends, this is…" His brow furrows.

"My apologies. I never asked for your name."

"Aphelian," I say without thinking. I've been loyal to my title—but in this moment, seeing the faces before me, clarity hits hard. "Keltania," I correct.

There are ten people total, six men and four women.

One of the women in the group, a plump redhead with deep brown eyes and a freckle-dotted nose, climbs to her feet. "You're an Aphelian?" I don't miss the note of accusation.

Ander clears his throat. He crosses the small space and rests a hand against her shoulder. "Keltania is here as a guest of Delkin's." He looks around at the group. "I trust you'll all make her feel welcome."

A soft rumble goes through the group, and most of them nod. Several smile, while the majority watch me with careful stares. A few, though… A few glare outright. Who can blame them? They've obviously been living here, protected. I'm an outsider. An unknown. They'd be foolish to welcome me with open arms.

For so long, we've been praised as heroes, the saviors of the Fae. But my kind are the disease, the infection that started it all. We saved the Fae—but we let our own race flounder. And for what? A fantasy?

"My people are the reason humans were wiped from Derriga. When Aphelian gave Servis the edge to win the war, she started a chain of events that led to the downfall of humanity." I drop to my knee and hold my hand across my heart. "My ancestor did not foresee the consequences of her actions."

An elderly woman at the back struggles upright. Several people jump up to help her as she wobbles to the front of the crowd, stopping a few feet in front of me.

"Poor child," she says. She places a weathered hand over my heart. Too stunned to react, I simply kneel there as her lips tilt upward in a strange grin. "You are broken in two and lost, but that is good. It saves you. And us."

I climb to my feet. "I'm *broken*?"

"In two."

Ander sighs and steps around me. He grabs the old woman gently around the shoulders and steers her back into the waiting arms of several of the others. "Forgive Eta. She's the oldest of us and sometimes doesn't make much sense."

I nod, but there's a chill in the air that wasn't there before the old woman touched me. "Valen and I came with someone. A…man. Where is he?"

"You speak of the kelpie, Daroose?" Ander laughs. "He's around somewhere, undoubtedly getting into trouble. From what I understand, he's an old friend of Delkin's. He's fine—I promise you."

I glance around the small group. "Do you all just stay up here? When was the last time you set foot on the ground?"

"Delkin doesn't want the humans to leave. He knows what Derriga is like now, and for us, there's no place there. He'll let some of the Fae come and go. Every once in a while, someone will get restless and he'll allow them to head back to the world below. Sometimes we'll send a party out to fetch something we can't get or create here. Other than that, we keep to ourselves and we stay put."

"So, you're not the group raiding villages in the Winter Lands?"

Ander tilts his head. "I can't speak for all of us, but I doubt it. Delkin wouldn't stand for it. And besides, we don't go that far north. Years ago, we had a small group step out of line. They were punished harshly."

"Delkin is a tyrant?"

Ander's expression darkens as a collection of gasps erupt from the small crowd across the platform. "As Delkin would say, he is many things. A tyrant *isn't* one of them."

"But you all just obey him? Let him keep you stashed away up here?" If that isn't the definition of a tyrant, then I don't know what is. The more I learn about this place, the more I want to get back down to the ground, back to the world I know. It has its flaws, but it's real. I would rather live in the pits of Lunal and look for a way to fix it than hide away in the treetops with my head in the clouds.

The red-haired woman shakes her head vigorously. "Delkin has his reasons, and we all trust him. You're a newcomer and can't possibly understand—"

I throw my hands up and back away several steps. "I'm not a *newcomer*. I was accosted and forced up your tree. I've got no intention of staying. As soon as I find Valen, I'm leaving."

"Tania?"

I whirl to find Valen standing at the top of the stairs. Next to him is a tall, broad-shouldered Fae with white hair and violet eyes that match his. Obviously, my first question should be, *Who is he?* Aside from Valen, I've never come across a Fae with eyes like those. But instead of asking, I throw myself forward and wrap my arms around him.

"Thank the Goddess you're okay." I'm alive and uninjured, so he's obviously fine. But in the back of my mind, something squirms. A thought so dark, so deep and impossible, that I can't acknowledge it. A feeling that has no place being there.

Valen returns the embrace, maybe squeezing just a little too hard. He chuckles. "I told you you'd be unable to keep your hands off me one day."

"Is she *yours*?" the white-haired Fae beside him asks.

His? And just like that, the brief spell is broken. I dislodge myself from Valen, and the sudden move sends him off-balance. He stumbles back, catching himself before ending up on the floor.

"If by *mine*, you mean the eternal pain in my ass, then yes." He runs a hand down the front of his leathers and gestures to me. "Delkin, allow me to introduce Keltania, my...friend."

A look passes between Delkin and Ander.

"Tania, meet Delkin, my father."

"Your—"

"It's a long story," Delkin says. "One I would be happy to share over breakfast. After that, we'll see what we can do for your friend."

A quick glance at Valen tells me he wants to stay, so I nod. We're safe here. A little downtime will give us more space from the Winter Guards, should they have gotten lucky enough to track us this far. They'll never think to look *up* while searching. Plus, if there *is* something wrong with me and these Fae can help as Daroose insisted, we'd be smart to stick around until we know for sure.

My joints ache, but that could easily be attributed to the journey. The terrain hasn't been easy so far. My head throbs, but I blame Valen and Daroose for that. No. I don't feel wrong—but I don't feel right, either. It's the only reason I allowed Daroose to bring us here.

As the others chat, I look to the sky. There are several

birds circling, but one catches my eye. A large crow.

"You again…" I reach out, hoping to speak with it, but like before, there's nothing but silence.

It narrows in, swooping down, then flies away.

"Fine, be that way."

I turn to one of the other birds. A crane. She squawks and launches into the air, circling above me. I need Levina to know we're still coming to Ventin but there might be a small delay. I have no idea if this will work, but… *"Can you understand me?"*

Unlike the crow, I feel the creature's reply. A gentle nudge, warm and welcoming, against my subconscious.

"The Fae with me can understand you as I can, and I don't want him to know what we're talking about should he listen in," I say. *"Please keep your replies vague if you can."*

"Understood."

"Do you know where the druids live?"

"Yes."

"One of them will be traveling the road to Ventin. Can you find her and deliver a message there for me? She bears our priestess sigil and should be able to speak with you."

"Honored."

By the time we start back down to the lower levels of the village, the crane has taken off. Bound for Ventin to update Levina. We're getting closer, and that should put my nerves at ease, but there's a kernel of fear in my belly that keeps growing. How many more obstacles will stand in our way?

26

Valen

The entire community turns out for breakfast. Rows of tables are filled with foods fit for royalty.

"Is the meal not to your liking?" Delkin asks. Tania sits across from him, pushing the food across her plate but eating none of it.

"No. It's fine. Really." She sets the fork down and smiles. It's nothing to do with the link, but I know that it's forced. I've grown so accustomed to her moods, her expressions. "I'm just… This is a lot to take in."

"How so?" Ander sets his own fork down and leans back in his chair.

Tania looks between him and Delkin. "The druids thought we were the only humans left. You've been living with the Fae, sharing your homes, your resources—"

"Our lives?" Benj says. He leans sideways and plants a kiss on Ander's cheek.

"He is *yours*?" I clarify, and Benj nods proudly.

Tania's eyes widen. "Yours?"

The entire table bursts into a fit of hysterical laughter. "His," Ander says, returning the kiss. "As in his partner.

Husband, in the human tradition."

Her mouth falls open. "You married a *human*?"

Benj beams. "Most handsome one in all of Derriga."

Delkin sets his napkin on the table and leans back. "The Derriga you know is not the Derriga I come from."

"Which is one of my questions." I found my father without looking for him. I have a million questions about my mother and about the events that led her to flee into the woods that night with me in her arms. Possibly more than that, though, is the need to understand Delkin himself. His odd eyes and long life. What does that mean for me?

"How is it you're still here?" I ask him. "How old are you, exactly?"

"My precise age doesn't matter, but I will tell you that I was born long before Servis."

Tania chooses that moment to take a bite from her plate, and she nearly chokes on it. "Servis has been *dead* for over a thousand years!"

Delkin winks at her. "Indeed." He stabs a piece of food with his fork. Some unappetizing purple thing I'm not brave enough to sample. "But let's talk about something better. Wouldn't you like to know about Mori?"

Amoriel Icekeeper. Orbik's sister. Her face is nothing more than an image in a painting that hangs in one of the dining halls at the estate, done long before she had me. She was young. My age, probably. With long raven hair and storm-gray eyes teeming with mischief.

"You said she stayed of her own free will. Why? Why didn't she go back to her family?"

Delkin's shoulders go rigid, and his fists clench tight for a moment. "She wanted to. In the first few days, I fully intended to have Benj escort her back home."

"But something changed?" Tania asks.

"There are Fae among us who choose to come and go. While they are here, they are cared for. Content. On the ground, they need to survive on their own. Doing that sometimes means they resort to less-than-civil means of monetary gain."

"So, the Fae who kidnapped her were going to hold her for ransom?" It makes sense. The daughter of the only Fae monarch left standing, sister of the next in line to the throne, would fetch a hefty price and make for an excellent bargaining chip.

Delkin's eyes narrow. "The Fae that kidnapped her were paid to end her life." He closes his eyes and inhales deeply, holding the breath before blowing out slowly. Like he's trying to maintain control over his temper. Maybe we have that in common. "I found them as the blade hovered above her neck. I brought her back to our village, saw to her wounds. It wasn't until I interrogated my men that she decided to stay."

"Why?" Acid bubbles in my gut. "What could they have said to make her remain here, with you?"

"The assassins were hired by her brother, Orbik."

The air chills so fast it's suddenly hard to breathe.

Something about my expression must give me away, because Delkin narrows his eyes and says, "It's true, boy. He had her removed so he could take the throne from his father."

"Why? He was next in line to the throne. What did she have to do with it?"

"Valen…" Tania's voice is low, a shadow hovering on the edge of my consciousness.

"Orbik was *not* next in line," Benj says with a scowl.

"Mori was to be given the throne. The day she was taken was to be her coronation."

"Valen," Tania says again, her tone sharper. I can't focus on anything other than what Benj and Delkin are saying, though. How is it possible that I've lived under the roof of the Fae who ordered my mother killed without knowing? Orbik is cold and cares little about the people, but to murder his own blood? He is lazy and arrogant and greedy, with a very short temper, but ruthless? I never saw that in him.

"Orbik now sits on *your* throne. He killed your mother and then your grandfather."

Delkin's words penetrate my haze, but with each syllable, they grow fainter. From the corner of my eye, I see Tania stand. She rounds the table and yanks me from my chair. There's something wrong with her. She's pale, and a twinge of discomfort filters through the link we share, but it isn't enough to break the fury building inside. If anything, it stokes the flames and makes the anger burn hotter.

"You are the true monarch of the Winter Court, Valen," Delkin says. "*You*, not Orbik."

Tania shakes me. Her eyes widen, and she stumbles backward, and it's the scream that rips from her throat—one that gouges me to the very pit of my soul—that drags me from the haze.

Tania's body goes rigid, and the tips of her fingers crystalize as her lips turn blue. Her eyes glow, taking on a cerulean hue.

"Everyone back!" Delkin yells. He jumps from his seat as everyone scatters away from the table.

Smoke wafts from her now iced fingers, solidifying

and taking the shape of vines made entirely of ice. They coil around her body, wrapping like a snake until she's engulfed. Then they spasm once before exploding, sending shards of ice in every direction.

Tania collapses, and I lurch forward to catch her before she hits the ground—but I don't make it in time, because everything goes dark.

27

Keltania

arch my back, aware that I'm on some type of bedding.
Every inch of my body aches, and the chill in the air is
far more prominent than it was before.

"How do you feel?"

Forcing my eyes open, I meet Delkin's hopeful grin
with a grimace. "Like I fell from your tree into an ice
cube." With his help, I pull myself up into a sitting position.
"Valen?"

"He seems all right. He hasn't woken yet."

"I suppose the secret is out." I stretch, cringing as a
knot forms in my lower back.

"Secret?" He's seated beside my bed, watching me
curiously, arms folded in his lap.

"That Valen has magic."

"That was no secret." Delkin smiles. "We knew from
the moment he was born. It's fitting, really. He's the son
of the true Winter Lady. He's extremely powerful, which I
suspect is why Orbik kept him alive all these years."

"They use him," I blurt out. Delkin is Valen's father.
He needs to know what Orbik has been doing to him over

the years. Crap. What did he call it? "Something called... panashere?"

Delkin pales and makes a soft choking sound.

"They drain his magic. Use it for themselves."

He flinches. "If I had any idea he'd survived, I would have torn the world apart to retrieve him. I was given false information. That he and Mori... When he arrived here, I hoped she was still out there, too." He squeezes his eyes closed for a moment, and when he opens them, there's nothing but an inferno of fury. It's the same look I've seen in Valen's eyes. "The pain he must have endured during those extractions..."

"It's no walk in the park." I think back to what Valen said about his mother. How she was found running through the woods. "How did Mori end up back at the estate?"

His expression twists into a painful grimace that causes my chest to ache. "Mori had gotten restless. She convinced me to take her and Valen on an outing, to the ground." A shudder goes through him. "She missed the Winter Lands so much, craved the snow... We ventured too close, and we were attacked and separated. I went out with members of Vey Brill. We searched for days until we found bloodied items belonging to her and Valen not far from a tragon nest."

"And you thought she was dead." I can't imagine how hard that must have been. Losing his love and his child... "I'm sorry."

"Mori would be happy that Valen found me. I take solace in that fact." He leans back and studies me for a moment. "That show you put on at breakfast was quite impressive."

"Was anyone harmed?" The thought that I might have

hurt someone twists in my chest.

"Everyone is fine." He cocks his head to the side. "Of course, we're all quite curious... Mind explaining how you channeled Fae magic?"

I run a hand through my messy hair, praying to the Goddess that he can't hear the sudden thunder of my heart. "It's complicated." I hold up my hand to examine a red leather braid tied around my wrist. "What—what's this?"

"I no longer have magic, but I can still *see* magic." He touches my forehead, to the left of my initiation sigil, with the tip of his finger. "Daroose brought you to me for a reason. Whatever is allowing you to tap into my son's power is coming at a cost—one your body is not designed to pay. That braid is soaked in jalva oil. It will dampen the magic—for a time."

"I made a mistake," I say. The admission is a foul tang against my tongue. "When warding Valen, I accidentally linked our life forces."

"Meaning?"

"Meaning what happens to me, happens to him, as well as the other way around."

Delkin laughs. "Fitting, I suppose. In a twisted way, I mean." His smile fades, his eyes narrowing just a bit. "He's your partner, correct? Based off that ridiculous Aphelian bond excuse?"

"Not a fan of the tradition?" I swing my legs around and over the side of the bed. The room sways and dips a bit, but it clears quickly.

He snorts. "Aphelian wasn't the person your people believe she was."

"You knew her?"

He frowns. "I thought I did, at one time." The hint of sadness in his voice falls heavily between us.

Something about the way he says it… "I don't suppose you'd like to elaborate?"

"I was forced to flee my homeland several years before the war. Anything I elaborated on would be nothing more than speculation." He leans back and scowls. The expression is so much like Valen's that it's haunting. "Besides, it's ancient history."

"It doesn't seem like ancient history. If she wasn't the person we think she was—who was she?"

Delkin's brows lift, his posture stiffening just a bit. "Aphelian was so blindly in love with Servis that it clouded her judgment."

"Judgment about what?"

He smiles, but it's not genuine. "Many, many things."

Another thing he and Valen have in common: the ability to talk in riddles. I know there's no point in pushing it. He's not going to tell me, and really, do I want to know? Aphelian was the hero of our people—and Valen's. What's in the past is in the past. I hesitate, then say, "Please don't tell him his magic is hurting me."

Delkin quirks a brow.

"If there's something wrong with me as a result of Valen's magic, it shouldn't affect him, right?"

He frowns, and it's impossible not to see the resemblance between him and his son. "No. Despite the link, the magic is Valen's, and he should suffer no ill effects."

I nod. "Good. Then I would appreciate keeping this between us."

"Daroose knows as well."

"I'll handle Daroose. Do I have your word?" Maybe it

isn't fair to ask him to keep this from his son, but I don't want Valen to find out. I know him. If he discovers the truth, he'll undoubtedly do something reckless to try to "save" me—and we can't afford that right now.

"I won't tell him if that's what you wish—but I think you should."

"I will. Eventually." I slip from the bed, and when I wobble a bit, Delkin is there to steady me. "We need to go. We're on our way to see my high priestess in Ventin Peaks. She can sever the link between us. I sent word of our progress to her a few hours ago."

"Days, you mean."

"What?" The air chills, and the bottom drops out from my stomach.

"You've both been asleep for four days now. We were starting to worry."

"Damn it!" I push past him and step into the sunshine. Across the way, Valen also appears. We stare at each other for a minute, and I'm not sure when I start moving, but soon I find myself in the center of the platform, face to face with him.

His brow furrows, lips twisting downward. "What Delkin was saying about Orbik...about my mother. I was so angry."

"I know."

His hand twitches like he intends to reach for me, but it stills. "I didn't mean for you to get hurt. Are you going to be okay?"

There's pain in his voice so deep that it steals my breath. How am I supposed to tell him that there's a chance he's hurting me each time the magic inside him flares? It's not something he can control. Maybe deep down, a part of him already knows. Maybe that's why I feel such strong spikes of guilt through the link sometimes. How can I confess to something that will make that worse?

I'm not sure if it's his desire to wrap his arms around me, or mine to him, but I'm suddenly cold from lack of contact. I shake it off and take a step back, slugging him hard in the arm. "Of course! You're a big baby. If I got hurt, you'd get hurt. Then I'd have to listen to you whine about it for days."

He fights a grin. "I'm glad you're — "

A commotion behind us is followed by a familiar voice shouting, "My druid!" Daroose flings himself across the platform and throws his arms around me. "I was so lost without you!"

I untangle myself from him and step away. "I trust you've stayed out of trouble?"

Delkin snickers. "Daroose will find trouble even when there's none to be found."

"How do you know each other?" Valen probably hoped we'd managed to ditch the kelpie, but I'm oddly happy to see him. I'm starting to realize how small my life in Lunal was, how constricted. There's so much more to Derriga than I imagined, and the individuals I've met along the way have kept me on my toes.

"We're old friends," Daroose says with a wink.

"Well, say goodbye." I gesture toward the floor. "We need to move. We've been asleep for four days."

Valen's eyes widen. "What?"

"I'd already sent a message to Levina. We need to hurry if we're to meet her in Ventin."

Delkin motions to Benj, who is hovering at the edge of a growing crowd of Fae. "Supplies," Delkin commands.

"Enough for five."

Benj nods and is gone.

"Five?" I ask.

"Benj and I will go with you. Do you honestly believe that after almost nineteen years, I'm going to let my son out of my sight?"

"Who will look after things here?" I ask. I can't tell how Valen feels about Delkin inviting himself on our little quest. I don't even know how he feels about meeting him. We haven't gotten a chance to talk, and I'm not getting anything through the link.

"Ander will watch over the village while I'm away."

"Really?" I balk. This whole situation is getting stranger and stranger by the minute. "You're leaving a human in charge of a Fae village?"

Valen groans.

Delkin simply smiles. "This isn't a Fae village. It's a village. A home. Everyone here is equal. I hope that by the end of our trip, you'll realize that."

It's a nice sentiment. One I would have believed at one time. Now? I'm starting to wonder.

28

Valen

Ander walks us to the southern edge of the village. Delkin, Daroose, Tania, and I start down another set of stairs, leaving Benj and Ander to their goodbyes. No one wants to intrude on such an intimate moment.

We hike in silence for a long time. Occasionally, I catch Tania looking at me. I get a spike of concern mixed with the smallest hint of fear, but it's fleeting, like she's trying hard to suppress something. Every time I meet her gaze, she turns away and the link goes cold. Does she know I'm hiding something world-changing? Is she getting suspicious?

We make it just over the old Summer Court boundary before stopping to set up camp for the night. Delkin and Daroose chat quietly on the other side of a roaring fire while Benj carves what looks like a small dragon out of a fallen tree branch.

"Bet this wasn't where you saw yourself ending up," I say to Tania. "Camping with three Fae and a kelpie." I laugh.

"Not in my wildest dreams." Tania plucks a weed from

the ground and twirls it between her fingers, watching as it transforms into a flower. "There was no point while I was growing up when I thought one day I'd know what it felt like to connect with someone."

Our eyes meet, and an entirely foreign sensation spreads through my body. Warm, almost electric. I fight the urge to brush a lock of stray hair from her shoulder. "Someone?"

"Some*thing*." She flushes, letting the small flower fall to the ground and dropping her gaze. "Obviously that's what I meant. The magic… What about you?" She clears her throat and inclines her head toward Delkin. "Unexpected, right?"

"I was raised to believe my father was a monster. A piece of rebel scum who kidnapped my mother and forced himself on her. To find that my entire life has been a lie? I'm still processing it all."

"But finding Delkin *was* a bonus."

Was it? It unlocks a way to get the answers I seek, but more than that? I'm still not sure. What am I supposed to do, moving forward? Stay with him in his treetop village? Spend this trip getting to know him, then forge my own way in this ruined world?

Then there's what I've learned about Orbik… I can't just let that go. Dealing with him will leave a vacancy on the throne—one I have no desire to fill.

"I have no idea where I am with Delkin—or where I want to be. Right now, I'm focused on dealing with this link."

"You mean fixing it."

"Huh?"

"You said dealing with the link."

"Oh. Well, obviously I want it fixed." The link was unexpected—and unwanted—but now that we've learned to live with it, is it really that bad? A part of me likes the connection. Sure, it was strange at first, but once we learned our way around it, it became oddly comforting. Just knowing, without a doubt, that Tania is here, relaxes me on a level I never imagined possible. It gives me... peace knowing that wherever she is, we're connected.

I can't lose her.

But telling her this? No. It seems like far too intimate a confession. Besides, keeping the link will only lead to disaster. Once I tell her about the tear, things will be different between us. That change is inevitable. Tania won't be able to look at me without seeing lies and betrayal and pain.

She may never forgive me...

"Obviously." She lifts her head and pins me with a stern glare. "Remember something, Valen. You have a chance that has passed me by. I don't know who my parents are, and I never will. I'll never meet my brothers or hear stories from their childhood. I'll never have the opportunity to speak with my mother or father."

She's right. There's no point making a rash decision when it comes to my newfound family—we still have some ways to travel. I pick the flower that she dropped out of the grass. It's small and delicate, and when the wind kicks up, the petals tear from the center and flutter away on the breeze.

I sigh. "I envy the druids of the past. The things they must have created..."

"You have an opportunity to change everything, Valen. To create something more beautiful than any flower."

The excitement in her eyes makes her entire face glow, and I can see her for what she truly is. Stunning and strong and full of far more hope than she'll have anyone believe. On one hand, it's breathtaking, and I wish I could see her like this more often. Yet on another, I don't like it. I don't like where this is headed. I don't like that a part of me hates the idea of breaking our link.

"Those villagers your uncle refuses to help—you can improve their lives now. You can help them fortify their home."

"How am I supposed to do that?"

Her brows furrow, and her confusion nearly knocks me over. "You heard Delkin. *You're* the true heir. Orbik isn't the rightful monarch—you are. The Fae won't turn away from you—you're not a bastard. You can turn it all around."

"The rightful— Are you—" How can she think I could—I'd *want* to—replace Orbik? "Why would you think I'd be pursuing the crown?"

Excitement sours and turns to anger. An acidic fog washes over me, burning my lungs with each breath as she says, "So, you're just going to let Orbik go unpunished for what he did to your mother?"

No. Orbik isn't going to get away with what he's done. My mind has churned with possibilities since Delkin revealed the truth. For the moment, I've settled on freezing him, inch by inch, and shattering the pieces. At least until I formulate a more gruesome end.

"I'm going to kill him myself."

She folds her arms. "Then who will rule the Winter Lands?"

"For all I care, Liani can take over." We're getting loud,

and the others are trying not to notice. Well, all except Daroose, who stares openly while chewing on something small with a tail. "She dealt with him all these years. She deserves it. She'll be a fair, kind ruler."

"Of course." Tania jumps to her feet. "Wouldn't want to exert yourself. Taking the crown would mean responsibility. No more days of lying around with a gaggle of girls and gallons of wine."

"No responsibility? Do you have any idea how much pressure it is to entertain that many women?" I flick my wrist at her. "As for the wine — if I don't drink it, who will?"

"You are unbelievable."

I open my mouth, then snap it shut. There's no point arguing with her. She's stubborn, and as far as she's concerned, she knows better than everyone else. I stand and storm into the woods. The more distance I put between us, the better. The weight of her disappointment is suffocating and unfamiliar. I never used to care what others thought about me. Then this damn human comes out of nowhere and suddenly decides she's going to be my conscience? Fuck that.

Fuck *all* of this.

How is it that someone so small, so unassuming, can cause me so much aggravation? From the moment she entered my life, the Aphelian has been nothing but trouble. This link must be messing with my head. To look at her and feel— Gods. What is wrong with me? To think I wanted to keep this infernal curse?

"Arrrrgh!" The roar echoes off the trees, bouncing through the valley before fading with an eerie warble.

"Does that make you feel better?" Benj emerges from the brush behind me. He eyes me for a moment before his gaze falls to my hands, to the icy mist rolling off of them.

"Is that what *he* thinks?" I flex my fingers, willing the cold to recede. "That I'm going to swoop in and save them all by stealing back my mother's throne?"

"I doubt Del has any expectations right now, aside from getting to know his son." He settles on a fallen log a few feet away. "Mori once said she hoped you would grow to right the wrongs of her ancestors. As for my older brother? Do I think he hopes you fight for what's yours? I do. He believes that the throne has never belonged to anyone more than it does you."

"He's your brother?"

Benj shrugs and throws up his hands. "Surprise. In one fell swoop, you gained a father and an uncle. Aren't you lucky?"

"Remains to be seen," I mumble, leaning back against the nearest tree. I take a closer look at him and can't believe I missed it. He has the same jaw as Delkin, the same crooked smile. But his eyes... They're deep blue. "What's up with the eyes? Mine and Delkin's are violet. Not a normal color for Fae. Yours are blue."

"Technically, Delkin is my half brother. Same father. His mother died in childbirth. We never saw it that way, though. I would die for him, and he, me."

"Must be nice..."

"You should know that when Mori found out the truth— the whole truth—she was all in. She didn't stay because of Del. Not at first. She stayed because she wanted to see her family fall. She wanted what was right."

"I'm not her. I don't know what I want." I sigh. "I don't even know how to hold my own life together right now."

"I imagine it's complicated."

"What is?"

"You and the druid. Being linked to someone while trying to hide something from them must take an enormous amount of energy."

"I don't know what you're talking about." I push off the tree and start to pace. "What could I possibly be — "

Benj shakes his head. "I have no idea what, but I can see it. So can Del." He shrugs. "Whatever it is, it must weigh heavily on you."

"I...know something." While I'm not ready to trust Delkin and Benj with my entire life's story, I feel the connection between us. I know, deep down, that they'd never purposefully hurt me. "I have information that Tania should— That she needs to know."

"And you don't want to tell her?"

"I do. But when she finds out, I'll lose her."

"And you don't want that..."

"Of course not!" The words come out in an impassioned rush, and Benj cocks his head to the side. "And then there are all these expectations she has..." I kick at a small red pebble. It skitters across the ground and bounces against a tree trunk. "I'm not a leader. I never will be."

He shrugs again. "Then so be it."

"But I'm going to kill Orbik."

His lip quirks, and he tilts his head again. "I think you and your father might disagree on that, but that honor is for you two to hash out."

"If I kill him and refuse the throne, who does that leave?" Can I really let Liani shoulder the burden herself? Liani, the only one who truly loved me growing up? She was there for every tear, every bruise... Can I really heap this burden on her?

"Kid, you gotta relax. Take one day at a time. Tackle things in priority order."

"And that would be?"

"You came out here to unlink yourself from the druid, right?"

"Right."

"That hasn't changed, has it?"

"Why in the Gods' names would it have changed?" The way he looks at me suggests he thinks it might have, and I wonder if Benj can see inside to the darkest parts of my mind.

Benj snickers. "She gets under your skin. No one has the power to do that unless they mean something to you." He studies me. "You're so worried about how she'll react to this big secret you have. That you'll lose her. Why worry if there's nothing going on between you?"

I snort. Something going on? Between Tania and me? I care for her, but not the way he's insinuating. Anyone with eyes could see that she's stunning. I'd have to be dead not to feel an attraction. That isn't the same as getting under my skin, though.

"We won't be swapping love stories, *uncle*." I tap my chest, directly over my heart. "I was warded as a child. A druid sigil that ensures I cannot ever fall in love—thank the Gods."

"If that's true, then I pity you."

"Please, don't. We fall in love just once in our entire existence. Once. If we're lucky, it's mutual and we create a claim. What happens to those of us like Delkin? My mother is gone. He will never know that kind of happiness again." I stare at him. "And you? Claiming a human? What will you do when Ander grows old and dies centuries before you do?"

"Your father was alive a very long time before Mori came along. It's true—he'll be a shadow of himself for the rest of his days, but the time they had together is enough to get him through." He frowns, and there's sadness in his eyes, but there's also joy. "As for Ander? You're young. Perhaps because of the ward, you cannot understand. When the right one comes along—human, Fae, male, female—it doesn't matter. Gender, lifespan—allegiances— you love who you love, Valen. It is the simplest thing there is."

It sounds anything but simple. I don't want to talk about this, but I also don't want to head back yet. Tania needs time to cool off, and so do I. Maybe spending some time with my uncle can help.

"How is Delkin able to become a wolf? He has no magic, right? I thought the Fae with animal souls were tied to magic?"

Benj frowns. There's an odd look in his eyes—a cross between annoyance and regret. "Delkin's wolf isn't connected to magic. It's who he is. Part of his soul."

"What about you? Do you have an inner animal?"

The lore tells us that Fae outside the royal line can transform because they're wild. Parts of their souls are still untamed, belonging more to nature. I should hate that part of myself, but I don't. I love the feeling that comes from running untethered and free.

And who knows what old stories are true? The more I learn about our history, the less I understand the life I've lived.

Benj grins and stands. "Would you like to see?"

"Is it a wolf, like Delkin and me?"

He doesn't say anything. Instead, he backs away. One step. Two steps. Three, four, five… Benj drops to all fours, and his body contorts in a macabre mangle of stretched flesh and twisting bone far more gruesome than I've ever seen. The sound of it turns my stomach. My own change is relatively quick. I suppose someone on the outside looking in might hear things, might be repelled by the sight, but I don't think it's anything as involved as this.

Slightly smaller than the tragon, Benj now stands covered in white scales, staring back at me with deep-blue eyes. A massive wingspan, fourteen or so feet, arches above us, flapping once and nearly sending me to the ground.

He huffs, then shakes his tremendous body before letting go of his dragon and slipping back into his Fae form. He grins. "Better than Del's, right?"

"Impressive," I say. "I'm a little jealous."

"Don't be. The wolf is noble. He's a leader, as are you."

"That's debatable."

He laughs and slaps a hand against my shoulder. "We should get—"

A horrible wail shatters the forest, shaking the ground and causing the trees to shudder. I sprint in the direction of the camp, and I'm only halfway back when my leg gives out.

Benj, who's right on my heels, drags me upright. "You're bleeding."

I am, but it's not my wound. "*Tania*." The name is both a curse and a prayer on my tongue. "The camp is being attacked."

29

Keltania

I duck as the creature strikes again, crashing through the trunk of a tree like it's nothing more than a twig. Splinters scatter in all directions, several impaling my hip and torso. I bite back a scream and tuck myself behind the nearest rock to take inventory.

A spike of pain courses through me, and I touch the smallest of the three barbs protruding from my body. "Damn it." They're too deep to simply remove. Two in my side and one in my hip, my leg is bleeding, and I'll have several brightly colored bruises when this is over.

If we survive.

I turn to the nearest tree and wedge my foot into the bark, but when I lift my arms to begin climbing, the air rushes from my lungs and my vision blurs. The splinters of wood still embedded in my side make it impossible to haul myself up.

Limping, I throw myself behind a massive boulder as the snakelike creature rounds for another go. This time, it catches sight of Delkin perched on a branch a few feet from me. The monster races for him, and Delkin smiles, spreading his arms and free-falling from the tree. Just before he hits the ground, he changes, a white wolf dropping in place of the tall Fae.

With massive fangs and a threatening snarl, the elder Fae is a sight to behold. The creature backs away several feet, and Delkin whirls. He catches a mouthful of my tunic and hefts me up the tree, to the lowest branch. "How badly are you hurt?" he asks after changing back.

I grimace as I try to straighten my leg. There's blood down the front of my leathers, and I don't have to inspect the splinters to know they've embedded even farther in my side. "These wounds won't do much to a Fae. I'm sure Valen is fine."

"I'm sure he is. I was asking about you."

"I doubt it'll kill me." I bite down hard against an involuntary shudder and survey the ruined camp. "What is that thing?"

"Yorger. They used to be docile, except during mating season. But the landscape, the ecosystem—it's all changed now. Apparently, they've become predators."

"The braid—" I lift my arm. "Does this block the druid magic as well?"

His brows furrow. "Druid magic? I don't understand. You said—"

Valen obviously hasn't told him about the rabbit or the forest. "The theory is, since Valen has Fae magic, he's... predisposed? He seems able to tap into the latent druid magic in the Winter Lands. Maybe because he's lived there his whole life? We don't know." Below us, the yorger howls. "A section of forest was rejuvenated. I—*we*—made it happen. Being linked to Valen, I seem able to tap into the Fae power as well."

Delkin's expression is unreadable, but I get the feeling there's something he's not saying. "Valen is very powerful. We knew that the day he was born. It doesn't surprise me he's able to harness it."

I nod. It's what we thought; still, it feels better to have someone else make the connection. "There was also a rabbit on the path—" I have an idea.

The rabbit...the bird back at Delkin's village... The strange crow seemed to be the only animal I was unable to contact. This is worth a shot... "We were able to communicate with it," I tell him.

His gaze goes to the yorger. It rages below us, shredding the remains of our camp. "You mean to try speaking with the beast?"

"I'm not sure if it will work without Valen." In Vey Brill, he was closer. Now, well, I have no idea where he's gone off to. I hold up the arm he tied the bracelet to. "If I take this off, is it possible?"

"Jalva oil is known to dampen all inner magics. The amount on the braid won't block the power completely, but since you'd need to tap into Valen to access it and it's not even clear how he's using the magic, I'm not sure it would work."

"So, I'd need to remove the bracelet?"

He frowns as the yorger flings itself at the base of our tree. We both wobble but remain perched on our branch. "I don't recommend it."

"I can take it off for a minute, then put it right back. If I can communicate with it, we can see what has it riled up."

Delkin doesn't look convinced, but he nods once. I undo the knot and slip the band from my wrist, then close my eyes and focus on the creature as it thrashes and howls beneath us.

"What do you want?"

The yorger stills. *"Stole my hatchlings."*

"Who?" I glance at Delkin. "It says someone attacked its children. Took them."

He shakes his head. "Yorger nests are impossible to miss. We haven't passed one. I've only seen one in a decade, and that was miles before our village."

The yorger lets out a howl. *"You."*

"I promise, we've done no harm to your offspring."

"Like you."

Acid churns in my stomach.

"Fae with weapons. Caged them. Took them."

If Orbik's guards are still following us and they're the ones who raided the yorger nest, they can't be far behind. I grip the edge of the branch and ease myself down to the ground. Delkin tries to stop me, but I shake him off. The yorger's anguish is like a knife in my gut. Valen can live his life while others suffer and not lift a finger? Fine. But not me.

"I will find them. I will return your hatchlings. I promise."

"Honor, Druid."

With a final snort, the yorger slithers into the brush, and I retie the red leather band to my wrist. A second later, Valen and Benj erupt from the tree line like they're being chased.

Benj skids to a stop, eyes immediately finding Delkin. The relief I see there would have stolen my breath if someone aimed it my way. "What—"

Delkin jumps down from the tree and claps Benj on the shoulder. "Yorger." He gestures to me. "Our fair druid friend handled it."

"You're bleeding," Valen says. He pushes past Benj and starts toward me.

"You are, too." I gesture to the matching bloodstains on his leathers and limp off to search the scattered remains of our supplies. The yorger displaced them throughout the campsite, and I'm sure some ended up in the river. I just hope the first aid supplies survived.

Daroose emerges from the brush moments later. He has an armful of wood for the fire, and when he surveys the site, he sighs. "I leave you all alone for a few minutes…"

"Everyone's fine." I sift through a pile containing several pieces of ruined fruit. "Except the supplies."

The kelpie inhales, then scrunches up his nose. His lips pucker like he tastes something foul. "Is that…yorger I smell?"

I give up the search and straighten, hobbling to the nearest tree. "We had a visitor. Did you see any of the medical supplies on the way in?"

Daroose drops the firewood and takes my arm, winding it around his shoulders to support my weight. My leg is numb, and the shards in my side dig deeper with each movement. Shooting a glare at Valen, he helps me to one of the large boulders on the edge of camp. He removes his shirt and hands it to me. "Try to stop that bleeding. I'll see what I can scrounge up."

Daroose sifts through the yorger's wreckage as I unlace my leather cuirass. I gingerly slip my arms from the holes and let it fall to the ground as I hold my breath, the smallest motion doing its best to coax out a scream.

"Let me help you." Valen holds his side as he kneels in front of me. There are traces of blood on his pants and tunic, but not nearly as much as mine. "If for no other reason than because I'm not in the mood to feel those sticks poking out of my side all damn day."

"Not your strongest argument." I grit my teeth as I reach back to unlace my red linen shirt. "Right now, I'm kind of thrilled at the idea of you in pain."

From across the camp, I swear Benj snickers.

Valen grumbles something I can't quite hear, then stands and swats my useless hand away. He undoes the string himself, then carefully lifts the cloth. I let him tuck the material under my biceps. I'm still covered as far as modesty is concerned, yet I feel more exposed with him sitting there than I ever have.

Daroose returns, glaring even harder at Valen. "You can turn around now, little Fae. Nothing for *you* here."

"Just pull out the wood, Daroose." I roll my eyes and meet Valen's gaze. He hasn't turned away. If anything, he's more focused, eyes locked on mine. I tamp down the involuntary shiver that races up my spine and clear my throat. "Valen will dress my wound, and then we'll go find the yorger's hatchlings."

Everyone's heads snap in my direction.

Oh. I haven't told them yet.

"I think Orbik's guards are following us," I say.

Valen tries to cover one of my bleeding wounds with a cloth, but Daroose slaps his hand away. "That's impossible. They couldn't have tracked us here. We're too far from the Winter Lands."

"Well, someone raided the yorger's nest and stole its hatchlings. It said the thieves were Fae with weapons."

"That could be anyone." Benj finds the bandages and throws the sack to Daroose. "The depleted still roam these parts."

I suck in a breath and dig my fingers into the leather of my pants as Daroose gingerly pulls out one of the bigger shards of wood. "Depleted?"

"Years after the Great Drain, some of the Fae—the ones who relied most on magic—started going into withdrawal." Benj shudders. "They *changed*. Became vacant and driven by rage."

"Their minds essentially rotted," Delkin interjects. "They became feral. We've seen a few around these parts, though they're not really organized enough to raid a yorger nest."

Daroose finishes securing the bandage on my midsection, then starts on my leg. He's surprisingly gentle. "We can handle the big bad worm stealers if you're frightened, little Fae. I'm sure you could stay here and babysit what's left of our things."

Valen kneels in front of me as Daroose goes to join Delkin and Benj in trying to scavenge what's left of our supplies. He nods to my wrist, toward the red braid Delkin gave me. "Where'd you get that?"

"One of the human kids back at Delkin's village," I lie. I want to tell him more—the truth that this small braid is what's probably responsible for keeping me upright—but he has enough to worry about right now. As soon as we get to Ventin, as soon as Levina fixes my mistake, then it won't matter anymore. Until then, I just hope it's enough. I start to stand, but he stops me.

"We're in this together. You know that, right?" His voice is soft and rings with a level of concern that makes me squirm. His gaze keeps flicking to the braid.

"I—" My throat is suddenly tight, the words lodging like stale bread. Sickly sweet and cloying, my belly churns, and my heart thunders an erratic beat, rebelling against a flood of emotion.

"It's not just the link, Tania," he says. "I don't want— I know there's something you're not telling me."

There's no anger in his tone. It sparks a wash of guilt, which, judging by the flash of justification in his eyes, he feels. "Valen—" Why the hell do I feel so bad about keeping a secret from him? I'm doing it for his own damned good! Let's not forget that he himself is hiding something from me, too! "How about we trade. You tell me what you're hiding, and I'll tell you what I'm hiding."

He stares at me but says nothing.

"Well then, there's your answer."

He stands and shakes his head. "You're stubborn and ornery and refuse to compromise, but you've become… important to me. I always respected you—our partnership— but it's more than that now."

"So serious!" I tease. "Who would have thought it possible?"

His gaze meets mine, and a shimmer of challenge gleams. "You might be surprised at what's possible." He turns on his heel and goes to join the others.

I watch him for a moment, wavering just a bit in my choice not to tell him the truth.

It doesn't take long to find what we're looking for. The party of five is stomping through the brush, making little attempt at stealth. They're dressed in the Winter Court's colors, and in the back of their camp, there's a small cage with three yorger hatchlings.

"Told you so."

Valen snorts. "Fine. I'll just ice them, and we can grab the slimy bugs and be on the way." He lifts a hand and takes a deep breath, but Delkin snatches it, pulling him—and me—past Daroose and Benj, away from the tree line.

"Stop. No magic."

Valen narrows his eyes. "Those are Orbik's men. We have two choices: allow them to see us and keep following—or kill them."

Delkin drags us back to the trees and points at something through the leaves. "That's a sniffer. Probably how they tracked you this far."

By the fire, off to the right of the men, there's a huddled figure wrapped in a hooded purple cloak. It's small and slender, and when it shifts and the hood of its cloak moves aside, I see dark blue scales covering a long, pointed snout. The thing brings a gnarled finger tipped with wicked claws up to swat away several flies buzzing around its head.

"What's a sniffer?" I ask.

Valen shudders. "You mean besides hideous?"

"Sniffers are rare," Delkin says. "Old, old blood, back from before the Fae walked in Derriga. They're able to smell magic from miles away."

"So every time we…" Valen pales. "Gods. We've been making it *easy* for them."

"You couldn't have known," Delkin says with a frown.

"Now what? With no magic, how are we supposed to get the worms without them seeing us?" We've wasted so much time already.

"We could always just kill them," Benj says with a shrug. He stands behind us, sharpening his blade. "My dragon is feeling a bit peckish."

"No. These Fae are hunting us, but they do so at my uncle's command. Who knows what lies Orbik told them? They might believe Tania and I are true enemies of the court. Or, more likely, that Tania has kidnapped me. If they think that, they'll injure me badly—not enough to kill me, but more than enough to take down a human."

Benj snorts and opens his mouth, but one look from Delkin and he clams up.

I steal another quick glance at the camp. The sniffer sits unmoving by the fire. "Then I don't see why we don't charge in, take the hatchlings, and fight our way out. Aim to incapacitate. In, out, on our way."

Benj slips his sword into its sheath. "Valen and Delkin cannot be seen together. If anyone were to—"

"If word gets back to Orbik that Valen found his father, they might think he'll betray them. No way to know what they'd do with that information," Delkin says. I don't miss the way Delkin aims a subtle shake of his head toward Benj or how the warrior cringes just a little at the nonverbal scolding. "But if there was no way to tell we were related..."

Benj laughs. "Good idea."

Delkin turns to me. "Your sigils are not traceable magic."

A mask sigil. He wants me to change their appearance.

"I wouldn't ask, but—"

"No. It's a good idea." I hold up a hand and step back. Digging into my belt, I untie the pouch containing my ink. "It has to be close to the eyes. I need something reflective so I can see myself."

Benj rummages through his pack and pulls out a small glass box. "Will this work?"

I settle on a large rock and prop the box up in front of me, then dip a finger into the ink. The sigil is simple: a crudely drawn eye. It's the first sigil I've done since we ended up linked, and as I move my finger and try not to cringe, I know Valen feels the sting of the magic as it seeps into my skin. It takes all my strength not to show how badly it hurts. When I'm done, Valen is staring at me, his expression a mix of pain and confusion. I told him the sigils don't hurt.

He knows I lied.

30

Valen

I didn't expect the rush of needlelike pain when Tania traced the sigil below her eye. That day she warded me, she said it didn't hurt. Was it like that for her each time she used a sigil? That sharp, biting pain that, even now, close to ten minutes later, still lingers?

"Amazing," Delkin says as he leans closer to the small glass box. With her finger, as she did to me at the estate, she traces the same symbol onto his cheek that she put onto her own skin. At least he doesn't have the same reaction to it I had—that feeling of euphoria. "My eyes are brown now."

"I don't understand why it makes so much of a difference," I say. "It's not like we're going to allow them to gaze into our eyes as we're stealing the yorgers back."

"If you want to break the link, we need to take every precaution possible." Delkin's gaze meets mine. "If they were to make the connection, I promise you, you would not make it to Ventin."

"And why is th—"

The bushes behind us rustle, and a second later, several

Winter Guards burst through. "Don't move!" the one in front shouts.

They emerge from the brush, one by one, the last coming through holding the end of a chain. At the end of that chain is the sniffer, and Gods, it's worse than the brief glimpse we got before. Its long snout twitches as it snaps at the air, twice in my direction. Thick yellow-tinted mucus drips from the corners of its mouth.

"Valen, nephew of the Winter Lord, are you safe? Have they harmed you?"

So, I was right. They spun it as a kidnapping. Liani knew the truth, but what could she have said? If she admitted to helping us leave the palace, surely Orbik would have punished her. Knowing what I now know about him, I can only imagine what that penalty would entail.

I step to the front of the group and bow. "Warriors, it is honorable that you came, but I assure you that I'm well. The Aphelian did not force me to leave the estate. I chose to do so of my own free will."

The guards exchange confused glances. The one in charge—I've seen him around the estate a few times—stiffens. "Be that as it may, we'll have to ask that you return with us. Your uncle worries for your safety. These are dangerous lands."

"I'm sure you wouldn't mind conveying my good health to my uncle. Tell him I'll return to the estate shortly."

The leader frowns. "I'm going to have to insist you return with us."

"Have I suddenly become a prisoner in my own home?" I offer them a lazy grin.

He shifts from foot to foot, clearly uncomfortable. His gaze lands on Tania, and he scowls. "I can't imagine there's anything out here that you can't do back at the estate."

Tania shifts. If she goes for her sword—like I know she wants to—they'll cut her down in an instant. "I'm fine," I tell him. "My current...guides...are well acquainted with the area."

The soldiers exchange glances, then turn to Delkin. The Fae in charge steps forward. "By the order of Lord Orbik, I demand that you stand aside and allow us to return Valen to his family."

Delkin is quiet, but the subtle shift in his demeanor is unmistakable. Relaxed but cautious, to eerily, silently enraged. Three steps. That's what he takes until he stands in front of the guardsman who leads the group.

"Return him to his *family*?" His voice is like ice, eyes pinning the guard in place. Fury blazes like I've never seen before. Something dark and primal. I wonder what a force he must have been back when the Fae were at their strongest.

The guards must see it, too, because they all reach for their weapons. "Stand down, or we will use deadly force."

Tania draws her sword and swings the blade, twirling it in an intricate series of swipes and twists. "I'm fairly sure you have no idea what that entails."

"Del," Benj says quietly.

My father is beside me now, still staring at the guards.

"Del," Benj tries again, this time with more force. "She's a *druid*, remember? You need to—"

Daroose sighs. The kelpie's posture is casual, but there's an unmistakable spark of concern in its eyes. "Someone really should have explained druid empath abilities to her."

Empath abilities? That definitely sounds like something Tania should have been given a heads-up about.

"How about I offer an alternate choice." Tania steps between us and the soldiers, blade still in hand. "Turn around and slink back to your lord. Tell Orbik that no harm will come to his nephew so long as you leave us be. When I'm finished, I'll return him, safe and sound."

Benj groans.

"Stand aside," the one in front demands.

Tania smiles again, this time wider. It's dark and full of promise and makes the hair on my arms jump to attention.

There's movement at the back of the guard, followed by a flash of silver. In the distance, the echoing sound of a crow's caw shatters the air, and someone in the back row hurls a blade through the group. Tania ducks aside, deftly moving from its path. It strikes Delkin instead, embedding in his forearm.

The air stills, and no one moves or says a word. Delkin stands calmly, the blade protruding from his skin. He looks more irritated than anything else. Benj wears a similar expression, while Tania... Her face twists with fury. A moment passes, and then another.

She turns her back on them, and our eyes meet. There's something unsettling in her stare. Something older than both of us, and more raw. Her feline grin promises darkness, and my stomach clenches.

I move to stop her, but she says, "I warned them."

Tania's fingers knot tight, the skin of her knuckles turning pale. When she releases them, each digit is rigid and frosty. A second later, the temperature plummets, and the sound of crackling ice fills the clearing. It creeps across the ground, coating the dirt and bracken with frost. Encasing everything in ice...

Orbik's men, the sniffer... They're all frozen solid.

31

Keltania

Finally, they shut up. These bastards who will tread on anything—anyone—with the simplest word from their *Winter Lord*. A false king. An imposter. A thief.

A murderer.

I hate these Fae, but in the back of my mind, I know something is wrong. The ferocity of my rage toward them borders on unearthly. Like they've wronged me personally. Taken everything I love and forced me into the darkness. Not to mention I shouldn't be able to do what I've done since Delkin gave me the braid. I look down.

The braid soaked in jalva oil is gone.

No…

Daroose positions himself between me and the frozen guard. He takes my hands. "Keltania, it is done. You've subdued them. We can return the disgusting little young to their mother and be on our way."

I glance down at my hands, clasped in his. "Step away."

Daroose, of course, doesn't listen. He's still speaking, but with each word, his voice grows more distant until the only sound I can focus on is the thundering of my own pulse. I grip his wrists and hold tight, and a thin layer of ice creeps across his skin.

The kelpie yelps, and Benj drags him away.

"Tania." Delkin takes Daroose's place. "Listen to me carefully." His voice breaks through the haze, but I can't focus on it. It's the guards, trapped in ice yet still breathing, that hold my attention.

Valen tries to push his father aside, but Delkin holds his ground.

"You are the first druid in centuries to tap into this level of power. It's been a very long time, and your people— they've forgotten what it's like. Now that you can access magic, you have a chance to form an empathetic bond to all living things around you. I imagine it's getting stronger, and it will take time to understand how to control it. Add to that the bond you have with Valen and his magic, and you are lethal—to others and yourself. The anger you feel? That red-hot rage? That is mine. It's my fault, and I beg you to hear me, to concentrate on my voice before you do something you'll regret."

In the deepest pit of my soul, his words pluck at something tangible. Some small part of me that fights for control. It twitches, remembering the newly thriving patch of forest, given life—not death.

Valen finally manages to push Delkin aside and takes my face in his hands. I'm numb, frozen to the most inner parts of my body, yet in all the places his skin touches mine, something pulses. A spark I don't quite understand.

"Tania, let it go. We can take the yorgers and leave." His brow furrows, and his lips pull up at the corner. Like there's an odd taste in his mouth. "I…I know you. Fae or not, you wouldn't harm these men for no reason."

He's right. I wouldn't harm the Fae—or any living creature—without provocation. The problem here was, they attacked us first. Some small seed deep inside me refuses to let that go.

I tear myself from his grip, fighting hard against the two warring impulses raging in my mind.

Walk away.

Destroy them.

Walk away.

Destroy them.

They are whispers fighting for attention, and with each passing moment, they get louder and louder, threatening to split my head in two. My knees buckle, and the world around me swims violently. Something wells in my chest, a bubble that will surely suffocate me if not released. I lift my head, meeting the frozen gaze of the Winter Guard leader the moment a scream tears from my throat.

Monster. He serves a monster and deserves to die!

A second later, they all shatter.

As we make our way farther into Kanadia, the former home of the Summer Court, Delkin repeatedly apologizes. He explains that not only do I have to deal with Valen's moods and bad habits, but there's always a chance I can pick up the strong emotions of others in proximity. The stronger the personality, the better the chance. It makes me wonder if we, as druids, were given a gift in disguise when we lost our magic.

I tuck my legs in tight, curling into a ball a few feet from tonight's campfire. I still see their faces the instant before it happened. The broken pieces, the chunks of icy limbs, all scattered across the land I turned into a battlefield with a single flick of my wrist. Is this what Valen has to deal with daily? The constant fear that he might hurt someone if pushed too far?

And if I have to worry about the emotions of others, should I fear Delkin? What if his temper is just as volatile as his son's? On some level, I understand his reaction. His son and his mate were taken from him. I can't even fathom that kind of loss.

"I know you're awake," I hear. On the other side of the fire, Valen shifts.

I'm not comfortable with this new turn of events. How far will this link push me? "Would you like a medal?"

"I would." He snickers softly. "Of course, it would have to be awarded for most charming personality. Or perhaps most perfect ass."

"You forgot Fae most likely to be tossed off a cliff."

"You'll have to present the award to me personally, of course. Preferably wearing—"

"I'm sure that troll from the bridge would rather do the honor. And you'd be roasting over a spit, no doubt."

"I'll miss that, I think."

I uncurl and sit up. My mind is racing, and I'm not going to get any sleep. "Miss what?"

"That bitter sarcasm."

"Is there some reason I would stop being sarcastic?" I nudge a small spider from the edge of my bedroll. It pauses, almost as if apologizing, before scampering on its way.

He watches me for a moment before shrugging.

"You're not always going to be around, Tania."

I lift a finger to my throat and make a slashing motion. "Planning something, Valen?"

He laughs. "I doubt you plan on sticking around after we get this link broken. I know I can be…a bit much. I'm sure this whole ordeal has been eye-opening." There's something in his eyes that tells me he wants to say more, but when he doesn't, I don't push. After all, I'm keeping a secret from him, too. I have no place to demand that he bare his soul to me if I won't do the same.

"I know who you are, Valen. I've learned to live with it. Trust me, I'm not going anywhere." Where would I go, anyway? Back to Lunal? Not a chance. They're my people, yes, but that place holds nothing for me. Valen is all I have, now; my duty is all I need.

"Too bad I've no interest in the crown." He sinks back to the ground, shuffling to find a comfortable spot. "I might have asked you to be my head of security."

I snort and lie down as well. "Like I would ever agree to something like that. You'd have a better chance convincing Daroose to let *you* ride him."

"Over my dead body," Daroose interjects sleepily from across the fire.

"Seriously, though… We don't know what will happen. You could discover something…" He pauses. "About my personality you can't stand."

"Or one of us could die," I say quietly. I need to tell him. In case something happens. "Valen, I—"

"Good night, Keltania," he says softly.

I sigh. "Night, Valen."

. . .

We travel through the woods for three days, avoiding trails until we hit a small piskie hamlet. Delkin announces that we're far enough away from prying eyes, saying he and Benj have some business to see to.

I can't imagine what business they have in a piskie town. Piskie and Fae aren't natural enemies by any stretch, but they aren't notorious allies, either. Our history books tell us they fought together in the Ogre Wars out of necessity, and that piskies favor the warmer lands but don't usually stick their necks out for outsiders—they keep to themselves and expect everyone else to do the same.

Before he disappeared into the town, I cornered Delkin and asked if there was any way to get our hands on jalva oil. Since losing the braid—his theory is that the power surge during our encounter with Orbik's men ate it up—the power has been building again, the pressure threatening to force its way from my body in a violent explosion I fear would hurt someone. But we're out of luck. The jalva plant only grows in a small section of land near Vey Brill. We don't have time to double back.

"I haven't been to a piskie town in over six hundred years." Daroose wedges himself between Valen and me, then slings an arm lazily around my shoulder. He inclines his head toward the tavern on the other side of the square. "Then again, I haven't been anywhere in six hundred years, so…"

"How long did they say they were going to be?" I take in the square. There are several piskies going about their day, offering us confused glances. Slightly shorter than average humans, the piskies are winged Fae with an affinity for nature. They can shrink themselves to the size of a rosebud and are said to commune with animals. There's a theory that the druids weren't one hundred percent human and shared a common ancestor with them, but I never believed it.

Valen stretches. "They didn't say. But if it's safe enough to be here now, maybe we could spend a night. I wouldn't say no to an actual bed."

I shiver. "And a warm fire." Ever since I lost the braid, I've been cold. Not freezing, but definitely colder than I should be given the warmer climate.

"I'd love some ale!" Daroose exclaims and sighs. "How I missed ale…"

Before I know what's happening, the kelpie drags me across the square and straight to the tavern doors. It's still early; the sun is just beginning to set, so the place is quiet.

He stops short as we get to the building, then reaches around and tugs my hair free from its bindings.

"Hey!"

"Shh," he says, shooing away my hands. "You need to cover those round ears of yours. We don't want anyone asking why a human is keeping company with a Fae." He sobers and points to my face. "Can you…"

My sigils. The initiation sigil and the one under my eye.

I close my eyes and focus on unmarked skin. The mask sigil warms for a moment before going cold.

"Perfect!" Daroose exclaims. He makes a show of arranging my hair around my face, then pushes me inside. Valen trails behind.

There's a purple-haired piskie in the corner, nursing a red drink from a large glass. Every few seconds, he hiccups, sending a burst of pink bubbles into the air. He pops all but one, letting the sole survivor float until it crashes against the ceiling. With a hysterical chortle, he begins the process all over again.

The only other patron is a stocky piskie with beautiful, bright-orange hair and golden eyes. She's dancing in the center of the room, twirling and laughing and humming to the lively tune played on a lute by a Fae at the far side of the room.

Daroose leans against the bar and grins. "Have you ever had piskie ale?"

"Can't say that I have." I glance back at Valen, who is hovering by the entrance, peering out the window.

"Then allow me to buy you your very first." He taps the bar. "Barkeep. Two glasses of your finest ale, please!"

"We don't have any money."

"This is a piskie village." He reaches over and unwraps one of the decorative leather strands on my sleeve, around my forearm, then slaps it on the bar. "With *this* we can drink like kings."

The barkeep's eyes widen as he lifts the leather. With an assessing once-over, he nods at Daroose and disappears. When he returns a moment later, he has two small glasses filled to the brim with dark-red liquid.

I sniff the drink. A cross between hilpberries and sandalwood. "That doesn't look the least bit appetizing."

"Trust me. Would I steer you wrong?" He nods to my neck, where his collar hangs. "Even if I wanted to—which I don't—I couldn't."

Aside from the unintentional taste I've gotten through the link with Valen, I've never had alcohol. It isn't allowed at the Order. On the rare occasion we went into the main town, the barkeeps knew we weren't to be served. Curiosity piqued, I pick up the glass and take a sip. The taste is surprisingly sweet and has a slightly fizzy sensation as it slides down my throat. "Not what I expected."

"Told you. Now, just be sure to—"

The glass is small, so I tip it back and drain the remainder in one, satisfying swig.

"—take it slow." Daroose's eyes go wide, and his mouth falls open. "Um…"

Valen appears on my other side. He glares at Daroose. "Um?"

The kelpie pushes away from the bar and throws up his hands. "You're really not supposed to chug it…"

"Was that bad?" I pick up the cup and swirl the tiny bit left at the bottom. The red liquid coats the glass, and for some reason, it's the funniest thing I've ever seen.

I laugh, and Valen, who's been glaring angrily at Daroose until now, joins me.

"Everything all right?" The barkeep leans against the counter. He has my leather ribbon draped around his neck like a prize. "She only had one. Don't normally hit the Fae like that."

I open my mouth to tell him that I am most certainly not Fae, but Daroose slaps his hand against my lips. "First drink. Girl's a lightweight." The piskie nods and shuffles off, and Daroose turns his attention to Valen, who is tapping his foot to the beat of the piskie girl's humming. "What in the Goddess's name is wrong with *you*?"

Valen jabs a finger in my direction and snickers. "Tania's drunk."

"I am not!" I hurl my empty glass at him. He manages to move, and it shatters against the wall behind him. It's the single most amusing thing I've ever seen. A giggle escapes my lips, then turns into a hysterical chortle. I catch the bartender's annoyed gaze as I topple off my stool.

"Apologies." Daroose hefts me off the floor and scoops me into his arms while Valen continues to laugh. "I'll just get them out of your hair."

Out into the fading light, Daroose carries me to the edge of the square as Valen trails behind. I wave to him, giggling as he skips after us. I can't recall ever seeing him so damned happy! The smile on his face makes everything about him more extraordinary. His eyes are brighter, his cheekbones sharper. Several shorter strands of inky black hair escape the ponytail he's pulled them into, fluttering into his face. He's beautiful.

"For the love of— Stop staring at him!" Daroose grabs my face and turns it away from Valen. "You look like you're about to start drooling."

"Sorry. He's just so pretty."

Valen stomps his foot and jabs a finger at us. "Ah-ha!"

The kelpie is furious, and I don't understand why. Doesn't he feel what I do? He had the same amount to drink as me. He should be dancing and singing and laughing his kelpie heart out in appreciation of all the beauty around us! "Kelpie needs to smile more." I pinch his cheek as he sets me down under a large hickory tree.

Valen lumbers up and throws an arm around Daroose's shoulder. "She's right, you know. You might not be as irritating if you smiled more." He waves a hand in front of his face. "And bathed."

Daroose snorts and ducks out of Valen's reach. "Says the little Fae with a permanent scowl on his lips." The kelpie inclines his head toward me. "Except, of course, when you're sneaking a peek at *my* druid."

Valen scrunches up his nose. "*Yours?* Don't you belong to *her*—not that she actually wants you." He whirls to me, his lips turning down. "You don't actually want the stupid man-horse, do you?"

"Stupid horse?" Daroose stomps his foot. "Hang on a minute."

I stand and wedge myself between them, throwing one arm over Daroose's shoulder and the other around Valen's waist. "What if I said I wanted both of you?"

The kelpie's eyes widen, and Valen pales.

I lean over and kiss his cheek. "Or if I said I wanted neither of you!"

I dislodge from them both and bound across the square, to the edge of the farthest row of trees. This morning, I had so much to think about, so many worries and fears. Now they seem to have slipped away, and I wonder how I haven't suffocated beneath the weight of them all.

The tree closest to me is tall with tiny, waxy leaves and delicate, bright-pink blooms. "These are amazing. What are they?"

Daroose groans and joins me at the tree. He picks one of the flowers and places it in the palm of my hand. "Piskie bell. They only grow in areas where the piskies have settled. The piskie's natural pheromones promote growth. It's what they use to make the ale."

The pink flower is so fragile, so small that it's hard to see. I can fix that, though. I'm a damned druid! Closing my eyes, I imagine the flower growing larger. The smooth skin of the petals stretches, and the weight in my hand increases.

"What are you doing!" Daroose snatches the thing and

hides it behind his back. "Are you trying to give yourself away? If someone sees—"

I try to get the flower back, but he steps out of reach.

Thankfully, Valen is closer. He snatches the bloom. "It *is* pretty. I know what would make it prettier, though." He blows out, and a cloud of frosty air engulfs the flower. When it clears, the thing is encased in ice. He hands it to me. "Here. Something worthy of such a being of beauty."

Daroose makes a gagging sound. "I'm going to be sick."

"Do I want to know why the barkeep told us to come round up our children?" Delkin stops a few feet from the tree line, arms folded and scowl firmly in place.

Benj, on the other hand, is grinning from ear to ear. "Being of beauty? Really? If I didn't know any better, I'd say someone ingested a fair bit of piskie ale."

"I might have accidentally given Tania some while we greeted the locals," Daroose says. He sounds apologetic, and I don't understand why. He did me an amazing favor. I've never felt so free, so alive.

Benj snickers, and Delkin grumbles something too low for me to hear before saying, "Come on. I got us a room for the night. They can sleep it off, and we can get moving in the morning."

Sleep? And miss this? Not a chance. No, there's too much fun to be had...

32

Valen

Tania is sprawled on her back on the narrow bed next to mine. She's been humming for the last half hour. It's a vaguely familiar tune, and I wonder if it's something I heard once or if the link between us has gotten so strong that I've started remembering things from her memory.

"That's pretty. What is it?"

She stops humming and sighs. "There was a tale Levina told when we were children. That was the tune the minstrel played as she spoke."

"Sounds like it was a happy story."

"It was a horribly violent tale." Her soft laugh slowly turns into an all-out chortle. A month ago, I would have found the sound grating. Now? I wish she'd do it more often. "Everyone died in the end."

"What are you thinking about?"

I turn to find Tania watching me. She tilts her head to one side and says, "You, actually."

From the moment we crossed the threshold, I've secretly stolen over a dozen glances at her. Somewhere along the line, the sight of her started making my chest feel heavy in the most amazingly confusing yet electric way. I want her. Want her in a way I've never wanted another.

The piskie ale is still working its way through her system, making *my* head swim. That has to be it. That, or the fact that she's so different from the others I've grown up with. No Fae I know has hair like fire and a mixture of hard and soft curves that I itch to touch. We don't question everything or fight when there is no hope.

The Fae at court treat me as though I'm just as much a royal as my uncle. Most bow and scrape and fight for my approval. None of them get under my skin like Tania. None make me feel supremely weak yet able to freeze the world at the same time. I've never been challenged or questioned, and I'm not sure I can go back to the way things were.

"I bet I would fall in love with you," I say absently. "If I weren't warded against it."

She swings her legs around and dangles them off the edge of the bed. "One *proper* kiss, and I'd probably shatter that sigil to bits."

"You already kissed me, remember?" I thump my chest. "Sigil still stands."

"Well, I wasn't really trying. That was a peck at best. Not a proper kiss at all."

If that was a peck, then there's a good chance I wouldn't survive a real kiss from Tania. "Sounds like a challenge to me."

I sit up and face her as my pulse hammers. Part of me feels the ale fading from her system, but another part refuses to acknowledge it. If the ale is still present, then anything we do, anything we say, can be written off as an inconvenient side effect.

"I'm very curious to see if you're right," I tell her.

She stands and crosses the small space between the beds, stopping next to mine so that she towers over me. Another might find it intimidating. As a society, Fae don't generally yield to the fairer of our race. I, however, find it intoxicating. Not knowing what she'll do—yield to the desire I feel emanating from her or slit my throat in response to the secret I carry. She wants me the same way I want her, but what she'll do about that is anyone's guess.

She leans in, painfully close. A strand of her fiery hair falls forward and tickles the side of my cheek. "What of my ward? Think you're man enough to break it?"

I stand to meet her, eyes pinning hers with defiance. "I guarantee I'm *Fae* enough to make it interesting."

She laughs. Not a sound of amusement—more like pity. The kind of laugh you might offer a poor soul intent on pursuing a fool's errand. "Do you really think your kiss is something special?"

I boldly wrap my arms around her waist, then pull her several inches closer. She's warmth and life, nearly flush against me, and my gaze falls to her lips. My head is nearly clear now. Hers has to be close. Still… "I think there's no reason to answer that. If you're wondering, find out for yourself."

Hesitation filters through the link. But the pull of desire, of the remaining ale still lingering, is a siren's call. It beckons her—beckons me—to cross a line both of us agreed not to. It wars with the sensibility slowly returning to us both. Instinct that screams *move away and never think of this again.*

I can move away. But we're here, and the pull is strong. Much stronger than it should be. But it has to be her choice.

"Come now, Aphelian. Don't tell me you're scared…"

Her lip twitches. Just once. Her brow furrows like she's concentrating very hard. I think for sure I've dissuaded her, but she claims my lips with a thunderous pulse I feel in every inch of my body.

My hands move of their own accord, sliding up her back to cup her head. She, in turn, winds her arms around my waist and backs me toward the bed. My knees hit the edge and buckle, taking us both to the soft griffin-down comforter.

"Your lips are so warm," she says between kisses.

"Yours," I say with a gasp. "Yours are cold." The sensation is amazing, sending tiny chilling prickles down my spine and to parts lower. Her touch is cool yet blazes in a way that lights me on fire from the inside. Frost rises from the tips of her fingers, wafting around us and turning to steam as the warm air vanquishes it.

I pull away and nibble the edge of her ear, breathing the scent of her in deep. "You're the first human I've ever kissed." She shudders and exhales sharply. "What do you—"

And just like that, the mood in the room shifts.

She throws her leg around and slides off the bed. "Are we finished here?"

"Are we— What? I don't get it."

"The ale effect is gone. I'm thinking clearly. Obviously, you are, too, so I assume this is just another attempt to— how did you put it back at the estate—*pass the time*?"

I stand. How is this my fault? "If I recall correctly, *you* kissed *me*."

"Only because I was under the influence of piskie pheromones and reacting to your interest in brashing anything in sight!" She jabs a finger into the center of my chest. "It's not like I'm going to *fall in love with you*."

Reality comes crashing through the room. What am I doing? *I would fall in love with you?* Nothing I've ever said has been falser. More than all that, why do her words coax the cold from my blood? "I said that because of the ale—obviously."

"Obviously," she snaps back.

"Doesn't change the fact that you kissed me first. And you *liked* it."

Her face pales. "I liked it? Valen, I've never felt sicker than I do right now."

"That so?" She's not lying. Not entirely. A wave of something—pain mixed with fear—shoots through the link.

I don't see what the big deal is. It was a kiss. Granted, it's one I'd like to experience again, but still. Just a kiss. We both liked it. Does she really think she can hide that from me? The link has surpassed anything we imagined—and feared. She's attracted to me, and I to her. What is her problem?

"I might vomit."

"Uh huh." Lies. Something lingers in the link. An emotion muddled and deeply buried. But nausea? No. Confusion? Maybe. Shame, guilt, and self-revulsion? I can't get a proper read on it.

"There's not enough soap in all of Derriga to wash away the taste of you," she says.

The words are meant to convince her, not me. They aren't working.

"Well, since you can't get the taste of me off your lips, how about we do it again?" On one hand, I can't believe I suggested it out loud. On the other, though, all I can think about is that kiss.

She leans forward, slowly bringing her lips to my ear. My pulse quickens, and a shudder goes through her. "Valen... Not even if you were the last of *anything* in Derriga."

She shoves me out of the way and stalks to the door, almost slamming into Delkin and Benj on her way out. Delkin watches her leave, then turns to me. "Feeling better?"

I ignore him and follow Tania. Down the stairs, through the lobby of the inn, and right out the front door. She's nowhere to be seen—which is just as well. What had I intended to do when I caught up to her? Continue bickering? As annoying as it was in the beginning, I've grown fond of our verbal sparring. Try to kiss her again? No, that was a huge mistake.

Apologize... For some reason, I feel like I should. She enjoyed the kiss as much as I did, but she was furious—no, *hurt*—when she stormed out. I'm sure of that much, even if I don't understand why.

Night has fallen, and the only sound is the crickets chirping in the distance. When I get to the edge of the square, I slow. Tania is across the way, standing with Daroose. Our eyes meet, and I feel... I have no idea what radiates down the link, but when she grabs the front of Daroose's shirt and drags him close, all I see is red.

The kiss to his cheek is short, and when she pulls away, she meets my gaze again, this time lifting her pinkie up and stalking away from both of us. Daroose follows her. I stay where I am, fearful that if I go after them, I might rip the kelpie to shreds.

"What happened?" Delkin comes up behind me.

"Damned kelpie. Foolish human." I pace like a caged animal, my mind spinning as I go over the whole thing in my head again. "Tell me we'll reach Ventin Peaks soon. I need to be rid of this damned bond."

"We're a little over a day out." He settles on a narrow bench carved from a fallen log. "And you should calm down, or you're going to freeze the town and give us away."

I look at my hands. Icicles have formed around my fingernails as cold air seethes around me. "How does she always do this to me?"

"Do what, exactly?"

"Everything will be fine, then"—I snap my fingers— "just like that, I want to throw her over a cliff."

"What did she say that has you ready to ice the piskies?"

"She kissed me." I feel ridiculous the moment the words leave my mouth. "Then she got upset and left with Daroose."

"And why does that bother you?"

"Because the kelpie is a manipulative bastard."

"Have you considered the possibility of another reason?"

"Besides not wanting to watch her run off with someone else?"

"Someone else." Delkin leans back. "You mean, besides you?"

I stop mid-step and whirl on him. "What are you trying to say?"

"Maybe the reason you're so angry is that you've developed feelings for Tania."

I told her I would fall in love with her—not that I had. Or *could*. "Even if it were possible for us to tolerate each other, neither one of us can fall in love." I tap my chest, right over my heart. "We were both warded."

Delkin folds his arms. "The druids are powerful but not infallible, son. Wards *can* be broken."

I have a slight headache the next morning, and if it's attached to the piskie ale, I bet Tania feels a thousand times worse. According to Delkin, she probably won't remember a thing. There's a reason humans don't generally partake in Fae alcohol.

Unfortunately, my memory is crystal clear.

We pack our things, refill what supplies we can, and set off again with little conversation. Daroose does his best to give me a wide berth, but by midday, when we make it to the edge of Ventin Peaks, he's back to his usual, annoying self.

"Half a day to climb, if I had to guess," the kelpie says with a sniff. "Could cut that back if everyone shifted."

"Too risky." Benj sets his pack down and stretches. "If anyone were to see—"

"The courts have dissolved, but there are still Fae in these lands—some even rumored to be loyal to Orbik," I tell them.

It's impossible to miss the look the two elder Fae exchange. There's more to their involvement than Delkin has told me, but right now I have one goal. Break the link. The longer this tie exists, the more complicated my life gets.

"Better get moving, then." Tania's pack is almost as

big as she is, yet she adjusts it and starts up the hill like it weighs nothing more than a pile of feathers.

The terrain is uneven and littered with large rocks, making the trek up the mountain slow and dangerous. Sharp edges and steep cliffs that end in jagged trees and wicked rock outcroppings taunt from below. Delkin and Benj take to the front, while Tania and I follow. The kelpie brings up the rear, and with each step, it's an effort not to turn around and push him over the edge.

"Why Ventin Peaks?" Benj steps around a large boulder and carefully navigates through a narrow channel. "Why not simply head back to Lunal?"

Tania hops from rock to rock, gracefully traversing the constricted section. "There's an herb that grows in Ventin. Levina says she needs it to break the link."

"Which herb?" Delkin asks.

She shrugs and hops off a larger boulder. "She didn't say. Why?"

Delkin slows but doesn't stop. "I'm just not aware of any region-specific herbs in Ventin." He shrugs and readjusts his pack. "I'll be interested to see which one it is. Druid magic has always intrigued me."

And that's it. The last thing any of us says until Benj announces we should stop for the night. We've made it several miles up the hill. Not horrible progress, but still slower than any of us liked.

While the others set up camp, I volunteer to get firewood. My intention is to put some distance between Tania and me. The plan backfires when she insists on going with me.

"You've been weird since the piskie village. Why?"

I set the sticks I've collected down to search for something dry to use as tinder. "Tired. That bed was lumpy."

She snorts and drops her pile of wood at my feet. "I'm human, Valen. I can see the way you look at me."

I freeze. Delkin assured me there was no way Tania would remember what happened in the piskie village. He said the moment she fell asleep that night, the ale would wipe it all away. Piskie pheromones are tricky things. Daroose, being as old as he is, should have known that. He should have never allowed her to drink that crap.

"What do you mean?" I ask.

She steps closer. "The way your eyes follow me. The hungry gleam." She slings her arms around my neck. "You've been dying to kiss me all day."

"I— You— What—"

She holds my gaze for a moment longer, then bursts out laughing. With a slug on my arm that makes her cringe a little, she says, "You should see your face. Obviously, I was just kidding!"

"Obviously."

"Because kissing you?" She wraps her arms around herself and shudders. "I'd need to scrape my mouth out."

"Right." It mimics what she said back in the piskie inn.

"I mean, the idea is vomit-inducing, right? Just the thought—"

"Tania?"

She stops laughing and looks up. It's the spark I see in her eyes that tells me without a doubt that Delkin was wrong. Maybe it's the link between us. Or maybe Tania is just something special. Regardless, she *does* remember the inn. "Yes?"

"For once, shut up." I cross to where she is and take her face in my hands. Still, I don't move in all the way. Like before, I leave the decision up to her.

Whatever she was angry about is seemingly forgotten. Just like before, she makes the choice I hope she will.

The kiss is intense, and it's brief, and when we pull apart, I say, "I don't have *feelings* for you."

"Since that'd be impossible," she replies with a wave of her hand. "Not to mention *technically* not allowed."

"Fae and Aphelians *do* engage in physical relationships…"

"But it's against the rules."

"I know how you love rules…"

"It's been a while, and you're not *horrible* to look at."

I trace the lines of her face, letting my fingers linger at the curves of her ears. "It was curiosity."

"I'll admit I was a bit curious myself. I wanted to see what it felt like sober."

"You were sober in the woods, remember?"

She keeps her expression neutral, but I feel her amusement through the link. "Huh. I keep forgetting about that."

"You're going to give me a complex."

She snickers. "Add it to the many you already have."

"Anyway, now that we've tried it, I can't say that I'm interested in doing it again." My fingers itch to twine into the long strands of her hair, but I pull away.

Her lips twist. "Have to agree with you there. So, if we're finished, shall we head back to camp and never, ever speak of it again?"

"I'd agree, except…" My heart pounds. "There's something going on here."

She moves her head, but it isn't immediately clear whether she's agreeing or shaking it in denial. "There really isn't."

I tap my chest, directly over my heart. "I hate admitting it as much as you do, but I want to kiss you again—just like you want to kiss me." The way she stormed out at the inn replays inside my mind. The emotion I felt still roils in my gut. "You weren't just angry with me in the piskie village. You were hurt. Tell me why."

She hesitates.

"I'd just like to know. Was it something I did?"

"You…" She watches me for a moment and, with a shudder, says, "Being linked to you is killing me."

"Ouch."

She shakes her head and blinks several times. A wave of regret rolls through the link. "I just mean, you know, the way you act sometimes. The things you say…" Her voice is soft, and the sudden spark of vulnerability in her eyes makes her seem so much younger than eighteen. "When you said you'd never…"

Kissed a human before. That's what I said. Basing her assumption on what she's seen of my life before we left the estate, of course she'd think my interest was experimental.

"I didn't mean it like you think," I say.

She moves a little closer, the spark of innocence dissolving, replaced by the semi-hardened shell I've grown so fond of. "And aside from that, I find you vile."

"I believe you've mentioned that once or twice."

"But this damn link—"

"Exactly. It's the link. I don't think we've got any choice. Ignoring it doesn't seem possible."

She drapes her arms around my neck again. "I still find you repulsive."

"Right back at you, Fungus," I say, leaning in to plant

several kisses at the base of her neck.

She leans into my touch and sighs. "But you're warm. So damn warm, and I need that right now. I need—"

I kiss her. Hands, body, mouth. Anger, frustration— every emotion we've both been feeling bleeds into the kiss. It's passion, and it's pain, and I—

"Where did you two run off to?" Benj shouts.

We break apart like guilty children, eyes locked and breathing heavy.

That's when I notice her bare wrist. "Where's your braid? The one you got in Vey Brill?"

"I lost it." Without another word, Tania gathers her pile of wood and starts back toward camp. I wait until she's gone, then run my finger over my lips. I know she'll feel it.

That was so much more than a kiss. And even though it's technically impossible for something more than a physical attraction to bloom between us, it's there. Something real and tangible and utterly foreign.

Unfortunately, neither of us will ever admit it to the other.

33

Keltania

I told Valen the truth…
Being linked to you is killing me.

Is it my fault he misunderstood?

By nightfall, we make it halfway up the peak. Delkin is sure we'll make it to Ventin by midday tomorrow.

"Knowing what you know about Orbik, what are you going to do when this is all over?" I ask quietly.

Everyone but Valen and I are asleep. I don't know why he's still up, but I'm too nervous to nod off. Tomorrow, we'll meet up with Levina, and I have no idea what to expect. What if her plan fails? Where will that leave me? Or Valen?

He stretches out his legs. "I'm not sure, to be honest. Maybe I'll go back to Vey Brill with Delkin and Benj for a while. Get my bearings. Would that be okay with you?" He twirls a small twig between his fingers.

"Where you go, I go. That's the deal."

He drops his gaze to the ground for a moment, and when he lifts his head again, there's something unreadable in his eyes. "It doesn't have to be."

"What?"

"I know you believe your duty is sacred, but what about your freedom?"

"Last I checked, I was free."

"Technically, yes. But isn't there anything else you ever wanted to do? Something that was out of the question because of your loyalty to the Order? To the Aphelians?"

"Haven't we gone through this already?" While I appreciate his stance on the matter, I still believe in our partnership. Just knowing he believes what he does makes him worth protecting in my eyes. "I've never given it much thought. Aside from finding my family, there's nothing else I've really had interest in other than the vow."

"So do it. Go find your brothers. Your mother."

"Valen, I like being your partner." Is he still trying to get rid of me? After everything we've been through? Maybe being linked has given him too clear a window into who I am. Maybe he's decided he's better off without me. "Besides, I wouldn't even know where to start looking. I've made peace with the fact that they're lost. Just knowing they're out there is enough." I shift, suddenly uncomfortable. "What brought this up?"

"I'm telling you that if you wanted to, I would be okay with it. If…if something happened to change your mind, I wouldn't want you to feel guilty."

I can't tell what he's really saying. I know we agreed not to pursue any kind of entanglement, but that promise seems to keep slipping through the cracks. Of all my previous encounters, none have stayed with me the way Valen's kisses have. None have made my blood boil and my heart race. Maybe he feels the same way. Maybe he's worried we'll cross a line we can't come back from.

I believe him. He would let me walk away without the shame of abandonment, but it stings that he seems so casual about it. It's just his way, I decide. He uses physical relationships to work through his issues. He said there was something between us, but I can see now that he was probably just trying to save me from feeling awkward about the fact that I can't seem to keep my lips off of him.

I lay down on my back to watch the stars. "I think I understand what you're trying to say."

"You do?"

"Yes. I'm not a fool. You don't have to push me out the door because you fear I'll react badly the first time you show some other girl attention. I told you—I know who you are."

"Show some other girl attention? Now I'm really confused."

I roll onto my side so that I'm facing him. "You seem like you're trying to get me to leave."

"Get you to— No! That's the last thing I want." A blast of panic hits me through the link, and it nearly steals the air from my lungs. "I've never had anyone…like this." He holds out his hand, and a small vine made of ice springs from his palm. "Obviously I'm out of practice talking to people. I mean, I've had plenty of someones. Fae throw themselves at me all the time. I've never wanted for company. But no one has ever *known* me like you do. We bicker constantly, and you're always threatening to kill me—" He laughs. "But I like not being *alone*."

"I—"

"I like you, Tania. So much more than I like anyone else. So much that I want you to be truly happy. That's, um, new for me. I usually don't give a shit about what anyone else wants. If you being happy means leaving to do something else — or because you feel the need to go for whatever reason — then that's what I want." He tosses the ice vine into the air above our heads, then sends a frosty projectile straight for it. The vine explodes, sending a shower of icy, glittering dust flittering down on our heads.

The chill in my bones intensifies. Ever since I lost the jalva braid, each time one of us uses Fae magic, it takes more and more of a toll on me. I'm human, after all. My body might be able to handle druid magic, but Fae power is something entirely different. Without the jalva-soaked braid, I'm not going to make it much farther.

"There's something I need to tell you." Maybe it's the cold pressing down on me, or maybe it's the raw confessions we've both offered today. Either way, I have to get it out of my system. He needs to know the truth about what's been happening to me. He wouldn't keep something this big from me. I have no right to keep it from him.

"Wait." He gets to his feet, and I feel... What is it? Shame? Anger? "I need to tell you something first."

"What's wrong?"

"I found out something before we left the estate. I found *something*."

"Okay…" My head begins to throb. "Why does it feel like your head is about to explode?"

"Because it's something I should have told you about. I wanted to, but, the truth is, I was worried about how you would react. I couldn't stand the thought of lo—" He cuts off abruptly.

"You're making me nervous." I get to my feet, and he backs away several steps. His emotions and his thoughts are all over the place. I can't get a solid read on anything other than that he's terrified of what he's about to say.

"Your people are wrong. The history they base their lives on? The bond they've fostered all these thousands of years? It's all a lie."

"What are you talking about?"

"Servis didn't honor Aphelian. At least, not in the end. He betrayed her."

A chill that starts at the base of my spine claws its way up, swallowing every inch of me. "You're wrong. Servis would never betray Aphelian. What in the Goddess's name makes you think that?"

"I found proof. I heard the truth."

"What proof could you have possibly—"

"I found the tear, Tania. The one that Aphelian used to loan the druid magic to the Winter Court."

What he's saying is impossible, and I would have written it off as exhaustion if I didn't feel the truth of it pulsing through the link. Still, to accept what he's saying... "That's not possible, Valen. Whatever it is you found, you must be wrong. Confused—"

"I'm not. Liani told me everything." He frowns. "Well, not everything. There are still quite a few holes, actually. But the basic fact is there. The druid power—the tear Aphelian lent us—sits in a vault in the Winter Court estate. It was never destroyed. I *saw* it."

"That's— No."

"It's true. I wish it wasn't, but it is. Servis wasn't the man you thought he was. He betrayed the druids. He betrayed Aphelian."

The entire mountain begins to spin.

"When I found it, I...I touched it. I think that's how

we've been able to tap into the druid power. I poured a small amount onto the tip of my finger. It soaked in and—"

A million tiny voices whisper inside my head, from denial to furious threats and everything in between. I lash out, grabbing the nearest tree so I don't topple over as my vision swims. "When? When did you find this out?"

He's quiet, and I know this isn't a secret he uncovered right before we fled the estate. This is the thing he's been hiding from me. He's known for a while.

"All the guilt I've been feeling… It was this," I say. I force in a breath. It feels like a million blades scraping down my throat. "How long have you known?"

He opens his mouth, but instead of answering, he shakes his head slowly.

"Answer me!" I snap, trying hard to keep my voice low. Delkin and Benj stir, and Daroose rolls onto his side, but we're still alone. "Tell me how long you knew."

"It was weeks. I found the tear weeks before we left the estate." Regret swirls between us, but the anger I feel washes it away.

"You— Why didn't you tell me?"

"I didn't want to lose you. I didn't know how to tell you."

He reaches for my hand, but I swat his away.

He isn't the one who betrayed the druids. He never even met Servis. Still, his neglecting to tell me is a betrayal in its own right. It's a betrayal of my trust. The one person I'm supposed to be able to trust implicitly kept something world-changing from me. Something that could have shifted the existence of all my people.

"This tear—the magic—it's at the estate?"

Not only did he know about Servis's betrayal and the

tear, but he hasn't offered to give it back. It's rightfully ours, and I'll see it restored. By any means.

"Yes. In the basement. I—"

"Then when this is finished, I will bring an army to take it back."

He pales, and for a moment, surprise filters down the link. Surprise—and anger. It's gone within moments, replaced by a cool void of indifference. "I see."

"If they try to stop me, I will cut them all down."

"And what of me?"

"You?" I lean close, bringing my face inches from his. We're breathing the same air, sharing the same space. There's a vulnerability to it, but also a danger. Either of us could slit the other's throat with ease. "If you get in my way, I will do the same to you."

The lie rolls effortlessly off my tongue. It's so convincing that Valen winces and backs away several steps.

Good.

"If you return that tear to the druids, you'll start a war." His voice is hollow. Empty. It's like he's reciting some script he's memorized. "The remaining bits of the human race will be wiped from existence."

"Is that a threat?"

"It's a fact, Tania. What's left of you is no match for the Winter Guard."

Dropping to my knees, I roll my linens and collect my pack. Tying it all together, I take one last look at Benj and Delkin, who are miraculously still asleep on the other side of the camp. Daroose is gone, and though I wish I could ditch him, he'll find me eventually. The bridle will see to that. "I can't stay here. Not with you. Being tied to you might destroy me, Valen, but one good thing will come from it. My people will come back from the brink."

"Destroy you? A bit dramatic, don't you think?"

"I'm going on ahead. I'll meet you in Ventin. Levina will fix this, and then we'll see where it leads."

I wait for him to stop me. To say something—anything—to keep me from walking off into the darkness alone. But he doesn't. And why would he? I just threatened to kill him. Him and his family. His people. Anyone who got in my way.

Whatever is blossoming between us withers in that moment. I feel it die just as plainly as I can now feel the animals and trees around me. The forest takes a collective breath, like it feels the pain as fiercely as I do.

With each step away from camp, my insides grow colder and colder. The farther from Valen I get, the heavier the weight inside my chest becomes. I might think it was guilt eating away at me after all the horrible things I said to him, but deep down, I know it's the link. While it may have helped bring *us* together, it's tearing *me* apart. He's using his magic. Maybe it's unintentional. His emotions tend to be a trigger, and if he feels betrayed by the things I said, I might not survive long enough to get to Ventin, much less long enough to get the tear back.

I walk for miles. Navigating the woods in the dark is trickier than it should be, and even with the forest animals' help, I still manage to fall twice and get my pack caught in a tree.

Has it only been a few months since Levina sent me to the Winter Lands? My entire world has been turned upside down.

The longer I walk, the clearer my head becomes. Valen was wrong. He should have told me the truth right away.

But the villain of this story isn't the Fae with magic—it's the long-dead Fae without it. I can't hold him responsible for something a long-dead ancestor did. And all those things I said? I could never hurt him.

I do intend to get the tear back, but what happens if Valen fights me? How far could I really go to take back what belongs to my people? It might get complicated.

I place a hand over my heart. Just thinking about him makes it beat faster. I can't love him, but my feelings for him are strong. Far stronger than they've ever been for another. I want him safe and happy. If love is much more than that, then I don't know how people survive it. Simply caring about someone pulls you in too many directions.

I make it several miles from our camp by the time the sun starts to break through the cloud cover. With a little distance, I hate that I left things the way I did. After all the things I said, I'm not sure he'll talk to me when we arrive in Ventin.

Do I even want to talk to him?

"You've been impossible to track," Daroose shouts, emerging a few feet away. I jump, so absorbed in my own thoughts that I never heard him stomping through the brush. "It's like you've been hiking in circles."

"What are you doing here, Daroose?" Though the question is pointless. I knew he'd follow eventually.

"Might I inquire as to why you left camp in the middle of the night?"

"Didn't you ask Valen?"

He nods. "I did. He said to scurry off and ask you."

"Valen made a mistake."

Daroose opens his mouth—no doubt to insert some sort of snarky anecdote—but I stop him.

"I reacted…badly."

Daroose's eyes narrow. "And he told you to leave?"

"Of course not." Would he have if given the chance? "I was angry and said some horrible things. I stormed off to think."

Daroose rolls his eyes. "What is there to think about?"

"When this is over—when the link is broken—I have no idea where I'll be."

"You'll be wherever you want. I imagine there's a certain icy-tempered Fae—"

"It isn't like that," I insist. I don't know exactly what it *is* like, but it isn't that. Especially not now. "Valen is…" What is Valen? He's annoying and cocky and, as Daroose points out constantly, ill-tempered. But he's also funny. He's compassionate in a way most humans aren't—even though he does his darndest to hide it. He's the first thing that comes to mind when I think of home.

But he also betrayed me. Maybe his intent wasn't malicious, but it was enough that I'm not sure I can ever trust him again. The right thing would have been to give the tear back. He thinks it would cause a war? The fear might be valid, but with me by his side, I'm sure we could have explained things well enough to stave off a serious conflict.

Liani told me everything…

Unless someone else has convinced him otherwise.

"I need something from you."

Daroose bows. "Anything—"

"You have to go back to camp."

"—but that."

"Daroose…"

He shakes his head. "They got an early start. Left for

Ventin hours ago. They'll beat you there, too. Delkin knew a shortcut."

"Then shift and catch up to them. I need you to stay with Valen."

He stomps his foot. "The little Fae is insufferable. Leave him to his kin, and we'll be on our way."

"I'm not asking, Daroose." I never wanted his bridle, and I hate to give him an order, but I need to be sure Valen is safe. I'm angry at him, and I'm hurt, but regardless of all that *and* the fact that our entire relationship is based on a lie, I'll still honor my duty. "If I'm your master, then consider it a command. Catch up to them. Don't leave Valen's side. Protect him at all costs."

The kelpie's lips twist into an angry scowl. "And what of you? Who protects you?"

I rest a hand atop my sword and resist the urge to shiver as another, more powerful wave of cold barrels through me. "I can take care of myself. That's how it's always been. That's how it always will be."

"Why? Why are you doing this?"

I want to tell him my reasons are selfish. I want to insist that if something happens to Valen, I would likely die. But I can't push the lie past my lips. "I care about him. I don't want to right now, but it's not something I can turn off."

"Have you tried?"

I touch the necklace at my throat. "If something were to happen to me, what would become of your bridle?"

He watches me for a moment. The weight of his gaze is like a rock, dragging me down. "What was wrong with you before we arrived at Vey Brill—it's getting worse, isn't it?"

"Delkin gave me something to help with the problem,

but it's gone now." I swallow back a rush of panic and square my shoulders. "I can't say with certainty that I'll survive long enough to break the link." Saying it out loud is terrifying.

"In the event your heart stops, the bridle will automatically revert to me." His lips turn downward. "But I don't want it back. Not like that."

Good. One less thing to worry about. Valen doesn't like the kelpie, but he's grown on me. If nothing else, I'm glad to have been able to free him from his lake. "It's an honor to have met you, Daroose. It's been…"

"Illuminating? Educational?" He shimmies his hips and spins in a circle, spreading his arms wide. "Wonderous?"

I step forward and wrap my arms around him, squeezing just once before standing back and smiling. "It's been fun."

Daroose sighs. He turns and starts back the way he came, pausing for a moment. Without looking back, he says, "Valen doesn't deserve you, Keltania." And then he's gone, swallowed by the mountain.

I turn my head to the sky, searching for a bird to take a message to Levina. She needs to know what's going on. Unfortunately, I can't feel anything. Either I'm too far from Valen to tap into the druid power or there just aren't any birds around. Given the state of the forest, the lack of wildlife isn't surprising.

Eventually, I give up and decide to try a bit farther down the way. Resigned, I make my way back to the path, but I'm cut off by a small reddish-brown blur that streaks across my field of vision. *Fae! Fae are here! Fae!*

My first instinct is relief. Valen regrets how we left things and sought me out so we could continue to Ventin together. I close my eyes and concentrate on the forest, on the trees and the plants. I'm able to pinpoint which way someone is coming from—but by the time I realize it isn't who I hoped, it's too late.

"Hello, Aphelian," Valen's aunt Liani says with a snarl.

34

Valen

I should have gone after her. Letting Tania wander into the woods in the middle of the night was foolish. Her anger was justified. Her words cut deep, but when my mind cleared, I knew she didn't mean them.

Not entirely.

Delkin stands at the top of the ridge, hand extended to Benj. Once he's up, I take his place, and my father pulls me onto the next ridge. "Another few miles and we'll be there. Are you sure she'll meet us?"

"There's no doubt in my mind." Tania wants the link broken just as much as I do—if not more since learning the truth. If she doesn't show, she'll be stuck with the shadow of my presence for the rest of her days. "She'll be there. She wants me gone because, apparently, being tied to me is *destroying* her."

"It is," Benj says casually.

I stop walking. "What's that supposed to mean?"

Delkin glares at his brother, then turns to me. "Tania is very ill. She has been since before you reached Vey Brill."

"Ill from what?" Daroose said she'd smelled wrong.

Was that what he meant? But when I asked, she told me it was nothing!

Being linked to you is killing me... Shit!

"Maybe instead of trying to hide things from each other, you should have talked." Benj shakes his head. "Things would have turned out differently."

"Humans aren't compatible with Fae magic." Delkin frowns. "It's been killing her for weeks now. I gave her a way to keep it at bay—"

"The braid. She said she lost it sometime after the sniffer."

Delkin nods. "I don't think she lost it. I think the magic simply was too powerful. I believe it dissolved when she froze the Winter Guard. If her high priestess doesn't break the link soon, Tania won't survive."

"What do you mean, she won't survive?" Panic wells in my chest, and a bubble of anger begins to form. How could they know about this and keep it to themselves?

Benj shakes his head. "She's human, Valen..."

Maybe they're wrong. "She's human, but we're linked and I feel absolutely fine."

"Since the magic is Fae, it's only affecting her. Probably why you didn't even realize anything was wrong. It's likely that each time you used your magic, it got worse for her. Neither one of you could have possibly known..."

But he's wrong. I felt...something. But I was so self-absorbed that it never occurred to me. *Fuck*. She even told me and I brushed her off.

"But you knew." The accusation is bitter and full of venom. "You knew how sick she was, and you said nothing to me?"

"I understand your anger, Valen." Delkin rests a hand

on my shoulder. "But she asked me not to tell you. I was honoring her wishes."

"How honorable of you," I snap. "That's not really the kind of thing you keep quiet."

I don't know where we stand, but I know that I care for Tania. I'm still not sure what it means or to what depth those feelings go, but I know one thing with absolute certainty. I will not allow her to suffer and die out here alone.

We arrive in Ventin just after midday. I hadn't known what to expect, but an actual town wasn't among the possibilities.

"It's been deserted for years," Benj says. "It was an unaligned village. After the Great Drain, when Fae started turning on one another, the chaos eventually spilled over into the town."

Delkin spins in a slow circle. "Any idea where in Ventin we're supposed to meet this high priestess?"

I scan the area. There are a handful of rotting, vine-covered shop fronts and a decrepit square, but there's no sign of human or Fae life. The decay doesn't mean Ventin is completely dead, though. The fountain in the center, long dried and cracked, now serves as a container for colorful weeds. Flora I've never seen before grows taller than me and attracts all manner of birds and butterflies. While not flourishing like it might have centuries ago, Ventin doesn't seem as dead as other parts of Derriga.

The road we came in on, leading into the center of

town, is lined with tall perchling trees. Since wivryn feed on perchling fruit, as a safety precaution we always cut them down before they go to flower. Here, they flourish, allowed to stretch taller than I've ever seen, their branches winding well into the clouds, much like the hilpberry trees in Vey Brill.

"Tania?" My voice echoes through the empty square. The sound bounces off the trees and buildings, fading into an eerie warble.

"There are other ways to get into town. We hiked the most direct route," Delkin says. "She might not have made it yet, especially if she's not feeling well."

"That's probably it," I agree. Tania could navigate the woods better than any Fae I've ever seen. There's no doubt in my mind she would have made it here first with time to spare—if she was feeling like herself. "Maybe if we spread out, we can find her. This place isn't that big."

I focus on the link, trying not to panic when I feel nothing but an odd kind of static. Since she left, I've been doing my best to ignore it. Practicing my magic, talking with Delkin and Benj, overanalyzing the terrain as we went… Shit. Had I really been making things worse for her every time I used my magic? What if it's already too late?

"I don't think we should split up." Benj squares his shoulders and looks from me to Delkin. "There are far too many dangers."

"There's no other choice. If we have any hope of finding Tania in time, we can't afford not to separate." I glare at Delkin. "I'm not taking no for an answer."

"All right," Delkin says. Benj opens his mouth— probably to protest—but his brother shakes his head. "But be cautious. There's no way to know what kinds of creatures dwell here now. If Ventin looks empty, it's only an illusion." As if to confirm, the screech of a wivryn, high above us, echoes to the ground.

I nod, and we go our separate ways.

I walk through the center of town, to the main thoroughfare. It's overgrown with trees large enough to indicate Ventin has been abandoned for a very long time. The stone pathway has all but crumbled, yielding to persistent foliage. There might be lingering depleted Fae here, but it's the wildlife that own this town now.

I come to the largest building in the square and pause. The door is missing, and the roof is partially caved in. I take a single step inside. It's as far as I dare go. "Tania?" No answer. Not that I expect one. I can't imagine her hiding. If she were here, she'd be standing tall in the center of town, quietly gloating because she'd gotten here first.

The next three buildings are more of the same. After that, I search the alleyways and find no evidence of anything other than animals that might have passed through at one point. There are no birds, no bugs—even the wind seems to have abandoned this section of Ventin to the forest. Maybe this is why the priestess wanted to meet Tania here. This town once thrived under Fae rule. Now, the forest has reclaimed it.

"Valen?" a familiar voice calls as I round the last corner. My aunt runs toward me. "Thank the Gods!"

"Liani?"

She throws her arms around me, and I return the embrace. Gods, I wasn't sure I'd ever see her again.

"What are you doing here?"

I've never seen her wear anything but the most fashionable gowns and expensive jewels, but the Fae

standing in front of me now could pass for common. Her
long hair is knotted into a simple braid that hangs over
her shoulder, and her gown has been replaced with simple
traveling leathers of black and gray.

"I've uncovered an awful truth, Valen. The Aphelian is
plotting against us. She plans to have her priestess break
the link, then take you hostage. She plans to use you to get
the tear back. I see you told her the truth…"

"What?" That's not possible.

"I told you telling her the truth was a bad idea." Tears
gather in the corner of my aunt's eyes. "I fear what will
come of this now."

"The Aphelian has no intention of harming me. We—
we had a falling out, though." I sigh and pull away. "We
separated, and she agreed to meet me here to break the
link, but she hasn't shown yet." I shake my head. "How—
how do you know this?"

"She's here. We found her on our way up the peak and
took her into custody when she couldn't tell us where you
were. She…she attacked me, Valen. She attacked me, then
told me what she planned to do." Just coming over the
ridge, on the other end of the square, are ten estate guards,
five on either side of Tania, who is bound in chains.

Oh Gods—

"I feared the worst, Valen. I thought she'd already… No
matter. She's paying for what she planned to do."

"You misunderstand, Liani. She does know the truth, but
she would never…" Another, longer look at Tania, and my
chest contracts. She looks horrible. Too pale. Gone are the
confident stride and bright eyes. Posture that was tall and
proud is now stooped and haggard. She shuffles forward
between the guards, her movements slow and unsteady.

"Don't look at her with pity! She is *not* your ally."

"You're wrong. And if she attacked you, it was out of fear. She—"

"Did you tell her I knew about the tear?"

"Yes…" Still, would Tania attack her? Knowing what she meant to me?

"There is all the motivation you need." She cups my face, bending her forehead to mine. "My child… I know that you try to see the good in others, but this time I fear it's pointless."

"Please, just let her go and allow us to talk. We can clear it up."

Liani snorts. The most unladylike sound I've heard her make. "I will not allow her to wander free. You cannot ask me to take a chance with your life."

The guards stop a few feet from us, and I find myself moving toward Tania. She looks horrible. "Are you okay?" I ask. She doesn't answer.

"Fae magic is obviously too much for a pathetic human. If I were a wicked one, I'd insist we simply wait and let it take her slowly." Liani sneers at her. "Painfully. But, given your fondness for the traitor—"

"Let me die," Tania says with venom. She glares at Liani, who regards her as little more than a gnat. "That magic belongs to us, and even if I don't take it back now, eventually, one of us will."

Liani laughs. It's a hysterical sound, almost unhinged. "Pathetic human. You really are clueless, aren't you?"

"Liani, let her go. Please."

Tania struggles against the bonds. It's a weak attempt, hardly rattling the chains. "Let me go and I'll rip your head from your body!"

"Tania! You're not helping."

"Why would I let her go?" Liani says. "You heard her with your own ears. She intends to steal back our magic. She wants to harm me."

I grab her arm. "It's not *our* magic."

Liani shrugs me off and squares her shoulders. "Semantics."

Tania forces a smile. She snickers to hide a cough. "I'd think you'd deem this rather poetic."

Every time I used my magic... "Why the hell didn't you say something?"

She looks away. "I did."

"Yes, but you made it seem like—" I shake my head. "I thought you were referring to whatever was happening between us."

She shakes her head and the action almost sends her toppling over. "It wouldn't have changed anything."

A small flicker of something passes through the link. It's weak and it's guarded, but I feel it nonetheless.

As we're standing there, her sigils begin to shimmer. The lines begin to change. "Your face..." It takes every ounce of control I have not to reach out and run the tips of my fingers over what just yesterday was the dull red sigil below her eye. Now, the red lines are turning smooth, glittering white. Like fallen snow made into paint. I take her hand in mine, flipping it to look at the sigil on her forearm. Just like the fresh one on her face, the older one, from her first day at the estate, is changing as well. It's beautiful.

"Must have something to do with your magic." She squares her shoulders for a moment before faltering and curling inward with a series of coughs.

"Is the druid priestess here?" I turn back to Liani. She's trying to protect me, and I appreciate it, but she doesn't know Tania the way I do. "We have to break the link. Now."

"She is," Liani says. "I left her just outside of Ventin. She's preparing the ritual needed to separate you." She motions for me to follow. "Come. Let's get this done so we can return home to our people. They need you."

I start to follow but pause. What about Delkin and Benj? They're out there searching for Tania. And even if I could let them know I found her—should I? The way they reacted at the possibility of someone seeing our resemblance... There's something Delkin isn't telling me. The question is, how bad is it?

I nod. "Agreed." If there's some reason they don't want Liani to see them, they'll stay hidden.

I follow Liani past the building and the guards. Instead of keeping her head bowed, Tania meets my gaze with defiance. "We'll get this sorted out," I promise her.

"You better hope not." Tania inclines her head toward Liani. "Because as soon as I'm out, I'm killing that bitch first. You might have an excuse for not returning our magic, Valen, but she knew all along, right?"

Liani sighs. "Honestly, Valen. I have no idea why you told her the truth. But I suppose this solves the druid problem. Now we don't have to feed and clothe her and put up with her holier-than-thou attitude."

"Unchain me, and I'll show you attitude."

It's nothing more than frustration and posturing. Tania is angry, but more than that, I feel a twinge of fear and the bitter sting of betrayal lingering in the link. Had I confessed weeks ago, this whole situation could have been avoided.

I could have told her sooner.

I *should* have told her sooner.

Whatever would have happened, it couldn't have been worse than this.

I shake my head and move to the front of the small crowd, where Liani leads the way. "I'm asking you—for me—let her go. She's the wronged party here, not you. Not me…"

Liani glares at me. "You can have any female you want, yet you're begging for this one? A human? Pull yourself together, Valen. She's beneath you."

I'm so shocked by her tone, by her words, that I can't even formulate a reply. I've never seen Liani act this way. It's unsettling.

She's never tried to keep the lengths to which she'll go to keep me safe a secret, but this? This is something more. There's a venom in her voice I've never heard before. A flame in her eyes that I've never seen. When I've asked her for something—not that I did it often—she went out of her way to oblige. Asking her to release Tania should have been more than enough.

Maybe it's jealousy. Liani had always been a bit jealous of Mika. She'd been the only one in my life for so long… But, with Tania, things are different. I might not have seen it right away, but it's impossible to miss now.

It isn't long before we've navigated the rocky landscape and end up in a massive clearing. In the center is a thick stone with several metal hooks.

The guards push Tania forward, then attach her chains to the end of one of the hooks. To her left is an older human woman I assume is Levina. She watches Tania with sorrow in her eyes, looking away as the guards all but force her to the ground.

"They have our magic, Levina!" Tania struggles with a seemingly renewed sense of fury against their grip, and to her credit, they have a hard time keeping her down. She looks to me for confirmation, but I stay quiet. We can deal with the magic later. Right now, we have to break the link. We don't have much time left.

"Shh. One problem at a time, Keltania." The priestess gestures to me. "Might I ask you to remove your shirt so I can inspect the ink my student placed upon your skin?"

"Oh. Yes. Of course." I do as she asks. "But there's nothing to see."

"I will be able to see." Levina leans in and ever so gently brushes her fingers over the spot where Tania's invisible mark is. The woman smiles, then nods to Liani. "It is exactly as I said it would be. There are several things we can do."

"Thank the Gods." Liani turns to her guards. "Leave us. Wait in the square."

The Winter Guards exchange confused expressions, but after a moment of hesitation, they obey, marching toward the town.

Levina produces another set of chains. "Do not be alarmed," she tells me. "It is a safety precaution and nothing more. The process can be a bit jarring, and from what I understand, you're a powerful young Fae not quite in control of your magic."

I look to Liani for confirmation, and she bows her head. She's acting strange, but I'm not worried. The druid priestess will find herself gutted if she tries to harm me in any way.

The chains are oddly cold against my skin, and when

she snaps them into place, something in my gut stirs. I look to Tania, but she isn't looking at me. She's watching Levina with an odd expression. "What's going on?"

Levina cocks her head to the side, brows furrowing. "What do you mean?"

Tania yanks hard on the chains. They rattle and snap but don't give way. "These chains are soaked in jalva oil."

Levina can't hide her surprise. "How do you know that?"

"I can smell it."

"Jalva has no scent."

There's a pained gleam in Tania's eyes. She pulls at the chains again, rattling them against the stone. She turns to me. "This is what my bracelet was soaked with. It suppresses magic."

Levina's frown slowly gives way to a wicked grin. "Well, of course I smell it. I'm the high priestess. And if you can smell it, then Liani was right to put the chains on you." She digs into her robes and pulls out a small blade. "Kill him, and we'll have our birthright returned to us."

A rush of anguish barrels down the link, and Tania's shoulders slump. "You already knew about the tear…"

She holds the small knife out to Tania. "Yes. And now we're moments away from reclaiming what's rightfully ours. All you have to do is stop his heart."

"What are you talking about? I can't kill him! I won't…" Tania's eyes meet mine. Guilt floods the link, and I'm not sure if it's mine anymore—or hers. "I would never hurt him."

Liani stands there, impatiently tapping her foot. "Well? Get it over with!"

I stare at my aunt as a bubble of anger begins to form in my chest. "Get it over with? What the hell is going on?" I tug at the chains. "Liani, let me go. The priestess just told

Tania to kill me!"

"And yet here you still stand. Still breathing." She glares at me, the ice in her eyes far colder than anything I could ever produce. A sick feeling forms in the pit of my belly.

Tania brings her leg up, kicking the blade from Levina's hand. "This is wrong!"

Levina and Liani exchange a look I don't understand before the priestess sighs and bends to retrieve the blade.

"I'm not going to kill him—and what would even be the point? The rebirth sigil will just restart his heart. And the wound would kill me!"

Levina and Liani both laugh. The sound of it turns my stomach. "That's not what the rebirth sigil does, child," Levina says. "It's a power transfer. You drew it on him, so when you stop his heart, his power flows into you. It will save you from his death by breaking the link."

"I— What— You planned to steal Valen's magic all along, didn't you?"

"Poetic, don't you think? All things considered."

No. No, this is wrong. All wrong.

"Don't you see what the magic is doing to me?" Tania lets out a strangled cry, and I'm nearly suffocated by a rush of emotion. "Humans aren't made for Fae power. If I end up with all of it…"

"It will kill you," Levina says. "Eventually."

Liani laughs. "But it wouldn't kill me."

Dread creeps from my gut and filters through the link. A rush of fury from Tania. "Liani? *Please.* What's going on?"

She leans down and grips my face, the tips of her nails digging into tender flesh. "I'm finally getting what I deserve."

35

Keltania

Kill him, and we'll have our birthright returned to us.
I'm drowning, struggling to catch my breath. I don't know if it's Valen's pain or mine, but I'm hollow. Gutted. What's unfolding is unthinkable. Something I would have sworn on my life was impossible. Yet…

I swallow back a mouthful of bile and shake my head. Tears gather in the corners of my eyes and spill down my cheeks. They leave blazing trails in their wake and make it hard to see.

"Whatever this is, it's unnecessary. Valen will give the tear back, and we'll all go our separate ways." I glance at him, then quickly look away. The pain in his eyes is too much to see. It's bad enough that I have to feel it, to choke on it. His aunt—the person he loves most in this world—has betrayed him.

"But what of the Fae magic?" Liani asks. She gives Valen's head a final, brutal shake before rounding on me. "I need it to rule the Winter Lands."

He snorts. He squares his shoulders and stands a bit taller. To the unknowing onlooker, he's furious and hard.

But to me, to the one person who can see inside him, he's a mess of anguish and fury and utter confusion. The storm of it all makes me nauseous. "Orbik would put your head on a pike before he gave you any kind of power."

Liani laughs. "Orbik? That fool has been under my control since before you first came to the estate." She inclines her head toward Levina. "Thanks to my druid friend here."

Something inside me cracks. The foundation our beliefs are built on is made of lies and duplicity. The discovery of the tear, hidden away in the Winter Court estate for centuries... To find out Levina had been working with the Winter Lady... "You helped her? Knowing they had our magic?"

Levina's eyes narrow as she jams the blade into my palm and wraps my fingers painfully around it. I grit my teeth against the sting, and on the other side of the rock, Valen hisses.

"Do it quickly, and he won't suffer," she says.

I let go of the blade. It clatters to the floor at our feet, catching a glint of sunlight when it falls still. "I won't kill him."

Levina narrows her eyes. "What mercy do you owe him?"

I peek at Valen through the curtain of my hair. "Mercy has nothing to do with it." I think about our journey here. About the times we fought and laughed. The times he saved me and the times I saved him. I think about the kisses... When I lift my head, it isn't Levina's gaze I catch. It's his. "Valen has his faults. Many, *many* faults. But I... I care about him."

Not *he's my friend*. Not *he doesn't deserve this*.

I care about him.

It isn't until I speak the words that I realize something else *has* been happening between us. Something I'm not quite sure what to call. It's strange, and it's strong, and it scares me a little bit, but I don't want to lose it. I can't.

My family, my beliefs, my mentor, my past... I've already lost everything else.

Levina laughs. "You *care* about him? Are you trying to say you have feelings for that filthy Fae?"

"I—" It's impossible, yet...

"Watch your mouth, druid," Liani says with a growl. "This alliance is tenuous as it is."

But Levina doesn't seem to hear her. She keeps laughing, growing more and more hysterical by the minute. "Do you have any idea how they *truly* view us? We are things. Toys to be used and abused, and when they've decided they've had enough, they punish us. They steal from us!"

"I'm not going to kill him," I whisper, forcing the words past my lips. "And what good would it do you if I did? The rebirth sigil is inked to me. If what you said is true and I don't die, why would you ever believe I'd give the power to you?"

Levina chuckles. "Don't you think I planned for this? Not your disgusting sentimental attachment to the boy, but your refusal to hand the magic over? I placed my own rebirth sigil on you the night before you left."

"No, you didn't."

"I did. Obviously, my intention was to reason with you. I don't want you dead, Keltania. But just in case..."

"No..." Though when I think about it, that night is hazy. I chalked it up to Levina keeping me up all night so I could memorize the sigil, but there has to be more to it. She'd given me the drawing to memorize, then brought me tea in the early morning hours. "You drugged me."

I surge forward, fingers hooked and itching to tear into her flesh, but she simply smiles and moves just beyond my reach. I come to the end of the chain and am jerked back violently. Valen catches me before I fall.

"I went to great lengths to ensure you ended up here. Everything from giving you the improper placement of the sigil, which dissolved the Heartbreaker, to showing you the altered version, which caused the link. Then, to be sure, I followed you every step of the way. Kept my eyes on you—"

"The crow..." I shiver. "It was you."

"It was," she says with a smile. "Being tuned so closely with nature that we can become nature is just one more thing the Winter Fae stole from us. You should be *thanking* me."

"That still doesn't make sense. You're human. It would just do to you what it's doing to me."

Levina smiles. It's wicked and wrong and turns my stomach to lead. "I'm...a little something more. I would be just fine."

"You... How could you do this to me? You raised me. You were like a mother to me."

"And I still am. I told you—I don't want you dead. I want you by my side."

"As long as I kill Valen."

"Yes."

"*No*," I snap.

"Enough chatter." Liani pushes past Levina and picks up the knife, then presses it painfully into my hands. "Do it now."

I slacken my fingers, and it tumbles to the ground again. "How can you let this happen? Valen loves you."

But it isn't Liani who answers. It's Levina. "Did you think her the dutiful aunt?" She smiles at Valen. "All this time you've loved her, thought her on your side, but do you know what she's done? She's used you, knowing what you are—knowing *who* you are." Unlike Liani, her voice is soft, mellow. Her words are razor-sharp, but she delivers them as if plated with sugar.

Liani sighs. "Must we do this?" She taps her foot impatiently.

"Surely you wish to clear the air?" Levina flashes a mock frown. She's the picture of calm, but there's something I can't quite put my finger on. Something chaotic churning just below the surface. "There's nothing to fear from him. He can't hurt you now."

Liani says nothing, but the fury in her eyes blazes bright.

"They knew, from the moment your mother was brought back into the estate." Levina taps her cheek, just below her eye. "There's only one family with eyes like those. One bloodline in all of Derriga."

"Orbik would be stronger than Amoriel, with my guidance." Liani's face is a mask of fury. "We deserved to rule, not her. But their father, *Lord Envrill*, wouldn't hear it. The only choice I had was to get rid of her."

Valen's face pales. The confusion in the link turns to fury. "What are you saying?"

"I'm saying Orbik was weak. He was happy to stand aside and let his sister take what should have been his. I stepped in and did what needed to be done. I hired a band of rebel Fae to kidnap and dispose of Amoriel, but something went wrong. They didn't finish the job, because two years later, they found her wandering around the woods with *you*."

Valen stares at her. I feel the storm brewing inside him, so similar to the sensation I felt when Delkin told him the truth. But it's muted. Trapped. It has nowhere to go but inward, and Valen crumbles. "It was you all along…"

"The guard found her while on patrol. She fought them—she didn't want to come back. She must have uncovered the truth about her abduction. But I soothed her, telling her Orbik was away. Some diplomacy thing with the piskies. She was safe. I brought her in, and when I saw you, I knew… Those damned eyes…"

"What do his eyes have to do with anything?" Things are starting to come together. The insistence to disguise Delkin's eye color. The longer travel routes to ensure we wouldn't be seen. There's a reason the elder Fae made his village high in the trees.

"Amoriel's injuries were superficial. Cuts and scrapes and bruises. But no one had seen her save for me and a handful of guards—all loyal to me. A single blade to the gut, and she expired by the time Orbik returned."

Valen's expression is the very definition of rage.

"Your mother told me your father was killed the year before, in a hunting accident." Liani laughs. "There was no chance he'd come after you, but to be safe, I spread the word outside the Winter Lands that you'd both perished."

"Are you finished yet?" Levina asks. The bored expression on her face morphs into irritation. "Because I'd like to be on the road home by morning. Wrap this up while I go find the abis root." She walks away, strolling like she hasn't a care in the world.

Liani glares after her. "You started this," she calls over her shoulder as Levina disappears from view. "Now I'll finish it. After all, it seems fitting the boy know who his father was."

Leaves rustle as Delkin and Benj step from the trees, towering figures of power and fury. "I think you mean *is*."

Liani starts, and for a long moment she simply stares. "Violet eyes... You must be Delkin Frostreaver. You never do seem to die, do you?" She offers a mocking bow. "All hail the king."

I don't know if Valen is too confused, hurt, or simply unable to soak in the events of the last fifteen minutes, because he just stares wordlessly and open-mouthed.

"King?" I ask, though in the back of my mind, the pieces have already fit perfectly into place.

Benj steps to the side and bows to his brother. "Delkin Arrell Frostreaver, the true Winter Lord."

36

Valen

Liani glares at my father. "Servis was a visionary, and he could see the current rule slipping from the old ways. Tensions with the other courts were high because of the liberties, the *equality*, the court extended to the humans. Something had to be done."

"You're saying the current Winter Lord stole the throne from my father?" I knew Delkin was hiding something, but this?

Liani waves offhandedly at my father. "Servis hated the humans, but when he met Aphelian—a very young, very powerful druid—he found that keeping her close and happy benefited his agenda. So young and impressionable, she was ripe for shaping."

"So, he never loved her?" Tania's voice is like ice. "He used Aphelian right from the start?"

"Wholly." Liani smiles. "Servis knew Fae magic was waning. It's happened before, though very few remember it. He kept Aphelian close, kept her happy and safe, and when the time was right—when she'd grown into her power—she helped him displace Delkin Frostreaver and claim the Winter Lands as his own." She sighs. "Of course, then the fool brought his most prized possession to the Autumn Court and started a damned war over her."

"So Aphelian did start the war." There were rumors, stories, but I thought that was all they were. Tales.

"Contrary to what everyone thinks, the Great Drain wasn't caused by the war. The war made it worse. Sped it along. But it started years before. Most just didn't notice."

"Autumn Lord Avastad knew the power was fading," I say. "He wanted the druid magic for himself."

Liani nods. "It wasn't long before all the courts got involved and the war destroyed them all."

Delkin's eyes narrow. "I'm still not sure why it mattered. Why fight such a bloody war, slaughter millions of innocents, all to come out just as powerless?"

"Powerless? He had the druid magic he stole from Aphelian," Tania says. "That would make him the most powerful Fae at the time, wouldn't it? If no one else had any magic?"

"It would have—if he'd been able to use it." Delkin takes a step toward Liani. To her credit, she remains where she is. "That's why you didn't kill my son. He was your chance for a real show of power. Magic you *could* manipulate."

She doesn't bother looking apologetic. "I began siphoning magic from him that very first day. Kept a reserve of it, just in case."

"The Icekeeper clan is not of royal blood." His eyes change, distinctly canine. His front teeth elongate, sharpening into fangs. "Royal Winter Fae have an animal soul." Another step. "Royal Winter Fae have violet eyes." One final step, and they're nose to nose. "Royal Winter

Fae are *Frostreavers*."

This time, Liani takes the smallest step away. She glances nervously over her shoulder, probably wondering if she could call loud enough for the guards to hear or Levina to return.

"Listen carefully, son. I'm about to give you your first *real* history lesson." Delkin taps his forehead. "Only a true Winter royal could have accessed that druid magic."

"But the war? Servis used the druid magic—"

"*Aphelian* used the magic to win the war. When she channeled it back into the tear, he stole it." Delkin takes another step closer. He's right in front of her now, between Liani and Tania and me. "He took credit for wielding the power, but it was her all along."

I think for sure he'll grab her. Maybe he would have if he'd gotten here earlier, if he'd heard she'd been responsible for my mother's death. Instead of attacking her, though, he grips both mine and Tania's chains and yanks them from the stone. The stone cracks and crumbles, and Liani has to dodge several flying chunks of debris.

One of our wrists in each of his hands, he closes his fingers around the cuffs and squeezes just tight enough to crack the metal and release us. I ball my fingers tight and produce…nothing.

"I don't understand," I say. "If the chains were subduing my magic…"

Tania tries—and fails—as well. "It's the jalva oil. The chains were coated in it, so it had to get on our skin. It'll take time for it to wear off."

Liani shoves Tania, and she stumbles back. Luckily, Benj sprints forward to catch her.

"You are the druid's problem, but you…" Liani turns

to me with a wicked grin. "I won't lose Fae magic. I will drag you back and chain you in the dark for the rest of your life if I must."

Delkin growls and grabs Liani by the throat. Lifting her several feet off the ground, he says, "I owe you for every moment of pain you've caused my son."

Liani scratches at his grip, thrashing wildly.

"For every ounce of magic you bled from him, you will suffer!"

Liani continues to claw at him. "Gu—guar... GUARDS!" she manages to belt out.

Delkin curses as ten Winter Guards charge over the hill. He drops Liani. She gags and coughs as she scampers from the fray.

"I suppose first I'll have to deal with them." Delkin releases his wolf and charges through the center of the men, grabbing the nearest by the throat as he plows through.

Benj smiles. "Finally. I haven't had a good fight in ages." He releases his dragon and charges into the battle after his brother.

For a moment, I'm mesmerized. Delkin and Benj move like they were made for battle. Delkin grabs a guard by the thigh, flinging him high into the air. Benj swoops down with fierce enthusiasm, catching the Fae and banking back up toward the heavens. Moments later, there's a terrified scream, followed by the Fae plummeting to the ground. On impact, his body shatters, sending the nearest guard scampering in fear.

Unfortunately for him, Delkin is behind him, waiting. He wraps his massive jaw around the guard's midsection and bites, essentially cutting the Fae in half. They're down to three guards when several more crest the ridge, letting out a war cry that echoes across the battlefield.

"Go," Tania says, seizing Delkin's discarded sword. I have no doubt he left it for her while he utilized his other *talents*. "Your hand-to-hand is good, but we both know your specialties lie elsewhere."

"You're not well." Some of her color returned, probably because of the jalva-soaked cuffs, but there's a heaviness in the link. A lack of *life*. The amount of my magic suppressed by the jalva oil is waning. "I can't leave you defenseless."

"I think we both know that I'll be fine," she says.

As if to prove my point, one of the newly arrived guards rushes us from behind. He dives for Tania, and although the move isn't nearly as graceful as I've come to expect from her, she lifts Delkin's sword and deftly dispatches the enemy by dragging the blade across his midsection.

"The jalva oil on the cuffs will keep the symptoms at bay while we deal with this."

She's right. I'll be able to do far more damage with my wolf—but I won't risk it. Having heard what the priestess said about the Heartbreaker, I understand why Tania reacted so badly yesterday. Why my failure to tell her the truth struck so deep.

Because she's in love with me.

And I'm in love with her.

"We'll fight—*together*."

For a moment, I swear she might argue, but in the end, she simply smiles—a mischievous, beautiful grin—and lifts the sword. With an echoing roar, she launches herself into the fight, and I follow, eager to spill whatever blood I can.

I dive for the closest guard, releasing my animal before hitting the ground. He pulls up short when, instead of the somewhat lazy, troublemaking nephew of the Winter Lord, he's faced with a giant angry wolf. I snarl and snap at the air, and he turns and runs, but I'm faster.

And far hungrier for blood.

I catch his ankle, clenching my jaw and coaxing a scream from him.

"Please! I was just following orders!"

My response is to bite down, tearing his foot from his leg and leaving him to bleed. I'm different now. Changed in ways I could never have imagined. But I still have no desire to take a life unless I have to. He could still die, but he's got a fighting chance—if he leaves to tend to his wound.

Back on two legs, I search the chaos for Tania. She's across the field, face to face with the largest of the guards. He swings; she pivots. She slices; he dodges. They're evenly matched. Or they are until she seems to hesitate. Mid-swing, she pauses and visibly shivers, as if overtaken by the cold. Her opponent uses it to his advantage. His attack is brutal and swift, knocking her to the ground. I feel the air leave her body, feel the spike of fear as he stands over her. He has her pinned by the tip of his sword, and I sprint forward.

I'm almost to them, several yards away, when he draws back his blade. It's impossible. I won't make it. "Tania!"

I hold my breath as the blade plunges toward her chest. A rush of determination surges through the link, and she twists at the last second. Bringing her leg up, she catches the guard behind his knees. His balance tilts. His momentum is thrown. The sword sinks into the earth, and her attacker crashes down.

One by one, we take them out. Benj sweeps in and hauls several of the guards away—I have no idea where, and I don't care. These are Liani's squadron. Possibly the same ones who looked the other way when she murdered my mother.

When the final guard is down, my gaze goes to the spot we last saw my aunt. Of course, she's nowhere to be found, but she can't have gotten far. "I'm going to find Liani," I say to Tania. She isn't going to get away with this. "She's mine."

Benj shifts back to his Fae form and points across the field. When I look, Liani is there, blade in hand, facing off against a massive black horse. "Looks like someone else beat you to it."

"Is that—"

"Daroose may come across as nothing more than an irritating distraction, but trust me, the kelpie is far more than he appears." Delkin smiles.

On the other side of the field, Liani swings her blade with skill. A lady of court, yes, but she was more than that, once. A fighter. A huntswoman. It wasn't just her beauty that attracted my uncle. She was fire and she was strength—and she has no intention of going down easily.

But Delkin is right about Daroose. The kelpie is far more than I thought. Liani slashes, dragging her blade across the horse's flank. Daroose lets out an otherworldly howl and sprints forward. Liani dodges and starts to run, but the kelpie is faster. Its teeth clamp down on her arm, coaxing a pained scream from my aunt, and it starts dragging her toward us.

"I believe you misplaced this, little Fae," Daroose says in a muffled voice. It—*he*—stops a few feet in front of us. The kelpie's true form is nothing short of magnificent. Black as the starless sky with teeth sharper than a warrior's blade, the kelpie has eyes that glow deep purple. The

glow matches his tail and mane, which seem to pulse with energy. *"Is anyone searching for a false queen?"*

I can't believe it. "You went after her?"

Liani struggles, and Daroose bites down harder. Blood oozes from his mouth. *"One more time, and I will bite it off."* To me, he says, *"I was doing as commanded by my druid."*

Tania comes up beside me. I look from Daroose to her, brows raised. "Protect Valen at all costs," she says, looking at the kelpie. "Thank you."

"Wait a second…" I study him, taking in his true form. "I thought you said you couldn't talk to us like that."

Daroose lets out a soft whinny. *"I lied."*

"What do you plan to do?" Liani shouts. "March onto the estate and reclaim your throne? They will crucify you."

"How is it that the people just forgot the Frostreaver name?" Tania glances back at Delkin. He's watching Liani with barely contained fury. "How do you simply forget the real royal family?"

"With magic," another voice says. Levina emerges from the trees. She walks to the center of the clearing and stops in front of Delkin and Benj. With a mock bow, she says, "It is good to see you, Majesty, after all these years."

"You know Levina?" Tania asks. I don't miss the slight wobble in her stance or the shiver she tries so hard to suppress. Underneath it all, there's a shimmer of hope. Like somewhere deep down, she's still hanging on to the idea that this was all a big misunderstanding. That her mentor, the woman who raised her, hasn't just betrayed everything they both stand for.

Delkin's face is pale. He's rigid, the muscles in his arms coiled, fists clenched and ready. "I know her. But this woman's name is not Levina. Her name is Aphelian."

37

Keltania

Delkin has never called me by anything other than my name, so it's a bit of a shock when he refers to Levina as Aphelian.

"This is Levina, our high priestess." I glare at her. What she'd been willing to do to Valen — *to me* — is unforgivable. Part of me is furious, while another part is devastated. She's supposed to be our example. The standard to which we hold ourselves. Instead, she's just as bad as Servis.

Inside, I want to crumble. I want to curl up and cry, to weep for everything I've lost — all the things I never considered might slip from my grasp. But on the outside? I am as Levina taught me to be. Nature's sword and her fury. "She's also a dishonor to the Order."

Delkin shakes his head. "No, Tania." His voice is soft, and the look of pity in his eyes makes my stomach clench. "She *is* the Order. This isn't *an* Aphelian. This is *the* Aphelian. The very same druid who channeled half of druid magic to win the war."

The weight of his words settles like a thick fog, and I find it hard to breathe. What he's saying is... No. Not on top of everything else. It's too much. Too impossible.

"How could that be?" I ask. "Aphelian was a human, and that was thousands of years ago."

Levina—*Aphelian*—laughs. The sound is grating and cold, skittering down my spine like razors against skin. "Indeed, it was." Her expression darkens. "And I have spent every moment of that time waiting for an opportunity to repay the Fae for their cruelty."

"But you were *helping* the Fae." My head spins. "You were working with Liani to steal Valen's power."

Aphelian waves toward Liani and shakes her head. "I knew where our power was. I simply bided my time until someone came along—someone I could manipulate like Servis did me—and struck a deal. She's nothing more than common Fae scum clamoring for power. The daughter of a simple healer determined to claw her way to the top by whatever means possible. I never had any intention of giving her what she wanted." Turning, she flashes Valen's aunt a saccharine smile.

"You bitch," Liani spits. She struggles in Daroose's grip, but the kelpie holds tight.

Aphelian sighs. With a wave of her hand, the ground beneath Liani's feet rumbles. Daroose lets go of his prisoner and jumps back as the earth cracks and thick, thorny vines sprout from the dirt. They slither upward and wrap around Liani—up both legs, around her torso and arms, then encircling her neck. The assault continues across her face and mouth and stops just shy of covering her nose.

When I find my voice, there's a slight shake to it. Now is not the time to fall apart. I refuse to let her see the devastation she's caused me. "She said you helped put

Orbik into her thrall. And this—" I point to the now-bound Winter Lady. "This is more power than a priestess sigil would afford. If you gave Servis half of everything, how can you do this?"

"When I created the tear, I left myself with a little something extra," she says. "A modicum of what I used to have—but more than enough to fell each of you should you decide to act foolishly."

Delkin must know this because, if not, he could have destroyed her ten times over. But, as fierce a warrior as he is, he is still just a Fae. And a Fae without magic would be no match for her.

"How did you fool the druids? How did you get them to believe you'd killed yourself?" They hailed her as a hero, a true protector of life. They created the Order to celebrate her...

"My first disguise, the very first incarnation I took after shedding this skin, was of Lily Rose."

Valen's confusion slides down the link. "Lily Rose was the druid who created the Order," I tell him. "She was Aphelian's daughter."

"Did you kill her?" Valen's revulsion hits me hard.

"Of course not, you disgusting beast. After Servis betrayed me, I fled the Winter Lands. I had Lily and hid her in Harabin."

Valen shakes his head. "Wait. Was Servis—"

"Her father? Goddess, no. I became pregnant after I left."

"Harabin was destroyed not long after the war," I say.

"Indeed. It was." Anguish blazes in her eyes for a moment before turning to rage. "I created the Order, disguised as her. As what I believed she might have looked like had she been given a chance to grow. I've had several children over the centuries. Their offspring continued my line so that the Order could survive."

"Why didn't you try to get the tear back?" Valen asks.

"I almost did. My plan was mapped out, a trap laid. I could have been in and out before Servis even knew I was there." There's a flicker of guilt in her eyes. "But an opportunity presented itself, and revenge burned within me. I failed to kill him, and as punishment, Servis bound me to his bloodline. While any one of his male descendants lived, I would be unable to act against his bloodline and, by extension, the Winter Fae."

Understanding filters through the link, and Valen nods. "You somehow convinced the courtesan to assassinate him."

Her lips slip into a sly grin. "With his death, my next step was to be rid of your grandfather, Envrill, so I bided my time. It was during his reign that I met a young Liani." She winks at the Fae. "We conspired long before she married Orbik, playing the long game in order to gain the power we both sought. I convinced her that as long as she won him over and didn't give him an heir, she would be the most powerful Fae in the Winter Lands one day. But alas, you were never destined for the throne, my old friend. And now that you've given me a way to be rid of the Icekeeper line..."

With the smallest flick of Aphelian's wrist, the vines finish their ascent, covering the rest of Liani's face. For a moment, her enshrouded form trembles and shakes as she fights like a banshee for air.

It's over in moments, and as the shaking form stills, I draw my sword and step in front of Valen. "I stand by what I said. I will not allow harm to"—another involuntary shiver wracks my body as the jalva oil fades from my system—"come to him."

Aphelian shakes her head. Her lips lift in a knowing grin. "You need not protect him any longer, child."

"But Valen—"

"Is the son of the *true* Winter Lord. As he was born of Delkin and Amoriel, he is not directly descended from a male in the Servis Icekeeper line. I will not harm him—for now."

For now...

She focuses her attention on Valen. "With Liani dead, Orbik is no more. The sigil I placed upon the Fae of the Winter Lands to shroud the history of the Frostreaver line has lifted. If you choose to return and claim your throne, they will recognize you as their lord." She smiles. "However, I would caution against it."

She turns to Delkin. With a slight bow, she says, "You never treated me or my kind with disrespect, and I regret what happened to your court. For this, I will allow you and yours one single chance to avoid my wrath. Take your son and go back to your village. Live there in secret and do not get in my way."

Challenge gleams in Delkin's eyes. "And if we end up in your way?"

"The Fae of the Winter Lands must pay." Her eyes spark with a hunger for retribution. "If you choose to align yourself with them, then you will pay as well."

Another chill, this one stronger. There isn't much time left. "I—" A blast of cold knocks the wind from my lungs and brings me to my knees. Valen catches me before I crumble completely, threading my arm up and around his shoulder.

"Only the future knows where we will all end up. Now, though, we are here. You are here, and you can help her." There's the smallest tremble in Valen's voice. "Please."

Aphelian studies me for a moment. "She's a human trying to process Fae magic. We're not made for that."

"She is one of yours—your own flesh and blood," Benj says. He's been so quiet that up until now, I almost forgot he's here. "Surely you won't stand by while one of your druids falls."

Desperation floods the bond between us, making me dizzy. Valen stands and meets her steely gaze. "Break the link." Unflinching power, a command worthy of true royalty.

"And what will you give me to save her, young king?" She runs a finger across his chest, right above his heart, then taps it three times and smiles. "What will you give me to save *this*?"

"The tear," he answers without hesitation. "I will return the tear to you."

Aphelian shakes her head. "Not good enough. You've already promised it to my protégé." She flashes me a wicked grin.

"I've made no such promise."

Aphelian clucks her tongue. "Ahh, but the intention is there. We both know you were always going to give it to her."

"Valen…" The chill grows stronger, but I manage to lift my head to look at him. There, in his eyes, is everything I should have seen before.

"Of course I was going to give it back, Tania." His fingers knot into a fist for a moment before the tension drains from him. "I didn't have a chance to tell you before you stormed off."

"I—" If he'd told me sooner, would I have simply accepted it? No. He was afraid of losing me, and rightly so. Granted, I probably would have come to my senses eventually, but I understand, now, his fear of losing me.

It's that fear I feel through the link.

It's that fear I worry will doom us all.

He takes my face in his hands and shakes his head. "Stubborn fungus…"

"Yes, yes. Very sweet. Shall we continue?" Aphelian snaps her fingers. "I'm not foolish enough to believe she'll willingly hand over the power, so I'll simply bide my time. No. If you want me to save her, you will need to offer something else."

Valen glares at her, then turns back to me. Our gazes meet, and something sharp and overwhelming, a sensation that's both warm and icy, shoots through the link. He turns back to Aphelian and says, "When the time comes, I will ensure you have no opposition inside the walls of the Winter Court estate. I will return and take the throne. You have my word." There's no hesitation in his voice, no uncertainty. He's just offered his kingdom—his people—to the slaughter. He just sacrificed his own freedom…

For me.

Delkin gasps. "Valen, no—"

I shake my head. "That means you have to go back, Valen. That's not what you want. All those Fae—"

"Done," Aphelian says. "With a minor adjustment."

"What does that mean?" I understand the caution in Delkin's voice. Aphelian is the queen of lies.

"The link cannot be broken."

Valen's arms tighten around me. "You said—"

"I can, however, manipulate the link. Make it so that Keltania can survive it. Is that something you want?"

Valen's "Yes" is instant and uncompromising.

My response is a bit more cautious. "Why does it sound like there's something you're not telling us?"

"This link will still work both ways but will create unpleasant side effects for each of you."

"Such as?" I can't think of anything more unpleasant than what we've already been through.

"Valen is Fae. His death will mean yours. However, you are human, so if you are to fall, he will survive it." She smiles. "Probably."

"Okay." That isn't necessarily a side effect—just another jab from the Goddess, pointing to the inequality between Fae and humans.

"A severe enough injury that would not kill him might still end your life."

"We know how the link works," Valen says with a growl. "Just fix this."

"There is one final thing you must know. This link will continue to grow. It's unprecedented, so even I do not know its depths. You're in uncharted territory. It's quite fascinating, actually."

It's the link or nothing. I can let Aphelian amend the bond between us and live to see tomorrow, or I can die.

"Am I required to stay with him?" I catch Valen staring at me from the corner of my eye, but I can't look at him. His hurt flows through the link, leaving a coppery taste in my mouth. "Am I bound to his side?"

Aphelian laughs. "You, my dear druid, are free. The first of my bloodline in millennia able to do as they please. I would encourage you to take advantage." She leans forward, expression tightening for an instant. "Because he *will* betray you. They all do."

"I—" I gasp, and when I expel the breath, it's frosty. I try to swallow, but the muscles of my throat simply won't contract. It's like I'm freezing from the inside out.

"Do it now," Valen shouts.

"We should think about this, Valen." I don't want to die, but I don't know if I can handle being linked to him for the rest of my life. "This isn't something you should—"

"*Do it*," Valen repeats fiercely.

Aphelian looks to me, and I nod. It's now or never.

38

Valen

The journey back to the estate is somber. There are a million things I should be thinking about—the unwanted crown about to be placed upon my head; facing the Fae who once saw me as nothing more than a spoiled playboy as their leader; what will happen between Delkin and me moving forward; how I'm going to comply with the promise I made Aphelian, *without* betraying my people—but all that occupies my mind is the thought of Tania leaving.

Coming home is like returning to an entirely different world. As we approach the gates, the guards all stare before dropping to their knees, both in honor of my father and me. One after another, Fae fall at my feet, offering promises of penance and loyalty. It's more of the same as we make our way through the estate to find Orbik being laid to rest in the grave marked by a traitor's symbol. At every turn, Winter Fae slowly come to their senses, remembering the world—the ways—that have been stolen from them by Aphelian's magic.

The moment the magic dropped and the memories

began returning, nobles stormed the throne room. Orbik had been perched upon my father's throne, cold and hard. They'd dragged his body into the streets, burned his banners, and trashed the grounds.

The healing and cleanup started the next day.

Tania hasn't said much in the two days since we returned, and I haven't seen much of her. Late in the morning hours of our first day back, I went into the tunnels below the estate, deep into the changing hallways and moving doors. The estate had welcomed me, guiding me to that icy room right away. I swallowed my magic Liani had bottled and retrieved Aphelian's tear. I intend to give it to Tania today.

In a week, I'll be crowned. I'll reveal my magic and begin to fix the things Liani has broken. Right the wrongs that the Icekeeper line created and tell everyone the truth—about Servis, the druids…Aphelian. I intend to bring hope and aid to the remaining Fae villages and maybe build new ones, as well as send supplies to the human village outside the Order. If they'll let me—after learning the truth—then I intend to help them build new villages. Start new lives.

"Have you left this room for more than ten minutes since returning?" Delkin lounges in the doorway, casually leaning against the frame. He has an apple in hand and is dressed in the Winter Court colors—white and silver; sadly, no hint of orange or green to be seen—the wolf crest on his chest proudly displayed.

"A few times. I was about to go find Tania."

"Oh?"

"I've kept my word." I hold up the small tear-shaped vial that holds half the druid's magic. "I'm giving the druid magic back as promised."

Delkin smiles. There's pride in his eyes. "Well, then I'll leave you to it. We'll talk later."

"Wait." I grab his arm as he turns. We're still getting to know each other, but I have no one else to talk to about this. "My Heartbreaker is broken." It's the first time I've acknowledged it out loud. I've thought about it constantly, but saying it to someone, verbally acknowledging it, somehow allows me to breathe easier.

Delkin's expression is sad for some reason. "I know."

"Tania is…" I honestly have no words for what Tania is. She's strong, and she's brave, and she's by far the most stubborn being I have ever encountered. She's beautiful, and simply the sound of her voice calms the churning in my soul. Before I returned home and was treated with respect, I was alone. I mourned for the mother I never met, felt hatred for the father I'd been fed. I was angry, and it slowly poisoned me. From the moment Tania entered my life, some of that venom eased. It continues to ease. "Tania could be *mine*."

"Please don't say that."

"What?"

His expression is pained, and he drops his gaze to the floor for a moment. "Tania is a human, Valen."

"She is," I agree. "And it makes no difference to me. I've decided to tell her how I feel. I believe she feels the same way." I start for the door. "She is just too proud to admit it first."

"Valen, wait." Delkin catches my arm. "Tania is a druid. An *Aphelian*."

"I am very glad I found you, Delkin, but I do believe you've entered my life a bit too late to tell me who I should and shouldn't love."

He closes his eyes and sighs. "I am sorry you feel this way. Under any other circumstance, I would be proud. She's a fine choice, and I believe she would keep you on your toes. But it cannot be."

"Why not?" My father, the advocate for humans, is telling me I can't love one? It's too late for that now.

"When you sacrificed your freedom to save her, you also sacrificed a future with her. At least an immediate one."

"You're making no sense."

"The Winter Lands have been asleep for a very long time. They've been misled, and they will be wary. You have thousands of years of damage to repair. In time, you may be able to change things, but right now…"

"Change what things?"

"In the days of Frostreaver rule, humans were treated not as servants but as friends. They were allies, and they were, on occasion, *entertaining*. They were never equal. Not in the eyes of the general population."

I can't believe what I'm hearing. "You looked down on them?"

"No. But the life we live in the village, where everyone is equal, isn't the life we lived here. That kind of change takes time. I was working toward it when we fell—and I believe you will finish what I began. With *time*. Right now, you need to focus on undoing the damage Liani did. You need to gain their trust—and that won't happen if you're amorously linked to a human. A druid, no less. The truth about Aphelian will unsettle the majority and cause doubt to flourish. It will not win you their trust."

"This can't be happening." I sink onto the edge of the bed.

"I should be telling you to make her leave. Her presence at the estate, when the truth comes out, will cause you problems. But I know better than to suggest that."

"I really can't be with her?" After everything we went through, all the pain and suffering and obstacles—we deserve to be happy. Of everything Liani did, all the things she stole, this is among the worst.

"Not in the way you want."

It isn't his fault. He is the messenger, and I know that. But I'm angry regardless.

He continues. "If she was willing, you *might* be able to take her as a courtesan, but it can't be what you want. What she would deserve. Not right now."

I try to speak, but the words won't come. The anger, the pain, the regret—but no words. Maybe I *should* ask her to leave. Gently suggest she go back to help the druids. They have just as much healing to do as we. If I do that, though, there's a chance I'll never see her again. That she'll disappear and become nothing but a painful memory. One I'm reminded of each and every day through the inseverable link.

I won't take her as a courtesan. Not with what she truly means to me. That would be an insult, and I won't betray her—Aphelian is wrong about that. But I can't ask Tania to leave, either. With her or not, my heart has already made its choice.

"I know this isn't what you wanted, but you were born to protect these lands. It's in your blood."

"But what if it's true? What if I'm the Omen?"

"What if you are?" He rests his hands on my shoulders and gives me a gentle shake. "Who says the Omen is a sign of destruction? Prophecies are open to interpretation.

I believe you are the sign of things to come, yes, but I believe they are good things. Things that will bring these lands back to what they once were."

There's a soft knock on the door, and a moment later, Tania pokes her head through. "Oh. Sorry. Didn't realize — "

Delkin smiles. "I was just leaving."

"*Leaving?* Or…?"

"I've sent Benj back to the village. He and Ander can keep an eye on things for a bit. I'm going to stick around and help Valen settle in and learn what he needs to run things smoothly."

She smiles. "I think it will be good for him." Her gaze flickers to mine, and she flashes me a mock frown. "Goddess knows he'll screw it up without your help."

Delkin snickers, then slips out the door, leaving Tania and me alone.

39

Keltania

Goddess, why is my heart hammering so hard? I'm a warrior, capable and strong. Yet the idea of admitting out loud that there might be something more going on between Valen and me turns me into a sweating, fidgeting mess? I should be ashamed. But I'm not.

I'm terrified.

"I wondered if we could talk?"

He straightens and nods. "If you've come to worship at my perfectly shaped feet, then by all means…" He grins and gestures to his shoes. "Have at it."

"You are insufferable," I say, fighting a smile.

"I…" He runs a hand through his hair, and he might as well have skimmed my own scalp for as real as the sensation is. In the beginning, I hated it. Now, it's like a breadcrumb—something I want to chase. "I have something for you."

I smile. It feels like the sun coming out after so many years of darkness. "Just so you know, I'm not a jewelry type of girl."

Valen doesn't return the smile. In fact, his face is a

bit grim. Instead, he reaches back and grabs a glass case. Inside is a small, clear crystal. "As I promised. Aphelian's tear."

"You never promised, remember?"

"If you had used your fungus brain, you would have easily known that's what I intended to do."

I hesitate for a moment before taking it from him. It's so small, so unassuming. Looking at it, you'd never know what kind of power that small drop of magic contains.

"Well?" He forces a smile, but it doesn't fool me. There's something on his mind. "Aren't you going to crack it open? Be the hero?"

I want to. More than anything, I want to head back to Lunal and give our people back the piece of themselves Servis had stolen. In that moment, I understand Aphelian's anger. Her desire for revenge. We've become shadows of what we once were, and here I am with the ability to change it all.

But I can't do it.

"I think it will have to wait."

His brows rise. "But you've been—"

"Think about it, Valen. If I bring this back to Lunal, the magic will begin to return. It will find its way back to all druids, everywhere. In a month's time, we'll be as strong as we were the day Aphelian gave it all away."

He nods slowly. "And that would mean Aphelian's powers would grow as well."

I can't give her any kind of edge for what's coming. "Until I can figure out a way to deal with her, to reason with her, I don't think I can let that happen. Think of what she could do to the Winter Lands with all that extra power."

"So you're keeping the magic hidden to protect the

Fae of the Winter Court?" There's the smallest hint of amusement through the link.

I jab a finger at him. "If you ever tell anyone, I'll deny it with my last breath."

He throws up his hands and laughs, and this time it's a genuine snicker. "So have you given any thought as to what your plans might be now? Aside from protecting the tear, I mean."

"You're asking if I plan to return to Lunal?" He's nervous but also sad. I walked in on something between him and Delkin. Even if I hadn't seen it, I'd felt it.

"I suppose I am."

I take a single step forward. It feels bold and brave and makes my heart hammer even harder. "Do you want me to stay?" In so many ways, for so many reasons, I want his answer to be yes. But the reality of our situation makes what I want impossible.

Valen closes his eyes. "Yes," he says, the word barely a whisper. When he opens them, there's regret there, and I know, despite his answer, that we're on the same page. Good. It makes this just a bit easier.

I force a smile. "You do know that if I stay, Daroose will stay as well. Are you certain you want a kelpie living on the estate? From what Delkin's told me, he's quite a handful when he gets bored."

"Then we should be sure he doesn't grow bored."

I punch him playfully, doing my best to tamp down the sick feeling in my gut. "One week and I bet you kick us both out."

"I need… We should stay close. For a time, at least. Aphelian said she didn't know how the link would change. We'll deal with it easier if we're together."

His reasoning makes sense, but it isn't what I want to hear. I narrowed my next move down to two choices. Neither decision will result in a truly happy ending for me, but I've always done what needs to be done. Lived my life for the greater good. That doesn't look like it will be changing any time soon. But, to choose between my two paths, I need him to tell me the truth. I need to know.

"Is that the only reason?"

"No." Again, it's low and comes with a spark of regret. "I trust you, Tania. More than I've ever trusted anyone. We joked about it, but I want it to become a reality."

The air heats, and it's hard to swallow. If my heart thumps any faster, it will explode from my chest.

"I'd like you to stay at the estate and become my official second."

The air rushes back, and it's cold. Icy. I still can't breathe, but it isn't for the same reasons. "Your second? I— Is that it? Those are the only reasons you want me to stay?" A streak of boldness forces the words out before I can stop. There can't be anything left unsaid. When I make my choice, I need to be sure I have all the facts. Know all the truths despite the heartache that will come with both. "Think carefully before you answer, Valen. Give me the truth because it will be the base of my decision. Is there or is there not something between us?"

"There *is* something between us, Tania." He hesitates, then reaches out to touch the newly transformed markings on my face. Delkin's theory is that the druid power, mingling with the Fae magic, recreated the sigils. Like the Order, the Fae magic has staked its claim on me. Marked me with lines of white like newly fallen snow. They're beautiful, but in some ways, they feel like just another set of chains.

"It's strong, and who knows how much stronger it will become with the amended link." I lean into his touch for a moment, then pull away. With all the Winter Fae magic I've experienced, nothing has been as cold as the loss of his warmth.

"We can't put a label on it. Not right now. Not *yet*." He draws in a sharp breath. The words cut him from the inside as they spill from his lips. They cut me just as deep.

"There are no promises to be made today. Not tomorrow or the next day," I say, then swallow the lump forming in my throat. "There are far too many things to fix, things to prepare for. Levina will not forget her revenge. Nor will the people."

He nods. "If you stay—and I want you to—it must be because we make a good team. Do it because you have a place by my side, regardless of the capacity, and because the Fae, and in time, the humans, will benefit from your presence here. Stay because you are my *friend*."

"Your most trusted *friend*," I say.

Friend...

The way he says it tells me everything I need to know. I love Valen. I love him, but when I walked into the room, it was to tell him that we can't be together. Not right now. He understands.

He agrees.

It isn't what I want. On the way back to the estate, my mind spun with possibilities. The opportunities stretched before me like an open road, filled with hope and happiness I never expected to find. But with each mile closer, I saw the problems we would create.

The Winter Lands, as well as the humans, I suspect, are not ready for us. Magic is coming back to Derriga, and that will cause things to shift further. Balance will change, allegiances will be threatened, and fingers will undoubtedly be pointed. With Levina's looming threat, we need to reduce the fracturing that will inevitably come with a shift in power as well as the truth about the history no one knew.

If there was nothing between us, I planned to stay. If he admitted to feeling as I do, my plan was to leave. We can't be together, and I don't think I could live each day so close to him, yet at such a distance.

I was so sure I could do it, too. Simply turn around and walk out the door without looking back. But standing here in front of him, trying to imagine what tomorrow will be like without looking into those strange violet eyes, without hearing that annoying voice... I can't do it.

"I will stay. I will stay, but my life won't stop." I don't realize I've done it until I feel my hand resting over his heart. The slightly quickened *thump, thump, thump* mirrors my own. "For the first time, I'm truly free. I can finally move forward. You know how I feel—just as I know how you feel. If we choose to have this conversation again in the future and can freely discuss that, I can't promise you won't be too late."

It's a lie, of course. My heart belongs to Valen—and he knows it. But the lie will help me move forward. I will repeat it to myself as many times as I must. A mantra I fear I'll need.

A painful spike shudders through the link, followed by one I can only describe as *determined*. A hand on either side of my face, he rests his forehead against mine. When he pulls away, he brings his lips to mine but stops just shy of touching them. The pain that wells inside my chest overpowers my ability to breathe, and for the longest moment, we just stand there, not breathing. I have no idea where he starts and I end. There's no distinction between his anguish and my agony.

"We will have this conversation again. That, I can *promise* you."

I nod and turn without another word. Across the floor and into the hall. I'm nearly back to the entrance of the east wing. He's moving today. Not into Orbik's room but another in the main estate. No doubt he'll want me to move as well. Sad as it is, I'll miss my little closet.

"Our lives cannot stop, Valen. They will all be watching us," I say to the empty corridor as I slump back against the wall. The flowers that line either side of the hallway turn frosty, then translucent, making them look like glass. "But I am *yours*."

As I push off the wall and head through the door into the courtyard, one of the guards comes running up. He looks panicked.

"Where is Val—the Winter Lord?"

He's not the Winter Lord yet, but there's no point correcting him. "Why? What's wrong?"

"We have a situation."

Acknowledgments

This one... This one was a long time coming. I've been obsessed with fantasy stories since I was a kid. To have the opportunity to put one of my own out into the world is a dream come true. A dream that would never have happened if I wasn't lucky enough to have such wonderful people in my life.

First, to my husband, Kevin. My rock, the voice of reason, and the keeper of what little sanity I have left. No one understands me like you do (and, let's face it, no one else would put up with me). So, even though I still have no idea how I got so lucky, thank you. None of this would be possible without you by my side.

Thank you to my mom, who has been cheering me on for as long as I can remember. Whatever I said I wanted to do, whatever I insisted on pursuing—you were always there. Always supporting me. I wouldn't be the person I am today if not for you.

And my dad... You're not here to see this book come out, but I know you'd be proud of me. I realize now that my imagination, the very creative spark that allows me to do what I love, comes from you. It is the single most amazing gift you could have ever given me.

A massive thank-you to my agent, Nicole Resciniti,

whose faith in me has never wavered. You believed in this book even when I didn't, and for that I'm eternally grateful. I'm so thankful that we're on this path together!

Thank you to my earliest readers, Tiana Warner, Lisa Brown Roberts, Costa Richards, and Melanie McCarthy. Your insight and thoughts on this story were invaluable, and this book is better because of them.

The WiPs! A big thank-you to Nina Croft and Lynn Crain for reading *Omen of Ice*, and the rest of the WiPs for their thoughts and suggestions on the early chapters. You are all awesome, and I'm lucky to have you in my life.

To Liz Pelletier and Lydia Sharp, my editors, and the rest of my team at Entangled Publishing—as always, thank you. Your continued faith in me and dedication to putting an outstanding book into the world never fail to impress me.

To LJ at Mayhem Cover Creations and Bree Archer... Thank you for the most amazing cover! There's a certain amount of stress that comes from waiting to see your cover for the first time. Will it embody your story? Will it scream READ ME? When I first saw this cover, I instantly fell in love.

And, of course, to you... Yes, *you*. The one reading this book. There would really be no point in all this without you. Thank you for tagging along as Valen and Tania made their way through the wilds of Derriga. Thank you for allowing me to share a small part of myself. It means more to me than you will ever know.

Omen of Ice is a thrilling epic fantasy romance between an icy fae prince and a fiery druid, with a happy ending. However, the story includes elements that might not be suitable for all readers. Violence, blood, death, anxiety, trauma, familial estrangement, life-changing injuries, hostage situations, and alcohol use are shown in the novel. Death of a parent and child abuse are mentioned in character backstory. Readers who may be sensitive to these elements, please take note.

Let's be friends!

𝕏 @EntangledTeen

◎ @EntangledTeen

❶ @EntangledTeen

♪ @EntangledTeen

📰 bit.ly/TeenNewsletter

entangled teen

an imprint of Entangled Publishing LLC